After the Hunger

Stories

MaryEllen Beveridge

Fomite
Burlington, VT

Copyright © 2020 MaryEllen Beveridge
Cover image — Detail from *En unge pige, som hoelder af en kande (Young Girl Pouring Tea - the Artist's Sister)*, Vilhelm Hammershoi

Epigraph from *Great Systems of Yoga* by Ernest Wood with permission from Philosophical Library

All rights reserved. No part of this book may be reproduced in any form or by any means without the prior written consent, except in the case of brief quotations used in reviews and certain other noncommercial uses permitted by copyright law. This is a work of fiction. Any resemblance between the characters of these stories and real people, living or dead, is merely coincidental. The places in this collection that are real do not necessarily correspond to geography.

ISBN-13: 978-1-947917-20-0
Library of Congress Control Number: 2019943850
Fomite
58 Peru Street
Burlington, VT 05401

For Ron Allen

and

In memory of Clayton and Beth Banks

"There is no travelling on this Path, it is stated, for one is not going from one place to another, or even from one mental condition to another. The goal on this path is most occult, hidden from both sense and mind, but is revealed when there is cessation of the ordinary manner of life, which could well be called the way of error and sorrow."
— Ernest Wood, *Great Systems of Yoga*

"We live in succession, in division, in parts, in particles."
—Ralph Waldo Emerson, "The Over-Soul"

These stories originally appeared in slightly different form in the following literary magazines.

"Out of Season," *War, Literature & the Arts: An International Journal of the Humanities*
"Blue Sky," *Eclipse*
"The Great Salt Marsh," *Crab Orchard Review: A Journal of Creative Works*
"The Émigrés," *Cottonwood*
"Holiday," *Louisiana Literature: A Review of Literature and the Humanities*
"The Last Good Day of Summer," *Emrys Journal*
"The Halloween Witch," *Owen Wister Review: A Literary & Arts Journal of the University of Wyoming*
"The Rock Gardens," *Pembroke Magazine*

Contents

Out of Season	1
Blue Sky	36
The Great Salt Marsh	58
The Émigrés	88
What Some Men Dream	117
Holiday	149
The Last Good Day of Summer	182
Four Evenings	207
The Halloween Witch	233
Opening Day	248
The Ruins	273
The Sisters	292
The Rock Gardens	315

Out of Season

Dirty. Dirty earth endless dirt. Five acres of it outside the kitchen door, falling in clumps from the pads of the Basset hound walking heavy with milk across Sasha Greenwood's floor. In summer the earth kept its heat, it was cool inside, what could she do. A mother said Woof at the screen door, Sasha let her in, the hound settled among her pups boxed in the open space under the sink, suckled them contentedly. The puppies were sighted now, unsteady. They fell roughly onto each other climbing the patient and immobile flank of their mother, fed noisily, and were licked clean by a tender pink Basset tongue. The mother came to Sasha for a pat on the head and a biscuit, wagged her hound-dog tail, pushed the screen door open with her big wet nose, and left dirt all over the floor. The child watched alertly from her highchair, testing the atmosphere with outstretched fingers.

And there was Clifford, making offerings of root vegetables at Sasha's feet, practically. Should she pat his head too, say Well done? Had she known, what could she have done when Clifford lay down their old life like the burden it had become? After a two-day journey by car he took her on secondary

After the Hunger

roads bordered by woodland and up a steeply inclined road, the entrance guarded by boulders deposited during the glacial retreat. He drove up the long drive to the house and told her it was theirs if she would have it. He walked her across the abandoned, silent land, past weeds, brambles, bare, dry earth, and through the rooms of the shuttered house built a century before, with its root cellar smelling of underground things, its pantries, closets, and storage areas containing the odor of must. Sasha looked into her husband's war-weary face and knew she must accept.

Now there was too much. Too much to pare, boil, brown, chop, to pickle or can or put by. She would succumb to blisters on her fingers, fevers from fire burns, the sudden vertigo from standing over a hot stove, regret for the life Clifford had left behind, where she had known exactly what to do. In the dry season the winds sheared across the soil and blew fine grains of mica and quartz into the noses of the dogs and they sneezed and bit at the wind as if it were a living thing. In the shadows of early morning the surfaces of the furniture glittered with a layer of mica dust that had blown in through the window frames during the night. The dogs howled at midnight over a cloud that obscured the moon or a possum that had come out of its den to forage. In the evening, Sasha heard the beat of moths' wings at the screened windows in the darkness beyond the light of the lamps.

Clifford brought beets, carrots, spring onions, and potatoes across the field to her, his large shirtless body finely gridded against the screen door. Dirt was clumped in the eyes of the potatoes and caught in the long, pale root hairs that anchored the tubers to the soil. *What must it be like to take a spade and turn the soil and uncover a bed of potatoes, as if they were a cache of copper coins.* Sasha took the strange bouquet from Clifford's dirty hand. He winked at the child Lucinda in her highchair, eyed the puppies under the sink. The screen door closed after him. His work boots left muddy prints on the floor.

Sasha, witness to the morning mew, moil, and feed and to Clifford's harvest lying on her now dirt-strewn countertop, lifted Lucinda from her highchair and held her against her blouse. The child spread her arms and tried to arc backward out of Sasha's grip. Sasha held on, felt the child's bottom. Not quite two, all was well. *Maybe I am dehydrating her instead*, Sasha thought. What did she know about not quite two-year-olds anymore? She settled the child back into the highchair.

Lucinda wore yellow overalls and a yellow cotton T-shirt. She had a blonde ponytail and bangs cut halfway around her head. Wisps of hair stood up along her ponytail, as if it had been electrified. The stray hair that didn't fit into the ponytail was held by two red barrettes. Her bangs were pushed to one side of her forehead, as if her mother had tamed them with fingers rather than comb or brush. Sasha wanted to undo the band that held the child's ponytail and calm the electrified hair. But then what would her mother say? Sasha was careful to return Lucinda to her mother just as she had been delivered, even if that meant she always seemed hurriedly assembled, which made her look neglected.

Sasha tore fresh thyme into a tomato and basil soup and stirred the applesauce that simmered on the stove. She shook Clifford's vegetables out the door, glancing down the border of honeysuckle bushes along the driveway. Clifford had set the woven basket under the shade of a honeysuckle bush by the edge of the drive. The basket was large, with woven handles and a deep interior, and with a patina of wear that had turned it a silvery brown. It went each week from Clifford's hands to the child's mother, Hannah Baines, and returned to him empty and vegetable-stained and sweet-smelling. Sasha had seen the older Baines girl, Felicity, try without success to lift the heavy basket at the end of the day to give it to her mother.

Clifford's work shirt hung on a peg outside the kitchen door. The shirt belonging to Lucinda's sister Felicity was draped over his. Felicity wore a thin sleeveless undershirt that showed the bars of her ribs. She had waited outside the kitchen door for Clifford to complete his errand. Now she followed him at a near distance, her digging stick in her hand, and they moved in miniature past the flower garden toward the kennels, dwarfed by the detail of color: beds of phlox, gladiolas, hollyhocks, snapdragons, and the open faces of the tiger lilies, Shasta daisies and deep orange California poppies lifted to the sun.

Clifford had built kennels for the hounds under an ancient oak on the rim of land that overlooked the field. The hounds lounged on the soft dirt within the wire mesh pens or in the shade of the kennels. The hounds had droopy ears that flirted with the ground when they walked, and their long tri-colored bodies were supported by stumpy legs wrinkled at the knee, but they were an old, noble breed and they brought a good price as hunters. Clifford tried to keep the bloodline vigorous, but Five-star, acknowledged head stud, lay claim to each litter, first working his way through the rope tied to his collar and then under the fence erected between the male and female hounds. Five-star sat watchfully on the roof of his kennel. Each year Clifford negotiated trades with breeders as far away as Maine and Pennsylvania to strengthen the line. Still, when the females birthed, all the pups were marked with Five-star's white forepaws.

Clifford spread his tools on a clean rag. He began to repair the wire mesh where Five-star had dug another hole under the fence. He straightened the mesh and filled the hole with rocks and dirt and twigs, an intermediate measure before he could try again to outwit Five-star. The dogs sprawled on the dirt near Clifford, thrusting their noses through the mesh into his hands as he worked. Felicity dug a succession of shallow holes in the dirt with her stick. Clifford respected her projects, little mounds of earth dug with uncommunicative concentration near where he worked and filled again by the end of the day.

Sasha opened a tap at the kitchen sink and dampened a cloth. Through the window she could see the flower garden, the kennels, and the field beyond. The hounds wagged their tails lazily at Clifford. In his work boots and khaki pants he was a big shaggy god the color of a betel nut. Sasha turned from the window and wiped the table with the cloth. The kitchen had a deep brick fireplace for cooking, and the living room and dining room and bedrooms had fireplaces for warmth. The kitchen was low-ceilinged and comfortable; the floors were pine, wide and worn, the walls horsehair plaster, and the ceilings timbered with oak. The house smelled of wood, from the floors, the beams, and the logs burned in the fireplaces. The fires were fed from the trees Clifford had felled to further clear the land. Almost two cords remained. On the far side of the house, the front door opened onto two large, flat stone steps that led to an overgrown trail once used for horses and carriages. Clifford had stacked the firewood near the trail, under a border of firs.

He put the tools away in the shed and gathered a spade, a handful of stakes, and strips of cloth cut from his discarded dress shirts. He released the wheelbarrow from a brake of bricks. He came into the house on those first mornings of hard labor with sawdust caught in the graying hair on his chest and arms, carrying muscles that were losing their tension after the last difficult year in Germany, following the war. He was building kennels then, a garden shed; he was sinking fence posts; working the land with axe and saw. He came back to Sasha from the war wounded in his spirit and unsure how to begin to talk to her about it, or if he could. He brought her to the place that he had begun to imagine in the rubble of Berlin, and cleared and sowed and weeded and harvested; it was the only way he was able to talk to her about the war.

Intelligence had assigned him to debriefings of survivors of the labor camps and concentration camps, and the information he gained from them was more cruel than anything he had witnessed during the war. In Paris he read the exhausted, passionate conviction in the eyes of the men and women of the Resistance in the same way he read in the eyes of the camp survivors in France and Germany and Poland and Czechoslovakia the knowledge of death. First the survivors had to be fed; they had to be brought back before they were able to speak of their experience. Too much food will kill a starving person; Clifford had seen it happen. The body shuts down. You cannot touch a starving man or woman without causing bruising, breaking the vessels under the skin. A sneeze will cause a tooth to fall out, or a nosebleed that can't be stopped. A cough will cause a hemorrhage in the lungs. He saw men and women who were alive only in the eyes, and they looked sad and crazy and visionary in a terrible, Biblical way, and yet determined to live, and to tell men like Clifford about the experience of the camps and about their missing families, even when they could not stand or swallow. Their skin was disfigured with numbers tattooed on their forearms; they would take this evidence of a fate they had partially escaped and see it ever after, when dressing in the morning, saying a prayer over a plate of hot food, embracing a child.

Clifford guided the wheelbarrow to the field. He moved between the rows, checking the plants for insects. He took the spade to the ground then tapped the stakes in, pushed the soil around them, and tied stalks heavy with tomatoes with the strips of cloth. He straightened his back, shaded his eyes.

Clifford moved to a section of the field he had planted with beans—yellow, pole, and green. He snapped a yellow bean from its stalk and tasted it. It was more texture than taste—firm and sharp when he bit into it. Then its taste crept forward, mild and sweet. He dug precise holes, pushed the stakes in and tamped the soil around them, and tied the stalks with the cloth.

Felicity roamed the field in a row next to Clifford. When he stopped to examine a leaf, she did too. When he pulled a weed, she found one. When he spaded a hole, she dug one with her stick. Clifford halted his labor and massaged the muscles at the base of his spine. Arms at her sides, Felicity turned and turned, cutting circles with her body. The field revolved around her: its deep, variegated green, the house above it, the surrounding woods. She stopped and the field stopped too. Above it, new green tendrils, like fingers, like fingertips, sought space, air.

Rinsing the cloth at the sink, Sasha observed the child as a dart of browning skin. There was dirt on her elbows, a paint of dirt streaked across her shoulder blades. Her brown hair was chopped straight across her forehead and fell in tangles to her chin, its luster marred by the dirt and twigs that collected in it. Felicity, Felicity, the dirty one. Not quite five, she ran through the field, elbows pinned to her sides, bony shoulder blades jutting, head and chest thrust forward. It was an odd posture for a young girl. Sasha could not acknowledge the pure absorption, pure response, watching and waiting for the buds that grew secretly under the leaves to become a zucchini, an eggplant. Sasha would get the child alone, away from Clifford, if that were possible, and talk to her about posture and pleasing qualities in a girl, how dirt was not appealing. Gripping her by the arm if necessary.

Sasha draped the cloth over the faucet. *What was the odd contentment her husband found with the little aborigine Felicity Baines,* Sasha wondered, *who performed strange rites in the dirt and didn't say Boo to anybody, at least in her hearing.* Sasha thought of her as low to the ground, conducting some private ceremony with the earth. Sasha had broken her of digging the ground near the cords of wood off the old trail, where she had found her that first day, and she no longer walked the yard with a glass peanut butter jar in which she had captured the furious bees, but Sasha suspected that the jar was hidden somewhere on the property, full of dead things.

She scrubbed the vegetables under the tap and arranged them on a sheet of newspaper to dry. She left the pots simmering on the stove and the blonde child in her highchair, dreamily sucking her thumb. Walking down the hall, she brushed her palm against the wall switch by the bathroom door, illuminating the room with a hard blue fluorescent light. Her tinted hair was curled around her temples from the heat of the stove. Her face looked older under the harsh light. Since Clifford had taken her from their home at Fort Bragg, where she had waited for him to return, lunches with the wives of the other officers, volunteer work at the base, even the ceremony and danger of the coming war seemed distant and unclear in her memory. Now there were dogs and children who were not hers and the relentless green field. Sasha ran the water in the sink until it was ice cold. She dabbed it on the nape of her neck and the pulse points on her throat, then plunged her forearms into the water until she felt the heat, like a physical complaint, leave her body.

She dried her arms and folded the towel over the rack. The bathroom still held some remnant of military order, like all of the rooms that she and Clifford had inhabited during their marriage. She was surprised when Clifford made the decision to leave the Army, then she was alarmed. He had fought in Greece and Italy and had helped liberate France (and she had raised their two sons alone). When the discharge papers arrived he folded his uniforms and stored them away. Then he brought her here. His body, which seemed fuller now under the weight of axe and saw, had a different bearing entirely. At Fort Bragg he had left her in the mornings and sometimes for weeks at a time, and in the war years she lived among the other wives who waited. Then he put his uniforms away and took his shirt off and raised vegetables and flowers and dogs. Sasha could not admit to him that she felt left behind. She put her hand on the countertop, disoriented and unsure why she had walked so quickly down the hall to this room.

She fingered through the Bakelite box next to the sink, trying to locate her purpose in leaving the child unattended and pots simmering on the stove. More by touch than sight, she reacquainted herself with eye shadows and rouge, face powders and lipsticks. Until Clifford retired, under other hard blue lights she had selected and applied the colors from the Bakelite box. She had chosen them carefully, after consulting with the women at the make-up counters in the department stores. She felt herself flush slightly, remembering the inordinate expense. She had sat at lunch with women whose husbands were of similar rank. The dining room attendants bowed as they brought each dish to the table. There was something cautious about their meetings, something unsaid, and Sasha found herself exhausted afterward, the luncheons always unsatisfactory, because she had wanted women friends, she had wanted true friendship. But they were military wives and they lived in a kind of war as well, over rank and privilege and ambition. She became adept at public life, the parades and shows of arms, conversation across a banquet table with men of rank and their wives. She stood in receiving lines next to her husband and extended her hand.

Sasha opened the curtains. Beyond the flower garden the land dropped toward the road. The house from which Lucinda was delivered to her each weekday morning lay directly across the road, built on a rise so it overlooked the neighborhood, a cul-de-sac bordered by woods. The house needed paint. The windows in the front porch, cracked from bitter winters, were covered with sheets of plastic. The steps were chipped and crumbling. Small yellow flowers were beginning to open in the broom grass growing in the yard, tall and dry as hay. On the patio in the side yard John Baines sat, his injured leg positioned in front of him. Those mornings Hannah emerged from the house in her dress and white gloves, carrying Lucinda across the road while Felicity, walking next to her, looked up at her silhouette. She put Lucinda down at the end of the drive and waited for Sasha to appear at her kitchen door. Hannah was neatly dressed but always hurried and looking, like her children, somewhat neglected. They called each other Mrs. Greenwood and Mrs. Baines. Before relinquishing her to Sasha, Hannah knelt in front of her older daughter and held her at arm's length by her narrow shoulders, as if surprised that she belonged to her. She spoke in a soft, pleasant voice to Sasha, but she always seemed to be elsewhere, as if in some dream that had left her.

Sasha uncapped the lid of a pot of rouge made of plastic so heavy and black it had the sheen of onyx. She admired the texture of the pure red substance within it, its perfumed scent. She ran her fingertips along the black tubes of lipstick. When she and Clifford went out for an evening (they had a military car then, a driver), or entertained the other officers and their wives, she wore a shade of lipstick that complemented the color of her dress. Then the war came. Sasha hoarded the pots and tubes, wore the colors sparingly. She painted the seam of a stocking on her bare leg. She shook the Bakelite box on the countertop, scooped the tubes of lipstick into her hand.

Lucinda sang to her from her highchair. She sang some unknown song. She sang, "Hh, hh, hh," as if she had just discovered her own breath. "Hh, hh, hh."

Felicity ran through the field. She stopped at the tomato plants that made her skin itch and examined a stalk. She twisted a tomato from its stem. She sat among the plants, hidden from Clifford, and bit into the fruit. She knew where the blackberries grew in the woods, where the wild pear trees dropped their fruit. In the ruined orchard she ate windfall apples, their meat so tart her eyes watered. Corn eaten from the cob made her stomach turn, and a cob was difficult to bury. The wild strawberries that grew along creepers on the ground were sweet and delicious. The berries were hidden by leaves the shape of spades, and Felicity competed with the swallows and crows for them. She finished eating the tomato and licked the juice from her fingers. She scratched a hole in the dirt with her stick and buried the stem, hiding the evidence of her hunger.

Sasha took hold of Lucinda's outstretched hand and kissed her palm. She put a finger to the soup and tested it. It was done. She opened the oven door and checked the firmness of the baking bread. Lucinda reached toward the odor of yeast and wheat flour and honey. Sasha opened a can of sardines and took a wedge of cheese from the refrigerator to soften. Lucinda kicked her legs against the highchair and breathed, "Ha, ha, ha." Then she spoke to Sasha, "Ah, ah, ah."

Sasha carried Lucinda to the stove and gave the applesauce a final stir. She spooned the sauce from the rim of the pot, blew on it, and offered it to Lucinda. The sauce was made from green apples stored on the floor of the root cellar, not in season again till autumn. The applesauce was part of Sasha's commentary to Clifford for having taken her to this place in ignoring the freshly picked vegetables and giving him something out of season to eat. It was all from Clifford's hands anyway, in season or out, but she enjoyed setting something in front of him that would not have existed without her intercession. The child turned her head and the applesauce spotted her cheek. Sasha offered another spoonful. The child accepted it and grinned at Sasha.

"Uppy," the child said, struggling to be free of Sasha's arms.

"Another visit with the puppies?" Sasha asked. She wiped Lucinda's cheek and nuzzled her neck, smelling the child smell under the soap and powder, sweet and musky, like wet earth in early spring. "The buyers will come soon," Sasha said. "We'll have more litters again in the fall. By then maybe you'll be able to say a word or two in English, and then what will we do?"

Lucinda formed a bubble of spit between her lips. She breathed rapidly and shallowly through her nose. She shrieked at Sasha, a tropical sound. A few discontinuous syllables followed. Sasha returned a few syllables of her own; she liked making them up. The child listened to the still air. Then her smile compressed and disappeared. She sucked her thumb.

"We have a few things to do before lunch," Sasha said. "Do you want to help me?" Lucinda nodded her head. Sasha cradled the child against her side. She held the child as if she were a football, a hold she had learned from witnessing her two sons' backyard scrimmages in the years before Roosevelt took them into war, when Clifford already had been called away to England, and their sons played the rough sports of boys. Sasha held Lucinda as if she were a football, from the memory of her grown sons' childhood games. Encircling Lucinda's waist and hugging her to her hip, Sasha carried the child to the bedroom and laid her gently on the rug. She straightened the bedspread, erasing the impression of Clifford's body where he had sat to tie the laces of his boots. Lucinda ran across the rug to stand next to Sasha as she plumped the pillows, her blonde head a small light at the edge of the mattress. Sasha carried the child to the living room. Lucinda played on the rug while Sasha arranged the newspapers Clifford no longer read in a stack on the table next to his chair. She squared the jigsaw puzzle on the card table in front of the fireplace. It had been missing a piece since spring. The piece was of a woman's eyes and one high-colored cheek against a sliver of sky. In the puzzle the woman, in a long white dress, walked in a summer garden with her companion, her expression incomplete, unclear.

Sasha touched the space on the card table where the missing jigsaw piece should be, as if trying to apprehend its whereabouts. She lifted Lucinda from the rug and checked her bottom. Holding the child to her chest, she carried her back to the bedroom. She put a towel on the bed and changed her diaper, cooing at her all the while. Lucinda waved her legs in the air. Done now, Sasha brought her back to the kitchen and set her down near the puppies.

At not quite two, Lucinda heard Sasha's words spoken to her as though through a long tunnel, echoes and reverberations, something lost to her between vocal cord and ear. She had known a vague liquid light before her birth and before that other voices, sounds that burst upon her with random clarity then static, along a frequency transmitted with less force as she moved day by day from it.

These intrusions awed her, as did her not quite two-year-old life. There was the liquid light, then a bright light that made her cry, and her own crying startled her, so she cried some more to test and relish the sounds she could make after so much silence. Hands and breasts and warmth, the smell of perfume on skin. Milk, mush, urine and shit. A pair of bigger hands, a face that loomed close to hers, dark brown eyes with great silences in them, a close-shaven beard that scratched her skin and made her cry. The hands and face went away and her mother lifted her up. Her sister's rough hand took hers every morning as her mother carried her across the black surface. Brittle colors fell to the ground, large blue spaces opened above. The colors at first were motionless and gray then pastel, then bright and chaotic like her drift in the liquid light. A profuse fragrance enveloped her. She was awed by everything, too awed yet to form the words spoken to her, to speak them back to the voices coming across the scented air. They came too along the frequency that had pulled her from that other place she no longer knew.

Across the black surface and into the chaotic light Lucinda was placed in a chair high off the floor in a house with words and odors very different from the words and odors of her own house. She spent the day deciphering and coding words and odors while her feet touched air. A woman not her mother turned from her walking, reaching, chopping, mixing to speak to Lucinda in languages not the language she usually spoke. What is the language you speak? she seemed to be asking Lucinda, murmuring unfamiliar sounds to her.

Along the frequency echoed the words the woman spoke in her search for the language of not-quite-two. The words formed in the woman's throat and vibrated across the room and Lucinda heard each word belonging to the woman. She tried to speak them, but now the man arrived, bringing colors in his hands, and the woman spoke the language of Lucinda's mother, and Lucinda felt the transmission cease and her effort at words fall back on her.

There was all of this to do: walking, chewing, seeing, hearing, swallowing, warm, dark, light. Sun, snow, mother, father, sister, hands over hers, color, earth, fur, tickle, milk. Everything the way it was. She closed her eyes and the world dropped away. She opened her eyes and it came back. *What do words do? Give something a word and what does it do? Could she give something a word and change it completely, a tree in the kitchen, her mother and father?*

Lucinda chirped, laughed, gurgled, kicked her legs on the living room rug. She swung her head. The room careened to the right, careened to the left. The woman took the flashing ponytail as a signal, brought Lucinda up into her arms, checked her bottom, took the wet away, wrapped a fresh cloth around her, made her dry and cool. The woman's fingers were long and slender. She smelled of cooking spices and clean clothes. The woman straightened a strap on Lucinda's overalls and set her on the kitchen floor. Lucinda walked tentatively to the sink and sat under it. The woman allowed Lucinda to sit not in the boxes but on the floor next to them. Lucinda touched the fur and it moiled and nosed toward her, pink tongues on her face. She coded the odors of their bodies, not unlike hers: newness, spit, uncertainty.

Clifford moved among the rows. The field released its heavy perfume. He wrestled a clump of weeds from the soil and heaved it into the wheelbarrow, its metal belly dull with rust. Felicity ran to the wheelbarrow. She slipped into the space between the handles. Clifford directed the barrow along the rocky edge of the field. Felicity wrapped her fingers around the handles, in front of his.

Felicity felt the long pull of the season like a great watery undertow. Her memory seemed to have begun here, walking behind the wheelbarrow with Clifford, or crouching near him, digging into the yielding soil. Each week the woven basket was placed under the honeysuckle bush and readied for her mother, a bribe of sorts, a temptation to bring her across the road when the shadows began to slant across the flower garden, to take her children home. Felicity wanted to give something of her own to her mother, to place deep within the basket, a blue ring, the wing of a faerie. She ate secretly from the field, and followed Clifford, and searched with her stick for something to give to her mother.

Clifford tipped the wheelbarrow and the weeds fell into the underbrush. Felicity spirited across the field, her browning arms and her undershirt smudged with dirt. Clifford took a handkerchief from his pocket and wiped his face and neck. He glanced across the field, to the kennels and the hounds, and the house that Sasha had retreated to. Felicity ran past the kennels, holding a red pepper. At the woven basket she placed it on top of the yellow beans and purple eggplants, their colors clashing and vibrating.

Felicity tried to break a stalk of rhubarb and fell flat on her back. She said, "Ugh, ugh," and struggled with the rhubarb as if it were a dog that she couldn't coax to come with her. Clifford opened his Army knife and cut the rhubarb and Felicity stood next to him until he had cut enough, and she carried the stalks to the basket.

In the flower garden Felicity picked tiger lilies for her mother. The long stems holding the outward-curving orange petals looked like torches burning above her head. She lay them on top of the basket.

Clifford surveyed the field. He thought of the small pleasures of the little blonde girl who gurgled rather than talked, and of Felicity and her mother, of John Baines who was tormented by memory. Clifford, tormented also, lost himself in the land to try to unbind himself from memory as well. He returned his handkerchief to his pocket and walked to the basket, handfuls of green beans plump between his fingers.

Felicity dug at the soil in the garden. She was looking for a golden flower to uncover, hanging heavy on its stem, that grew in darkness. She found roots, small jagged quartz rocks, slugs. An earthworm tunneled into the soil. She looked up to where Clifford had been releasing the green beans into the basket, lifting the tiger lilies from it, brushing spider webs from the stems. The space he had filled in front of the honeysuckle bush was empty, a blank background of green and yellow. Felicity rose to her feet. She ran into the field. Then, remembering, she looked toward the kennels at the hounds, whose muzzles always pointed in the direction of Clifford's movements. He was standing at the rose bushes at the front of the house, pinching a petal. He held a coffee can under it. Felicity ran to the rose bushes. The air was sharp with the smell of gasoline. She scratched the ground with her stick, concentrating on the scars it made, as Clifford continued his work. He took her arm gently and led her to a rose bush.

"This is a Japanese beetle," Clifford told her. He showed her an insect, feeding from a petal. Its back was metallic green, and when Clifford touched it, its back opened and the brown wings showed briefly. Clifford named everything in the garden and field for her—aphid, sparrow, Monarch butterfly. "They can kill an entire rose bush," he said.

Felicity knew from what Clifford told her that the Japanese beetle was bad. The Japanese beetle seemed to have something to do with her father. It seemed to have something to do with a place her father had come back from, though she did not understand how this insect had harmed her father when he had been so far away. She did not understand how a beetle could make her father so.

She looked up at Clifford and tried to form a question about her father. The beetle had harmed her father, it was in the past a long way away but here too, in the rose bushes, surely too in the tall grasses of her own yard, and this is what had harmed her father. It was in the past and not; it was far away and close by. This was in the past and the Japanese soldiers would come through the side yard that led to the patio where her father sat, and he would hold up his hands as if to stop them, and the soldiers would come out of the sunlight into her house in their bloodied uniforms, their rifles held in front of their faces.

She tried to respond to what Clifford had told her about the beetle. But there was her father and the soldiers who would come into her yard with their rifles. She pleated her shoulders and made her body small.

"They won't hurt you," Clifford said. "We'll take care of them." He took her arm again and watched her body unfold. He showed her how to pinch the beetles off the roses without hurting the petals, and they shared the coffee can with its inch of gasoline between them. Felicity pushed a beetle into the can with her stick, and she watched it swim in the slick of gasoline, its brown wings issuing helplessly from its back.

Sasha opened the screen door and called to Clifford. The basket of vegetables and flowers was like a complicated jewel lying at the end of the driveway. Across the road, John Baines sat at the table on the patio. A chess board was opened on it. He had turned his chair toward the deep woods behind the house, and his eyes were fixed on it, as if danger lay within it, or escape.

Hannah had left Felicity in the house with the new babysitter and driven to her first day of work, her gloved hands arranged on the steering wheel. Her pelvic bones were spreading; she could feel them in the night, the ligaments stretching and cramping. Late that afternoon Sasha watched unmoving at her kitchen window as Hannah searched the overgrown yard for her daughter, a crack appearing in her voice as her calls went unanswered. Sasha had found the child behind the cords of wood at mid-morning, her knees splayed, burying a peanut butter jar with three bumble bees in it beating angrily against the sealed glass. She was dirty and mud-streaked. Sasha brought her to the house and ran a warm washcloth over her face and arms as Felicity tried to twist her narrow shoulders away.

The child was out of earshot of her mother's voice, solemnly piecing together the jigsaw puzzle on the card table in Sasha's living room. Sasha brought Felicity down the driveway. Hannah ran wildly into the road and began to cry. She held Felicity, and the child's arms were wrapped around the taut curve of her mother's belly. "The babysitter. Oh— A slow, heavy girl," Hannah said to Sasha, after she had stopped crying. "I must call her mother." Hannah released Felicity's arms and gently pushed her away. The babysitter had arrived promptly at eight on her bicycle, Hannah explained to Sasha, but then she had pedaled down the road guarded by great glacial boulders, surely called away by the silent house from which she forgot to return.

Hannah spoke to Sasha in front of the honeysuckle bushes while Felicity chipped pieces of moist dirt from the peanut butter jar. The bees, now dead, lay stiffly at the bottom of the glass. Sasha had been too frightened of the bees' anger to uncap the jar. Clifford was at the farm-and-garden center, and Sasha did not tell him that Felicity had been trying to bury something in the dirt behind the firewood or that she had allowed the bees to die.

"My husband isn't able to work yet," Hannah told Sasha. "He isn't gaining weight as he should. I often wonder, will he ever gain it back. He was so thin already, when he was called up."

"I'm sorry, Mrs. Baines," Sasha said. She began to walk back up the drive. "Your daughter seems to have suffered from all these miscalculations."

Hannah turned her slender back and walked across the road with her child. She climbed the crumbling front steps and took her inside. Sasha did not want to see the interior of the house and be shocked (she was certain) and then feel bad but then not at all surprised at the way the family lived. Even though she had been willed by her husband to forsake the old ways, the other part of her, trained as deeply and well as Clifford, felt absolute justification in appearances, in presentation as creation, as reality. She knew if she went into the house that needed paint, with its cracked windows and a yard one could hardly see the end of, she would be confronted by a sink full of dishes and clothes in a laundry basket in need of ironing and a tear, perhaps, in a lampshade. There would be testimony to desire, to hunger, beyond the relentless demands of breath, and bone—a figurine on a mantle, a row of good books leaning against brass bookends, a glass vase—small protestations against the divination of the ruined lampshade.

At dinner that evening Sasha said, "That woman across the road, that Mrs. Baines, left her child unattended and drove off to town. I found her in the yard, dirty as a muskrat."

"Sasha," Clifford said.

"What could I do?" Sasha asked. "She wouldn't speak to me. She wouldn't go home. I washed her face and hands and kept one eye on her until her mother came back. Mrs. Baines is expecting another child; her dress can't hide that. Her husband must have been sent home again in time to— He must have been well enough to—"

Clifford folded his napkin on the table and walked across the road. The next morning he waited at the end of the drive for Hannah and watched as, grateful and shy, she put the palm of her hand on her daughter's back and guided her across the road, where Felicity entered into his care.

Now, hearing Sasha call him from the kitchen door, Clifford cleaned his hands with a rag and put the coffee can away in the shed. The dogs stirred in the pens and bayed at him. Clifford spoke to the hounds and calmed them. At the rose bushes he spoke to Felicity in the same even voice. She put away her stick and walked with him. He took their shirts down from the peg outside the door, and they each pushed the buttons through.

Sasha picked Lucinda up from under the sink and brought the child with her while she reapplied her lipstick. The child tried to touch the colored stick, but Sasha held her fingers while she closed the tube and returned it to the Bakelite box. She blotted her lips, then arranged her hair quickly with her free hand. She kissed Lucinda's soft cheek, leaving an orange smudge. She wiped the smudge clean and kissed Lucinda again, and Lucinda gurgled at her.

Clifford ran his fingers over a puppy's paws, felt its chest. The puppies mewed and climbed over each other, searching for his hands. He changed the newspapers that lined the box and shook and refolded the blanket where they slept. The puppies scrambled around on the floor. They fell on their sides. Clifford returned them to their box, one by one.

Sasha smoothed the collar of his work shirt and placed a hand to his face.

He stirred the soup, tasted it. "The tomatoes in the field are still ripening," he said to her. "There may be enough to can in the fall. We've never tasted better tomatoes, have we, Sasha?"

"I daresay we haven't," Sasha said. After all the want of war, food was good again. Clifford's presence was good again. Every aspect of him—his body muscled now, relaxed into its own strength; his eyes, made older by war, yet indebted now for this moment, whatever it held—seemed to have come into being from the dirt-encrusted vegetables he brought from the field to her door. But she still woke in the morning and couldn't quite locate herself in the place her husband had brought her to. Lying in bed she would hear the dogs barking and the brush of fir tree needles against the roof and meet again the slow awakening of the land. Before dawn the mourning doves

After the Hunger

began to call. Robins pulled earthworms from the ground, black crows heckled from the branches, white butterflies and yellow-and-black striped bumblebees and black-spotted ladybugs coursed across the flower garden, and at dusk swallows swept across the field. Sasha turned off the burner, got a ladle out. Felicity hung back by the door, unsure of herself in the house, with Sasha.

Clifford took Lucinda from Sasha's arm, chucking her gently under the chin. She looked at him with recognition and curiosity. "Felicity," Clifford said, "take your sister here and help her wash her hands." She looked at him with her dark eyes. He rested his hand briefly on her tangled hair, an unfamiliar gesture between them, and sent her down the hall with Lucinda. Clifford and Sasha heard the scrape of the stool under the sink and the running of water, and Felicity as she did every day before lunch telling Lucinda about the sliver of soap that had disappeared in their father's hand, like magic, while he was helping her wash for supper. Soon they reappeared, sparkling slightly. Sasha settled Lucinda into the highchair. She tried to tuck in Felicity's shirttail, but Felicity wrenched herself away and sat next to Clifford.

Sasha took a tray down and placed a soup bowl and plates on it. "Why don't you have Felicity take the tray today?" she said to Clifford. She didn't like Clifford crossing the road to the house, for any reason.

"You know she's too small to carry the tray," Clifford said. "The last time I brought her there, John started singing to her. 'Waltzing Matilda.' He sang it like it was a lullaby. He tried to lift her but his hands shook, and he had to put her down. She climbed up on his knee herself—his good knee—and picked up the spoon and began to feed him. I think it was your zucchini soup. She was perched on his knee like a sprite. John ran his hand through the ends of her hair, as if he had never seen her before. After lunch Felicity hid in the woods and I had to get Five-star to find her." The hound had tracked soundlessly through the woods and found her crouched in the bracken. Five-star had licked her downturned face until she allowed him to lead her back to Clifford.

Clifford brought the tray down the driveway. John Baines sat at the table on the patio, absently nursing his injured leg. Clifford had seen the leg, the previous summer, on a hot day when John uncharacteristically had worn shorts. It was badly scarred from a Japanese bayonet. John had been too long at Cabanatuan for it to heal properly. Clifford, whose eye had been educated in the camps of Europe, had guessed that John suffered from malaria, a standard disease of the tropics, and he probably was still recovering from dysentery, which compounded his struggle to gain back his weight. Malaria, dysentery, malnutrition, Pacific Theater. Tuberculosis, dysentery, malnutrition, European Theater. It was just a matter of geography.

John Baines was dressed in trousers and a white long-sleeve shirt. He was clean-shaven and his hair was cut in military style, like Clifford's used to be. Under his pallor he had the color of a fair-skinned man who had spent time in the tropics. Clifford could not read in the *Iliad* of the relentlessly detailed slayings on the battlefield without getting sick to his stomach, and it seemed strange to him that the trauma of war had only been officially recognized and given a name in this century, following World War I. Clifford, keeping a benign eye on the household across the road, speculated to Sasha that John Baines frequently returned to the Veterans Administration hospital, and came home often looking the worse for it. *We survive,* he thought, *and then where do we find life possible again.*

"John," Clifford said. John looked up from the chess board and stood in greeting. Clifford put the tray down and shook John's outstretched hand.

"Clifford," John said. "Can you sit a while?"

"How are you, John?" Clifford said.

"Very well," John said.

"And Hannah? I see her sometimes on her way to work and then of course when she fetches the girls."

"Hannah," John said.

John had returned from the Pacific Theater, he had returned to Hannah. He had night sweats and nightmares that woke Hannah into whatever battleground he lived in during the night. The house began to deteriorate into wasps' nests hanging under the eaves, paint that chipped from the walls, floorboards on the stairs leading to the rooms where Hannah put the children to bed and where Hannah and John slept that creaked as if a heavy foot walked on them.

Hannah's dreams had fled. Night was darkness and then the day came. John heard her weeping over the baskets of vegetables she carried up the front steps to the kitchen. They seemed like a rebuke because she was empty, she had become empty in various states and now she was empty completely. She placed the vegetables on the kitchen table and cried. She took them down the back steps and left them in the high grass because how was she to chop and pare and simmer and turn? Her children were full of need.

John lay on his back in the night and tried to see only darkness. *How can I love anyone, ever again? I have used myself up in trying to be alive. My body is reduced to a small flame which must be guarded.* Hannah was crying. Someone was crying. He went to the patio and smoked. The stars were formal and ancient. John signed himself into the Veterans Administration hospital. The doctors had him on a regimen to gain back his weight, and they were trying to help him with the nightmares. John was in and out of the VA hospital, in and out. He had only returned again in the spring.

The day was bright and vivid. The woods whispered around him. There was a bird somewhere. John couldn't be in the house as another man could, who hadn't seen war. He sat at the table in the early afternoon sunlight. He looked again at the chess pieces, arranged since his homecoming for the game to begin.

John pulled a chair out for Clifford. He looked with disinterest at the tray of food. "Is Hannah bringing your lunch?" John asked.

"This is from Sasha," Clifford said.

"Sasha," John said.

"I bring her too much food. But it's become my duty. After all that hunger."

"Yes," John said. "After the hunger." At Cabanatuan he had dreamed of food. He had dreamed of tables of food.

"Would you join us for lunch today, John? The girls are with us at the house. And Sasha, of course."

"Hannah wants me to read this book," John said. "She said it would help focus my mind." Clifford saw that it was a book of winning chess games by world champion Paul Keres. John had it opened on the table. "We made the pieces from bamboo," he said. "The tan bamboo was the king. The green was the queen. The bishop. I can't remember the bishop. We scorched one side of the bamboo piece, so we would know which was black and which was white." He closed the book between his hands.

Clifford stood. John stood and shook Clifford's hand again.

"I'll come back," Clifford said. "To see how you're doing. If you want, I'll show you the dogs. Great hunters. Lucinda likes to play with the puppies."

John sat at the table again. The beautifully carved chess pieces were of smooth, yellowing ivory. "I played a pretty good game with the bamboo pieces," he said. "I got used to the feel of the bamboo."

Clifford walked back to the house. Felicity sat mutely at the kitchen table, waiting for him. He ladled the soup into the bowls and took them to the table. All the other dishes were laid out. Sasha swung Lucinda's highchair around next to her and she and Clifford took their places across from each other.

"I told this one to have her mother bring her hairbrush next time," Sasha said, looking across the table at Felicity. "The child always has litter in her hair."

Clifford inclined his chin at Felicity. "Hungry, Little One?" he asked. He placed a tea towel over the warm loaf of bread and cut a slice for her. She began to eat.

Sasha helped Lucinda with her soup, wiping her cheek after each mouthful. She looked at the dark-haired girl across from her. Sasha granted her her silences, preferable to a story she might tell about the house across the road. When she was smaller and allowed Sasha to accompany her to the bathroom, Sasha, ashamed of herself now, looked for marks on her body. There were none, only the dark eyes that followed her, until she had Clifford take the child out of doors with him again.

"I have the oddest feeling," Sasha said, "that there's something I can't find. This morning I found myself walking down the hall, looking for something. I don't know what."

"The old days," Clifford said. "Is that it?" He had wished for her something else, something more.

"The old days," Sasha said. Now there was this. The field gave up its fruits, dogs birthed in winter, flowers bloomed all year long. In December golden-orange flowers opened on the vines clinging to the house, looking to Sasha like the trumpets of angels. The Christmas cactus on a table in the living room bloomed with fuchsia flowers from October to March. Three of the Basset dams gave birth late that first winter. The puppy boxes stayed under the sink. Watching the mothers clean their newborn pups, Sasha felt betrayed by the seasons that were no longer regular in their cycles, and by Clifford, who needed life, abundance, all from his hands, as a way to annul memory. She tried to follow. She tried to locate something that would belong to her.

Sasha fed Lucinda a spoonful of applesauce. Lucinda chirped at her. Sasha had almost put aside the old loneliness she had felt while she waited for Clifford to return. In Berlin he had resigned his commission under protest from his superiors. He came home and took her away from all she had known. *The new days*, Sasha thought; *what were these days: a field surrounded by woodland, its depths and quiet and insulation, which were helping Clifford fully return to himself. Did all this space and quiet (except for the excitable dogs) help John Baines too?* She had forgotten to ask, she never asked about him; Clifford seemed to accept that she needed a certain distance from the place he had brought her to, and from a man who had been wounded too deeply to fully return, and a woman who took her husband's car hesitatingly down the road every day to work. *The Baineses must have married just before the war,* Sasha thought. *These were to be the new, bright days for them, after his return. Hannah must have thought of them often, waiting for him.* Sasha put her hand on the tray of the highchair and Lucinda grabbed her thumb.

After lunch Sasha helped Clifford clear the ground where he had harvested the summer squash. They gathered the dead vines and threw them into the wheelbarrow. Clifford wore his shirt buttoned to the collar. His muscles worked under the shirt as he loosened the soil with a hoe. Lucinda sat in a portable playpen nearby, swinging her ponytail. Felicity moodily dug with her stick a few yards from Clifford. She collected acorns from the trees at the edge of the woods and buried them. The hounds barked at them intermittently, wanting attention. Felicity carefully wiped a smooth gray stone and slipped it into her pocket.

Sasha took Lucinda in for her afternoon nap, leaving Clifford to finish clearing the ground. She washed her hands and wiped the remaining lipstick from her mouth. She lay down with Lucinda on the bed she shared with Clifford, covering her with a light blanket. The child closed her eyes. Sasha gazed idly out the window, waiting for sleep.

Felicity walked past the bedroom window and Sasha saw her vanish behind the cords of firewood. A crow called from a fir tree. Sasha waited. The child next to her breathed softly through her mouth. Felicity emerged from behind the firewood and walked out of Sasha's line of vision, around the side of the house.

When it was time to return the children to their mother, Sasha brought Lucinda to Clifford and he waited with the children for Hannah to turn the car into the driveway and walk across the road. At Clifford's feet was the basket he and Felicity had prepared for her. Clifford said to Hannah Baines, coming pretty and shy to the edge of the yard in her white gloves and belted cotton dress, "How are you, Hannah?"

"Oh, how beautiful!" she said, bending over the basket and holding a tiger lily by its stem. "It's so kind of you and Mrs. Greenwood." Felicity stood next to her mother.

Lucinda, in Clifford's arms, sucked her thumb. Clifford lowered Lucinda gently next to the basket. Hannah took off her gloves and lightly massaged her hands, working the exhaustion out of them. "They have me typing," she said. "I've never seen such typing. I'm afraid it's ruining my hands." Clifford offered his hands, brown from the sun and hard as leather, and they laughed. Hannah said, resting her hand on Felicity's hair, Felicity stilled, calmed, by her mother's caress, "Were they good today? Did you help Mr. Greenwood today?"

Sasha draped a cotton sweater over her shoulders. She opened the front door and, stepping off the old trail, found the square of earth behind the cords of wood that had been dug and covered over. She crouched to the ground, as she had seen Felicity do, and dug into the soft earth with a stick of kindling. The jar was wrapped in a piece of clean rag. Inside it were the dried remains of the bees, a smooth gray stone, a couple of acorns and the missing piece of jigsaw puzzle of a woman's high-colored cheek.

Beneath the jar Felicity had buried a package, wrapped in another clean rag. Sasha lay it in her palm and opened the rag. She was careful not to touch the objects inside. The black tubes of lipstick were laid side by side. She held them in her palm. A mother-of-pearl button from one of Clifford's dress shirts was pressed between them, the white threads thick and ragged, as if they had been torn from the cloth or bitten free. She shook it into her hand, losing it briefly in the dirt. She loosened the dirt from the button and rubbed it between her fingertips. She stood and walked away. She had left all of the buried things where they were.

Clifford spoke to Hannah in the shade of the honeysuckles. Lucinda played at her mother's feet. Felicity looked up at her mother. Across the road, in a slant of sunlight, John Baines's hand drifted above the white king.

Sasha walked down the drive. Her hands were full of dirt. Felicity took a step toward her mother. The baby reached into the worn basket and pulled a tiger lily from it. A glove, like a white leaf, fell from Hannah's hand. Sasha spoke to her husband. "Clifford," she said. "Clifford," she said again.

Blue Sky

It was past ten o'clock and Nell sprawled on her bed, dressed for lunch, one arm flung behind her head. She lay half awake, alert to the voices below, trying not to resent her mother, who had raised Nell with few certainties but her insistent punctuality, and who was now quite late. During the years that Nell lived in New York her mother waited faithfully in the train station at the end of the Metro line, anticipating those irregular weekend visits in the smoky waiting room as she kept an anxious lookout for Nell from a seat in the corner, her pocketbook guarded on her lap. Nell's mother had failed to meet her only once, and that was during the period when she was practicing meditation. Nell had found her, waiting for their visit to begin, in a trance in her car in the railroad-station parking lot.

The curtains at the windows above Nell's bed fluttered against the sills. Too drowsy to think, Nell lay in the current of the cross breeze. The cottage that Nell rented was built on a rise and held fast to it by no visible means except the tenacious beach grass that grew in the sandy soil. Beyond the branches of the Austrian pine that rose miraculously from the sand, the cottage overlooked a clutch of similar cottages that were bordered by shell-and-gravel footpaths. The voices of the tourists who rented the cottages, whose faces changed every Saturday, came to Nell faint and discordant on the cross breeze, as she strained to hear the sound of her mother's voice.

The footpaths trailed into a smoky green landscape, part marsh, part meadow, that was dotted with the roofs of wood frame houses built on the long curve of the harbor. The harbor was at too great a distance from Nell's windows for her to see, though she was always aware of it. The breeze brought sensory messages from the harbor and the ocean beyond— salt spray, wet sand, ruined wood, ships' bells, gulls' cries, and the quick, muscular movement of underwater creatures: cod, flounder, mako shark, humpback whale. The sky was an even wash of blue, a hue found only in spring. Nell knew from its high, translucent blue that the harbor would be the same color, chipped white by the sea wind.

The road to Nell's cottage ran perpendicular to the harbor. Nell had drawn the road for her mother on a map that a child could not fail to understand. A narrow driveway, partially hidden by wild beach rose bushes, snaked onto the property from the road. At the end of the driveway an open wooden staircase climbed to the cottage. A child could understand that, from the directions Nell had sent to her mother in the mail.

Nell got up from the bed and straightened the spread. She washed the dish on which she had peeled and eaten a blood orange for breakfast. She took last night's dishes from the drainer and stacked them in a kitchen cabinet, and put away the bottle of Bordeaux—the line of dark red liquid now just below the half-way mark—which had eased her into sleep the night before and into a mild headache in the morning.

The curtains on the windows were sheer, and they blew inward, and the breeze stirred the fine grains of beach sand on the floors. The floors were laid with mottled blue linoleum, and the walls were painted bright yellow. In the living room, three straight back chairs remained, as they had all winter, in a semi-circle around an ornate potbelly wood stove. Nell dragged the chairs away from the wood stove and arranged them around the coffee table. She gave the room a brief inspection, and returned to bed. She closed her eyes, then opened them again, too alert to enjoy the sensation of borderline sleep. She put a pot of coffee on the stove and heard her mother's voice through the low background noise she had been decoding all morning. Her mother's voice was clear, somewhat high, musical, as familiar and mysterious to Nell as her own. She opened the cottage door and walked down the long wooden staircase to find her.

Her mother stood next to her friend and neighbor Irene on the path at the end of the staircase, trying to get the attention of one of the tourists on his way to the beach. Her mother's car made a rapid ticking noise as its engine cooled under the inconsequential shade of a giant yucca plant. Her mother's rental of a cottage with Irene on a northern stretch of shore had diminished the distance that Nell tried to keep between herself and her mother to twenty miles, and now there she was, standing practically beside her daughter, still trying to find her.

"Mother," Nell said. "Mother."

Her mother turned to Nell. Her look of pleasure was overset by a look of surprise. She looked astonished at arriving at this latest of many impossible places to find her daughter, after having traveled at the mercy of forces that she did not entirely believe supported her.

Irene smiled pleasantly and benignly at Nell, the expression she wore in the company of Nell and her mother. A blissful otherness, a good defense. Nell embraced them. Their bodies, which had borne a dozen children between them, were on the other side of middle age, not plump, but soft. Even their shoulders were soft. Nell's mother and Irene wore almost matching outfits, loose white cotton blouses over elastic-waist pants and splashed with bouquets of summer flowers. Little bees and butterflies trembled among them.

"There you are," her mother said, the look of surprise still with her. "We've been wandering around for an hour, trying to find you."

"I drew you a map. I told you about the cottage on the hill," Nell said.

"First we drove up that driveway back there," her mother said, gesturing behind her, "and a very nice woman told us she hadn't heard of you. Then we came here, and tried to speak to that man there."

"You can see the cottage plain as day from the road," Nell said. "I told you all about it in my letter. You couldn't have missed it."

"She said she knows a woman named Eleanor, but she looks nothing like you," her mother said. This fact seemed to intrigue her. "I described you to a T." She touched Nell's face with her fingertips. "You never change."

"How many people did you ask?" Nell said. She couldn't let it go.

Nell's mother withdrew her hand from Nell's face and laughed pleasantly, as if Nell had said something amusing.

Nell took Irene's soft, freckled arm. They followed Nell's mother to her car. "Do you have trouble finding your children?" Nell said to Irene.

Irene's laugh was like a bubble in her throat that wouldn't burst; it seemed to both tickle and concern her. "Even when I misplaced a few," she said, laughing until the bubble retreated, "there were still plenty more underfoot."

Irene patted Nell's arm, while Nell read a warning in the set of her mother's back. Nell's mother didn't need to follow directions; she sought strangers as guides, hoping they knew Nell and would lead her to her daughter. Nell thought that her mother hoped she would find a friend of Nell, who knew Nell in another way and could help her mother find her. But Nell's mother never asked anyone who knew Nell for directions. There was a part of Nell's life that had been spent hearing her mother say, "Where are you?" while Nell gave detailed directions and said, "I'm here." She had been calling, "I'm here," for years, while her mother misplaced or misread or forgot Nell's directions. She never found Nell easily or completely.

"We're here now," Nell's mother said. She opened the back door of the car. It hurt Nell that her mother had such a difficult time finding her, no matter how easy Nell tried to make it for her, and that she was unconcerned, even cheerful about her failures.

Her mother leaned across the back seat and rummaged through a number of brown paper bags, rolled tight like small pillows. Neatly arranged next to the paper bags were a straw beach bag, a cloth hat, a stack of beach towels, a pair of rubber flip-flops, and a thermos bottle.

"I have that map of yours," Nell's mother said. "It's right here." She poked unsuccessfully around the paper bags. "It got us off the highway and into town. I must have left your letter at home, there was so much packing to do. I'll look for it again when we finish our vacation."

"Fine," Nell said, knowing her mother wouldn't.

Her mother handed Nell one of the paper bags. Inside it was a plastic bag secured with a twist tie and filled with granola. Her mother's granola, baked with honey and coconut flakes, tasted heavy and delicious and took a lot of energy to chew.

"Thank you," Nell said, surprised and pleased.

In Nell's memory of her mother's car, the back seat was filled with thermos bottles of coffee and of Kool-Aid, paper bags containing apples, raisins, pears, and peanut butter and

After the Hunger

jelly sandwiches, a pile of sweatshirts, and flashlights and extra maps. Her mother took long, random drives in her car at night, revealing a small desperation in the way she stocked it, provisions against catastrophe. She lifted her sleeping children from their beds and carried them one by one to the car under the dark blue sky, wrapping them in blankets against the night chill. The headlights of the car wavered along the dark roads as her mother made her way to the coast road. Nell sat in the front seat, gripping a blanket around her. Nell's younger brother and sister sat confused and drowsy in the back, flanked by the mysterious paper bags, while their mother searched the coast road in the deep blue night for a place to rest that did not seem to exist for her.

Nell took her mother and Irene up the wooden staircase to the cottage her mother had been unable to find. Her mother and Irene settled into the straight back chairs.

"It's cozy here," Irene said.

"Would you like to look around?" Nell asked. She put the granola in a cabinet next to the bottle of wine.

A minute later Nell's mother and Irene were back in their chairs.

"Would you like some coffee?" Nell asked.

"Don't make it too strong," her mother called after her into the kitchen, raising her voice unnecessarily.

Nell set mugs of coffee, spoons, honey, and cream on the coffee table. She sat in one of the chairs. Her mother poured cream into her coffee. She stirred the coffee until the cream evenly colored it.

"Is there a grocery store nearby?" her mother asked.

Nell's spine straightened. "Yes," she said. "There's an A&P up the street. It's to the left on the road you crossed as you came into town."

"I hope you're taking advantage of it," her mother said.

"Why, yes," Nell said. "Yes. Very much so."

Her mother spooned honey into her coffee. She wore her diamond engagement ring on her right-hand ring finger; her wedding ring was in a jewelry box on her bureau at home, among the costume jewelry.

"The cross-ventilation is good here," her mother said.

The curtains blew softly. The breeze would pick up when the sun set, fiercely red, framed by the kitchen window. Nell could live now with windows exposed to a darkness undiluted by the lights from the town. There was promise again in the night air, in the wind that eddied through the rooms and seemed to sweep through her body. She sipped her coffee. Her mother, who so easily lost or misplaced her directions, was discussing with Irene the direction of the light and the sea breeze.

This is what her mother had been able to give her children: healthful meals, shelter, open windows and good air. Nell's younger brother and sister had married young and moved away. They owned homes now, and had children. Nell rarely saw them.

"How are you getting on, Nell?" her mother asked.

"Very well," Nell said.

"Do you need anything, dear?"

Nell tried to imagine what her mother meant. She said, "Thank you; I have everything I need." She got up to pour more coffee.

Her mother leaned forward in her chair. "Waiting on tables is a hard way to earn a dollar," she said.

"It's a portable profession," Nell said. "Like being a circuit judge or a physical therapist."

"It's not a profession," her mother said. "It's something you do to get by while you're making other plans."

"Well," Nell said, "I guess that's what I'm doing."

"But honey," her mother said, "you've been doing it for three years."

"I got to see California," Nell said. "I didn't like California. I went to the Grand Canyon. Have you been to the Grand Canyon, Irene?"

Irene looked up politely from her coffee. "No," Irene said. "I don't think the desert appeals to me."

"It didn't appeal to me, either," Nell said.

Nell's mother got to her feet, abruptly changing the subject. "If we don't eat lunch now," she said, "we won't have time to go to the harbor." She ushered Nell and Irene out of the cottage and down the stairs, even though she had no idea where she was going.

Nell and Irene followed Nell's mother onto the road that led to town. The day was clear, the sky an unmarred blue; days of this weather lay ahead, rolling in across an undisturbed sea.

Her mother put her arm around Nell's waist. Nell felt its assuring pressure and with it something that only her mother could do, touching a part of Nell that belonged to her mother and waited for this. Her mother's face was in profile as they walked together, her eyes on an undefinable middle distance. Nell draped her arm around her mother's waist. With her arm there Nell would be able to sense her mother's body tighten before Nell crossed the invisible line that marked their time together, waiting without temper for Nell to overstep it. If she kept her arm around her mother's waist she would be able to feel her mother's body tighten and step back in time.

Irene walked beside them, amiable and accommodating. Irene and Nell's mother had been taking vacations together for ten summers, beginning the year after Irene's husband had died. Nell took Irene's arm. "How is your family?" Nell asked.

"Oh," Irene said. "Everyone is fine. I'm having a family cookout on the Fourth of July. All the grandchildren will be there."

Nell remembered Irene's sons and daughters as a swarm of knock knees, skinned elbows, runny noses and limp blond hair, roller skating crazily down their street. Irene's husband, a practicing Catholic, had stopped speaking to Nell's mother, even in his own living room, after she divorced Nell's father. Irene's children gradually stopped asking Nell to roller skate with them down their street. "How many grandchildren do you have now, Irene?" Nell asked.

"Ten," Irene said. She laughed her bubbly laugh.

"Mother will never catch up with you," Nell said.

"Oh! A couple of grandchildren won't confuse a person too out of proportion," Irene said. "But ten! I still can't get their names straight. Or who they belong to." Irene found this very amusing. Nell liked her enormously.

Nell's mother released her arm from Nell's waist and moved away from her to pick a wildflower by the side of the road. She rolled the stem between her fingers, looking up at an old cemetery on a hill, its scarred and slanted stones overrun by flowering weeds. Nell let go of Irene's arm and took a step toward her mother. She was wildly afraid, suddenly, that her mother would walk off, into the old cemetery, or a part of town that Nell didn't know, and Nell would lose her there. Her mother threw the wildflower down. She hesitated by the side of the road, then came back to Nell and Irene. They resumed their slow walk into town. Her mother pulled at the diamond ring on her right hand, as if it irritated her finger.

The wisteria was in full bloom, the thick brown vines climbing the porticoes of the houses they passed. The lavender blossoms moved heavily in the breeze, like a piece of architecture on the houses that appeared only in spring.

Nell took them to the sidewalk café where she worked, on the main street. She had switched shifts for the day with one of the waitresses when her mother's letter arrived informing Nell of her visit. The café was a large flagstone patio that flowed outward from a small white building where the cook grilled, flambéed and sautéed, and yelled at the waitresses. The patio held a breeze that masked the cook's bursts of temper, and the waitresses, used to him, emerged from the building carrying trays with the poise of ballerinas. Nell ate most of her meals at the café during the summer season. After hours the waitresses and the cook, no longer under artistic pressure and subdued and friendly, walked down the street to a restaurant on the harbor and sat in the empty dining room, lit obliquely by floodlights that made pools of light on the harbor. They drank beer with the restaurant's staff while the sous-chef threw a line into the harbor and pulled baby squid from the water under the dazzling floodlights. The sous-chef brought bottles of white wine to their table and they drank it in the darkened dining room with the sautéed squid and Caesar salads he had prepared for them.

In the fall, after the restaurants closed, the Portuguese women gave Nell kale from their gardens and she made soup from the bitter-tasting plants, spiced with sausage and garlic. The fishermen who still went out to sea brought fresh catches of flounder and lobster to the wharf and Nell ate as she never had, the meat sweeter than she ever imagined it could be. She bought a license from the City Hall, "to take SHELLFISH and SEA WORMS from the tidal flats and waters," and went out at low tide, with a pail and a short-handled metal rake, to search for bubbles in the damp sand, signs of the quahogs' breathing.

In November the entire world was blue-gray—flats, tidal water, sky—its borders blurry and magical. The figures of the people of the town, dressed in the muted colors of late fall, bent over the flats with their rakes, harvesting quahogs from the wet sand. Nell made patterns in the sand with her rake and filled her pail. Of the men in the town she was beginning to know from harvesting the flats, one would always come to her, exactly at the moment her pail was full, his face lined with

After the Hunger

weather, and pull a knife from the sheath at his hip. He would take each mollusk from the pail, stick the point of the knife into the seam of the thick shell, and open it for her. She made chowders the way the men taught her, with the ingredients they named as they bent over the resisting shells: chopped celery, garlic, sea salt.

Nell, her mother and Irene sat at a table on the restaurant's patio under one of its wide blue umbrellas, which didn't quite shield the sun from their eyes. Their waitress held menus and her order pad high as she walked toward them between the crowded tables.

"Hi, Ann-Marie," Nell said.

"Hey, Nell." Ann-Marie smiled at her. "Is this your mom?"

"My mother, and her neighbor. Mother, Irene; Ann-Marie."

Irene nodded; Nell's mother said, "And how do you like working here, Ann-Marie?"

"Oh, fine," Ann-Marie said, looking puzzled.

"I'll have a glass of iced tea, Ann-Marie," Nell's mother said.

"I'll have a Bloody Mary," Nell said.

"I'll have a Bloody Mary," Irene said. She grinned conspiratorially at Nell.

Nell's mother searched her pocketbook for her reading glasses and studied the menu. Ann-Marie brought their drinks. Nell's mother asked Ann-Marie to bring her some Sweet 'n Lo. Ann-Marie quickly searched the nearby tables and brought a supply of packets to her. Nell's mother shook the packets and ripped them open. Nell had seen her mother open the letters that came from her father in the same way, with the postmarks from towns that Nell didn't know, until they stopped coming altogether. Her mother would shake the envelope and rip it open and take the folded letter out. She would open the letter, blow into the torn envelope and look into it. Then she would refold the letter, unread, back into the envelope, tear it up and throw it away.

There was a loose, steady crowd on the sidewalk. Irene laughed and the bubble in her throat rose and fell. She tried to catch her breath. She wiped her eyes with her napkin. "Why," she said, "everyone is so informal."

They watched the crowd on the sidewalk, women in shorts and halter tops, men in T-shirts that barely covered their chests, children shouting and racing each other down the street in wet bathing suits, ahead of their parents.

"The season is just beginning," Nell said.

A grand matron walked by, leaning lightly on a silver cane, in a large straw hat and a linen caftan.

"She owns a huge house on a bluff outside of town," Nell said of her. "I've never seen her in town but she's not covered from head to toe. She usually has her driver take her around. She must suffer no end in the heat."

Irene turned her chair slightly to keep the crowd in view as she squeezed the juice from a lemon slice into her Bloody Mary. "Is there a hospital in town?" she asked.

"Do you mean," Nell said, hungrily eating a stalk of celery dipped in vodka and tomato juice, "do people have babies here?" Nell's mother looked up quickly from her menu. "There's a hospital about twenty-five miles away,"

Nell said, "but there's a health center here, and a library, and schools—" She checked herself; she was becoming too elaborate. Nell shielded her eyes from the sun and turned her face to the breeze coming from the harbor. "From here," Nell said to Irene, "it doesn't seem as if anyone could be sick or ever want to read a book."

Her mother flagged Ann-Marie to take their orders. Her mother was displeased with Nell, Nell knew it by the restless fetching of her reading glasses from her pocketbook, the set of her mouth as she shielded her eyes from the sun and pointed to the menu as she gave her order, the pitch and scrape of her chair on the flagstones. Long ago, in her mother's car, still disoriented from sleep, Nell had held a flashlight over the map on her lap. They had missed the exit to the coast road. With her reading glasses her mother had pointed vaguely toward the vast, blank space at the edge of the map, colored blue, the Atlantic Ocean, and said, "Find the turnoff that leads north. Not the highway, but the two-lane road. It will be the red one." The map flowed over Nell's lap and onto the upholstered seat. It was full of red lines, like veins.

Her mother took off her reading glasses and conferred with Ann-Marie, changing her French fry order to coleslaw, and after Ann-Marie left with their orders she decided, putting her glasses away and snapping her pocketbook shut, that she wanted a Bloody Mary too. Nell followed Ann-Marie into the restaurant. She waited in the doorway for her mother's drink, locating the table on the crowded patio where her mother and Irene sat. The breeze ruffled the edges of the umbrellas, and the entire patio seemed to move as if in a slow current. Nell's mother leaned toward Irene and said something to her, then sat upright, looking impatiently across the patio. She tapped her fingers on the table, and Nell saw in that gesture the minor discomforts that were unnecessary and in some way unkind, but provoked by a greater, unnamed discomfort. Her mother turned to Nell to fix them, to run after a harried waitress, complicating everything, while the other discomfort remained unfixed, unexorcised.

Ann-Marie brought the drink to Nell. "Thanks," Nell said. Ann-Marie winked at her. Nell lifted the drink from Ann-Marie's tray, holding it high as she walked between the tables. Nell gave the drink to her mother. She sipped it under the umbrella. Nell sat close to her in the bright sunlight. Her mother and Irene had bursts of laugh lines in the delicate skin at the corners of their eyes. Their skin was surprisingly luminous, as if deep springs of health flowed under its surfaces. The lines between her mother's eyebrows were straight and flat.

Ann-Marie served their lunch of lobster salad and sliced cantaloupe. Nell and Irene turned their chairs toward the sidewalk. "Oh look," Irene said. "That boy there, on that platter with wheels, I should know— Oh yes, on that skateboard, my grandchildren have them, the boys anyway. Look, he's running up the side of that building." The bubble in her throat almost burst. Nell's mother's chair was turned slightly away from them, toward the wide blue umbrellas on the patio rippling in the current of air, as if she were seeing something else altogether.

After the Hunger

Nell's mother folded her napkin on the table and called to Ann-Marie for the check. She scrutinized it with her reading glasses and left a bill under her iced tea glass. She led Nell and Irene away from the patio and into the swirl of tourists, seasonal workers, and day-trippers that flowed along the sidewalk and into the street. There was a deep solitude expressed in her mother's posture, the stride of her walk. Nell noticed with a small shock that her mother's shoulders, once squared with resolve, were rounded now, giving in. Her mother moved farther ahead of Nell and Irene, putting more and more distance between them. Her mother's walk excluded everyone and everything but its own purpose; in it was the memory that she, too, had been left behind.

Nell and Irene walked down the sidewalk. Nell took her hand. Nell's mother was far ahead of them. "I think my mother is trying to lead us to the sloop," Nell said, "but she missed the turn-off to the wharf." Then she would come back upon them, anxiety ready to distill into anger at missing the boat ride on the harbor. Irene laughed; this was her medium. Nell laughed too.

Irene walked farther down the street to find Nell's mother, while Nell turned onto a side street and down the wharf. The sloop was tied to its berth, murmuring the sounds of a boat at rest: the strain of rope against wood, the slap of the lines against the furled sails, the ping of the sloop's bell with each slow roll of the boat in the harbor's swells. The afternoon sun was hot. A caravan of skateboarders and bicyclists flowed past Nell as she queued for tickets.

Nell paid for the tickets and folded them into her pocket. She walked toward the concrete structure at the wharf's end, where the fishermen unloaded their catches. The wharf was old and scarred, almost a relic. The waters were depleted; there were quotas or bans altogether on certain catches. The wharf smelled of time and history, of struggle and conquest that had nothing to do with men. It had the depth of the ocean in it, the scent of creatures that spawned and migrated, hunted and ate according to another clock, another understanding of time altogether, that were hauled out of the liquid environment to die in air by men who knew the tides, seasons, storms; men who knew about hunting and sometimes dying in water too.

The fishing boats were out, beyond the breakwater and the harbor, out of sight. The harbor smelled salty, ripe, alive. The smell of the harbor soothed Nell, like the first shock of salt air through the open windows of a car at night. It was all from memory, timeless; when had she first known the bite of salt air in her nostrils, the taste of the ocean? Something was good then; the memory of comfort was in her nostrils, from a time when driving on the coast road had tricked her, distilling itself into scent: here is comfort, here is danger.

At the end of the wharf, on the far side of the concrete structure, the ropes for tying the fishing boats were secured to wooden pilings. All along the wharf the pilings were cracked and brown from the salt air, and below the high-tide mark they were eaten badly by sea worms. The water was a deeper shade of the washed blue sky. Gulls hung in the air currents.

After the Hunger

On the far side of the breakwater the wind raised whitecaps on the water. The town curved gracefully on either side of the wharf. The houses, close against the shore, were white and the silvery brown of weathered cedar.

Nell leaned against an aged piling and lifted her face to the sun; behind her eyelids the sun was vivid yellow-red, warm. The harbor sounds were far away: the cry of sea birds, the drift of boats at anchor, the slow lapping of the waters. Nell let a small spasm overtake her shoulders, of relief and pleasure.

Then she heard her mother's voice, the memory of it distilled into sound as old as she could remember; she would hear it until she died. Her mother's voice was calling to her, as far away as the sounds of the harbor, a constant undercurrent. Then it emerged from all the other sounds, with its own urgency. Nell opened her eyes and got quickly to her feet. She moved down the wharf, following her mother's voice, old as memory: this is comfort, this is danger.

Nell and her mother and Irene queued at the sloop with their tickets. A member of the crew helped the passengers onto the vessel. The passengers were led to low chairs on the deck, to port and starboard. The view was clear and unobstructed. The crew untied the ropes from the dock and Nell, sitting between Irene and her mother, heard the vibration of the engines starting below. The heavy wooden ship eased out of its berth and voyaged slowly beyond the breakwater and into the harbor.

The engines ceased and the crew unfurled the sails; the sails billowed and strained against the masts. The sloop picked up speed and glided into the harbor, turning its bow into the wind, and Nell was alone on the water in the graceful boat. The cottages at the far eastern curve of the harbor swept by, and then crew and passengers were traveling out, toward the open sea, with no land to guide them.

The wind was stronger there; one of the crew offered blankets, but Nell and her mother and Irene refused them. The wind filled the sails and urged the sloop onward. Irene took Nell's hand and said, "Imagine being here, on the water, in winter, coming to this shore in a boat after months at sea, and sickness and starvation, and your old life behind you." Irene looked toward the blank blue water and the even blue sky. "I can't imagine it," she said, "the hardship and loneliness."

Nell looked at her mother, who seemed to recognize that hard blue sky and sea, the voyage into a territory of hardship and loneliness. Her mother sat upright in the chilly wind, her fingers gripping her pocketbook. "You would travel by the stars at night," she said. "You would find a point of reference there and travel by it. They must have known that then. And in the daylight there is the sun to follow."

This is the stock you come from, Nell thought, *reducing hardship to equations made from stars in the night sky, and depending on the charity of the weather, the direction of the sun, and your own determined heart.* Nell saw the lines of hardship and loneliness in her mother's face that didn't obscure the soft hope that lay beneath them, the perseverance that kept her face beautiful and alive. Nell wondered if, on those long journeys in the car that her mother stocked with provisions against calamity, she found a sign in the night sky to travel by, if those journeys were necessary to reaffirm for her that beyond rage and abandonment lay a harbor for her, however foreign and frightening, somewhere that she could leave behind the burden of exile that she believed marked her.

The sloop sailed out past the harbor toward the cold blue horizon. There was the roar in Nell's ears of the wind, the rush of the sea against the wooden hull, the splash of spray like a baptism. Her mother's body leaned into hers as the sloop turned and began to tack toward shore. The wind blew her mother's hair and her cheeks were flushed. The lines of worry between her eyebrows were deeply furrowed. Nell wanted to press her fingertips against them, rest her palm over her mother's brow. The wind was against them; the engines started up to help ease the sloop back into the harbor.

The pressure of her mother's body withdrew from Nell and her mother sat upright again under the engines' power as the sails, tied close now to the masts, no longer worked against the wind. "That was a long way out," her mother said, adjusting her vision from the trackless horizon to the fringe of houses along the shoreline. Nell was aware, like the knowledge of loss, of her mother's body no longer pressing against her side. She looked at her mother's hands, so much like Nell's own, holding her pocketbook on her lap.

"Yes," Nell said, and a frozen memory leapt out at her, of her mother's car home now, safe, the engine cut and dying under the deep blue night, and her mother lifting each dozing child wrapped in a blanket against the chill, to sleep again in their beds. The car doors opened one by one and Nell's brother and sister murmured in their sleep as they were carried inside. Then Nell's mother opened the car door and lifted her up. Nell lay her head heavily against her mother's shoulder and looked up at the night sky gone lighter now as her mother wrapped the blanket around her and carried her into the house. She tucked the sheets around her and sat in a chair next to Nell's bed as Nell drifted back into sleep to the memory of the vibration of the car's engine, which seemed to her now like the sound of full sails in a strong wind.

The Great Salt Marsh

The church was built of fieldstone on a narrow corner of clipped grass and frost-worn sidewalks. Its true height and depth were difficult to apprehend because of the two perpendicular-running streets with their cars and taxicabs and buses, the nearness of other buildings, and the portion of land that held the church, giving one a feeling of vertigo on looking skyward or a false idea of one-dimensionality when standing before it. The grounds had great beauty because of the two yellowwood trees that grew on either side of the walkway from which one approached, their trunks knotted and gnarled. They bloomed in June with flowers like hanging white bouquets. The trees were almost the height of the church, and so, even from the Common across the street, one saw only the dense branches and leaves. Above the trees was a rectangular steeple, also made of fieldstone, crowned with a gold weathervane in the likeness of a bantam cock with a feathered tail.

Patricia knew these things, paid attention to them. How the grass grew poorly under the yellowwood trees. How, on a Sunday, passing under the trees, crossing the loosely fitted slate walk and a brief set of steps and opening the massive wooden doors one found oneself in a vestibule and one could see, beyond it, the sanctuary and its pews and the altar and the stained-glass windows. There someone gave Patricia a bulletin and it was mostly someone she didn't know. Another walkway was on the near side of the church, longer, more recently tended and repaired, which led to another door where, on stepping through it, one was in a hallway with a bench, as if for waiting or resting, and beyond it was another door to the sanctuary, nearer to the altar, and to the right of the hallway were the church offices. Patricia knew all these things and she often saw the church in her mind, its heavy proportions occupying the land. She carried the image of the church with her, a beautiful thing made of stone and wood and glass.

The sidewalk was patched with ice. Patricia walked carefully toward the intersecting streets, carrying the evening's reading in her gloved hand. In the early dark, the church seemed to be slumbering. The great windows were as if turned away, the figures in them without form. All the lights were off, even the spotlight that lit the face of the church. Only the window in the minister's office was lit. Other days, other evenings there were services and meetings of committees and coffee hour after church, and lunch in the meeting hall, served the second Sunday of each month, and Saturday breakfast for men and Bible readings and people making sandwiches in the kitchen after services to give to

After the Hunger

homeless men and women on the Common. Then there were the organizations that used the church to give concerts of chamber music in the sanctuary and hold Al-Anon and AA meetings in the upstairs, paneled rooms, the oak there darkened with age and neglect. Patricia sometimes used to see the men and women from those meetings standing on the side walkway in the early evening, smoking cigarettes, trying to think or not think their way from pain, crushing the tooth-marked, stained filters under their heels and lighting another, until the stewards, having been approached by aggrieved church members, told them they couldn't smoke there anymore.

Patricia didn't know all that the church did, all that occurred in its many rooms, some lushly furnished with drapes and wing chairs, some bare except for a stack of folding chairs. She was a peripheral person who had once walked the half-mile there most Sundays and heard the choir and the minister and looked at the stained-glass windows, struck by the sun, and at the fans in the high ceiling, the blades turning in the summer heat. When she stopped attending with any predictability people had understood something about her and stopped calling to ask her to sit on a committee or to bring cookies for the coffee hour. When she did attend services she sat in a pew in the back of the sanctuary and took the hands of a few people during the greeting of peace and held the hymnal and lifted her voice upward, seeking to join the others in song. But Tom, their new minister, had called to invite her to a group that was to meet each week during

Lent, and so she had put on her boots to walk to the church to join them.

The minister's office was arrived at after opening a door to the suite of offices, the outer two rooms for staff and storage and copying. Tom's office was crowded with furniture and books; Patricia wondered on entering it whether he had inherited all the paraphernalia of the other ministers—Tom being the fourth to have led the congregation since Patricia had started going there—and perhaps the paraphernalia of all the ministers before them. There were voices in his office and the smell of wool coats hung in the overheated room. An old radiator clicked and hissed in a corner.

There were only two places to sit, at a chair pulled up, facing Tom's desk, or around a low glass top wooden table shaped like a wheel, with the carved figures of people and small flags like prayer flags all moving outward as if on spokes. Patricia took off her coat and gloves and sat in a chair in a circle with the others. She shook the hand of the woman next to her, who had offered it. There were eight people in the room, including Patricia. They were all talking in low voices among themselves. The group had missed the first meeting because of the weather and Patricia had missed the following week, having had the flu or some distress she couldn't name; and so they were already into the middle of March, Easter coming that year on the second Sunday of April. Patricia, to prepare, had spent a number of evenings reading chapters from the book they had been assigned.

After the Hunger

People stopped talking when Tom arrived and sat with them. He was dressed informally in trousers and a V-neck sweater, and under it an open-collar shirt. He was a man in his mid-thirties, with a large frame, and so he filled up spaces like chairs and altars and rooms. He said, in his trained, pleasant voice, "Hello, and welcome to the third week of the Lenten season." They greeted him with respectful silence. He said, "Patricia is new to our group tonight. Patricia, would you like to introduce yourself?"

Patricia looked down, then across the wooden table, and addressed the group. She said, "Hello, I'm Patricia Waring." Waring was her married name. She used it more and more easily now. She paused and thought about how she would introduce herself to the people in the room, whom she didn't know, who looked at her with mild expectancy. Her life seemed suddenly complicated and unclear, like a trail looping back on itself. She wished she had a story, a simple, clear story: this is what I bring to you. She said, "I've been coming to church for a number of years. Though not with any regularity. As I had so hoped. I'm glad to be here with you and I look forward to sharing this Lenten season."

The group looked away from her and turned to Tom. He asked them to introduce themselves to Patricia and she began to hear their names, and she nodded and repeated, "Bill," and "Ethel," and "Fiona," to each. Everyone seemed to be about the same age, within a range; she thought Tom must have planned that, he must have had some idea about how he wanted the group to be composed.

There were a few white stones clustered on the glass tabletop, and a metal bar and a hammer with a triangle-shaped head beside it. A honey-colored candle had already been lit. The burning wick illuminated the rim of the candle, and the flame flickered within it. Patricia imagined that Tom had lit the candle the first evening; the wick seemed to have burned that far. Tom struck the hammer to the bar and asked for a moment of silence and prayer. Patricia closed her eyes and bowed her head. The one, high note of the bar seemed to linger in the air. She heard breathing and the shuffling of boots on the worn wooden floor, and she saw where the office door was, in her mind, and the door leading to the hallway, and the door leading outside, and she breathed once deeply and told herself where she was, in a room with people of the church.

They continued to bow their heads. Tom had led them not into prayer but a prolonged silence. Patricia wondered what she was to do. She was to pray. But how to arrive at a prayer. Hers were usually so brief. For help, or guidance, or to celebrate gladness. She did not know what to do with the silence. It seemed as if a cloth, a loosely woven cloth, covered her eyes. She began to think about the weather and the walk home in a deeper darkness, and she remembered how the minister, the one who had died, had walked her home after a meeting. He had asked her to join a committee and afterward, after the meeting was done, he walked her home. The season cool, early spring; it held the smell of hyacinths. The setting of the sun had brought a mild, intermittent wind, and at the street corners there was a sharpness to it, as if it carried with it the end of the harshness of winter.

He walked her home through the spring darkness and talked about the oak tree across the street that was over two hundred years old, its bark that turned the color of metal in the dying light, and how old and drafty the parsonage was, and how he wrote his sermons by hand at a small hard desk in a cramped room that overlooked the flowering chestnut tree, should it ever bloom again, while he wore a heavy sweater and blew into his hands. She knew from a plaque on a wall in the church the year he had started his ministry; he had been there almost twenty years. She had come to the church out of loneliness, the kind of loneliness one can only have in New England, and there was her minister walking beside her in the spring night. She listened to his voice in the darkness, with only the faint contained light from a streetlight on each corner, and she thought she could walk with him into the night and the next. She went home and tried to understand how she was to think of that walk, with her minister speaking to her as they slowly pursued the evening under the trees.

Tom struck the metal bar again and the people in the room opened their eyes and raised their heads. He said to Patricia, "As you know, we're reading week by week as we move through the Lenten season. We should now be reading from the third week of Lent, but if there's anything else you want to look at from the earlier chapters, we can do so. We will continue to prayerfully contemplate Jesus' forty days and nights in the wilderness as we continue our journey."

People crossed their legs. They opened their books. Patricia said, "If I may say. I just wondered about Lent. How it came to be something we participate in at this time, in the days leading to Good Friday and Easter." She had placed her book on the glass top table. "In that," she said, "first Jesus was baptized by his cousin John, then he went into the wilderness, then he returned and called his disciples and preached and healed the sick. Then he was crucified. He was in the wilderness for forty days and forty nights, after his baptism, it seems to me as a way to prepare for his ministry, not later, not to prepare for his death. After his baptism, see here, our book quotes Mark, "The spirit driveth him into the wilderness."

Patricia looked at Tom. He had shut his book, and he held it on his knee. She wondered if she sounded to him like one of the impertinent Pharisees, trying to trip up Jesus. "Because," she continued, "he came to Jerusalem deliberately, from Jericho and Bethany and the Mount of Olives, and then he was betrayed. Before that, he went from a city, like Capernaum, say, or the coasts of Judea or the shore of the Sea of Galilee, he withdrew to the desert or a mountain to be alone and pray, but people followed him, the multitudes followed him, and brought him back to them."

Patricia was aware of the people in the room, that their attention was elsewhere; they probably were eager to speak, to discuss the book they held in their hands. Lent was a figment, she knew, it was a Catholic invention that some Protestant churches, at least her church, had decided to model. Perhaps the Catholics could get away with it, because at one time their congregants were forbidden or unable to read the Bible; it was left to the priests to interpret it for them. But anyone who read the Gospels could see that Christ was baptized, he went into the wilderness, he preached and healed the sick, he celebrated Passover with his disciples in Jerusalem, he was betrayed and tried and crucified. Anyone who could read could see that. After his baptism Jesus relinquished the world and went into the wilderness alone. He prayed and fasted. *He had been sent to learn*, Patricia thought, *to be who he already was.*

She remembered the Catholic girls in her high school, their foreheads marked by the thumb of the priest, discussing what they had decided to give up—chocolates or sneaking cigarettes or chewing gum in class. They skipped breakfast as a way of fasting and by mid-morning were sullen and petulant and often on the verge of tears. She did not know what people did now, even the people of her own church, what prayer was like, or penance, and if fasting brought on the hardships that Jesus knew, and then the revelation. She had been excluded by her own ignorance, her own disbelief.

Tom returned his book to the table with deliberation. He picked up one of the white stones, moved it an inch along the surface of the glass, then moved it back again. He looked at Patricia sternly, as if she were some reckless woman who had arrived invited to the table but now had placed herself outside the circle of believers.

Patricia adjusted her shoulders. She was trying to find a posture from which to speak. She did not look at Tom. "It seems the struggle Jesus had," she said, "was with something more, something we don't know about. He always seemed to know that he would be betrayed, that he would be abandoned by his disciples, that he would die. So perhaps in a way he was already preparing himself for his death. Maybe he was sent to the wilderness to learn how to be the beloved Son of God."

Patricia wondered if her church had celebrated Lent under the minister who died. She attended church irregularly, even then. She wondered if she would have questioned it, if she would have questioned the minister who died. But she believed everything then; she believed the minister who died as he gave readings from the Bible and spoke with formality and love to the people listening in the pews and led them in communion and lifted his robed arms and blessed them at the end of the service. But now she needed to know why the church would celebrate Lent whose premise was an event that had not occurred in the weeks before Jesus' crucifixion. It had something to do with the minister's death, she knew. Nothing had been right since then.

Around the table, a few people had pressed their fingertips against their foreheads. Tom, it seemed, had simply been waiting for her to finish. She looked at him now, her mouth slightly open.

He said, "We have entered a time of prayer and introspection with the advent of Lent. It is a time to make room for God." He was not speaking to her. Nevertheless, he seemed to be rebuking her, as if she had transgressed the agreed-upon, shared belief about the story of Jesus in the wilderness. To prepare for their meetings, she had read the Gospels again, to know again how the people who witnessed Jesus preach and heal the sick and cast out unclean spirits and perform miracles were amazed and astonished, they marveled, they were full of wonder, they trembled and were afraid. Shepherds saw angels and Jesus' disciples saw him walk on water and the multitudes saw him touch a person and make him whole. People were hungry and were fed. Lazarus rose from the dead. The priests were offended. Jesus wanted his followers to be silent about what they had witnessed, but they rejoiced and spread his fame. The people who had lived beyond the reach of hope or comfort wore robes and rags and wept in Jesus' presence.

"As we begin," Tom said, "I want to remind you that this is a place of safety, where we are free to speak our hearts." The old radiator banged. The room was hot and close. Patricia's mouth was dry. She gripped the underside of her chair with her fingers.

"I read here," the woman next to Patricia said, opening her book, "in the reading for Tuesday, about desire, and passion, and the promise of ecstasy, and I thought about my husband. He's been gone now for three years, and it's just occurring to me that we had a relationship of great distance, though he was always kind. We raised three children together. But now, thinking about him, I remember his courtesy and his carefulness, as if we were playing out an idea of marriage as a kind of obedience to God. Though something was always between us. A veil was always between us."

Patricia looked at the woman beside her, at her lowered eyes. She seemed to be looking at the space in front of the burning candle. Patricia thought that this was what was being sought by her, in Tom's office, some way to acknowledge absence, or an understanding of disappointment, and to share it. But no one made a reply to the woman who had spoken about her husband.

Tom struck the hammer softly to the bar and it returned a low, muffled note. They all bowed their heads. The radiator released a burst of steam. Patricia closed her eyes. The minister who died had joined a meeting after church. It was being held in a room with drapes and good chairs. He wore a light wool suit. She didn't know who he was. His skin was clear, almost radiant. After he died someone said to her that his radiant skin was a sign that he was a man of God. But she didn't know him then. No one acknowledged him and he sat quietly and listened to the progress of the meeting. A man with a bony face and rough-knuckled hands was proposing a protest against the limits imposed on their committee to give money to causes, to worthy causes; he wanted to march on the church in the way protesters did against the Vietnam war.

Patricia was uninitiated in the ways of the church, she didn't understand its history and its loyalties and its factions, but she said, "I can't protest against a church I have just come to." The man who had made the proposal looked like an old warrior, familiar with protest, but Patricia didn't want to be part of an estrangement. The man in the light wool suit stayed a few more minutes and left. Afterward, an hour or so later,

After the Hunger

he called her at home. So it was he. He was just ending his sabbatical, he said. He was spending the day in meetings. He said, "People in the church are too intimidated by that man to oppose him, but you had the courage to do so." She said, "I'm perhaps too new to know any better." Then he had to go away, to another meeting. She heard someone speak to him, respectfully, as if from across a room. After he said good-bye to her she sat in her living room and held the receiver in her open hand and then put it back in its cradle.

Another woman spoke. People raised their heads. The woman said, "I remember the birth of each of my daughters. They're both married now, but I remember their births so vividly." She looked at the woman next to her and they smiled at each other deeply. "I know that isn't what our book discusses, exactly, but in reading it I thought about my daughters. I had asked for love and found my husband. Then I had my two daughters. I was glad to have that, to know the love of a child."

Tom struck the metal bar. The note seemed to enter the room in waves. Patricia looked at the carved prayer flags under the sheet of glass. She did not know what to call what had happened between herself and the minister who died. He telephoned her sometimes in the morning, on a Saturday. She was always surprised. He said, "How are you?" and she felt buoyant, and she understood happiness as a physical thing. She said, "My grandmother left me a book of recipes when she died. I've begun to read it. It's written in a beautiful hand." The minister had the flat accent of the Plains. He told her that when he first came to the church, the women wore elaborate fur coats and looked at him reproachfully from their pews, as if to say, What can you do for me? He was a young man then, not even forty, called to the church that was set back from the frost-broken sidewalks, with its old ways and its politics and its patrician congregants. He kept the liturgical calendar, he had them sing the old hymns. He read to them from Paul's letters and from the Gospel according to John.

People were looking at Patricia. They seemed to be waiting for her to speak. Had she said something? She picked up her book. She had read the chapters, but she couldn't remember any of them. She thought about Jesus' ministry, how he often retreated to a mountain or the desert. That was surely what he did after he was baptized, he retreated to the desert in prayer. Although none of the Gospels described what Jesus had done there, what had really brought him to the desert. In John, Patricia had read about Jesus admonishing a Pharisee, "Marvel not that I said unto thee, Ye must be born again. The wind bloweth where it listeth, and thou hearest the sound thereof, but canst not tell whence it cometh, and whither it goeth: so is every one that is born of the Spirit." *So the Spirit was like a wind,* Patricia had thought, closing her Bible, *that one surrenders to. It comes from somewhere and it takes one somewhere, and it is impossible to know. It was the breath of God that drove Jesus into the desert to confront himself.*

She fumbled with the book in the overheated room. She searched for a passage she had marked. "I was moved by this chapter," she said, "this brief chapter, for Monday, on prayer, where it is described as meditation, as entering into an awareness of God." She thought when reading the passage she had understood what Jesus had done in the desert. The desert brought hunger, and hardship, and temptation, and finally, surrender to God. And afterward Jesus was able to return and begin his ministry. She ran her finger along the page in the book, touching the black letters and the margins and the spaces between the lines of print.

"Let us do so then," Tom said. He sounded the metal bar and they closed their eyes. All was blankness and darkness. Patricia felt the small living heat of the candle lit on the tabletop. The cloth in front of her eyes was loosely woven and its color was brown, like dirt or sand.

The minister who died hardly ever talked about himself. He called her in the morning when she imagined he thought she would be at home. He called her on a Saturday. He said, "Hello, Patricia." She thought him very kind. She loved him. This was what she could not say to him. She wasn't sure what he wanted to know about her. But he was, she knew, asking her to talk to him. She was going in the afternoon, she told him, to visit the shore. She would go to a clam shack on the water and order steamers and French fries. She ran her hand down the cord to the telephone. She heard him breathing lightly. "The sea," he said.

In the evening, after a meeting, when he walked her home, the shadows of the leaves were on the brick walls and the shadows made the bushes in the yards rise above themselves, their own doubles. The minister who died listened to her. She told him about picking strawberries, on a farm to the west, and how they had stained her fingertips red and the hard seeds on the new berries had made small cuts on her hands. She made a compote of the strawberries and stalks of rhubarb from a recipe she had found among her grandmother's papers. The minister who died walked beside her as the shadows of the leaves rose along the brick walls. She knew he was waiting for her to tell him something, but she didn't know what it was. When they got to where she lived sometimes she wrapped her sweater around herself or felt the long flow of her scarf, and in doing so turned slightly away, and he was gone, into the evening, and she couldn't hear his footsteps, all was quiet and still, and she felt alone and bereft.

"I wanted to return to Wednesday," a younger man said, speaking forcefully into the room. "The Wednesday of this week, the third week. I think it's especially appropriate. In that we are all wounded. You see, I've been estranged from my father almost all of my adult life. I can't begin to tell you why; it's too painful. And so that estrangement has led to an uncomfortable relationship with my mother, as you can imagine. So you could say that I am estranged from them both. And that has been difficult because often there has been no one. But I don't really see a way back, because the wounds are too deep." The younger man sat back heavily in his chair. His posture did not seem to invite comment. The room felt close, the air somehow fogged and tainted, as if the younger man, in speaking, had discharged something material into the room.

After the Hunger

Tom said, "We have discussed a lot of important topics this evening, many to do with our own needs, our own fallibility. And trying to live in the spirit of God. We will end our evening with a moment of silence." The people around the table folded their hands and bowed their heads. Patricia shut her eyes. She shifted slightly in her chair. They had been sitting now for over an hour. She was no longer afraid of the room, its closeness. There were so many wounded people in the Gospels. With leprosy, palsy, blindness; the lame and those inhabited by devils. A woman who bled for twelve years and people who died and caused great sorrow to those who loved them. People who were ill followed Jesus and he healed them. There were so many; almost everyone who came to Jesus seemed to be ill. Patricia thought they must have suffered in a different way, with some anguish of the spirit made into another anguish which Jesus healed.

Tom reminded them of the reading for the following week, and everyone, standing finally, complained about the weather and buttoned their coats and laughed as if expelling something out of their bodies, as if the evening had brought this about. Patricia walked toward home. The parsonage was a few blocks up the street from the church. Its windows were lit. Tom's wife was keeping the windows lit for him. Patricia had been to the parsonage only twice, more recently when its interior was painted after a wait of two years following the death of the minister before finding another, a man who did not follow the liturgical calendar as the minister who died had done, and Patricia felt lost within her own life. She had gone to the open house to see the parsonage again, to remember it as she had known it when the minister who died had invited her to Thanksgiving dinner. She had known him not even a year and he had become ill suddenly with cancer, and when he became too ill to preach and then to walk he removed himself from the church, its building and its congregation, as if preparing himself for death. He had died in the parsonage, but she didn't think of that when she walked through the rooms to see them again.

This time she was able to see the whole house, upstairs and down, not just the few rooms the minister who died and his wife and their guests inhabited over the course of Thanksgiving day, and the foyer where he took her coat and hung it in a closet and put his hand out lightly, briefly, as if to touch her back, and guided her into the house. The rooms were different now, the walls painted in bright primary colors. Patricia had liked the house so much better in its somber New England colors, the rooms with their marble fireplaces and the old rugs before them. She walked up the lovely curving staircase and found her way into the room where the minister who died had written his sermons, as if he had given her directions for finding it. The room was empty of furniture or drapes, a stark, small room with wide floorboards marred where the minister who died had thrust back his chair. Outside the chestnut tree was in bloom, the clusters of yellow flowers upright as if displayed with scores of candles.

That Thanksgiving, Patricia brought a green pea salad to the parsonage. She had tossed it in sage. She had been reading her grandmother's recipe book and it turned out it was not a recipe book, though there were some of the old recipes for stuffed tomatoes in aspic, apple coleslaw, and cranberry mold written in a careful, upright hand. It was a book; that is, a number of sheets of paper and note cards held loosely between moleskin covers, containing recipes mostly for healing illnesses. For coughs, nervous complaints, indigestion, headaches; burns and insect bites; feverish colds, female complaints, insomnia, anxiety, muscle cramps; to purify the blood, and to fortify the blood. Some were written in hands other than her grandmother's on yellowed onionskin paper. On quite a lot of them, in her grandmother's hand, was printed a woman's name and a date above the name of the recipe, and Patricia recognized some of the surnames as belonging to her grandmother's mother and her sisters and aunts. Each recipe was for a tea or a compress, a sachet or a salve. Patricia had tossed the green pea salad in a sprinkle of sage because it was once cultivated, she learned, in monastery gardens, and its Latin name, *salvia officinalis*, was derived from the Latin *salvere*, to save.

The dining room table in the parsonage sat twelve and it was fitted with a linen tablecloth, and Patricia and the minister's wife and the other women brought out the food and set it on the table. The minister who died said a prayer and Patricia bowed her head and listened deeply. A number of people from the congregation had been invited and Patricia sat at the table and was glad. Afterward they sang hymns in the living room with its high ceiling and oak woodwork and a fireplace fire burning. Later the minister's wife put together a plate for her and Patricia walked home with it held out in her hands. That was before she was married, and she was lonely and full of sorrow and rage and she loved the minister who died but she didn't know, would never know, if that is what he had wanted of her.

A thin sheet of ice on her front steps splintered under her heel. She unlocked the door and took off her boots on the mat inside the door. Fred was asleep on the couch. He had seemed to come to her out of nowhere, as if in a dream, and married her. They could have lived anyplace, within reason, but he moved into her small house in the neighborhood full of old trees and vines that crawled across the roofs of houses because he noticed the way everything was familiar to her, the front-door lock that had to be jiggled and the squirrels that ran across the telephone wires like trapeze artists and the dips and ruts in the road. Patricia sat on the couch so they were hip to hip and leaned over him and kissed him. He put his arms around her and she fitted herself onto the couch with him. He was still in his work clothes, a blue shirt and black trousers and a Jerry Garcia tie flung wildly across his shoulder.

"I thought you were going to call me," Fred said. His voice was arriving from the end of sleep.

"The walk was good, even in this weather." She had put the book down on the coffee table.

"So," Fred said.

Patricia sighed.

After the Hunger

"No?" He looked at her closely. "I thought it might be good, you know, good to be with a group of people at the church, have a conversation."

Patricia lifted the book and put it down again. "Do you think that a way to talk about Jesus' suffering in the wilderness is that we must talk about our own?" she asked. "The evening was like a confessional. I found it embarrassing. I think Tom encourages it. He has a candle and a bell; there were a lot of silences for prayer. We may as well have all been lying on horsehair couches draped in Oriental rugs."

"I would think not," Fred said. He had sat up. He was fully awake now. They were sitting together on the couch. He had smoothed his tie down his chest. "I would think we're supposed to try to replicate Jesus' experience in the wilderness, as if that were even possible, in terms of prayer." Fred was raised as a Baptist, and he had read the Bible, really studied it, but he had lost his belief in God. That continued to confuse Patricia. "And where did prayer lead him?" Fred went on. "That's the question. People seem to miss the point. Maybe it's too difficult. Who is able to forgive, for example? Maybe it's all beyond us."

"I wish we could just talk about Lent, whatever it's supposed to be, and not bring our own lives into it," Patricia said. "I felt that I couldn't really join in without confessing something. As if that would have made me a true part of the group. One man spoke about his father and it was somehow very disturbing. Although a woman spoke about the birth of her daughters, it was from the part of the reading about having the courage to ask for love."

"That sounds like it," Fred said. He kissed her hair. He watched her go into the kitchen. He was too tired to follow her. She turned to look at him. He had brought her love. She had cried a lot in the beginning, when she was alone again, after he drove her home from dinner or a film. She didn't know why she cried so. Already they had known they would marry. In the kitchen she prepared a plate with slices of apple and almond cake and brought it to the dining room table. She set down dessert plates and forks and they sat next to each other and she filled his plate.

They ate irregularly together; Fred often worked at his office into the evening. She had tried the old recipes her grandmother had left her but most of them were too heavy to eat at the late hour they often had dinner. Her grandmother had a recipe for corned beef and cabbage with carrots and potatoes, another for a lamb stew in a thin broth, its ingredients finely chopped then simmered, which Patricia remembered with complete clarity but could never replicate. Her grandmother's pies stood cooling on her kitchen table. She made a thin, delicious applesauce from fall McIntosh apples. Patricia had been able to approximate her grandmother's beef stew, which she made with cuts of Angus beef, and she and Fred ate it on winter evenings and soaked up the gravy with crusts of bread.

Fred placed another slice of almond cake on her plate. He said, "Are you going to talk to your minister?"

"I will," she said, "tomorrow."

They lay together under a woolen blanket. Patricia heard Fred's breath in sleep; it was like a ragged purr. Sometimes,

After the Hunger

when she first knew him, he would play a bit of music for her, to entertain her, and she would cry. He would hold her and pet her back. She learned how not to cry in front of him, for how then could he marry her? He brought her a bouquet of wildflowers. He held her hand. She no longer cried. It was as if she was one of those with some terrible affliction of the spirit, who had wept and cried and was saved.

The last time she saw the minister who died he was sitting among the congregants, listening to the service. From her seat in a pew at the back of the sanctuary Patricia saw him in a pew near the front. A guest minister, who was leading the service because the congregation didn't know what to do about being left so suddenly lost, introduced the subject of fear. He read a passage from Matthew where the angel of the Lord appeared before the two Marys at Jesus' tomb and said, "Fear not ye; for I know that ye seek Jesus, which was crucified. He is not here; for he is risen." Later, the minster recounted from Matthew, the women were met by Jesus as they went to bring his disciples the news. "Then said Jesus unto them," the minster read, "Be not afraid: go tell my brethren that they go into Galilee, and there shall they see me." The minister closed his Bible and asked anyone to stand who had known fear. A lot of people stood. The minister who died stood. Then they sat down. The minister folded his hands and led them in prayer.

Patricia had strained to see the face of the minister who died. His skin was pale. He no longer called her on a Saturday morning. He had stopped coming to meetings; he no longer walked with her in the evening past the wisteria vines heavy with flowers, their petals falling on the wind. She had learned of his illness, the fast-growing cancer, at a special meeting called by the church, and she had felt the blood drain from her limbs and she was ill and she tried not to show that she was bereft. She learned later that he had endured one round of chemotherapy and then refused any more. He had retreated to the parsonage. The hospice people took care of him. His wife refused all visitors.

Through an emissary who was allowed to the parsonage, Patricia sent him a recording of the Brandenburg concertos. She hoped he listened to it. She wanted to think of him listening to it. She thought about her grandmother's recipes and the cures the Indians used and the enslaved women brought from Africa and the West Indies. But there was nothing for an illness like that. She thought about the quality of the world we inhabited and what we breathed and that there must be something about the age that had begun to harm us in these ways. That if you could just walk together you would be cured of all sadness and longing, you would find God in the night, the breath of God in the sharp winds where the vines and the shadows of the bushes on the brick walls tossed and sighed.

Patricia was sleeping heavily when Fred sat on the bed and ran his hand down her back. She turned and looked at him. It was very early. He was already in his dress shirt and tie. He lifted her up, she was like a thing of lightness, without form or will, and held her in his arms. She clung to him. He was saying something to her, murmuring in her ear. It was like a song, something one strains to hear, some melody known all along.

"Are you going to stay?" he asked.

He meant the group at church. "I'll call Tom this morning," she said. She was up, walking him to the front door. She didn't like him thinking of her still lying in bed, to have that as his image of her as he left the house. He kissed her and held her, and the thin fabric of her nightgown slipped against his clothes.

She sat on the bed holding a cup of tea, then phoned her office with a vague complaint, a cold perhaps, some trouble with the respiratory system, some inability to breathe deeply into the lungs, and then she put down the receiver and was free. She ate a slice of toast and a black plum and got into her car, the one she owned before she married Fred that belonged to her in the way that one takes a car to places that belong to one. She headed north, to the throughway, and drove for almost an hour, and turned off an exit and drove north again.

On the narrow roads there were old stone walls and old houses with pitched roofs and high granite steps leading to doors with wrought-iron hinges. There was always the idea of the sea. The land seemed to fall toward it, arrived at finally by river or estuary or creek or marsh. At a certain point on the river one could glimpse it in the far distance, a strip of deep blue, moving swiftly, dangerously, the water buffeted by whitecaps, and the horizon framed with climbing white clouds. After the minster had died she had driven there, on the narrow roads with the scent of the sea at the open windows. She had gone to the memorial service attended by it seemed generations of the same congregation. The seats were filled in the pews and the balcony, and a trumpeter stood near the altar and played, the notes sharp and clear, and the bishops came as if out of the Middle Ages, wearing green damask robes and mitres trimmed with gold thread, and carrying their scepters down the center aisle like staffs.

Once, driving north, she took the car through a break in a stone wall and drove down a dirt road and saw in the distance a farmhouse and beyond it the river. The house was surrounded by fields. It was shuttered, its curtains drawn; it did not seem to be occupied. On a path near the house a smoke tree was in bloom. Patricia had brought with her a thermos of tea and a sandwich of sliced cheese and mustard. She sat under the smoke tree with her lunch. There was a mild wind off the river, and it rolled over the seagrass on the estuary. The dusky purple panicles on the smoke tree rustled and sighed.

Once she took a turn onto a farm with a handsome brick house and pastures marked by split-rail fences. There was a circular drive in front of the house and massive oak trees that shaded it. The farm, she realized, was a preserved version of itself in that it was now a place for parents to bring their children, a place to learn about the past. Patricia saw guides in blue T-shirts and children leaning over the fences petting horses and goats and sheep, and parents closely monitoring their children, and a big turkey strutting near the children's legs, its feathers in full display. Patricia walked along the fence line and then behind the house she discovered another pasture, and beyond it a ruined barn. Farther on was another house, newer, probably even grander, alone in a field, a wrecked gravel drive leading into the distance, the house's windows without glass and the floors damaged from rain and snow and a chandelier still hanging in the foyer, its few remaining crystals catching the afternoon light.

Patricia drove farther north. Along the roads were fences marking pastures where horses switched their tails and cows sat low to the ground on their huge bellies. A sign read, Hay for Sale, though it was too early in the season for hay. She had brought a thermos of tea and stopped on the side of a road and drank it. It was sassafras tea, and she remembered walking through the woods near her grandmother's house and bringing home the roots for her, and her grandmother looked troubled and alarmed, as she did with the least variation in the cycles she had entered into of meals and church and family and sleep; this was the prerogative of her advancing age. Her grandmother put the roots in a glass of water but they browned and died.

Her grandmother had a kitchen garden where she grew thyme and mint and rosemary and dill. Oil of thyme, Patricia had read in her grandmother's recipe book, was used as an antibiotic. Women medicated bandages with it for binding wounds. The ancient Greeks sprinkled its flowers in their bath water, believing it was a source of courage. Her grandmother pressed the leaves between her palms to flavor chicken breasts arranged in a glass baking dish. There were pills to take now from the pharmacy and medicines from the drug store. One ingested them using a glass of water or a teaspoon. To treat insomnia one stirred a splash of whiskey in a cup of warm milk. Patricia knew from reading the old recipes that the women would go with baskets and long-handled spoons into woodlands and fields, to shorelines, wetlands, and the banks of streams; under many of the recipes there were directions by foot and dirt road. She liked to imagine the women harvesting the leaves and roots, flowers and fruits. She wondered if her grandmother had accompanied them, perhaps as a child. But she didn't learn of the recipe book until after her grandmother's death, and so she couldn't ask, and she wondered often why this book had come to her, and what her grandmother would have her do with it.

Patricia put away the thermos of tea and brought the car back onto the asphalt. True spring wouldn't arrive for a number of weeks, but the trees already were turning, and faint streams of color, yellow and green, were rising into their branches.

Just above a stop sign Patricia saw the entrance to a dirt road. She turned onto it. The road led down a mild incline, and it curved to the right and the left, and Patricia braked lightly. She had entered a woodland. Then the road became flat and ended in a lot of packed sand. She parked and got out of the car. She had entered a marsh. She could see three horizons: to the right where the marsh opened to an estuary; to the left where it became denser and was bordered by brush; and ahead, where a narrow gravel causeway led to an island in the river signaled by a cluster of trees. Somewhere beyond was the sea. In the early season, not yet spring, the water of the marsh was like a mist, and the sky was pale blue, and along the horizon the water seemed to rise and dissipate like tendrils of steam. An egret flew low across the marsh, its long wings a flash of white against the shallow water, and landed, with legs delicately outstretched, and folded its wings to its body.

Patricia walked along the causeway. The shallow water on either side was brown, and in it was vegetation, brown also and spongy looking and filled with holes as if the homes of hidden creatures. In the water, where it was pierced by light, she could see minnows swimming. Across the marsh were the reeds and grasses from the previous year, leeched of color and brittle, and along the borders the cattail flowers were spent, wisps of cottony fluff still clinging to them. Patricia thought that other eyes, older eyes, would be able to look across the marsh and see a remedy to any ailment, a cure for any heartache.

After the minister's death, his wife brought with her all of his sermons in a number of paper bags and shook them out on a table in the meeting room during the coffee hour after the service and announced that anyone could have them, to take as many as desired. She walked around the room while people were sipping coffee from Styrofoam cups and eating lemon cookies and pointed to the pile of papers on the table and people looked at her in surprise. Then they put down their refreshments and went to the table. By the time the coffee hour was over, all of the minister's sermons were gone. People examined them carefully, pointing out to a companion the typed pages annotated in the minister's hand, and Patricia thought they were taking a sermon that held particular meaning for them, placing it into a pocketbook or a jacket pocket. Patricia watched from a distance. It seemed as if the sermons were the minister's body and by the time the morning was over nothing was left of it. She watched the minister's wife fold the empty paper bags against her knee and leave the meeting room with them.

Pieces of gravel on the causeway were held by clumps of ice. In the open, with the marsh on either side, Patricia became aware of a wind, a constant wind, bringing with it another season, and the sharp asides where the currents pitched against each other. It blew her hair. She unbuttoned her coat and let the wind blow her clothing. The wind caressed the old grasses and ruffled the surface of the water. She walked further into the wind. In the distance was the island with its cluster of trees. On the far side would be the river, then the sea. She walked toward it. The wind was on her face like breath.

The Émigrés

The two little girls ran across the grass, fleet as wind. They played together on the back lawn, drifting across the roots of trees, until the older girl spied Holly next door on her mother's deck, taking down the laundry. The younger girl stared boldly up at Holly, then fled with her sister behind the heavy blue flowers of a hydrangea bush. Holly worked a wooden clothespin from the line that traveled along a pulley above her mother's yard, releasing a billowing sheet. She pulled the line in, hand over hand, and dropped the pieces of laundry into a wicker basket. A red cardinal burst into her field of vision, sudden and swift, flying straight above the line of rope, and landed, now only a rustle of needles, in the far branches of a fir tree.

The girls' grandmother opened the basement door onto a patio under the deck of the house. She closed the door behind her and walked the yard, as if fixing its perimeters. It was enclosed by a chain-link fence with the exception of the driveway the family shared with Holly's mother, and even then she had had to convince the girls' grandfather of the impossibility of opening her car door should the fence be extended there. The girls' grandfather had begun the project of attaching green fabric to the inside of the fence; it was already in place at the other side of the yard and at the border of the property behind the house. Soon the yard would be barricaded by sight as well.

The girls ran to their grandmother and stood before her. She smoothed their hair and put her broad hand on their small backs and surrendered them to their play. She walked across the yard, from fence line to fence line, as if on a kind of watch. Holly waited for her to look up. She waved. The girls' grandmother waved back, at first automatically, then, having remembered Holly, with warmth. She walked up the stairs to the deck and went inside the house, back into the enclosed world the family inhabited.

Holly left the laundry basket inside the kitchen door and returned the old canvas clothespin holder to its place on the floor next to the refrigerator. Her mother Nora sat at the table over a cup of coffee, smoking a cigarette. It was one of the few indulgences of her entire life, and she persisted in smoking after almost everyone had stopped and there was nowhere left to smoke in public. She bought cigarettes by the carton and smoked three or four a day, one after each meal and sometimes one before she went to bed. Smoking made her still, almost dreamy; otherwise, when Holly and her husband Dean visited, she was quick, almost abrupt in her movements, and in her vigilant attentions to her house there was always some chore for one of them to do.

"I saw the cardinal again," Holly said.

Her mother blew a trail of smoke into the kitchen. Smoking had somewhat criminalized her, and so she consigned herself there. She looked at her daughter and smiled. "He's a beautiful cardinal," her mother said. She inhaled another lungful of smoke. Nora had gray eyes and hair rinsed light brown, set in short curls around her forehead and temples. She wore a pair of denim slacks and a cotton shirt. Even when she smoked there was a certain antique glamor about her, as if she brought with her cigarette case and lighter, placed near her elbow on the old kitchen table, memories of nightclubs and swing bands.

Holly carried the laundry basket into the house and folded the items it contained in her mother's bedroom. Her mother liked to do laundry on sunny days so she could hang it on the line to dry. She liked the smell of the sun on her towels and sheets. Holly put away the laundry in its assigned drawers and closets and left a few things for her mother to help her with later. She brought the basket to the basement, then poured herself a second cup of coffee and sat at the kitchen table with her mother.

Dean was upstairs, raising storm windows and pulling down the screens. Nora had given him the task of making the house ready for the new season. He had already changed the order of the storm windows downstairs and replaced the storm panels with screens on the front and back doors. The doors and all the windows were open. The air moved through the house. It smelled clean, like earth and new leaves.

The Émigrés

The house was almost the last on a street that had once been woodland, and many of the old trees were still in the yards, large firs and oaks. They towered over the houses, a mixture of Cape Cods, two-family homes, and shoebox-shaped bungalows. All of the houses were worn and blemished by age and requiring repair: paint on the front steps, a new window frame, a repointing of brick. Over the years, in defiance of want and need, Holly's mother had planted her yard with daffodils and tulips, climbing clematis, hellebore, and decorative cedars, and it looked verdant and welcoming, a surprising map of color on the declining street.

Nora stood and said, "I think I'll go read my book while you and Dean take care of things." She had crushed out her cigarette and placed her cigarette case on top of the ashtray.

"What are you reading?" Holly asked. She was following her mother into the living room.

"Oh, that war memoir by that French woman," Nora said. "She found her diaries abandoned in a cupboard. She doesn't remember a thing about writing them." Nora borrowed the books from the public library and read entirely from the nonfiction section. By now she could speak with some authority on the subject of the war years and the Cold War decades that followed. Sometimes, over the telephone, she related to Holly an incident from one of the books. There was always some unexpected element of human motive in them, men and women in crisis within a larger disruption, a larger crisis. But mostly she merely closed the covers and returned the books to the library, the only witness to her lengthy hours of reading a typed list of the books and the dates she had read them. She smoothed her denim slacks and picked up her book from the ottoman. She sat in the green plush chair and began to read under the light of the picture window.

Holly went upstairs. Dean had finished adjusting the screens and was sitting on one of the twin beds in the guest bedroom, trying to type on his laptop.

"I tried working in the other room," Dean said in a low voice, "but my legs began to go to sleep. At least I got the Internet up. There must be an open connection somewhere in the neighborhood."

The other room, directly across the landing, was an unfinished space that Nora used as an attic. In it were a few old chests of drawers, a trunk, a bookcase containing a dictionary and books on gardening, and plastic dress bags where Nora stored her out-of-season clothes. There was a small window across the room set in an unpainted frame. Strips of pink insulation hung between the beams along the roofline. To work, as Dean wanted to, there was nowhere to sit but the floor. "I'll talk to my mother about a table and a chair," Holly said. "Maybe there's something stored away." But she knew before she finished her thought that there was nothing stored away and that her mother would resist any request to remove a piece of furniture to the upstairs, to change the order of her house.

Holly turned the wedding band on her finger. She had good, sharp, deeply set brown eyes. She looked at Dean with a kind of habitual patience, as if she always observed the world, and him in it, from slightly afar. He closed the laptop and put it on the floor. He took Holly's hand and led her to the bed. They sat together on the chenille bedspread. The old springs gave, making a sound of protest.

Dean held her. His body was big and sturdy. He had a luxurious mat of hair on his chest. A tuft of it showed above the neckline of his sports shirt. When they were alone, when he held her in their own bed, his chest hair on her skin was like fur.

"The windows held up another year?" Holly whispered. She often felt, here, as if she had come to a place where there were acts penance to perform. As if she could only know her husband again after a number of labors.

"Yes ma'am," Dean said. His hand was at her waist; along the curve of her hip.

Holly turned and lay on her back. This was the room where she slept when she visited her mother, before she married Dean. The house had felt cloistered, immaculate; the habitation of women. Holly played gin rummy with her mother and Scrabble on an old board, stained with coffee rings, the wooden tiles worn to a patina. They both smoked cigarettes then. They breathed thin gray curls of smoke into the kitchen, and to Holly each exhale was like a sigh. Her mother had the cleaning woman in before Holly's visits, and she served their meals punctually over the space of the day and went to bed at 10, after the local news. Holly felt imprisoned in her mother's world of ritual and routine. But she had begun to understand, in the way her mother insisted on maintaining it over the years, on the most ordinary days, that it had saved her from something she didn't want to think or talk about, and that it would be impossible now to let go.

Dean brushed Holly's hair away from her face and began to kiss her. The bedsprings complained. He kissed her goodbye in the morning. He kissed her in airport terminals and after services at church and when they walked along the marshlands where the Asian water lilies grew. He kissed her after dinner. They had been married three years. They had each brought a certain sorrow, a certain deep consideration, a certain gladness to their marriage, because they had lost quite a lot beforehand. Other wives and husbands. It seems they had lost a great deal of people. They were aware of all the losses that inevitably come to one. Each year on their anniversary they stood under a flowering willow on a roadside near their apartment building and married each other all over again.

Nora was downstairs, opening cabinet doors, opening the refrigerator. Things were being taken down, taken out. Holly sat up and pressed her chest against Dean and kissed him goodbye. The twin bed was low to the floor and he took her hand and helped her up. The other twin bed, where she slept, was higher, with a new mattress so thick that the protector wouldn't hold; after a night of sleep Holly's cheek on waking was against the bare mattress, the protector all pulled away. At night she felt at an unbearable distance from her husband as she lay in the darkness in the uncomfortable bed, listening to his breathing.

The Émigrés

Nora moved around the kitchen. She handed Holly plates and dishes to bring to the dining room table. She said "Sit, sit," to Dean, and he sat in one of the chairs while the women laid the food before him. Nora had prepared a fruit salad, a lime Jell-O salad with cream cheese and grated carrot, and a plate of wheat bread and thinly sliced, rare roast beef. There was another plate of lettuce and sliced tomato. Nora had spooned mustard and mayonnaise into separate glass dishes. Lemon slices and cubes of ice revolved slowly in a pitcher of tea. The evening before, Holly and Dean had arrived late, at dinnertime, for Mother's Day weekend, with Friday afternoon traffic stalled ahead of them and on the northbound side of the throughway as well, and they met more traffic as they turned off the throughway onto North Main Street. They breathlessly sat down to a dinner Nora had prepared of roast lamb, crispy potatoes, and snap peas.

"Can I make you a sandwich?" Holly said to her mother. Dean had passed her the serving plate.

"No, no," Nora said. She took two slices of roast beef and tapped a spoonful of mustard onto her plate.

"This is very good roast beef," Dean said. He had built himself a towering sandwich. He was calm and polite with Holly's mother. Nora thought Dean a steady, good man, but Holly thought Dean hadn't been able to learn how to relax completely with her, and to be with her as a member of the family. She thought he was still trying to learn how to do that, or perhaps he had moved up to the border and decided to stay there.

"Do you remember your neighbor's name?" Holly asked her mother. "The grandmother next door, the grandmother of those little girls. I saw her when I was taking in the laundry."

"Something, something like Madeline or Marjorie," Nora said. "I wish I could understand her better. It would be good to have a neighbor to talk to. Though the girls are very sweet. So shy when they first moved here. But now when I get out of the car they come over and ask for hugs."

"Mirjeta," Holly said, with the finality of memory. "She told me when I went over to meet her, in the yard, before the fence went up. It must have been at least a year ago."

"Oh, that fence," Nora said. "The father is gone, did I tell you? He apparently wasn't ambitious enough for the girls' mother, so she sent him along. Now the grandparents come to the house while the mother is away at work. She has a very good job in a nursing home. The father used to take good care of those girls, in my opinion, but he was sent away nonetheless." Nora's eyebrows had knitted together in consternation.

"I remember him," Holly said. "I remember seeing him, that is. But hadn't they just come here, weren't they new?" *How does one begin*, she thought. *How does one begin in all of one's newness.*

"Oh, he was very nice," Nora said. "He did all of that beautiful stone work in the yard—the patio and the walkway in the front. He and his wife's father replaced my gutters. The needles from the fir tree overwhelm the gutters so I asked them if they could possibly take a look."

The Émigrés

Dean sent Holly a signal, a brief shift of his eyes. He flexed his shoulders minutely.

"Between the two of them," Nora continued, "they hardly spoke a word of English. We didn't have a language in common to discuss the matter. The grandfather showed me a receipt from the hardware store and I covered it and paid them what I thought was fair for their labor." She served the fruit salad in little lotus-shaped cups and offered them to Holly and Dean. "He didn't argue," she said, "so I guess my figure was correct."

"If I may ask," Holly, said, "what did you pay them?"

"Why, twenty dollars," Nora said.

Holly felt her lungs deflate, discouraged for the men who had done this work for her mother and who were too kind or new to counter her.

Nora passed a serving dish to Dean and he positioned a circle of Jell-O salad on his plate with a serving spoon Nora had taken from her mother's silverware chest. Nora's dining room was arranged with the furniture she had inherited from her mother and father: the table and chairs, a sideboard, and a china cabinet with a door of curved and beveled glass. Holly remembered the furniture in her grandparents' dining room. She had loved to sit at the table with her grandparents, who seemed so old to her, and at peace together.

Nora's bedroom contained a four-poster bed that had belonged to her parents, and a matching vanity table and chest of drawers. Elsewhere in the house she had a Hitchcock desk and chair, a set of matching side-table lamps, and a spindle-leg table on which in recent years to mark the Christmas season she placed a miniature evergreen of bristling plastic branches. She seemed to exist in a kind of Yankee obliviousness, full of manners and a certain brisk grace, while living in a Cape Cod house at the end of a neglected city street that seemed to Holly as if it could be stormed at any moment by whomever desired to. Years ago she had advised her mother to get deadbolt locks for the doors, and on her next visit the doors held small brass sliding-bolt locks, more the idea of a lock than a lock, which Nora most of the time forgot to engage.

All her early life Holly had lived with her mother in one shambling house after the next. In her childhood her mother rented an old house with a yard beset by crabgrass and small thorny bushes. Each room was accessed by a fieldstone step and built at an obtuse angle so no one room seemed to have any relationship to the other. The house always held a chill. Holly was too young to question whether it was from thrift or lack of funds. Even in summer the house was cold, like the impenetrable cold of stone. Her mother then rented the top floor of another old house with sloping ceilings and a staircase that led from the downstairs hall to a narrow pit, an architectural error, it seemed to Holly, from which one stepped up into the living room or into the hallway that led to the bedrooms. Holly had to stoop under the roofline when setting the kitchen table. Nora parked her car in the barn. Its entrance had a high threshold over which she would gun the engine, and Holly, her palms pressed to the dashboard, waited for the lift of the car, its sudden drop, and the urgent pump of the brakes.

The Émigrés

After her parents had died Nora took her inheritance and bought her house and moved her parents' furniture into it. The rental houses were isolated, separated from their neighbors it seemed now to Holly more by circumstance than actual geography, and the house Nora had finally been able to own seemed to exist in that same isolation. All of the places she lived, that were somehow inadequate, somehow wanting, seemed like a rebuke to Holly's father, who had quietly escaped the expectations of the hoped-for peace of war's end and its promised prosperity and of his wife and child that had all somehow confounded him, and had left Nora alone.

Nora topped Dean's glass of iced tea. "Did you notice the fence in the yard on the other side of the house?" she asked Holly. "The neighbors over there?"

"The white one," Holly said, trying to remember what had been there. "It looks new."

"They took down the swimming pool. They left all the parts leaning against the inside of the fence."

"Who lives there now?" Holly asked, though she barely remembered who had lived there before.

"I don't know their names," Nora said. "The trees block the view of the house. Maybe that's for the best. I just hear cars coming and going in the driveway."

An older couple, from Jamaica, had lived across the street, but they had moved away. Nora had liked them. She enlisted them to take in her mail when she went to visit far-away friends. Another couple, a barrel-chested man and a woman who often sat in a lawn chair drinking Cokes, had lived directly across the street. A magnificent cherry tree grew high above the house, which the new owners had had chopped down. Holly remembered how each season, over the course of days, its dense pink petals fell in drifting showers onto the lawn and the street. Somewhere lived a teenage boy, not completely right in the head, according to Nora, who shoveled the snow from her driveway during the worst months of the winter. She used to speak in passing about another family with a number of children, all very polite, she observed to Holly, but Holly didn't know what house they lived in or even if they lived on the street anymore. No one ever appeared to be about but the little girls next door. The street seemed to be inhabited by immigrants, passing upward, passing through, leaving the street in another stage of exhaustion with each retreat.

Nora and Holly cleared the table and Holly washed the dishes. Dean, unsure of what else to do, went upstairs to his computer. At home Holly got everything ready and Dean cooked dinner and afterward they cleared the table and he talked with her while she washed the dishes. It was a good arrangement, but when Nora inquired about her daughter's menus and meal preparation she put forth the opinion that Holly was neglecting Dean and her role as Dean's wife. Holly was happy to be getting something right. She had been married before, two times in her twenties, and how does one know anything then? How to measure distances, how to read the signs, how to travel a curved line. Then, after what had felt like permanent winter, a place of cold and dark, she had found Dean. During her twice-monthly telephone calls to her mother, her mother often said, "Oh Holly, Dean is a fine man, I know, but how I wish for the days when we used to sit at the kitchen table smoking cigarettes and playing gin rummy." She gave Holly recipes for spinach omelets and stuffed mushrooms.

Holly went to the car to get her old clothes. The little girls were in the front yard with their grandmother. The older girl was twirling on the stone walk her father had built, stepping one foot in front of the other. Her long brown hair lofted above her shoulders and seemed to weave in the air, following the turn of the girl's body. She looked up at Holly and stopped, her pink Crocs still, her hair falling and resting again on her shoulders, and slipped away, into the house. The younger girl climbed onto her bicycle and rode it in circles, showing off for Holly. Holly saw the grandfather lift a bag of loam on the other side of the yard and shake it onto the ground. The grandmother, Mirjeta, walked toward Holly. Holly took her hand.

"Do you remember me from last time, when we met, I think it was last spring," Holly said, and she repeated her name to her.

"Yes," Mirjeta said. "Spring." Then she said, "How are you?" The younger girl had jumped off her bicycle and stood next to her grandmother, boldly looking at Holly.

"I'm here with my husband for the weekend," Holly said. "We're going to plant flowers for my mother. Hello," she said to the little girl. The girl continued to stare at Holly. She thrust her little chest out.

"This is Elira," Mirjeta said. "She is four. Would you like some coffee?" The older girl studied Holly from the crack between the screen door and its frame. The front yard had been converted to a garden. The grass was turned under and the soil covered with loam. Pale green shoots stood in ordered rows in the furrowed ground. The garden took up the entire front yard, stopping just short of the stone walk.

"Kaltrina," Mirjeta said. "Come here. This is Holly. Kaltrina is five."

Kaltrina opened the door and took a step onto the walkway.

A white car drove up the street, made a U-turn where the street dead-ended, and parked in front of the girls' house. Willie Colón's trombone thundered through the open widows and abruptly stopped when the driver cut the engine. A young woman got out of the passenger side and followed the driver, a young man, to a one-story white house across the street. She crushed out her cigarette on the street with her boot heel and threw a contemptuous look at Mirjeta. Both wore baggy cargo pants sliding down their hips and black sleeveless T-shirts. Their upper arms where decorated with tattoos. They sat together on the front steps of the house. The young man lit a cigarette for himself and one for the young woman. The girl's dark hair hung in thick strands over her shoulders; the boy's was closely shaved. They looked like guardians of something alien and forbidding, sitting silent and unmoving at the door to the house.

"Come," Mirjeta said, and Holly followed Mirjeta and her granddaughters into the house. The living room was modest, like Holly's mother's, with a leather couch, a fireplace, a clock on the wall in the shape of a sun, two easy chairs, and a coffee table that held a number of children's toys. It was probably the girls' parents' idea of an American house, Holly surmised, everything new, clean, without a history. The girls spoke the language of children, soft whispers and little shrieks. Sometimes they spoke the language of their parents and grandparents, words with different intonations within the hesitant English. Kaltrina, more daring now in her own house, sat next to Holly on the couch. Elira stood in front of Holly, swelling her little chest. "I cut my hair," she announced. "She cut her hair with the scissors," Kaltrina explained. Elira pulled her short dark brown hair up and turned her head to show Holly what she had done. "Mama had to take her to fix it," Kaltrina said.

"Oh," Holly said, "you cut your hair! It looks very pretty." *Of course she had cut her hair*, Holly thought. *You come to a new country or you are born to a new country and you wear your hair like a guerrilla. You are at war with your own history. You are perhaps at war with a country you don't understand. You can be four and know this.*

Mirjeta brought a cup of coffee on a wooden tray and set it on the coffee table as she moved the children's toys out of the way. There were books on Cinderella and Pinocchio and bright pieces of paper that had been pasted onto felt and little magical looking balls made of clear plastic with sparkles suspended in them.

"Do you take cream?" Mirjeta asked. Her English was slow and labored.

"No, thank you," Holly said. "The coffee is delicious. You aren't having any?"

"My English," Mirjeta said. "It is not good." She had an accent that sounded to Holly as if from Eastern Europe, the words clear, with a throaty sound under each one.

"My mother will be home in four minutes," Kaltrina announced to Holly. She had begun to spread the toys out on the coffee table for Holly. Elira took some more from the end table next to the couch.

Mirjeta's face was calm and beautiful, but it held an old sadness. Her skin, a dark golden color, looked as if she had spent time in the sun, while her granddaughters' eyes were full of hunger for the day, for the strange woman sitting in their living room, and their skin was pale and clear. Mirjeta held her chin up slightly, as if that would help her in her search for English words. "My daughter speak English," she said to Holly. "I learn it from her."

"My mother loves your grandchildren," Holly said. She could only speak English to the girls' grandmother, so she went on. She said, "They give her hugs when she comes home in her car."

"My English not too good," Mirjeta said. "Kaltrina translates for me."

The Émigrés

But Kaltrina was five and she stood quietly at the mention of her name, as if hoping not to be called upon.

"You have children?" Mirjeta asked.

"No," Holly said. "I have a husband. Dean."

"We have four children," Mirjeta said. "Three here." Mirjeta lifted her palm and Holly thought she meant somewhere nearby. "We live a few streets over there. My other son, won't fight, go to Switzerland."

"Won't fight?" Holly said.

"He not fight. Terrible war. Make no sense. One day no more Yugoslavia. We from Kosovo. Now no more Kosovo."

"Do you know people here?" Holly asked.

"No," Mirjeta said. "No one care to. Close doors, stay inside. No one to visit."

"Have others come?" Holly asked. She meant to say, Do you have friends here from home, do you help each other, does it make it easier for you, do you cook the old foods, do you laugh again? but Holly was silent, suddenly confounded by her own language.

"The Roma come," Mirjeta said. "But the Roma bad."

The girls had run upstairs and then upstairs again and come down with a small plastic table and two chairs. They were showing Holly all of their things in the living room, and now some of their things from upstairs. They sat at the table to show Holly what it was all about.

Mirjeta's husband opened the front door and stepped into the room, tucking a cotton bandana into his back pocket. He extended his hand to Holly. "Leka," he said, and bowed, and Holly stood and gave her name and shook his hand. His skin was tanned and his forehead was deeply lined. He had graying, dark blond hair. His frame was muscular and agile, as if he were used to satisfying work with his body. He had a pleasant face. He sat in one of the easy chairs and spread his fingers over his knees and scowled. "I tell those kids to leave," he said. He looked at Holly but he was speaking mostly to his wife. "They sit in their car and play their music, I tell them park at their own house."

Mirjeta said something to her husband in their language. Holly put her thumbnail to a tooth. The young man and woman had disturbed her. They had seemed so hostile, so offended that she and Mirjeta would even dare to regard them, and so removed from any loyalties but to each other.

"I see your husband outside," Leka said. "You planting some flowers, eh? He would like a coffee?"

Holly called to Dean, who was standing on the grass, trowel in hand, surveying a patch of dirt under the lamppost. He put down the trowel. The men shook hands and sat across from each other drinking Turkish coffee from elaborately painted porcelain cups that Mirjeta had presented on the same wooden tray. The girls sat on either side of Holly, pressing for her attention. Dean sat ceremonially with his host, bringing the cup to his lips and taking sips of the coffee. Leka had taken an attitude of comradeship with Dean. He was talking to him about Clinton and the Dayton Accords. He said "Clin-tun" and "Day-tun," as if they were the same. "End of war," he said, "but not of troubles." He lifted his chin upward too, trying to find the English words with which to speak with Dean. Dean listened respectfully, his body canted toward his host.

Kaltrina, shy again with Dean in the house, began to fidget with her dress.

"Dean and I were going to work in my mother's yard," Holly said to Mirjeta. "We were going to start this afternoon." Holly thought that much of what people spoke to each other was something other than what was said, words intended to show affection, or concern; an acknowledgement that the mind sees one, understands one. They could be almost any words, about a garden or coffee or a warm pair of gloves. They helped with the other words, how one can begin to approach the inexpressible. Holly did not have the words to tell Mirjeta that she admired her and was glad to know her, and so she smiled at her, and Mirjeta, beholding Holly's face, smiled too.

Mirjeta turned to Kaltrina, her translator, but Kaltrina had hidden her face in her grandmother's side.

Holly wanted to ask Mirjeta about her homeland that was no more and what it was like to have to leave and then to come here and how does one leave a promise of a life when it has been taken away. Or was it always bombs and fear and was she glad to have left, even her home and her clothes and the graves of her parents and grandparents? What did you leave behind and how do you start again and how do you do, how do you do? Instead she said, "Maybe the girls would like to help us with the flowers."

Mirjeta said something to her grandchildren and they sprang up and went to the door. Holly said to Dean, "I invited them to help," and Dean stood slowly and the men ceremonially shook hands and Dean thanked Mirjeta and Leka and Holly said "Thank you, thank you," and Leka hospitably opened the door and the girls streamed out, into the sunlight, and across the double driveway to Holly's mother's yard.

Holly changed into her old clothes. Nora was at the lamppost, in a pair of old walking shoes, showing her the places where Dean had begun to mark the dirt with a trowel. A flat of pansies lay in the shade. "Now," Nora said. "You have to dig a hole, fairly deep, and water it, then separate out the plant and push the dirt around it, nice and firm. You won't need to water it again till evening. You don't want to overwater a new plant."

The girls stood close by Nora and Holly. Holly lifted the watering can and told the girls what she was going to do. Elira followed her to the side of the house, just beyond the trash barrel at the end of the driveway, and Holly showed her how to turn on the spigot and then how to squeeze the nozzle of the hose and fill the watering can. Elira crouched over her work intently. The can was half-way full and Holly showed her how to let the nozzle go and lift the can, though Holly took the weight of it by the handle and Elira, very seriously and with great care, brought the can across the lawn. Holly helped her set it down. Dean had finished digging the holes and Nora carefully took each plant from the flat. Holly helped Elira tilt the can and soak the dirt.

The Émigrés

Kaltrina had retreated to her own yard. She stood on the walkway her father had built and watched Holly and her sister move around the lamppost with the watering can and Holly lift it up and Elira jump up and down, up and down, and Elira tilt the bottom of the can and the water come out like a shower. Holly was taking each plant and setting it into the dirt and showing Elira how to tamp down the dirt around the plant. Her little hands patted the dirt like she was petting a dog, and Holly showed her how to press the dirt firmly with her fingertips. Elira held up her dirt-streaked hands for Holly to inspect, like their mother made them do before they sat down to their dinner.

Holly showed Elira how to hold out her hands and she held the watering can over them like a shower and then Holly held the can over her own hands, one by one, and then put the can down and waved her hands in the air, all the while smiling at Elira. Elira jumped up and down up and down, and waved her hands and clapped them and got a spray of water and some dirt on the front of her jumper. Holly raised her eyebrows in pretend shock and got some more water and cleaned Elira's hands. Then Elira looked around for more to do but the flowers were all planted, their little brown and yellow and blue faces tilted toward the sun.

Kaltrina ran across the walkway. She ran up to Holly and said, "My mother will be home in four minutes."

Holly said, "Would you like to help us till your mother comes home?" Kaltrina nodded her head and she helped Holly fill the watering can at the spigot as she had seen her sister help her and then watered the holes at the front of the house that Dean had made ready under the picture window and in front of the bushes. She and Elira helped Holly take each plant from its receptacle in the flat and she felt the resistance of the plants and saw the trail of roots as she laid them, as she saw Holly do, on their sides on the lawn. This time the flowers were pink and white and Nora was saying something to Dean about the spacing of the holes and so Holly had Kaltrina and her sister count the holes and there were nine, one, two, four, nine, in the rectangle of soft dirt on each side of the front door and Dean covered a few holes and dug them again, though Kaltrina had a hard time seeing that they were any different.

Nora said to Holly, "I miscounted. We'll have to get another flat tomorrow," and she picked up the empty flats and went around the side of the house. Dean spoke in a low voice to Holly and kissed her ear and went to the car and got a book and opened the front door and went inside. Holly had to fill the watering can again and again and sometimes Kaltrina helped her and sometimes Elira did, and they watched the holes fill with water and the water disappear into the dirt and then they set the remaining plants in and tamped around them with their fingers. Kaltrina splayed her hands onto the cold dirt that was like Play-Doh almost or something from her mother's kitchen, a cake a cookie ready to be put in the oven. Kaltrina and Holly and Elira all clapped their hands and waved them at the sky and the water shot in droplets over their clothes.

The little girls were like creatures that ran with lightness and squatted over the earth and said "Yes," when Holly said

The Émigrés

"Hold your hands out," or "Me, me" when Holly said, "Let's fill the watering can," and they swayed over the flowers very close to her and their breath was like the breath of something newborn, it came in little puffs, puff, puff, as if from a great exertion as they tamped the wet dirt around the plants. They all had droplets of water on their clothes as if they had been caught in a brief rain. Leka opened the front door as Holly was standing contemplatively over the plants and he looked at each of his granddaughters and smiled and nodded briefly at Holly and closed the door.

The boy and girl with the low-slung pants sat on the steps across the street again, in front of the one-story house. They sat with their knees together and their forearms resting on their thighs, in an attitude of malign alertness. The boy tamped a cigarette on the step and lit it. The flame flared, like a sudden fire. They seemed to be looking at no one but Holly knew they were aware of her and the girls and of Leka who had shut the door on them after checking on his grandchildren. The boy looked briefly at the closed door and seemed to speak to the girl and then went back into his pose of indifference, a figure guarding the entrance of a forbidding place. The little girls crowded close to Holly and Kaltrina held a finger over the plants and counted and said, "Twelve," and Elira said, "Huh, huh," as she tamped the dirt for its own sake and held out her hands for Holly to shower with water.

Holly assessed their work. The line of plants was orderly and straight. There were six additional holes ready to receive more plants. Then the girls looked up at Holly because

After the Hunger

their work seemed to be done. They looked around for more flowers to plant, at the yard with its mowed lawn and nowhere else for them to water and tamp. They crowded close to her and she could hear their breathing. She took their hands and said, "Tell your grandmother I'm sorry you got your clothes dirty." There were little flecks of dirt on their clothes. Kaltrina said, "My mother will be home in two minutes," and Holly took their hands and they went with her across the walk and she waited until their grandfather opened the door and they were inside.

She stood over the new flowers then took the gardening things to the basement and rinsed them in the old zinc sink and put them away and took off her sneakers and washed their soles and walked up the basement stairs in her socks. She stood on the deck. The cardinal appeared as if already in mid-flight, winging from tree to tree. It landed on a branch and flicked its tail, then flew across the yard again, just beyond the deck, a brilliant red against the green foliage, as if to be seen, as if to show himself to Holly. She knew then he must have a nest nearby, perhaps in the dense bushes next to the deck, and he was showing himself to her so as to divert attention from it. She went inside and shut the door gently, so he would not have to be concerned for the safety of his nest, so he could go back to his mate and his chicks.

At dinnertime Nora ordered take-out from the Chinese restaurant on North Main Street and they sat down together at six o'clock. After dinner they watched a movie on cable television. Holly sat with her mother on the deck in the darkness

The Émigrés

while she smoked her evening cigarette. They heard briefly, from across the two yards, through an upstairs window, the excited cries of the girls; their mother had come home. It was late and Dean was waiting for her upstairs and she lay with him under the covers in the narrow bed and he pulled her arm around his chest. Then she lay in her own bed, on her back. The street was quiet, the darkened houses filled with sleepers, their bodies turning, their breathing shallow and rhythmic, as if the houses themselves were dreaming. She woke to the sound of a car moving slowly up the street. Its motor seemed large and powerful in the stillness, like the slow thunder of tanks, and Holly was suddenly afraid. She heard two car doors slam shut and the fading sound of footsteps across the street.

She woke in another layer of darkness to the sound of songbirds announcing the dawn. They called from the depths of the trees, singing and singing, each bird calling its tribal song. She woke later as if having arrived again in her own body from another place. She tried to remember her dreams. Dean snored gently in the other bed. She slipped into her clothes and walked softly down the stairs and unlocked the back door. She walked the yard in the thin new light, to the far border and then across to either side. The birds were quiet. She heard a single low chirp, the shaking of feathers, from high in the trees.

For breakfast Nora made blueberry pancakes and bacon, freshly squeezed orange juice and coffee, and they ate together at the dining room table. Holly brought down their Mother's

Day gifts, tucked into a decorative bag she had lined with white tissue paper. Her mother opened the card and read it slowly aloud and read their signatures and placed it open on the table. She reached inside the bag and unwrapped a small box and pulled from it a long strand of pearls, colored pale blue, and ran it admiringly through her fingers. There was another gift, of soap and a companion hand lotion, and she squeezed a few drops of the lotion onto her daughter's hand and rubbed in the scent, then did the same for herself, and the air held the odor of lavender.

Nora said, "Thank you, oh, thank you, how thoughtful, how beautiful," with genuine gladness, and Holly thought how she often forgot that there was only herself and her mother, and then on other days a few relatives, and some friends here and there, and that to celebrate anything, anything in peace and plenty with one another was a gift. Holly kissed her mother's cheek and felt bad about everything, everything, and then she was glad and she blinked her eyes, blinked her eyes, and ran her fingertips under her lids, catching an eyelash, catching an eyelash; it was only an eyelash.

Holly put away the breakfast things and washed the dishes while her mother set her card on the mantle. Dean went out to survey their work in the front yard. When he had had another life entirely, he husbanded his property, pruning and mulching and planting. He owned a half acre and a good house and it was all gone, to the lawyer and to his ex-wife. Now in winter he would point out to Holly a few sticks growing out of the ground and name them. In spring he told her the names of all of the

The Émigrés

plants they discovered on their walks, and which ones he used to have in his yard. Now, after breakfast, he had a few rows of pansies and impatiens to oversee, and he checked the soil, as he had done the evening before, and packed a plant a little tighter, and stood up and ran the back of his hand across his cheek. Holly drove her mother to a farm-and-garden center to buy another flat of impatiens. As she backed the car out of her mother's driveway she looked across the street in the rearview mirror but nothing was there. Whatever car had come down the street in the night was not evident; all was quiet and still. The little girls' mother's car was gone, taking her to work again, and the door to their house was closed.

Holly's mother, having decided on a flat of mixed pink and white flowers, rested it on the floor of the passenger seat. Holly drove them home. She turned into the driveway, gave the flat of impatiens into her mother's hands and walked with her to the front of the house. She heard the clack of Dean's computer keys through the newly installed screen in the door. She looked for the little girls, who she wanted to help plant the flowers. They seemed to her to be a necessary part of this labor, two wood nymphs with powers that would help the plants take root.

And then there was Leka, walking across his daughter's front yard, across the furrows, stepping onto the soil that was birthing the seeds he had planted to feed his family. He knelt near the fence line that bordered the street, his knees disturbing the furrows. He was hunched over something on the ground in an attitude of dismay. Holly went to him. He looked at the garden with an old despair, as if he were witness again to something that had been irrevocably harmed. A mass of cigarette butts lay tightly together there, as if they had been dumped over the fence from a car ashtray. The boy and girl sat on the steps of the house across the street, watching Leka in their attitude of sinister guardianship. The white car was parked in the driveway next to the house. The girl had folded an arm loosely across her knee.

"Evil, evil, evil," Leka said, and he stood as if to accost them. He looked helplessly at the marred ground. Nora waited by the door, the flat of impatiens in her hand, her mouth pursed. She would probably tell Holly that they shouldn't be planting a garden in their front yard, as if they were on a farm instead of looking after a house on a street in a city. *But then,* Holly thought, *what does one know to do in a new land, in a new world, aside from try to survive.* Her mother must surely know this, having entered so early into a world incommensurate with anything she had imagined of it. Holly found herself covering her mouth with her fingers.

Every loss seemed concentrated in the defaced soil. She ran into her mother's house and pulled the tissue paper from the brightly colored gift bag and carried it across the yard to Leka. She knelt on the ground and spread the paper beside him and began to place the cigarette butts on it. When she was done she folded the sides over and dropped the paper into the trash barrel at the end of her mother's driveway. Leka watched her, paralyzed with an old rage. Holly returned to him and knelt over the soil and began to repair the furrows.

What Some Men Dream

Laurel glanced up at the wind-up clock on the shelf above the drawing table. The second hand moved in discreet measures across its face. Turning, leaning into her elbow, Laurel pressed a metal-edged ruler against a sheet of vellum affixed to the table and guided a No. 1 pencil along it, making a series of perpendicular lines. She shifted the ruler and guided the pencil again. The lines took form, becoming a cross, or an intersection. From her pots of colors she selected a deep shade of red, bent a sable brush into the pot and left strokes of color inside the lines. She blew the vellum dry. Checking the clock again, she dipped a fine-point pen into a bottle of India ink and drew question marks all over the edge of the paper.

In her bedroom, Laurel untied her bathrobe and buttoned herself into a skirt and blouse. She parted the curtains and looked out the window for her father. There was no buzzer in the downstairs foyer to announce a guest, or a lock on the front door. The building's inhabitants once slept on summer nights with their apartment doors held open by a brick or a heavy iron to encourage the movement of air. The landlord had installed a lock on the front door but it was quickly broken by indignant tenants, for without a buzzer the lock was an impediment; some of Laurel's neighbors had no telephone and so they couldn't be reached except by entering the building, climbing the stairs and knocking on their door.

Laurel sat on the bed and ran her fingers through her hair. She crossed one leg over the other and made loose circles with her foot.

She was startled by a light rapping on the door. She got to her feet, smoothing her skirt. "Who is it?" she asked, although she always knew who it was. Her father had called her into the afternoon to announce his progress toward her apartment. He often called from places she had never heard of: the far reaches of the Bronx, northern New Jersey, or Brooklyn where he had checked into the Granada Hotel as soon as he had cashed his is first V.A. check. She now knew the subways that departed from the V.A. Hospital in Brooklyn; when the Staten Island ferry docked next to the U.S. Coast Guard station; and exactly how long the subway took from Hunts Point.

He would call; there would be a delay; he wouldn't arrive. She would call the V.A. Hospital and be told he wasn't there. No, she was told, his bed was already taken; there were strict curfews; the hospital wasn't a hotel or a boarding house. No, they couldn't call her if he arrived. Yes, of course, she could call the hospital again. While she waited for her father, Laurel would return to her pots of colors and draw the forms of long-legged, handsomely tailored men on the smooth vellum.

Their features were blurred, unconvincing. There was noise over the telephone line when he called, of traffic, subways, wind. The spiral-bound book of maps of the city she had bought when he began to visit her trembled on her knees as she held the receiver to her ear, trying to locate the exact point where her father was calling from, and each time she had to remind herself that it was he, on the phone with her, he existed again, he was coming to see her.

"It's Webster Hammond," her father answered. Laurel opened the door. Her father was changed subtly each time from his previous visit, but to her he was like a beautiful animal, a lean, tawny cat, a mountain lion, arresting and unknowable. He was clean-shaven and dressed in an off-white linen suit, a light-brown shirt, and brown leather shoes. His veteran's records from World War II, which Laurel's mother still kept in a fireproof box on a shelf in her bedroom closet, stated: Height, 5' 11", but he looked different than she used to remember him. She was a small girl then, in a wool coat with a velvet collar and a matching wool hat, and he was the figure next to her, holding her hand, but already looking elsewhere, already not really there. In some of the photographs he looked straight at the camera but she couldn't remember if afterward he looked at her. Then in the photographs he looked away. His bones were long and elegant. But he was thinner now; he had been ill. His head was bent forward slightly from his shoulders; it was the only aspect of his bearing that was out of harmony with the rest of his body, as if he carried a secret burden. In one hand he held a leather valise, and with the other he braced a paper shopping bag against his hip.

She held the door for him and he passed through the doorway and into her apartment, having avoided any contact with her. She had learned that he didn't like to be touched. He called her frequently. From New Jersey and Brooklyn. The IRT and the BMT. When he visited her he wore a cream-colored suit; she wore a blue dress. He sat nobly with her in her living room, smoking a Pall Mall cigarette, even though smoking was forbidden. He was taking treatments at the V.A. Hospital; sometimes he came to see her still unwell from them. He wouldn't let her visit him at the hospital, where she would see him wearing a hospital-issued bathrobe and a pair of slippers with the backs worn down. Getting ready for his arrival, Laurel's breathing changed, as if she were running a long distance. Her chest sometimes hurt. In it her heart was that of a small girl, tiny and broken.

In her living room, her father sat lightly but with some difficulty on the couch and settled the valise and paper bag on the floor beside him. He pulled a Pall Mall from the pack in his breast pocket and lit it. The tips of the index and middle finger of his right hand were stained with nicotine. He breathed out a large smoke ring and floated two smaller rings through it. Laurel set an ashtray on the coffee table.

"You found your way from Brooklyn without too much trouble?" she said.

"Queens. Yes, Queens. Though I did have trouble. I got on the IRT, but at Seventh Avenue made a mix-up somewhere."

He patted the valise and paper bag. "The subway kept going straight on, downtown. I should have been on the Broadway line. It's the Broadway line, isn't it? When the subway began to slow, like a damned fool I stood up. It works on trains, you see. It's all right to stand on trains. I was under a bit of a strain. I don't like being in the dark like that, when the lights go out, underground, an occasional light flashing by. Standing up in a railroad car, on the other hand, is part of the arrangement between you and the people who run the train. Well, I missed the strap. It could have happened to anyone. There was a driver up front, a speed demon. He didn't know how to work the brakes. My valise took a fall."

"You're all right?" Laurel asked.

"Oh, sure. Hey," he said. He leaned over and pressed her hand, then quickly took his hand away. "It's good to see you."

At the end of their first visit, at the hospital in Philadelphia, his long forearm swept across his face, hiding himself from her when she tried to put her arms around him. Good-bye. She finally walked away.

Webster Hammond's case was problematic; he was ill and destitute. Costly to the hospital. Miss Priestly, the hospital social worker, was trying to find a way around it. A man cannot live to be—she checked the file on her desk—fifty-seven and have absolutely no one. Mr. Hammond sat across from her in the clothes they had found him in—cleaned and pressed, she noticed; he had probably told a tale and a nurse's aide had run off with them to the cleaner's—a well-cut sports jacket,

After the Hunger

a crisp gray shirt, burgundy tie, flannel slacks. Polished; a gentleman. He was flirting with her, telling her about France. No, she had never been to France. He would take her to the Champs-Élysées, Mr. Hammond said. In better times. To buy her a hat in Paris.

Mr. Hammond, Miss Priestly said, is there no one? Webster Hammond's expression became chilly. She encouragingly pushed a pen and paper across her desk. He clicked open the pen and wrote a name and a possible address—not an address, just the name of the state where his former wife lived. When he last saw her. No, he couldn't remember when. No date came to mind. Quite some time ago. Mr. Hammond, Miss Priestly said, you really shouldn't be wearing your street clothes while a patient in this hospital. Webster stood. A pleasure, he said, without taking her hand, and left her office.

Miss Priestly read his file: Often refuses to take medication, will not discuss case, often threatens to leave hospital. She wrote in his file: temperamental, easily affronted, high intelligence, often unrealistic, pursuing conversation with Mr. Hammond of this date. She examined the piece of paper he had left on her desk. She called the telephone company and asked if it would be possible to deliver to her at the hospital a telephone book from every county—she read from the piece of paper—in the nearby state, 150 or so miles northeast on I-95.

Laurel never saw any forms or charts related to her father, never met any doctors or nurses whose care he was in, only Miss Priestly. An official piece of paper was what was needed, one with her father's name on it. Someone at the admissions desk to take a form from a file and say, Oh, yes. Mr. Hammond. Room 530. Take any elevator over there.

The hospital was cavernous and silent. It was the weekend, and no one was about. No one had left instructions. Laurel looked each way down the long corridor then walked up to the information desk.

On the morning Laurel was to take the train to Philadelphia to meet her father, Miss Priestly phoned her with the news that Webster was dangerously depressed. It was interfering with his treatments. He cried and wouldn't eat. Miss Priestly said, A visit is not in his interest at this time. Laurel said, When, then? She had been crying; she had hardly eaten since Bettina, her mother, had phoned her the previous week. Your father is in Philadelphia, she had said. I got a call from a Miss Priestly. Just today. Imagine hearing his name again.

The night her mother called, Laurel felt her heart contract behind her rib cage. She lit every light in her apartment and lay on her bed. Now, after Miss Priestly's call, she couldn't bear the thought of her father sick and alone, and crying because she was coming to see him. Or the thought of, Miss Priestly had told her, her father at first having been taken to a psychiatric hospital by two policemen who thought there was something wrong with his mind, because he had been found on the street without identification, without, even, his eyeglasses, clutching the trunk of a tree.

After Laurel got off the phone with her mother she turned over the piece of paper on which she had written

Miss Priestly's telephone number, as if something would be revealed to her. When Laurel reached her, Miss Priestly said, Miss Hammond. Yes, a visit, lovely. Well, let me see. Any other family members? We could possibly make arrangements— Yes, of course. He does. He reads all the time. Newspapers and magazines. But days old, often weeks. The hospital, you see, is not that well supplied. Newspapers and magazines are not enough, she told Laurel, for a man of his intelligence; he needs something more substantial to engage him.

Laurel wanted to give her father something that belonged to her. She stood in front of her bookcase. Her collection of books seemed suddenly meager, as if her father was there with her, judging them. She pulled them down by their spines and dropped them onto the windowsill. One or two fell to the floor. She fanned the books' pages and slammed them shut between the palms of her hands, trying to imagine her father's life. He listened to music, he owned books. Bettina had seemed vaguely angry at his music and his books. He was not, Bettina told Laurel, what one would call attentive. To the present situation. Whatever that might be.

Dad, Laurel said to him as she studied the titles of her books, I was sent away on Saturday afternoons to eat a carton of popcorn and watch action movies in Technicolor in the theater on Main Street. Your former wife Bettina had an affinity for parades: high school marching bands, the Shriners, the Elks, the Veterans of Foreign Wars in particular; for Fourth of July fireworks bursting over the high school football field at precisely 9 p.m. She liked to play

"The Little Drummer Boy" at Christmas, serve lamb at Easter and pumpkin pie at Thanksgiving. She thrilled at the boom of firecrackers, the drill of the marchers, noise, food, the excesses of the holidays. After the celebration, as Laurel hung up her sweater and slipped off her patent-leather shoes, the aura of spent dreams followed her mother through the rooms of the house.

By the end of the week Laurel had narrowed the books on the windowsill to a reasonable number, and she carried them on the train to Philadelphia in a paper shopping bag. She never forgave Bettina for selling her father's books. Bettina said she hadn't meant to sell all of them, only some. But the man who bought some of them took them all, because Bettina wasn't paying attention when he took them out of the cellar and carried them away. Laurel was just a girl then; she couldn't remember the titles of the books that had remained in the cellar so long. She arrived in Philadelphia with her suitcase and her paper bag full of books, and she spent the afternoon in her hotel room lying on the bed behind the closed drapes.

Miss Priestly, on weekend duty, answered the page at the information desk, unsurprised to see Laurel there, and escorted her to the visitors' lounge on the fifth floor. Her father sat in a chair with one leg crossed over the other, in striped pajamas and a cotton bathrobe. His room was somewhere nearby. Laurel had black circles under her eyes. Her clothes felt badly constructed, and they pulled at her skin. She was aware of her footsteps on the linoleum, carrying her toward her father.

Miss Priestly said, "Miss Hammond, I would like to introduce you to your father," and sat expectantly in the chair next to Laurel's, lacing her fingers over a knee. Laurel and her father looked uncomfortably away until Miss Priestly, rebuffed, adjusted her skirt and walked to the elevators. Webster stood. But then he remained standing, as if he had forgotten who Laurel was, and why he was in a visitors' lounge in a hospital wearing a pair of striped pajamas. Laurel stood also.

You're so much like your father, Bettina would say. Exactly how much, Laurel wanted to know. Why, by a certain lack of connection, a certain drift away from the simplest conversation, looking into a distance no one else can see. Bettina flew into a rage when Laurel read a book. When she read a book, even in her own room, Bettina flew at her. Her mother liked cleanliness, neatness, punctuality. She liked the concrete, the ordinary, the easily explained. Laurel had to be careful not to do anything that would remind Bettina of her father, whom she did not even know. It did not seem fair to Laurel that she, a little girl, would so unfailingly, without provocation, remind her mother of a grown man to whom she was no longer married, who had left without a forwarding address.

Laurel walked across the linoleum to her father and held out her hand to him, as one would on meeting a stranger. Down the hall from the visitors' lounge, a piece of machinery turned over, an engine began to whir. Webster was thin and frail-looking. He did not take her hand. She waited for him to say something, anything. He said he had to sit down. Laurel sat next to him. He reached his hand toward the hand that she had folded on her lap, but then he withdrew it. He looked quietly, thoughtfully away from her. Then he said, "I would have known you anywhere."

Webster tapped the ash of his cigarette in the ashtray on Laurel's coffee table. His fingers were long, the nails cut straight across. He was telling her again about the convertible he had bought with the pale yellow seats made of leather. He told her about working on missile projects for the Army, top secret assignments during the early years of the Cold War, and taking long drives in the desert at night. "The desert," he said, "is a place that will absorb you. There are colors one doesn't ever see elsewhere. The mesquite tree against the sky. The sky that is so blue—how to even explain it—it seems to vibrate, and you can't look at it for long, because God is there. Well then," he said, blowing a smoke ring into the room. "So you see. Soon you learn you never want to find your way back."

Laurel tried to place him, to find her father in the sleek yellow car, driving west, while she was a girl in a house with a cellar filled with the books he had left behind. Sitting on her couch in his new linen suit, his body still had the gracefulness she knew from the photographs, or memory; she got them all mixed up. There was a Ferris wheel, her father lifting her up. Did he sit next to her? Training wheels on a bicycle in the back seat of his car. Perhaps that very yellow car. He had already gone away; then he had returned, he had come to the small house where Laurel and Bettina lived. Did he stay for

After the Hunger

lunch? Did he lift her onto the bike, hold the back of the seat and run beside her? Did he spin her in his arms?

He took her on the train to New York City, he brought her to F.A.O. Schwartz on Fifth Avenue and bought her a stuffed tiger with legs that moved. He taught her how to tie her shoes. Bending next to her, turning the lace into a loop, tying the other lace around, making another loop, pulling the loops tight. Two hands then four hands then two; the loops falling asymmetrically over the sides of her shoes. Laurel used to think she remembered her father until she tried to recall him outside the frame of the photographs, and then her memories all seemed to be made up or borrowed.

Laurel slept poorly on her return from Philadelphia. After midnight the trucks stopped shifting gears in and out of the lot down the street. The teenage boys had stopped throwing firecrackers off the rooftops and their mothers had stopped shouting at them. The lights in the windows of the apartment buildings blinked out. Laurel got out of bed and stood on the bare wooden floor. Her bedroom was never dark, even in the night. The windows faced west, onto the street. The fire escape cast its shadow on the window shades. She could smell the salt air from the waters of the bay that washed up the Hudson River. She heard the foghorns on the river; they woke her when they started sounding, imploring and mournful.

The foghorns broke loose some memory of the Sound in New England, a clapboard cottage her parents rented one summer, her father bending over her bed, his silhouette formed in the light from the living room, kissing her goodnight. When he closed the bedroom door some of the light shone through the knotholes in the wood. She heard the records he played, the shifting and settling of ice cubes in the tall glass her father liked to drink from. The smell of his cigarette smoke mixed with the smell of sand and salt water. She closed her eyes. Her father was there, in the room on the other side of the door.

The doorway to her bedroom was dark where the light from the street stopped suddenly, and the hallway beyond was in blackness. She was sure it was waking and looking into the dark hallway that kept her from returning to sleep. She strained her ears for the sound of her father's walk, expecting to see him there, on the other side of the doorway, no longer familiar.

She tied the belt of her bathrobe and sat at her drawing table. The streetlights threw shadows into the room; an image of windowpanes assembled on the far wall. She heard the sound of heels on the pavement; perhaps it was someone who couldn't sleep either. No other noises. Just a pacing back and forth, a restlessness. She spread her fingers on the drawing table and waited. She thought she heard a voice. She went to the window. A man stood on the sidewalk across the street, beyond the light of a streetlight. A man in a hat. No one wore hats anymore. But there he was. Long-boned, elegantly dressed, wearing a felt hat. He greeted her and then he pointed to her window, and to himself, back and forth. There was something he seemed to be imploring her to do.

After the Hunger

The man on the sidewalk pointed to her window again. He stood across the street, waiting politely for her invitation. He carried a valise. Or was he extending an invitation, was he asking her to come with him? To drive with him in the desert in his yellow car, his linen trousers and shirt wrinkled from the miles he had traveled to find her. Someone spoke; someone spoke to her. A light went on and a window went up. "Be quiet," a voice said. "It's 2 a.m."

Laurel and her father took the elevator to a basement cafeteria in the hospital, empty except for a few kitchen staff in whites on break. They sat at a Formica table near a bank of windows with dead leaves blown against them and shafts of sunlight poking through. Their cups of coffee steamed in front of them. Webster asked his daughter to buy him a pack of Pall Malls from the vending machine in the corridor outside. He stood when she rose to get them, and again when she returned, pressing the collar of his bathrobe down his chest as if it were attached to a linen suit.

Webster opened the pack and tapped a cigarette loose. He cleared his throat. "Our name," he said, "belongs to one of the great houses of the great highland families. Bloodshed and early death. War at any provocation. I wouldn't doubt if Shakespeare had borrowed a thing or two."

Laurel put her cup of coffee down. Webster lit his cigarette.

"There were letters to Europe," he said. "I came to know certain libraries there. I followed every miller and warrior, every woman who birthed a child, every generation, all the way to the Conquest. By then our name had changed entirely. It was unrecognizable, a Norman name. I lost all trace of it. That was when the work began." He blew smoke into the sunlit room. He leaned his elbow on the table and put his fingertips to his forehead as he spoke. Bettina used to yell at Laurel for making this gesture that belonged to her father, though how, Laurel had retorted, could she possibly know that. "The librarians took an interest," Webster said. "I picked up the thread again, among the armies moving north, out of France. I have it all, every generation, in the notebooks I kept. Ask me anything, about any century, and I can tell you. The land our ancestors farmed. The warring clans. The names of the men who won the great battles under our family's coat of arms." Webster sat back and dropped his forearm to the table. "You look for a name," he said at last, "and you find the accidents of history."

The library was built of stone; granite, the air inside cool in summer. Her father's yellow car was parked outside. On a table, a row of sharpened pencils lay next to the stacks of leather-bound books, some untouched for years. The high lead glass windows provided a good light to work by. Her father took a book from the top of a stack and opened it. A librarian walked silently by, turning an interested eye toward him. He read a page. On the table was a notebook, lost now, that he slowly filled with his even handwriting, flowing across the page.

"Tell me about your mother and father," Laurel said.

"What would you like to know?" Webster sounded suspicious; suddenly guarded.

After the Hunger

"I never knew your father," Laurel said. "He died before I was born. Of course you know that."

"He was the eldest of thirteen sons," Webster said, as if reading from his notes. "His mother died not long after the last was born."

"I can imagine," Laurel said, trying to share the awful joke.

Webster lit another cigarette.

"Your mother was very good to me," Laurel said. "I mean she gave me things, and they always meant a lot to me. I remember her big coat, and under it a flowered dress and a lovely brooch, and her snowy hair. She was very stately, she made much of those visits with us. I mean she made a fuss, and it was nice."

Laurel would sit close to her and she would snap her pocketbook open to retrieve an embroidered handkerchief, and Laurel would peer inside to glimpse its secrets: a change purse, a train ticket, a small silver-backed mirror, the mysterious and well-thumbed prayer book, which, Bettina told her, Catholics read.

"She sent a set of encyclopedias once," Laurel said. "She brought me pretty dresses and white socks with lace at the top. A Cross pen and pencil set. A book, *Tales of the Arabian Nights*, with pictures of people wearing beautiful robes, riding black horses. A little tea set, everything in miniature." It was coming back, the gifts wrapped in tissue paper, her grandmother sitting next to her on the couch and handing the wrapped present from her lap to Laurel's. These were the mementos Webster's mother brought to her, against the wishes of her family, her Catholic sister and brother and cousins. They were gifts that made Laurel happy, and that was all that had really seemed to matter to her grandmother.

Laurel had trouble speaking to her. She was shy around her grandmother, she was so imposing. She reminded Laurel of her father, of some connection that had been broken and that had hurt her. Some people were unkind to her because her mother and father were divorced, but her grandmother was good to her. She came to visit Laurel in spite of her family's disapproval. They didn't speak; Bettina was speaking, she carried on her adult conversations with her former mother-in-law, but Laurel sat near her and everything about her was loving and grand. *Maybe,* Laurel thought now, *my grandmother brought me things because her son could not.*

She remembered her grandmother, a tall, large, lonely woman, whose husband was dead and whose son had gone away, who took two trains to get to Bettina's house, stayed for lunch, and took two trains back. Her family was appalled at the idea of divorce because the Catholics forbade it, so her visits were infrequent and formal, and she came alone, representing no one. When she died, suddenly, Laurel still had been shy of her, and she hadn't known her, except for her gifts, and the tender way she presented them to her granddaughter.

"She got hard of hearing," Laurel said to her father, "and she couldn't hear me, and I'd raise my voice, and she'd tell me not to shout. But I wanted her to hear me, even if it was just to say, 'Thank you' or 'I love you.' After she died, it turned out she had put money away for me to go to school. She made that possible for me."

"I was going to send you to school," Webster said. "I was going to send you to Berkeley."

"I didn't go to Berkeley," Laurel said. "There wasn't enough."

"You should have gone to Berkeley," Webster said.

Laurel thought about her father sending her to Berkeley. About her father coming to visit her at Berkeley. Bringing her a gift perhaps. A book bound in leather. She thought about his own father, dead all these years. "Did your father want to send you to school?" she asked. "Was that a dream of his?"

"I studied under the G.I. Bill," Webster said. "After the war. The Romance languages. Martin Luther and the Reformation. Chaucer and the Greeks."

"I understand," Laurel said, remembering something her grandmother had told her mother, "your father made the crossing to Ellis Island with his father and all of his brothers."

"Yes," Webster said.

"Your mother mentioned," Laurel said, "that your father fought in World War I."

"The Great War."

"Did he meet your mother after the war?"

"Oh, I'm sure he met her in the spring. It would have been the spring." Webster's voice had become clipped. He crushed out his cigarette.

"Did you know your uncles?"

Webster looked impatiently away. "I followed the history," he said. "I followed the family names."

Webster sat across from her at the Formica table in the basement cafeteria of the hospital because his military records, along with most of the others from World War II, had been destroyed in a warehouse fire in Missouri, and so Miss Priestly had spent a month calling everyone with Webster's last name in the state where Bettina lived, until she reached Bettina. Bettina gave Miss Priestly all the information she required from the fireproof box in her bedroom closet. Now the Veterans Administration was paying Webster's hospital bill, because Webster had no job, no health insurance; he didn't even own a pair of eyeglasses anymore.

"After your mother died," Laurel said, "there was some hardship, you see, about staying in touch. A few too many priests and nuns in the family, I guess."

Webster brushed a stray piece of tobacco from his lap and lit another cigarette. "I would have assumed as much," he said.

Laurel waited for her father to ask her something about herself, anything. He was very sick. He walked with great effort. He was probably taking all sorts of dulling medicines. She looked across the Formica table at him. *I could break one of his frail bones*, she thought, in her fierce need. *I could touch him and break a bone instead*. Webster had finished his coffee. He seemed too tired to speak.

After he was discharged from the hospital in Philadelphia and had come to New York, Laurel boarded a train at Penn Station to retrieve his belongings from a woman who had rented him a room in her house on Long Island. He had left suddenly with nothing but a complete set of her house keys.

After the Hunger

The house was like the others on the street and the nearby streets: a strip of lawn, a peaked roof, a front door with an aluminum screen door, a detached garage, a picture window that looked across the street onto its exact double looking back. There was a street, Lewiston Street, which Laurel searched for on the identical streets, and a preposterous address, 112705, and a color, red, like all the other red-colored houses. Laurel rang the bell and from behind the screen door the woman, Mrs. Reed, told her to come to the back door, and already Laurel felt as if she were suspect. She dropped politely into a chair at the kitchen table. Mrs. Reed hung her elbows over the sink, washing two coffee cups. She dried them and put them on the table.

Laurel fumbled with her hands. "You see, Mrs. Reed," she said. Mrs. Reed moved about the kitchen. "He has always lived this way. There were books, stored in a cellar and then lost. Notebooks left open on a table. He listened to records. He never touched the grooves with his fingers, and he cleaned each record with a chamois cloth before putting it away. He was in the Army, in the war, then later, too. He went to the desert. I don't think he used to be much among other people. I think he got accustomed to living that way. He forgets certain considerations. He drove west in his yellow car. He left a lot behind. He had forgotten about your house keys, you see. He simply forgot. But you don't have to worry. He won't be back."

Mrs. Reed was low-keyed, suburban, baffled, anxious, and reserved. She served coffee and a plate of pastries and

Laurel started crying at the kitchen table of this stranger whose house it had taken her all afternoon to reach. She dragged her father's possessions from the garage, where they had been stored in plastic bags, and sorted through them on the back steps for her books. Mrs. Reed watched Laurel the way Bettina had done, for years, her eyes narrowed and cautious, for signs that she was like him.

Laurel set a tray on the coffee table with glasses of iced tonic water decorated with slices of lime. Webster said, "How very nice." He smoked another cigarette. He looked exhausted and distracted. There was a lawn, trees, lawn chairs, the air was warm and comfortable, a lot of people were about, relaxed and friendly. Her father sat in a chair, and Laurel stood next to him; he was talking to a man and a woman, and they were pleasant with each other. Webster said something and the man and the woman laughed, easily, and Laurel put her hand on her father's arm, wanting to be part of this circle, and he lifted her onto his knee. There was a beer bottle in his hand, and he held it to Laurel and she sipped it, one sip, pungent and golden and cooling.

He had friends, Bettina had told her, he brought them home and played the old 78s and Bettina served beer and soft drinks, pretzels and crackers, and they talked about things she didn't understand, Mahler and Moravia, the only names she could remember. He excluded her, she told Laurel; they never did have the same *point of view*, not really. Laurel sipped her tonic water and watched her father measure the weight of the glass then lift it. Sitting next to him, she felt as if she and her father were formless as apparitions, two ghosts who knew each other once, long ago. The man who had spun her in his arms. The little girl who spun in his arms.

"Do you remember," Laurel said, "giving me that sip of beer? On a lawn? I never developed a taste, you see; it never tasted so good as then."

"You wore a dress," Webster said. "A blue dress...." He pushed his hand into the air, as if he had just remembered something. "Oh," he said, "I have a gift for you." He pulled the paper bag around and reached into it, and held out two record albums to her.

Laurel reached for him and kissed him and then withdrew, quickly, from touching him, feeling a guilty joy, remembering her longing at other girls whose fathers bought them winter coats and educations. She held up the albums, held them to her. She put the *Piano Music of Erik Satie* on the turntable. She would save *Emerson Lake & Palmer* for later. Erik Satie belonged to her father; the other album was what her father imagined she would like to hear. Laurel listened with her father to Erik Satie's piano, its beauty and wit, its newness and fearlessness. She brought her father to her bookcase to show him the long row of Bakelite 78s that she had taken from Bettina's cellar. He bent his knees and looked closely at the cloth bindings, so heavy and old, the records sheathed within, and ran his hand over the spines of his collection: Mozart and Beethoven, Verdi and Stravinsky, Hayden and Mendelssohn.

"I wondered what happened to these," he said.

"I took them away. I took them here."

"I used to listen to them in the evening."

Laurel put her hand on his shoulder and he stiffened. He was so thin beneath his suit jacket. He put one arm around her, barely touching her.

"Are you hungry?" she asked. "It's almost dinnertime." She had moved away from him.

"I could use a little something," he said.

"I'll pick up a few things for us at the store."

"I'm coming with you," he said. "No daughter of mine is going out into the night unescorted."

She went to find her sweater.

They walked up the street under the evening sky. He put one foot uncertainly in front of the other, keeping a careful balance. In the small grocery store he selected artichoke hearts, smoked oysters, and marinated olives from the shelves. Laurel found endive, fresh cooked shrimp, string beans, a red pepper, a loaf of French bread, and a square of Parmesan cheese.

"Will this suit you for dinner?" she asked. "We can make a salad."

"A salad, yes," Webster said. "If you would indulge me so."

Webster stood impassively next to his daughter as she paid the bill. He carried the bag of groceries while Laurel walked beside him. He held the bag to his chest, each foot tentative on the pavement, as he escorted her into the evening. He stopped and crossed the street and guided her into a neighborhood bar.

After the Hunger

They took seats at the bar; it was still too early to be very full.

"I thought we could have an aperitif," he said. He held up two fingers and said to the bartender, "Vermouth. Two. On the rocks, with a twist."

"I had a birthday last month," Laurel said. She was pleased to be sitting with her father.

"I know you did. March twenty-fifth, right?"

"March twenty-sixth."

"When you were born you weighed seven pounds, ten ounces, and you were twenty inches long. I remember the day so well. The crocuses were just poking up. You were the prettiest little thing. I could hold you in the length of my forearm."

"What did you say?" Laurel asked. The bartender had brought their drinks.

"I said, 'Hello, my daughter.'"

Bettina didn't know what to do with Laurel's memory of Webster. What did she remember? Was it good or bad? Laurel loved her father more. Bettina didn't like Laurel very much. She didn't like raising a child alone, a quiet child who didn't seem interested in her own mother, who was interested instead in a fabrication. One day she said, "He'd come home and play with you and lift you in the air and do spins and call you all sorts of endearments, and you'd laugh and get all worked up." Bettina was looking sharply at Laurel. She was smoking a cigarette. Her teeth made marks on the filter. They all smoked from that generation. They smoked and drank. Bettina breathed smoke at her daughter, who was trying not to listen.

"Then just like that," Bettina said, "he would put you down and punch the newspaper out in front of him, and he'd sit behind it and want no more of you. Usually I'd take you by the hand and we'd play together while I made dinner. I felt so sorry for you, you see." Laurel was working over her fingernail. She was biting her thumb. "But once," Bettina couldn't help but say, "you were still laughing, because you had no idea he was tired of you. You tried to crawl onto his lap. You tapped the newspaper with the flat of you palm." Bettina crushed out her cigarette and snapped the leatherette cigarette case shut. "And what did he do? What did your father do?" Laurel got up and left the room. "He lifted you from his knee," Bettina said. She was shouting now. "He sat you hard on the floor and walked off to another room, rolling the newspaper tight in his hand." Bettina was at the doorway, shouting into the empty hall. "Your wonderful Papa. And what did you do?" From behind her closed bedroom door, Laurel thought she heard her mother spit into her hand. "You just sat on the floor," Bettina said, "a little, dumb, confounded girl, following him with your big eyes."

"Do you want another?" Webster asked.

"No, thank you."

"Bartender. Another here."

His spine curved sharply under his linen jacket. He drummed his fingers softly. *Who had he sat with, at bars, at tables over dinner?* She put her hand around her drink.

"Did I ever tell you about France in wartime?"

"No," Laurel said, "you never did."

"We were three men," he said. "Long ago. Traveling on foot at night to Le Chambon. We were to meet some people in the Resistance— It's a long story, and it turned out all right. We came upon a farmhouse, set among cypress trees off a dirt road. Most of the land lay fallow. The war ruined the planting seasons. There was no one to plant, nothing to harvest. A lot of people starved. The old man was housebound and practically deaf and his daughter was afraid of us, though trying not to show it. We gave her coffee and canned milk and chocolate. The old man smoked our tobacco. We meant them no harm. We told them what news we could." Webster stirred his drink and looked at his daughter and put his hand next to hers on the smooth surface of the bar.

"We billeted there. The old man showed me where I was to sleep. He took me upstairs, to his granddaughter's bedroom. Her photograph was on the dresser. He had sent her to America to wait out the war. The room looked undisturbed. Thin curtains, a bowl and pitcher on the night stand. The mattress was filled with straw. I slept like the dead in that farmhouse. And the wonder of it was that I dreamed the dreams of a French girl who had been sent to America, sleeping in her bed that night in the wood and plaster farmhouse. They weren't a man's dreams. I woke from the dreams of a young girl waiting to return to France."

There was not much difference in his appearance. In the photographs he looked intelligent, refined, removed. He had suffered somewhere in his life and had learned not to show it. He had an almost circular scar on his head, near the left temple. It was the only mark on his skin, and looking at him in the subdued barroom light, Laurel could not imagine that her father was dying. But he was dying, Miss Priestly had told her so. His hair, which used to be thick and a rich shade of brown, was white now at the temples and thin at the crown of his head. It was because of the treatments he was getting, she knew, but then she thought, looking closely, shyly, *He is bald; there is no hair on his head to grow back*.

"Honey," Webster said, "I'm a little short of cash today."

They had finished their drinks. Laurel paid the bill and left the bartender a tip. She lifted the bag of groceries and they walked home. They sat at the kitchen table and Laurel cut the vegetables and the jars of delicacies into a serving bowl. She spread butter and crushed garlic on the French bread and put it in the oven to warm.

Webster went into the living room and Laurel heard the rustle of his paper bag. He returned with a thick computer print-out and talked to her about FORTRAN and all the other computer languages. He sat across the table from her and explained about the language of those machines. Laurel served the salad in glass bowls. Webster ate a slice of artichoke heart. He told her that he was conversant in almost all of the computer languages, since he had programmed most of them during his career, in the west, after the war, but she didn't understand him, and she didn't believe him.

Miss Priestly took Laurel aside at the information desk in the hospital and told her about some irregularity with Webster's employers. Faulty records. The hospital was trying to locate any funds he might have. There was employment out west, in the desert. Something to do with computers, even then, many years ago. But he had had a disagreement, left under a cloud. Very smart, they said, but couldn't get down to it. Got angry over the slightest thing. There was a more recent job in Philadelphia, Miss Priestly told her. No, there were no computers to program, no new languages to talk to them in. At least that wasn't his job. Miss Priestly became vague, her voice dropped, she whispered something about the long blue-on-white pages of discarded language left on the floor, and in waste bins, and the empty plastic coffee cups sitting on desks at the end of the day. Some sort of service position, Miss Priestly said, cleaning up.

"Dad," Laurel said, "where did you go?"

"Why, I traveled west. I worked in the desert. I created things. I was on the ground floor of the computer revolution. I told anyone who would listen, years ago. I told them all. But who listened?" His voice was rising. "Your mother didn't listen. So I had to go alone. Out west. Where the future was. I wanted to take you with me, I brought you a bicycle in my car."

"I remember the car, I think," Laurel said. "The yellow car, pale, a beautiful color. The yellow seats, ribbed and plump. A bicycle wheel, side up in the back seat, spinning and spinning. I wanted to sit in the car and hear the tick of the wheel."

Bettina told Laurel how brilliant he was, when she was in that kind of mood. After the war. When she met him. Simply brilliant. That he had such promise; the whole country did. So many opportunities for a forward-thinking man. They were already divorced by the time he tried to lure Laurel out west with a bicycle, and it was, strictly speaking, kidnapping, not a word used then when a father wanted to take his daughter away. Bettina called the police. Everyone said how brilliant he was. But he had a temper, he was not one to pay attention, he listened to 78s in the evening and he and Bettina were, everyone said later, unsuited. Unsuitable. Bettina wanted a family and a house with a fence and everything pleasant and conversation at dinner. He took his car west. His trail grew cold. Laurel was left alone with Bettina. Things became difficult. Neighbors became difficult and teachers became difficult and Bettina became difficult. Divorce threatened Bettina. Divorce threatened people, absent fathers threatened people, in all the vast hopefulness after the war. Something was amiss; just look at that girl and her mother.

Webster and Laurel finished their dinner. Webster stirred his coffee distractedly. *Perhaps,* Laurel thought, *he was thinking of the desert*. She didn't know.

"What else did you bring with you?" she asked. "In the valise?"

Webster looked at her sharply and she thought he might rise from his chair and walk off. Then he said, "I brought my other things with me: a fresh shirt, another tie, a change of underwear."

"You aren't at the Granada Hotel any longer?"

"I've moved a few times since then. My government checks haven't caught up with me yet. But I'm working on it."

"Can you go back to the V.A. Hospital in the meantime; will they let you stay there again?"

"I suppose I could, if I had carfare."

Laurel washed the dinner dishes and left them in the drainer to dry. She stood at the sink with a dishtowel in her hands and looked at her father. He wanted to stay; he wanted to empty the contents of his valise into a dresser drawer and stay with her. Her father bending over her, kissing her goodnight. Playing the old records, softly so as not to disturb her. The smell of his cigarette smoke drifting down the hall.

"Would you like to stay here tonight?" she asked. Her father there, in the room on the other side of the door.

"That would be a relief."

Laurel made up a bed for herself on the couch. She fluffed the pillows on her bed and took down her heavy cloth bathrobe and laid it on the bed for him.

"I hope you sleep comfortably here. It was good to see you again, Dad."

"Good night, Daughter."

"Good night."

In the living room, Laurel gazed at the shadows of the windowpanes the streetlights threw on the wall. She lay still until she heard her father's breathing deepen. She lifted the covers and stole over to the valise and paper bag, which were lying where Webster had left them. The paper bag was empty; the valise contained the computer print-out, a shirt, a tie, and a change of underwear. There would be something else, she thought, in the valise he carried with him, but that was all. She stole back to the couch and fell asleep.

In his daughter's bedroom, lying on her pillow, Webster slept. He was dreaming of the deaf old man in France. The deaf old man spoke to him in his cracked voice. The sound of the old man's voice woke him. He looked at the illuminated dial on the clock on the night table. It was late. Across the street a window opened, and he thought he heard someone say, "Quiet." He parted the curtains. He saw an open window across the street, a light in the room beyond going dark, a streetlight above an empty sidewalk.

When he was dressed again, Webster pocketed the carfare Laurel had left for him on the kitchen table and settled his valise in the hallway near the door. He walked into the living room and sat beside his daughter. He smoked a cigarette and watched her face while she slept. She would have liked the desert. The sun fell across it in bars of light. The cactus plants brought forth flowers after a rain. Hummingbirds sped by like bold spirits. You could lose yourself in the desert; it was a place where you didn't have

After the Hunger

to be found. He saw her, driving with him in his yellow convertible, a ribbon in her hair. He looked at her sleeping form. She had the same pretty face, the features more defined now, lovelier; she was all grown up. But he would have known her anywhere.

Holiday

The two of them—it was almost always the two of them—drove around the rotary, Imogene wondering who would invent such a thing, to be caught up in, as if by centrifugal force, each time they went to the grocery store, cars entering, seeming never to exit but to circle and circle as if the physical world had been disrupted, as if one's will had been destroyed, then hurdling toward an exit, Imogene hanging onto the strap above the passenger door, and Joe somehow keeping steady at the wheel. She had almost completely stopped driving since their marriage. Often she missed it, though not in rotaries, not in snow or rain, not at night. When she reminded Joe that she used to drive, she used to drive very well, in fact she had driven him home quite successfully, quite without incident after his cataract surgery, the hospital insisting on a driver, he reminded her that she was behind the wheel because he was at that moment drugged and half blind.

But now he was driving from the grocery store, and she wondered if, had she been driving, she would have been able to take them directly home, instead of on a detour, which she was bitterly aware their life at that moment had become. There—the two of them—if it could be just that—they would empty the grocery bags and set the bottle of wine on the counter and go over their preparations for the holiday, and afterward listen to the Bose in the den and drift upstairs to bed.

There wasn't any snow that season, as the year drew to a close, and the temperatures under a gray sky remained in the low forties. The trees that bordered their yard had tall, straight trunks crowned with fans of branches seeking the winter sun. The woodlands along the roads and at the boundary of their back yard were the distant relatives of an ancient broadleaf forest, having risen from the spent soil after the old farmlands had failed. The woods were under a cover of fallen leaves, but Joe kept the yard raked and the walkways swept. At that time of year, surveying the yard, even now, on Christmas eve day—before their drive to the grocery store, walking around it carefully, as if what they imagined of it might shift and vanish and come back again as something even more fantastic than stony ground covered with crabgrass and shrubs stalky and feral—they could see, under the leafless trees, the old stone walls, loose and crumbling.

They said, stopping in their woolen sweaters at a sweep of shrubs, each saying, Azalea, yes; forsythia. A tree, its thin branches like a waterfall trailing to the ground. The woods, the yard, seemed like sleepers, insensate to any attempt at rousing. They looked up at the windows and could see inside the house from where they stood. The fall of a curtain, a chair, a bowl of fruit, nothing yet familiar, nothing yet theirs.

They had owned the house for a month. It answered certain needs for Joe. He seemed lighter now, as if his mind were full of land, space; and with it a kind of peace. At night they went outside to the light crunch of frost on the ground and they could see the constellation Cassiopeia the Queen, the North Star, and the Great Nebula, a distant display of galactic dust and gas, as if held in a moment of splendor. The night was black and pierced with starlight that guided Joe, holding Imogene's hand, around the yard, looking skyward for Pegasus, for Lyra.

At midmorning the female goldfinches came, like a pack of sisters, to the thistle feeder hung at the side of the deck, their tawny yellow bodies balanced on its perches, and they were bright and glorious against the naked trees and somber sky. A cardinal pair came to the feeder in the yard. Joe would see a flicker of red in the rhododendron and call to Imogene. They would watch the cardinal fly to the smoke tree while its mate waited for him among the furled leaves of the rhododendron, then wing to the feeder and land on the rim and dip its orange beak and fly away; its mate repeated its path and the feeder turned like a carousel as she ate. Joe took Imogene for walks under the trees to feel the tread of the land under them, to see all that was theirs now, in the front yard brambles and a swath of old mulch, the color of ash, and the tangle of fallen branches atop the bushes.

Everything needed work, or enhancement, or Joe invented another task for himself. Imogene saw only fallow land, and woods; and inside the house, the rooms with sunlight streaming through the windows or stark in the brooding cloud cover of winter. The house contained the few pieces of furniture they had brought from their apartment, and Joe had located a furniture store that supplied them with an outline of each room. But they had enough for Christmas, their first Christmas, though the house felt larger than it actually was, and empty, as if a creature waiting for nurture.

The former owner had deposited most of her accumulated belongings in a dumpster and assigned the house to the care of her agents. She had left them, or left behind, a bottle of Madeira, which Joe and Imogene drank on their first night there, whispering to each other as they walked through the echoing rooms. The house with its subdued colors and elegant fixtures felt stripped of its own history. They found here and there objects their former owner seemed to have lost interest in, or was unable to take away. The house had come to them from some undetermined loss, and the old land had been abandoned, and Imogene was aware of that, and of how she and Joe were trying to make something of the house again, to inhabit it in another way.

They had invited their family members to Christmas dinner. That was certainly the first thing. To open the curtains, to be thankful, to gather one's family in this new place. They bought two poinsettias and placed them on the fireplace mantle. Joe found a forsaken Flexible Flyer sled in the garage and carried it to the living room. Imogene arrayed their gifts on it, wrapped in heavy red and green paper, the gifts for each other, and for Joe's son Alexander and Imogene's mother Marion. This would be their first Christmas together; the first Christmas where Imogene's mother would sit at her table.

Joe was navigating the rotary when his cell phone rang, and Imogene could tell from the way he spoke into it that his son had called. They said "Hey" to each other in clipped, unnaturally deep voices, which Imogene thought of as a kind of code, the aural equivalent of a fist bump or a bear hug. Something that acknowledged the family bond. Alexander's voice came through the phone. Imogene tried not to listen. His calls usually involved an emergency arising from a misadventure with money or something to do with his car. Some crisis that Alexander demanded rescue from. Joe held the phone against his chest and said, "Alex wants to come for dinner and spend the night. He wants to bring his girlfriend, Erin."

Imogene turned to her husband. "He wants to spend the night at our house with his girlfriend," she repeated, her voice inflected upward.

Joe signed off and put the phone on the console. He had begun to circle the rotary. The exits rolled by. Imogene experienced a sort of vertigo. "You have to tell me if we should go back to the grocery store or go home," Joe said.

"Can't he wait till Christmas?" Imogene fretted. "Can't it be our Christmas, tomorrow, our first Christmas here, with your son and my mother? Must he invite someone? We don't even know this girl." An image came to her, of her parents, herself and her little sister under the lighted tree, and her father handing her a present across the open boxes on the rug. They wore their pajamas and bathrobes. Her father wore brown slippers that looked like shoes. Her sister looked up at him, her mouth slightly open, her wonder at the day bubbling in her throat. Her ponytail, mashed sideways from sleep, drooped between her shoulder blades.

"I worry about him," Joe said. "He spends too much time alone. It's good for him to be able to invite someone for Christmas. Good that he has this girl to invite."

"Isn't this all rather sudden?" Imogene asked. "It's almost sunset. He hasn't even seen the house."

Joe tapped his fingers lightly on the steering wheel. These occasions now of course involved conversations with Imogene, decisions with Imogene. Before they married, they—father and son, and Imogene—used to see more of each other, as a way to begin to become a new family, a new arrangement with each other, but something always took an unforeseen turn, like an accident, with its aftermath of broken parts. Every notion Joe and Imogene held about themselves and Alexander already had been undone before it could achieve whatever they had hoped of it, as if on each of their meetings a countermovement was at work. After Joe and Imogene married he reduced their mutual encounters with his son to a restaurant dinner at Thanksgiving and on Christmas eve, an hour or so in a public place, to give Imogene fewer causes for perturbation.

Holiday

Imogene looked out the passenger window. They had gone around the rotary a couple of times. Her body leaned toward Joe as the car completed another circuit. She tried to pull herself upright with the strap. They were about to get into an argument about sleeping arrangements, she knew. "Where are they going to sleep?" she asked.

Joe pulled the steering wheel into the curve of the rotary. He didn't respond. She could have been a crow or a box of fruit. A baseball mitt or a Pomeranian. In other, similar conversations about his son, seated together in the same room, Joe had the fantastic ability to vanish. His eyes would go blank and his face would empty of expression, as if he were in a vacuum, or in a sensory deprivation chamber, sealed away. It was the time perhaps when Imogene pointed out that Alexander never addressed her, never called her Imogene, never called her anything. How strange! Didn't he think it strange? To shift and slide though their celebratory dinner, to turn his shoulders so, away from her, as if she wasn't there? And she would say, Alex, how is?—while there was so little to ask him about, because what did he do, anyway, aside from work at that part-time job behind a counter and play his guitar? Sitting together in the same room, Imogene would tap, as it were, on the glass, but Joe wouldn't see her, wouldn't hear her.

"What are we going to do about sleeping arrangements," she started to say, but Joe had turned the car off the rotary, back toward the grocery store. He dialed his cell phone. The male voices greeted each other. Joe gave his son directions off the throughway; he and his girlfriend were, it appeared to Imogene, already somewhere on it. Imogene liked to think about things, to plan things; she liked to see things in her mind's eye. Joe's son often disordered her narrative. He interrupted the daydream of her marriage.

The sun was dropping behind the trees. There were lights in some of the yards, strung around the evergreens. *I am in the service of the Lord*, Imogene thought. It was a song from another time, another season. *Did they used to sing it at church, as she shared a hymnal with her father, and her mother bent over her sister and pointed to the words? Did their minister read it to them? It was something about the soul. Something about God.*

The muffled sound of the engine preceded Alexander's car on the driveway. Joe was up from the couch and unlatching the door that led to the garage and opening the garage door and waving in the direction of the windshield to come in, come in. The car looked road-worn, covered with a fine winter grit; it was a different car than when Joe owned it, before he gave it to Alexander. Joe was paying most of Alexander's bills, and at the end of the month he gave Imogene the totals, as if his act of recounting them and her act of writing them down, there in black and white, could at all influence Joe, influence Alexander. Sometimes Alex had a gasoline bill, the sum of twenty-odd dollar increments at gas stations near the apartment building where he lived, that required the tallying of a calculator. He could drive down 95 all the way to Key West on that much gasoline, Imogene said to Joe. You can't get to Key West on 95, Joe had replied. Imogene sighed, rattled some papers. Joe studied a candle holder, ran his thumb over the carved figures on it. He picked up the alabaster figurine of a swan.

The car doors opened, the engine ticked and died, the doors slammed, the two young people crossed from the garage up a brief set of steps into the kitchen where Imogene stood, stomping their feet though it wasn't particularly cold, at least not in the house. The girl, Erin, thrust her arm out and released something into Imogene's hand. It was a CD, a Leonard Cohen CD. Imogene said "Thank you," and the girl stepped back and Imogene realized that this was their Christmas present, to Joe and Imogene from Alexander and Erin, nakedly lying in her hand. It was a new CD. Imogene didn't recognize any of the songs. Oh, to hear "Suzanne," or "Dancing to the End of Love," but not there, not that day.

Imogene and the girl exchanged names, having to introduce themselves, while Joe clasped his hand on Alexander's shoulder and said, "Well, son," in a hearty voice. Alexander hefted a grocery bag onto the counter and withdrew a six-pack of beer. In a few deft motions he twisted the tops off the bottles and handed them all around. Imogene put up her hand. This was Joe and Imogene's new house and their first holiday in it and they were the hosts, and Joe especially was the host of his son and his son's girlfriend, whoever she was, and not Alex, pulling the tops off bottles of beer and handing them around. The table was set with water glasses and the wine glasses that Joe would ceremoniously fill, after they sat down, and where did bottles of beer, straight from the package store, fit into this? Alexander was disordering her daydream again. He took a two-liter bottle of wine from the bag and placed it on the counter.

Joe said, "How was your trip," and the girl was frightened, Imogene could see, a new girl in the home of someone's parents all on her own. "Alex is a great driver," Erin said. She was smiling at Alex. "We took that exit and here we are." They had set down their overnight bags and everyone but Imogene was lifting a bottle of beer to the ceiling. She looked out the window. A squirrel had climbed the smoke tree. It started across a branch. Imogene picked up the pair of binoculars from the sill, cupped them in her hand.

Joe led the young people on a tour of the downstairs rooms. He wanted his son to see the house. He had lost the house where he was raising Alex when he divorced his second wife, who was utterly crazy in Joe's telling and hell bent on entering the household into a permanent state of crisis. His first wife, Alexander's mother, died when Alex was a child, and it distressed Joe that his son had so little memory of her, the shape of her face or the way she used to hug Alexander to her side as they walked together across the yard. Imogene had spent her adult life living in old brick apartment buildings with large high-ceilinged rooms, elaborate moldings, temperamental windows, and leaking radiators. Joe bought their house for her, he often told her, to know rooms, stairs, grass, the deep arrhythmic beating of wings as a flock of starlings flew overhead, but it was a return too for him to the old way he was accustomed to, with rooms, too, a yard, too, and his family with him. Imogene heard Joe, in the living room, point out this object, this view to his son. She fitted the binoculars and saw the squirrel position itself at the end of the branch. She could tell by the arch of its tail and the tautness of its muscles that it was reckoning the distance to the bird-feeder.

After returning from the grocery store, Joe and Imogene had spent the remainder of the afternoon waiting for Alexander. Imogene sat on the couch, her open palms holding her chin, looking at the Flexible Flyer topped with presents. Joe went to the basement and emptied the dehumidifier into the kitchen sink. Imogene turned a few presents in her hands. There was a gift for her sister, a music box, for whenever she decided to return from California or New Mexico or Timbuktu—places that seemed impossible to bridge. When Imogene's sister was very small their mother put her hair up in a ponytail that fell in a wave down the nape of her neck. It was a beautiful blonde color and she was always smiling and she had a high abrupt laugh that sounded like Ah! Ah! Ah! Imogene sat with her on the floor and taught her patty-cakes and stood next to her when their mother put her down for a nap and watched her eyelids slowly close and heard her quick animal breath. She would walk toward Imogene in a stiff, uncertain way and Imogene would hold her and she smelled of shampoo and talcum powder and cotton clothes warm with the heat of her body.

The squirrel gathered the muscles of its haunches and leapt into the air. It missed the bird-feeder and fell to the ground. It sat there as if in disbelief, then stood, its body making quick nervous movements.

After the Hunger

Alexander and Erin were taking off their coats and Joe was putting them over the back of the pull-out couch in the den. The girl wore what looked like yoga pants over her slender legs and a gray sweatshirt. Alexander wore a flannel shirt and a pair of ripped jeans. He lifted his bottle of beer and drank it down. Imogene shut the half-full six-pack in a cabinet. Alex had come to Easter Sunday service with his father and Imogene the year before they married, meeting them on her street, parking behind Joe's car, and the three of them drove to Imogene's church together, Imogene and Joe in Sunday dress, Alexander in worn high-top sneakers and corduroys with the nap missing at the knees and a hoodie zipped over a wrinkled shirt. Imogene, having told him earlier, through Joe, her emissary, even then, that she would introduce him to her friends after the service, thought then, *How can I possibly?* and they left by a side door, avoiding the other congregants, avoiding the minister who stood greeting them at the wide front doors.

Alexander eschewed institutions, church, education—having dropped in and out but mostly out of community college for the past number of years—though he seemed to recognize and respect the law, having been coached by Joe about the dangers of smoking marijuana in the car, and told that if a cop ever stopped him to ask no questions and do what he was told. He lived within the more conservative reaches of his generation, smoking pot and drinking prodigiously, Joe told her, especially since having met Erin. He played his guitar. He seemed to Imogene to have invented himself as a character out of the movies of the 1950s, hoarding some inarticulate grudge. But Imogene found him self-absorbed and strangely entitled for the offspring of a man who was attempting to make his own life worthwhile, who went to work and paid his bills and hoped as they all did to stay on the other side of disaster.

Joe was telling his son and his son's girlfriend a story about a raccoon, a raccoon in a closet. It wasn't their closet. Imogene didn't know whose closet he was talking about. There were two squirrels on the ground now under the birdfeeder. The first twitched its tail aggressively and chased the other up a tree.

Alexander had lost his mother, and Joe had left him in the care of a neighbor at the end of the school day, had worked late, had somehow not been home, observing to Imogene that women, single mothers, are more able to renounce here and there a part of their day for the care of their children, while Joe knew he would have been released, eventually, from his particular ladder, had he done the same. When Joe was courting Imogene he lived with his son in the apartment they had fled to after his second wife proved to be intolerable. *There was always that,* Imogene thought, watching the squirrel scramble up the tree; *the intolerable wife.* She must be careful not to be an intolerable wife. She fidgeted with the binoculars, wrapped the strap around her hand. Joe came to visit her, late on a Saturday morning, having completed the weekly grocery shopping for himself and his son. He brought her in one of the grocery bags a cantaloupe or a Bartlett pear, and

After the Hunger

she would see the long tape, the accounting of his purchases, the bags of cookies, the prepared foods for Alexander to heat in Joe's absence.

The squirrel, having reclaimed its territory, was climbing the smoke tree again. It moved to the end of the branch and flicked its tail. Imogene banged her palm against the window. The squirrel turned and looked at her through the glass. It didn't move. She was, she realized, engaged in a stand-off.

"Im?" Joe called.

"Yes. Fine," Imogene said.

So maybe that was it. A sea change was at hand, another sea change, and Alexander saw it again in the groceries his father unpacked and placed in the freezer, in the cabinets, for him to heat in the microwave, to eat standing at the kitchen counter. All that day, their wedding day, Alexander, wearing a suit his father had bought him, kept apart from everyone, Imogene's mother and a few friends, and the minister with his robes and Bible and the organist who played the wedding processional on the organ in the chapel. Alexander's hair was long and unruly, as if having received an electric shock. Observing Joe, observing Alexander, Imogene wondered now if Alexander was angry at his father for having to raise himself, and if all he did now that tested Joe, that confounded Joe, came from that one injury as injury in kind. Imogene put down the binoculars and turned away from the window.

The tour was over. Joe and his son and his son's girlfriend stood together near the fireplace in the den. Joe began to lower the shades. Imogene picked up Erin's overnight bag.

"We have a bed for you upstairs," she said. The girl followed her to the guest room. Imogene set the bag down and said, "There are towels in the bathroom down the hall and an extra blanket in the closet. If there's anything else you need, let us know." She was saying this finally in her own house with Joe but she hadn't expected to be saying it to this girl. The girl was very thin, and her eyes protruded slightly as if she were frightened or astonished. Joe had that afternoon brought up a camp bed left behind in the basement and tightened the screws and pounded the mattress and Imogene had fitted it rather poorly with the extra set of sheets she had expected to use on their own bed. The girl said, "Oh thank you," and she was, Imogene knew, elsewhere, going through a formality in a strange house with a woman not Alexander's mother, married to his father.

Imogene decided not to show her the rest of the upstairs, the room she shared with Joe with the bed and dresser and the framed mirror on the wall, and the other room Joe wanted to make into a study, with its open boxes of books and a stack of empty packing boxes on top of which he had placed a reading lamp. Imogene liked to stand in the room at night and see the porch lights of their neighbors' houses and the dimly lit interiors, the houses at night seeming to inhabit their own private space. The moon rose through the east-facing window and Imogene watched it until it moved beyond the window frame. Once, in the early evening, returning to the house, they saw the full moon rising behind the trees, looming above the horizon, its color orange, as if an object of worship.

They got out of the car and watched it ascend the sky, its color fading and transforming into a pale yellow image high above the trees, as if flung upward from the earth. The ground was white under the moon, and the long shadows of the trees crossed the lawn.

Joe was making up the pull-out couch in the den. It was the only piece of furniture in the room. After its purchase Imogene wondered who Joe had expected to stay with them on a pull-out couch. Alexander rested his foot on the stone ledge of the fireplace. A pillow lay on it with a folded pillowcase on top. Next to it was a folded wool blanket. Joe moved around the couch, fitting the sheets. Alexander, lightly attending to his father's movements, was telling him about a new type of GPS. "You can fit it into a holder on the windshield," he was saying. "You can speak into it, too." Imogene said, "Alexander, why don't you help your father." Alexander glanced at her in mild surprise. The girl went to help. She and Joe pulled the top sheet up across the mattress and the girl smoothed the sheets together. Imogene went to the kitchen and opened the refrigerator. She didn't know what Joe had purchased on their second trip to the grocery store; she had remained in the car.

She broke the tape on the butcher's paper. Joe had purchased more of the same items they had planned for dinner. Alexander followed her into the kitchen. "Where's the corkscrew?" he said. She wanted to say, We have no idea, but there was their bottle of wine on the counter, so she opened a drawer and handed the corkscrew to him. He uncorked the wine bottle he had brought with a loud expulsion of air. He put the bottle down and returned from the cabinet in the dining room with two wine glasses. They had been a wedding present from Imogene's sister, sent by Federal Express from Albuquerque. There had been no card. Alexander filled the glasses and led Erin into the living room. The TV came on. Imogene heard a newscaster's familiar voice. The remote clicked through the channels. Imogene looked at Joe, but he was opening cabinets and taking out pots and dishes.

The girl helped Imogene bring the serving spoons to the table. Joe pressed a rub of lemon zest and sage into the chicken breasts and grilled them on the Jenn-Air. Alexander refilled the wine glasses and returned to the TV. Imogene sautéed zucchini and onions, and she checked the golden potatoes, which Joe had quartered and tossed in olive oil and rosemary and put in the oven to brown. The girl helped Imogene fill the serving dishes. Alexander had seated himself at the head of the table. Imogene sent an eye signal to Joe, but he was smoothing a corner of the tablecloth. Erin had waited to see where Imogene and Joe would sit, Imogene at her usual place near the kitchen, Joe now at the other end of the table, across from Alexander. Alexander was waiting for the bowl of potatoes to be passed to him. He had refused the zucchini.

"Alex is mostly a vegetarian," Erin said. "But he doesn't like vegetables."

"We understand you eat chicken and fish," Imogene said. "We had chicken planned for dinner tonight, before you called."

"I avoid red meat," Alexander said to his father. "I did a lot of reading up." Alexander drank his wine. The bottle on the kitchen counter was already a third gone. Imogene and Joe were drinking from their own bottle. It hardly seemed friendly. She lifted her glass.

Imogene turned to Erin. "Alexander told his father you were looking for work. He said you have a degree in management." Does one start with pets, parents, hobbies; she didn't know. "What kind of job are you looking at?"

"Oh," Erin said. "I've been making contacts. There's an organization. They have lots of contacts. I just have to get my car fixed. Then I can drive there, no problem. My dad says there's something wrong with the engine."

"What are you doing in the meantime?" Imogene asked. The girl looked to be in her early twenties, a year or so out of college. Alexander had turned twenty-five that summer.

"I help out my dad," Erin said. "But it's only temporary."

"You've been working for your dad since college?" Imogene asked. She recognized that she was beginning to sound like an inquisitor.

"Yah. But he doesn't really have that much work."

Alexander was talking to his father. "I saw that new James Bond movie," he said. "But no one will ever be as good as Roger Moore. I mean, there was a classic hero. He could wear a tux and beat anybody at anything."

Imogene's conversation with Erin had begun to wither under his voice. Father and son each had big voices, when they wanted to. That fall Imogene had witnessed Alexander, his voice in a paroxysm over some problem with the Registry of Motor Vehicles coming through Joe's cell phone, and Joe attempting to silence him by outshouting him. Then, eventually, he would be able to understand what the issue was. Joe had parked the car at a sharp angle off a main road and he stood in a patch of weeds, shouting at his son, while Imogene waited in the car, as if through a freak storm. Imogene remembered her father's voice, its timbre. He read to his daughters when they were old enough, **Little Women** and **Heidi,** "The Little Mermaid" and *Charlotte's Web, The Tale of Peter Rabbit.* There was never any shouting. Afterward, Joe took her to an elaborate lunch to try to soothe her disquiet at the outraged voices of father and son.

Imogene began to clear the table. Alexander's voice, speaking to his father, was like an element in the house, a foreign tone. Imogene tried to get away from it, but it was there in the kitchen too, a big voice, speaking across the table. Erin was silent. Joe said, "Ah but you should give Sean a chance. Now there's a man who can wear a tux. But perhaps he was too wry, that look of pained amusement always on his face.

"But Daniel Craig," Joe continued, "he has the torment. He has the melancholy. He's the Bond Ian Fleming envisioned."

"I'll go with Roger Moore any time," Alexander said. "And Jack Nicholson. Now there's a Joker. What an evil smile."

"But Heath Ledger, with that smudged make-up, and that nurse's uniform," Joe said. "Now there's derangement. There's evil."

Alexander stared at his father, feeling outdone. Imogene knew there was probably a thrust and parry about to start about the X-Men or the Avengers. A default conversation, in some zone of safety, where they could argue about the inconsequential.

Joe finished his wine and put the glass down. "How's the job," he said to his son. "Making good commissions?"

"The Haitians buy something and then they use it for a few weeks and come in and want their money back," Alexander said. "Or they come in and manhandle something and then try to bargain you down."

"What do you say?" Joe asked. He was leaning toward his son, his forearms crossed in front of him.

"I tell them about store policy," Alexander said. "But there's no talking to them."

Imogene brought out a bowl of sliced strawberries and a plate of macaroon cookies. She said, "I'll put coffee on."

Alex said, "I've stopped eating cakes and pies, that sort of stuff. Processed sugar can make you sick."

"You're looking very fit," Joe said.

Imogene served dessert. She handed Alex a dish of strawberries. He neglected to pass it to Erin. She handed him another dish. Joe said, "There, Alex, pass it along."

The girl helped Imogene bring out the coffee. They had it in the living room. Joe had put a CD in the Bose. It was Debussy's *La mer*. Joe often played it while they cooked, and the notes, conjuring great pulsing currents, blue-black depths, carried them through their work. Erin lifted her coffee cup to her lips in a quick delicate motion. She seemed restless under her good manners, a little at odds with the house. *Am I taking good care of this girl,* Imogene wondered. Her mother used to wear a lovely flared dress and a gauzy hostess apron when they had one or two couples in for dinner and a hand of cards. She had a table crumber with a small brush. *Imagine such an instrument,* Imogene thought, *for crumbs, cigarette ash, all swept away by a hostess with painted red fingernails.*

Joe had been saying something about a Christmas tree they had had no time to purchase and the sled arranged in front of the living room window and next year, next year. Alex was putting his coffee cup down, standing, leaving the room. There were strings in the background, and the sound of bells, very low. They heard the Bose stop, the sound of the CD being ejected. Then a silence. Alexander was doing something to the Bose. *Who owns sound, and space, and the whole movement of an evening?* The house felt strange to Imogene, as if its texture and arc and curve were being wrested away, and the house that she and Joe were so thoughtfully imagining, day by day, was being disassembled, each room folding inward, undergoing a slow implosion.

Alexander returned with the wine glasses in his hands. He had refilled them. He gave a glass to Erin. She seemed grateful for it. "I connected my phone to the Bose," Alexander said to his father. "All you do is key in the name of a singer or a band, and you have the whole menu." There was an electric guitar and drums, a male singer's voice raw in front of the instruments. Alexander sat back in his chair. The next thing to do, Imogene knew, according to the old legends, was to exile his father from the kingdom and declare himself king. *But*, Imogene thought, *there are many ways to defeat the father.* Later she would sing another song to Joe, a Joni Mitchell song, in a low voice, to undo the sound on the Bose. Joe was smiling at his son, his ear turned theatrically toward the music.

Would it always be Joe and Alexander, Alexander and Joe? They had gone to visit Alexander at his job at the electronics store. He was speaking into a telephone. They could see him dial it as they walked toward him, standing next to the cash register. He talked into the phone while they stood on the other side of the counter, not to a customer but to someone he knew, with whom he seemed to be making some sort of plan. He looked up and spoke to his father, then went back to the telephone. Imogene and Joe left the store and Imogene stood at the hood of his car talking to him with her arms crossed over her chest and Joe went back to the store and returned to Imogene and said, He's very sorry that he was so busy with a call and Imogene, risking all, risking it all, said, I am invisible to your own son, and Joe said then, We will never be a family.

Imogene put the dinner things away and filled and turned on the dishwasher. It was another sound in the house, a familiar sound. She returned to the living room and sat next to Joe. She put her hand lightly on his knee.

"Well," Joe said. "It's been a long day. Let's call it a night and we'll see each other in the morning."

The young people watched them leave the living room. Imogene left the upstairs hall light on for Erin. Alex had turned off the Bose; they heard from their bedroom what sounded like a movie. Imogene was standing in front of the wall mirror, as if it had captured her reflection. She frowned into it at Joe.

"It's from his laptop," Joe said. "He downloaded a film."

"I thought it was customary for the guests to go to bed when the hosts did."

Joe went into the bathroom.

"I wish he'd meet someone like Kate Middleton," Joe said on his return. He turned down the bedcovers.

Imogene arranged the sleeves of her nightgown. "He's not going to find someone like Kate Middleton," she said. "Not while he's a clerk in an electronics store. Except Erin has nice manners. As I've read about Kate Middleton. You didn't say anything to them about their drinking. They went through almost that whole bottle of wine."

She thought she was going to lose him again to wherever he went when she spoke about his son. But he said, "She has ADHD. She takes Adderall. She's too old for it, for one thing. It's like speed. Alex thinks she drinks to mitigate its effects. She smokes a lot of pot too, apparently."

"I thought they were broke," Imogene said.

Joe went away from her then. She could hear his breath deepen, then his light snore. The movie played on in the den. Later she thought she heard the repeated, pulsing noise of a video game. Then later a sharp, brief cry. Then silence. At 3:30 she turned off the hall light. At 7 she heard Erin climb the stairs and close the door to the guest room.

After Joe and Imogene had finished their breakfast, Alexander and Erin appeared at the kitchen door, wearing similar T-shirts and plaid sleep pants. The rooms seemed to hold people then discharge them into other rooms, as if by some strange magic. The house, and the rooms that Imogene was always aware of, their waiting emptiness, had begun to seem unknowable to her.

The young people came into the kitchen. Their feet were bare. Joe put his coffee cup down. "Merry Christmas," he said.

"Merry Christmas," Erin said.

"Yeah, Merry Christmas," Alexander said.

"How was your sleep?" Joe said.

"We only have cold cereal today," Imogene said. "There's coffee in the pot. We have to leave soon, to pick up my mother. Make sure your things are put away, the couch folded up."

Joe poured coffee for them. Erin curled her toes on the floor. Imogene got her and Joe's coats.

The throughway was almost free of traffic. They listened to the news on the radio. Joe took the exit ramp onto the parkway. Imogene opened the passenger window. A sharp wind glanced off her shoulder and the side of her face. They took an exit off the parkway and drove north. Imogene's mother lived in a small frame house with an imposing pine tree that each fall shed its cones with great crashing noise like little bombs falling onto the front lawn. Marion opened the door. Behind her, in the living room, was a stretch of carpet, a wing chair and a standing lamp, the framed black-and-white photographs of her family on the wall. She was dressed in

Holiday

the same Christmas outfit she had worn for years, a white sweater and red slacks, with a pin at her shoulder of a red flower with a green stem and leaves. She wore gold-colored clip-on earrings. She hugged them both. Imogene could smell her perfume.

Joe helped his mother-in-law into the car. Marion sat in the passenger seat and smoothed her gloved hand briefly over the seat belt Joe had fastened for her. Imogene listened to her mother talking to Joe. She was discussing with him the line-up for the teams that were playing the Patriots that season. Joe had sent her a list of the teams she should pay attention to. "Those Bills," her mother said. "Did you see that game?" "It was a close one," Joe said. He was patient with her, gallant with her. She liked Joe. She liked being taken care of, having him drive. Imogene opened her window and let the wind enter the car. Her mother said, "I've never seen such an arm as Tom's." Joe said, "He's the one, he's always the one to watch." Imogene closed her eyes.

They parked next to Alexander's car and took Marion around the yard. She named a number of plants, told Joe to remember to cut back the dead-looking branches from the hydrangea, to be sure to cut the spent daffodil leaves down almost to the ground. They showed her the path to the woods. Imogene said, "We can hear sounds, animal sounds, sometimes at night, that we're still trying to identify. Bears, maybe. Who knew." Marion laughed. Imogene took her arm.

Alexander and the girl had straightened the house— the pull-out couch was put away and their things were out of sight. The kitchen had been tidied up. They were sitting in front of the TV. Erin stood. Imogene introduced them. Marion took her hand. "Hello Alexander," she said. "Hi," he said from the couch. Alexander and the girl wore a change of clothes, jeans and long-sleeve T-shirts. Alexander returned to the TV. Marion said, "You're looking very well, Alex." Alex said, "Oh, thanks."

She had brought a few gifts. Imogene placed them on the sled. "Oh isn't that fun!" her mother said.

"Next year we'll have a tree," Imogene said.

Imogene took her mother around the house, showed her all its empty spaces. Upstairs, in the corner of a room, she made the impression of a table, a vase. Marion looked out of all the windows, traced the passage of the winter sun across the sky.

There was some kind of cartoon on the TV. A creature with blue and purple fur was talking to a little girl in pigtails while a green creature with one eye stood by. Marion sat in a chair and said, "I know that voice, don't I. Whose voice is that?"

Alex flipped though the channels and returned to the cartoon. The blue and purple creature was being yelled at by a creature with giant eyeglasses on a chain.

Alex and Erin laughed at something the creature said.

Imogene brought out glasses of cranberry juice splashed with club soda. Soon, in their new house, there would be Christmas dinner. Joe was grilling shrimp. Imogene got out the fig relish and the cod. She stood over the fillets.

Holiday

She went to her mother, who was trying to talk to Alexander over some frantic activity on the TV. She said, "Well, Alexander, what's new?"

Alex said, "Nothing really," and went back to the TV. Erin was leaning into him, as if for shelter. She smiled at Marion, who seemed too far removed down the family chain to know what to say to.

Imogene said, "Mother."

Her mother took Imogene's arm as if something new, something good awaited them. She was a guest now in Imogene's home with Imogene's husband. She lived in her house with its framed pictures on the walls and photo albums, its mementos and the old, familiar household things. Imogene's sister was absent. Imogene had returned each year to her mother's holiday table, by herself, a circumstance her mother couldn't comprehend, even though she herself was alone. But now Marion understood her daughter's life: a house and lamplight and a bowl of pinecones on a table; Christmas and then the new year and all the holidays like stones one uses in crossing the year, as if it were a river.

Imogene had laid out the fillets on a sheet of aluminum foil. She said, "The fish market told us we could roll the fillets around the stuffing and tie them with string, but I don't see how, the fillets are so thick." Joe was slicing the skin from an eggplant, readying it for the frying pan.

"Let me see," her mother said. She pressed her fingers flat on one of the fillets, as if taking its measure. She turned

After the Hunger

to Imogene. They stood together over the aluminum foil, pressing their fingers on the fillets. Imogene got a spoon for the stuffing.

Joe put out the shrimp. Marion sat next to Erin, and the others were at their places around the table.

Alex said, "We wonder when dinner will be, that is, how long it will take, because Erin has to get back to spend Christmas with her family."

"I thought you were spending Christmas with us," Imogene said. "I thought that was the point."

"The shrimp is— Oh," Marion said. "What a delicious sauce."

"We really have to get back," Alex said to his father.

Joe spooned some sauce onto his plate, dredged a shrimp in it. "It's the fresh dill that makes it," he replied to her.

"We have dinner and then presents," Imogene said.

Alex pushed his empty plate away. Erin helped Imogene clear the table.

Marion opened the oven door and prodded the cod with a fork. They had solved the problem of the string by laying one fillet over the other.

They all sat at the table. Marion had cut the fillets in two and placed them on a serving dish. Erin helped Imogene bring out the julienned carrots her mother had cut then steamed and sautéed in butter and brown sugar, and the grilled eggplant sprinkled with feta cheese. The table was scored with a green runner, and on it was a sprig of holly. They passed the dishes around.

The wine glasses had been filled. Marion lifted hers and said, "To a special holiday dinner with my daughter and new family."

There was the clicking of glasses, then the clinking of silverware against the china. Marion said, "Do you think we'll have snow this year?"

Joe said, "We forgot to put out the cookies and milk for Santa," and Alexander regarded his father as if this was who he was, a sentimental man, who wished for so much, who so stoically hid his disappointments.

Erin said, "Usually my parents have Christmas dinner at two but they're waiting on me."

No one replied. All around the table were the ghosts of the missing. Marion hardly mentioned her younger daughter anymore. Their father had left; Imogene could recall the sound of his voice—always measured and calm, always slightly amused, as if sharing finally a secret he had wanted to share all along, about a radio show, a story in the local paper, some antic by the neighbors' dog—less and less. Imogene's sister started to wear heavy black eye make-up; she looked already like one of the departed. She left after high school, in the same mysterious way their father had, and perhaps with the same unnamable emptiness. Their father was completely gone, except in Imogene's imagination. Her sister called occasionally, from Des Moines, from Seattle, as if from a stop on a quest. Imogene visited her in San Francisco and brought her the Christmas presents she had saved for her, soaps and sachets and scented candles, as if instruments for a rite. Her suitcase still smelled of them.

After the Hunger

Erin helped Imogene clear the table and bring out the coffee and pumpkin pie. Joe cut it into slices and handed it around. Imogene put out a plate of grapes for Alexander. He had abruptly left the table. He was gone for all of dessert. Joe shook his head imperceptibly at Imogene. Then Alexander returned. Imogene studied him closely, covertly. That she and Joe could do this, share this bounty, seemed to be its own miracle. *Had Alexander understood this, that he had been invited to his father's table, finally; had he been suddenly overwhelmed?* He had gone away, upstairs, and then returned. The sun was making its transit across the sky. The trees would be casting shadows on the lawn.

They assembled in the living room. Imogene asked her mother if she would distribute the presents. This is what they had done in her parents' house, the four of them, when her sister's ponytail hung down and her father wore slippers that looked like shoes. Marion handed the presents around. She recited a name, and the name of the person it was from, and stretched her arm out, the wrapping paper and bows like baubles in her hand.

Alex had taken his seat again on the couch. He turned on the TV. There was now another cartoon; two orange fish seemed to be arguing with each other. Alex had pressed the Mute button. One of the fish swam away. Imogene said, "Alex, please turn off the TV." He was disturbing her dream again. She turned to her mother. *We should have had lights this season*, Imogene thought, *lit in all the windows of the house*. They used to sing about it in church. She wanted to say, "Mother, do you remember that hymn? Was it a hymn? 'I am in the service of the Lord.'" *Was it a prayer? It was something about God.*

Her mother handed her gift to Joe. He opened it. It was a blue cashmere scarf. They had nothing for Erin; they apologized; they hoped she understood. Well next year, next year. Alexander turned on the TV. One of the orange fish was talking to a blue fish. "Alex," Imogene said, "will you put down the remote please, turn off the TV, it's not for today." He turned off the TV. Then he stood. "Erin's parents are waiting for us," he said. His opened presents were on the floor. He picked them up. Joe had bought him a good winter jacket, a wool hat, and a pair of leather gloves. The other presents lay opened in front of the sled. Imogene's sister's present was the only one that remained. Marion stood and took each of their hands. "Merry Christmas," she said.

Joe got their coats. Imogene heard doors opening and closing, the sound of an engine. She took her mother into the kitchen. "Are you warm enough," she said. "The temperature outside seems to have dropped. What I mean to say is, I could turn up the heat."

Marion hugged her daughter. She didn't seem to know how to act once Imogene's father had left. The apron and the crumber and the painted fingernails, laughing over something with the other couple they had invited to dinner. She was lost for quite a long time.

Imogene refilled their coffee cups. They sat at the dining room table. It would be long dark by the time she and Joe retuned from bringing her back to her house. She had wanted her mother to stay, but her mother's attachments were elsewhere, to her own home, its routines and its memories.

The sun was a pale glow behind the trees, like a meteor that was crashing to earth. The air was still, the fans of branches high up the trees like a gesture toward the darkening sky. They could hear the engine of Alexander's car and the rumble of the car under its power. Joe still didn't come inside. He was perhaps standing in the driveway, watching Alexander's car turn down the road. He would be cold, Imogene knew, in his shirtsleeves, waving goodbye to his son. Another time, he would be saying, though Alexander wouldn't be able to hear him.

Marion put her cup in its saucer. She took her daughter's hand. For a while Imogene's sister sang in the church youth choir. Imogene looked across the sanctuary at her, in her choir robe, and heard her voice, the strong contralto. *Did she remember the hymn to God? They were all hymns to God*, Imogene supposed.

Marion opened her daughter's palm, ran her fingers over Imogene's. The furnace came on and began its work. "Did you have a good day?" Imogene asked. It was not the kind of Christmas she had imagined. She wanted, of course, what had gone, what had left her behind. She glanced at the sled, the torn wrapping paper, the presents so haphazardly arranged. A tree next year, next year, lit with lights, lighting the way. She and her mother were both waiting, in their own way, for a return. Joe was still outside, standing in the street, his arms folded across his chest. His son was surely by now turning his car onto the ramp to the throughway, while Joe narrowed his eyes to await the miraculous, the headlights bearing his son toward him.

"It was a good day," her mother said. "The best Christmas I can remember."

The Last Good Day of Summer

Along the coast the season would not end gradually but suddenly, and the days of late September were stolen from the summer months they followed. It would soon be the season of withered leaves burning on curbsides, and of ice and blowing snows, but now the air was hot and parched. On the beach there was no shade except the slatted strips of dark under the pier. Melodie moved out of the sunlight and lay under the pier on the damp, hard sand. Her bones ached, the long femur bones of her thighs. Some days it was her hips or her shoulders, but today the ache had settled into her legs.

She lay beside the dog, which she knew she must not touch in the unbearable heat of the day. Its fur was a bristle on Melodie's skin each time the dog panted for air. Later when the sun had cooled and her family was home, the dog would come to her; she would bury her face in its thick, white crest, and its feathery tail would sweep across the floor. The animal turned its muzzle to her and the dry nose touched her forehead, and it turned away, the engine of its lungs trying to temper the heat on its body.

In the shade thrown by the pier, the water eddied in dark swirls, struck by the sunlight that fell through the slats. The six black hollow oil drums at the end of the pier rose with the tide, sending echoes through the water, the sound of sealed interiors, in the groaning effort to bring up the wooden dock that rested on them. The dock was built on an estuary of the river that coursed into the Sound, an emerald-green ribbon cut off from the river by beds of seagrass. Small boats navigated the estuary, and Melodie could hear a boat's motor, far off and hidden by the seagrass, above the flow of the incoming tide.

The beach was a thin strip of sand. Prickly tufts of beach grass grew fiercely in it, the knife-edge shadow of each blade marking the sand like a sundial. Sand and rock trickled noiselessly from the low embankment that formed the boundary of the beach, slowly altering its pitch and strength. The embankment sloped under the pier to a field of rank seaweed, driftwood, and flowering beach rose bushes. Beyond the blistering wooden stairs that led from the beach, and the lot that held the two cars, the cattail forest began. It was close-grown, dark, the flowers a furred, animal color, and halted only by the lot's poor gravel soil, each narrow spike held aloft by a reed-like, elongated stem.

At the far end of the beach, the embankment became a wall of steep rock, an eroding buffer against the tides. Beneath the fortress of rock, Melodie's sister Janine dug the sand with her pink plastic shovel. She filled the companion pail and carried it with great purpose past the tan blanket on which their mother and their neighbor Mrs. Finch sat in beach chairs sunning themselves. Mrs. Finch's husband stood apart from them, untangling a length of fishing line. Melodie heard her sister's laugh as she approached the water, a series of bright chirps, part of the language she spoke, which consisted of shrills, warbles, songs, and sudden collapses of her body into spasms of crying. The water was clean and clear; the pebbles under its surface rippled toward Janine in the pull of the tide and the sheets of glare the sun threw on the water. Janine dumped the pail of sand on the rim of the shore, and it melted into the water. She shook her head back and forth; her jet-black hair whipped her cheeks. Righting the pail, she followed her tiny footsteps back to the hole in the sand she had carved with her shovel.

The dog snapped at a green fly, then plodded to the water and lapped at it briefly. In the burning sun Melodie's mother called to her, "Don't bother the dog."

Melodie diffidently picked a grain of sand from her leg. Her mother waited for an answer. Melodie called, "Okay."

Her mother's legs were bent high at the knees, and her toes pointed into the sand, giving her back an aristocratic arch. Her wrists hung languidly over her knees. Her fingernails were filed to elegant half-moons just above the tips of her fingers. She wore a white bathing suit, and her skin, which she tended with the creams on her vanity table, was the golden color of the sand. She had painted her lips a light shade of pink, and her blonde hair fell softly around her face. In a drawer of her vanity table, she kept a pot of Max Factor rouge and tubes of Max Factor lipstick. Their perfume drew Melodie to her mother's bedroom; she would open the drawer and take off the top of the pot of rouge, and the tops of the tubes of lipstick, and the scents were of womanliness and glamour. In her beach chair, her mother tossed her hair, ran the tip of her tongue over her front teeth, and spoke to Mrs. Finch, looking cool and impeccable, even on the hard sand beach, where no one came.

Melodie rubbed the joints of her knees. The sun bothered them. She rolled her body in the sand. Her fingernails, bitten and ragged, had left trails on the skin that covered the joints that ached, beginning with her eleventh birthday, almost a year ago, trails fading over her shoulders, her elbows, her hands and feet, even the small bones of her neck. Her grandmother called it a growth spurt; she had gained three inches since winter. Under her turquoise bathing suit, Melodie's fingernails had left marks on the narrow leverage of her hips and across her back.

In her grandmother's house, she would lie on the couch after dinner, her head on a pile of pillows. The shades would be drawn over the windows, the crocheted pulls dragging on the sills. Her grandmother tucked an afghan around her. She brewed a pot of chamomile tea. The tea made Melodie drowsy and warm. Her grandmother filled a hot water bottle, and Melodie held it to the bones of her body. Her grandmother took Melodie's feet in her hands and kneaded the arches, the pads of the toes, the heels and ankles. Melodie's eyelids became heavy. She saw her grandmother through her eyelashes while her bones in her grandmother's hands were

After the Hunger

being made better, her grandmother's head bent, her white hair neatly held by a net, her breathing rhythmic and familiar. Her grandmother said, "Is that better now?" and Melodie, her joints loose, nestled her head in her grandmother's lap. Her grandmother eased the joints of Melodie's hands, and Melodie slept against her grandmother's body, her arms high and limp against the bodice of her grandmother's dress.

Before Melodie heard Mr. Finch's voice, she smelled the stogie he smoked constantly. On the Sunday nights it was the Finches' turn to entertain, her mother and grandmother returned from their games of pinochle with the smell of his stogies in their clothes and hair. Mr. Finch's hands were on his knees, bent in front of Melodie at the sharp line in the sand where the shade from the pier ended.

"Come out from under there, why don't you," Mr. Finch said. "Get some sun."

Melodie folded her legs under her.

"Come on, gal," he said. He held out a rough palm, striated with healed cuts from his fishing line.

"No," Melodie said.

"What's the matter with you, sitting over there?" Mr. Finch puffed on the stogie through his teeth. He wore plaid shorts and a short-sleeved shirt. The flesh on his elbows and knees was slack. His hair was thinning and gray, combed back and held with the grease he used. He had a hawk nose, and his eyes squinted at her in the sun.

He would go soon; he would take his car and drive to the place where he kept his motor boat, and he'd steer it into the Sound and cast his fishing line for the bluefish that ran in massive schools during September. All month he had come to Melodie's grandmother's back door with dead fish wrapped in newspaper, and Melodie's grandmother had cut off the heads and tails and gutted them. It was the one time Melodie did not want to be in the kitchen with her grandmother. Her grandmother wrapped the fish in butcher's paper and put them in the freezer. In the back yard, among the roses and chrysanthemums, her mother built a charcoal fire on the grill and cooked the fish. Her grandmother put lemon wedges in a cut-glass dish and made acorn squash and scalloped potatoes and complimented her mother on the tenderness of the fish, but Melodie couldn't eat the greasy flesh; the gift of the bluefish reminded her of Mr. Finch.

"Gal," Mr. Finch said, "how about helping me get a piece of fur from your dog." Mr. Finch took a pair of clippers from his shorts pocket and clicked them at her. "You know the blues love your dog's fur. Must be the way it looks to them in the water."

The animal's sides heaved in and out. A string of its saliva fell onto the sand.

"She's awfully hot," Melodie said.

Mr. Finch ducked under the pier and squatted next to the dog. He bit on the stogie, and Melodie coughed. "Here, now," he said. The dog sat up, martyred and put upon. Mr. Finch ran his hand admiringly over the dog's chest. He separated a tuft of fur and clipped it. He pulled a lure from his pocket and fixed the fur to it with a length of wire. "You'll eat good," he said to Melodie and walked back into the glaring sunlight. The dog's chest was stubbled with clipped fur. The dog dropped to the sand and thrust its nose into it, looking for a cooler spot.

"Melodie!" her mother called.

Her mother was pouring lemonade into Dixie cups from a thermos she had taken from the cooler. Melodie ran past the blanket and down the beach to fetch her sister. Janine sat happily next to the hole she had dug in the embankment, her plastic shovel in her hand.

"Sea monster, sea monster," Janine said.

"Let's see," Melodie said. Janine led Melodie to a patch of sand among the steep rocks. On it was a marker of three pebbles. She pushed the pebbles away and dug at the sand with her shovel.

"I make the stones," Janine said.

The shovel revealed the legs of a sea creature, brown and pleated over the brackish innards. Janine routed for the tail with her shovel and dragged it onto the sand. She flipped it over with her toe, revealing the hard shell.

"It's a horseshoe crab," Melodie said, "and it's dead."

"I found it, I found it, I found it," Janine said. "In the rocks, in the rocks, in the rocks." She pointed to the far side of the rock formation where their mother had told her she couldn't go. She dug her feet stubbornly into the sand. Her little belly bowed out above the frills of her pink bathing suit. Her arms and legs were freckled with sand, and deeply brown.

The Last Good Day of Summer

Melodie hitched the straps of her bathing suit, and they pulled on the aching tenderness of her breast buds. She was surprised by their willful hardness, like small eruptions under her skin. In the shadow of the pier, she had seen Mr. Finch's slitted eyes on the buds of her breasts, and on her legs that were marked with the trails of her fingernails. She did not yet want to think about breasts or lipstick or tossing her hair. She did not want to leave her grandmother's arms.

Melodie said, "We can come back to your sea monster later." She took Janine's hand.

"A big monster, a big monster," Janine said. She made the warbling noise at the back of her throat that was like a bird singing.

The blanket's satin borders were coming undone. The women's beach bags, the cooler, and Mr. Finch's fishing gear were spread on the blanket behind the beach chairs. Mr. Finch had drawn up a chair next to his wife. Melodie's mother shielded her eyes with her hand. "It'll be time for a swim soon," she said to Mrs. Finch. The Dixie cups, full of lemonade, were screwed into the sand at their feet. Melodie hovered on the sand near her mother. There was no room on the blanket for Melodie and Janine.

Melodie's mother took her hand away from her eyes and smoothed the plastic flower on her bathing cap. "Will you be coming in?" she said to Mrs. Finch.

Mrs. Finch said, "I think I'll be a landlubber today." Her legs were marked with small, broken red veins. She looked smoke-filled, dusty with the smoke of her husband's stogies.

Melodie's mother poured lemonade from the thermos for her daughters. Melodie took the Dixie cups from her mother's hand, briefly brushing the manicured nails. "Go on with your sister," Melodie's mother said to her. Her mother reached into her beach bag and took a cigarette from her cigarette case. A match flared bluely into flame. Her mother shook the match, and the flame died, and she tossed the match onto the sand and dragged on the cigarette.

"Go on, now," she told Melodie.

Melodie gave a Dixie cup to Janine. They sat together under the pier and drank the lemonade. The dog was asleep, dreaming. Janine said "Ah," burped, and giggled, and dropped her Dixie cup onto the sand. She began to dig with her shovel.

Melodie shook the sand from Janine's cup and walked into the sunlight on the other side of the pier.

"Where do we go, where do we go, Mellony?" Janine asked. She sprang up and followed Melodie.

Seaweed floated on the incoming tide. Bubbles of air broke the surface between the fronds where Melodie imagined larger fish hid, and sea crabs, and eels. Hundreds of minnows swam over the seaweed, and hundreds more swam crazily at the lip of the shore, in the slowly lapping water.

"I thought we'd sit right here, and then you can take me for a swim," Melodie replied to Janine's full and complete thought, uttered without shrills or warbles, wishing she herself knew how to say more, so she could help her sister with the sentences that were the communion between human beings.

"I'm six," Janine said.

"You're five," Melodie said. She gently pulled the crisscrossed straps at her sister's back, and Janine plopped next to her. They thrust their toes into the water, and the minnows frothed over them, their quick bodies brown and opaque, even where the sun struck them.

"I'm five," Janine said, and she spread her toes. The minnows swam between them. Janine began a series of shrills and calls that was the way she talked almost always, a lifting of her tiny voice. Her voice rose higher and higher in her excitement over the sensation of the spuming minnows, becoming a song sung before words. Janine's voice broke and ceased, unable to sustain the notes it sought. To Melodie, shoulder to shoulder with Janine in the sudden silence on the water's edge, the scraping wings of crickets among the ruined seaweed and driftwood were a roll of thunder, and the lapping water was a storm.

When Melodie and Janine lived with their father and mother, Janine stopped using her voice only to cry or gurgle as babies do and began to speak the language of her god. She spoke it only to their father, standing at his knee as he read the evening newspaper in his chair in the living room, her small fist clinging to the crease in his pants. She wore oxblood-colored shoes and corduroy pants and a striped T-shirt, looking like a tough little being as she sang to their father, only to him.

He would put down his newspaper. Melodie would look up from her puzzle book on the floor at her father's feet as Janine told their father of shining white cities, golden rooftops, the tale of the prophet, choirs of boys singing. Or the screaming of bombs as they broke through the sky, the ruin of cities, the taste of ashes. Their father would pick up Janine, her voice never ceasing, and sit her in his lap. Gently stroking a stray black curl at her cheek, he would look deeply into her hazel eyes as she sang to him.

When Janine lost the language of her god, or no longer spoke it, she came to her father again, and stood at his knee, and spoke in the same beautiful, insistent voice. Melodie could understand it now, because she had lost the language of her god long before Janine was born. Janine tested her new language, said Toe and Dog and Bed and Step, and sometimes the ancient language broke through, and she sang it to her father. Then it was gone and she spoke the other language only, of Play and See and Shoe and I, but only to him.

The winter their father left he took Janine's language with him. She spoke another one now, not the language of her god or the language she had learned incompletely from their mother and father but a language of shrieks and shrills, high laughter that ended in terrible, inconsolable sobbing, a language before god. Their father had taken a job in Ohio, or Indiana, a place beyond Melodie's imagining, far beyond the roads she traveled to school, or church, or to the beach in summer, or to her grandmother's house for Sunday dinner. The furnace broke down; Melodie's mother heated the kitchen with the bellow of flame from the oven and boiled water for their baths; they ate oatmeal and salt crackers and soup made from butcher's bones. Melodie and

Janine slept together in Melodie's bed for warmth. Their mother lit her cigarettes from a burner on the stove.

By spring they were living in Melodie's grandmother's house. Melodie's mother stored their furniture in the basement. In a corner, cylindrical storage bins held linens and blankets, and dishes and glassware wrapped in tissue paper. A reading lamp stood behind Melodie's chest of drawers. The coffee table lay face down on the couch. Felt-bottom lamps had settled together on the kitchen table. The beds had been raised against the wall, and a puff of dust clung to the wheel of a bed frame.

Melodie had crept down the basement stairs to look at the furniture where she had eaten and slept and played, shoved together and unused and no longer what they had been, just wood and metal, nothing. In the gloom of the basement, she had climbed over an ottoman and around an end table. On her father's reading chair were two photo albums and a Monopoly game. Melodie put them on the floor. She sat in her father's chair, her legs splayed over the upholstered seat, her arms held wide on the arm rests. Then she curled her body into a tiny ball in the large, empty seat.

In the sunlight on the far side of the pier, Melodie cupped the tidal water in her hands and sprinkled it over Janine's legs. Janine shrieked at her, thumped her outstretched legs on the sand, and broke into a gurgling laugh.

"Cool," Janine said. She scrambled up, sank her Dixie cup among the skittering minnows, and dumped the water on Melodie's legs.

Melodie shrieked and said, "Cool." She scooped her Dixie cup in the water, and Janine lay on the hot sand, her eyes shut. Melodie poured the water on Janine's arms, and on her shoulders, at the straps where the skin was turning red.

The sky was white with heat. A thunderhead had formed over the estuary, on the horizon, foaming upward into the heated air. The crickets buzzed. This was the last good day of summer. The boats would be brought in soon, the geese would fly overhead, the crickets would cease, the clouds would turn thin in the crisp air, the seagrass would begin to die. Melodie lay on the sand, her eyes closed tight, while Janine poured the warm water over her.

Melodie jumped up, ran into the water, and dove in. The water was spangled with green light. She surfaced farther out and pushed the wet mass of her dark hair from her eyes. Janine shrieked from the shore. Melodie put her face in the water, took two long strokes toward her sister, breathed, two more strokes, breathed. Janine bubbled over to her, plunging her feet into the water. Melodie circled around her, tickling Janine's feet. Janine laughed, hugged herself, drew her feet away, then offered them to Melodie again. Melodie picked up Janine and swung her over the water. She said, "We're going to take a swim, okay?" and Janine nodded but drew her legs under her. Melodie set her on the shore and swam a short distance, then stood and held her arms out. Janine splashed into the water and dog-paddled to Melodie, her chin high, her rosebud mouth pursed.

Melodie told Janine to hold the straps of her bathing suit, and Janine did, pulling hard. Melodie's breast buds flattened on her chest. She swam to the black drums under the dock with Janine's fingers locked to the straps, Janine's frog legs knocking into hers. The water here was cooler, deeper, and they rested under the shaded overhang of the dock.

Melodie showed Janine how to hold the rim of an oil drum, and Melodie grabbed the overhang of the dock and pulled herself up. She took Janine's hands in hers. Janine sought a foothold on the smooth drum, the overhang, and finally the firm, worn wood of the dock. She and Melodie were soaked and salty, and their hair hung in ropes around their faces. Janine hugged herself and laughed. Melodie brushed the water from Janine's arms and legs, and they lay side by side.

"I swim," Janine said. She took a big gulp of pure air, and her little chest swelled.

"You swam real good," Melodie said, and they fell into a sun-struck silence. Melodie's stomach rumbled. She heard the low murmur of her mother's voice, speaking to the Finches, over the echo of the oil drums and the creaking of the dock. Janine was singing a song about a minnow and a sea monster. She drummed one leg against the rough wood.

The evening before, in their grandmother's dining room, Janine sat on a telephone book, kicking her legs against her chair, and pushed the food around her plate with her fork. Their grandmother and their mother talked. It was the formal talk of the dinner table, of adults after their day. Their conversation climbed high above Melodie, invisibly, and stretched across the table. She sat beneath it, the currents and

After the Hunger

countercurrents not touching her, having nothing to do with her. Her grandmother spread Melodie's napkin on her lap and brushed Melodie's hair with her fine hand. Janine carefully picked up a pea and painstakingly balanced it on the end of her spoon, then tipped it and the pea rolled onto her plate.

Melodie ate, her body grew, no one noticed her. At school that day she had climbed the knotted ropes at the gymnasium all the way to the top; two boys fought on the playground; she got a 92 on a geography test. She could tell her mother exactly where Ohio and Indiana were: she could show her their irregular blue and yellow shapes at the center of the map of the United States.

Her mother put her napkin to her mouth and said to Janine, "Honey, eat your peas properly."

Melodie had helped her grandmother bring dinner to the table. There was the T-bone steak in its essence on a platter and the tenderloin her grandmother had cut into four pieces so they could each have a bite, Janine's garden peas, a cucumber sliced thin as paper and marinated in vinegar, and whipped potatoes topped with a pat of butter. In the refrigerator, cooling, were four servings of chocolate pudding, in glass dessert dishes.

Her grandmother baked apple pie, rhubarb pie, Concord grape pie, the strips of dough latticed over the fruit and smothered with melted butter so the crust baked to a golden color. She made Toll House cookies, blueberries in cream, strawberries in cream, lemon meringue pie, Boston cream pie. She made pot roast, roast beef; potatoes peeled, sliced, or pierced with the tines of a fork and baked; tomatoes fried in bread crumbs; succotash, the corn kernels bursting sweetly in Melodie's mouth. She cooked Wheatina and Cream of Wheat, made Bisquick pancakes, biscuits, rolls, and sugar buns. Her grandmother scooped another helping of whipped potatoes onto Melodie's plate. Melodie ate all the food at her grandmother's table, and this was love.

Janine ran lightly off the dock and along the boards of the pier. Melodie sat up and saw Mr. Finch swing Janine off the steps onto the beach. Janine picked up her shovel and ran down the beach to the rocks where the horseshoe crab shriveled beside the hole she had dug for it.

Later, Janine would swing the horseshoe crab by its tail and say, "Ai, ai," and put it in her plastic pail. She would want to take it home, and their mother wouldn't let her. Janine would cry, her little body trembling with a sorrow too big for a dead horseshoe crab. In those frantic moments when their mother would abruptly say it was time to leave and shake the sand from the blanket, Melodie would comb the beach for something to give to Janine—a crab's leg dried in the sun, a seashell, the spent flower from a beach rose bush.

Mr. Finch's footfall on the pier sent disturbances through the dock. He had put his stogie away, but he smelled of it.

"Hey, gal," Mr. Finch said, squatting next to her. "Want to come with me on my boat today? You can have your very own rod. I got two in the car. Ever catch any blues?"

"No," Melodie said.

"Look at you, gal," Mr. Finch said. "All dried out in the sun. You have salt streaks on your arm. See? Right here," and he traced the dried salt down her arm, to the tips of her fingers.

Melodie stood awkwardly. She looked across the water to the beach. Her mother lay on her stomach on the blanket, next to Mrs. Finch. Her bathing suit straps were pulled off her shoulders.

"The only way to get rid of those salt streaks," Mr. Finch said, "is to take another little swim. How would you like a little swim?"

Melodie stepped back, and the drums beneath her rolled in the tide. She was dizzy and sun-dazed. Mr. Finch stepped toward her, and she was lifted up, her wrist in one of his hands, her ankle in the other. He swung her over the water. She struggled to right herself, panting and kicking at his hand with her shackled ankle.

Mr. Finch said, "Gal, gal, gal," and he panted, too, holding her. Her free leg dangled over the water. He was trying to pull her toward him, but she was kicking at his shorts and punching at his face.

"What do you sleep in, gal?" Mr. Finch said. "Do you sleep in a pretty little nightie?"

The water careened toward her. She twisted her body and her ankle came loose from his hand. He lost his balance and fell to his knees on the dock. She crumpled next to him. She stood quickly and swung her fist at him, and he laughed at her. His greased hair stood up from his head and he smoothed it down with the palm of his hand.

"I'm just playing with you, gal," he said. "Didn't no man ever play with you?"

Melodie broke into a run across the dock and pushed off with the balls of her feet, jumping high and wide. Her legs shot out behind her, and she sliced into the water. She surfaced quickly and pushed her hair from her eyes. She swam toward the seagrass until she was breathless. She saw Mr. Finch stand, glance toward the blanket where his wife drowsed, adjust his shirt with a twitch of his shoulders, and walk down the pier.

Melodie drifted in the cool current that ran through the beds of seagrass. The shore was far away. Janine struggled with the horseshoe crab; her mother and Mrs. Finch turned like ripening figs on the blanket; Mr. Finch scanned the water as he collected his fishing gear. Melodie stirred her legs in the current, drew them up, searched for a warmer place. She stroked gently, her hands making shallow troughs in the water. Water and air were one element, without depth or color or sound or smell. The water soothed her bones; she rubbed her wrist where Mr. Finch had grabbed it and made it hurt over the hurt of her bones growing. She rubbed her ankle under the water, easing his touch off her.

The tan blanket was sinking into the sand. Her mother had put the beach chairs away, and Mr. Finch was gone. Melodie turned a swift, complete circle in the water. He could be anywhere; he could be here, next to her, under the water, holding his breath.

In her grandmother's house, Melodie was afraid of the dark. She coughed, trying to dislodge a strange dry tickle in her throat. Her sister sighed in her sleep. It was the middle of the night. Melodie could see Mr. Finch, the empty space that was her father, her growing bones glowing through her nightgown in the dark. Someone sat on her bed and she began to cry. It was her grandmother saying to her, "Melodie, dear." Her grandmother had left the hall light burning and her nightgown was pearly in the light. Melodie's grandmother handed her a glass of water and Melodie drank it gratefully. She coughed a few more times, weakly.

"Where is it?" her grandmother asked, her voice a whisper, her nightgown in satiny folds.

"Here," Melodie said, touching her throat. She couldn't get to it; she couldn't make it go away.

Melodie's grandmother got up from the bed and walked down the hallway. The floorboards creaked. Everyone slept. The medicine cabinet opened and shut. Her grandmother wore her slippers and her feet were heavy on the floor. She was old, how old; she had trouble walking, she walked with effort. When they moved into her grandmother's house, her mother had said, "You girls aren't to trouble her, or where would we be?"

Her grandmother sat on the bed and took a Sucrets from its tin and unwrapped it. Melodie put the lozenge on her tongue. It tasted of wintergreen, and her coughing stopped. Her grandmother said, "Sit up until the lozenge is dissolved," and Melodie worked the lozenge with her tongue until it melted away. All the while her grandmother held her against her nightgown, and then Melodie was lying again in her bed, and the hall light was out, and the house was completely still.

From the shelter of the seagrass, Melodie saw Mrs. Finch doing something to her hair, patting it, fluffing the helmet of false curls around her head. She and Melodie's mother sat up slowly on the blanket, drugged by the heat. Melodie let her legs sink. The water was up to her mouth; she breathed through her nose. Her mother brushed the sand off her legs and adjusted the straps of her bathing suit. She retrieved her beach chair and pulled the cooler around, in front of her, and put her feet on it. She lit a cigarette. Melodie's stomach growled.

Her mother had decided after breakfast that this was the one remaining beach day of the year. The shades were drawn in every room against the heat. Her grandmother made bacon, lettuce, and tomato sandwiches and deviled eggs. She packed them in the cooler with apples and Toll House cookies while Melodie's mother ordered Melodie and Janine into their bathing suits. Janine hopped up the stairs next to Melodie, shrieking and gurgling, saying "Beach, beach, be-be-be." Melodie helped Janine into her bathing suit. In the back yard the crickets scraped their legs across their bellies. The late roses were blooming in the garden. Melodie and Janine got into the car in the garage that smelled of spilled motor oil and cut grass. Melodie's mother slammed the car trunk, put on her sunglasses, and got into the car.

Janine banged her shovel in its pail and jumped up and down in the back seat of the car. The dog cantered to the open door, and Melodie said, "Stay." The dog bounded in. Its front paws gracefully curved over the seat, and its long tail swept around its paws. Melodie's mother backed the car out of the garage; she gave the horn a light tap and waved across the yard. Mr. Finch slammed the trunk of his car, and he and Mrs. Finch waved back. Melodie's mother took the car down the driveway. They followed Mr. and Mrs. Finch toward the beach. The dog was already panting. It sat up and sniffed the air.

Beyond the town center the street was lined with Dutch elms and chestnut trees, the leaves a dark green. Behind the trees were lawns and flower gardens and big houses, bigger than Melodie's grandmother's house, where the families of doctors and lawyers lived, the girls who asked her at school where her father was and why she lived with her grandmother, and Melodie opened her mouth to speak but nothing came out; pure silence.

At school, Melodie took her sorrow out on the high bars, the fifty-yard dash, the basketball court, the softball field. The girls who lived in the big houses feigned periods during gym class; they were constantly menstruating. They sat on the sidelines in their white gym uniforms with their smoothly shaved legs. Melodie climbed and ran and fired hoops and threw the perfect, seamed weight of the softball; she could hit it out of the field. Someday she would have her own car; she would drive it to Ohio or Indiana and would find her father there, sitting in his chair reading the newspaper, and she would say to the girls who lived in the big houses, "Here he is, he has always been here, I knew it all along." Her bones would no longer hurt; she wouldn't be afraid of the dark. Her father would look over the top of his newspaper and smile at her, and she would sit on the floor next to his chair.

Melodie kicked her legs in the incoming tide. The water stirred. The tide swelled through her; her flesh was glass, her bones were glass, sand, dissolvable.

Melodie's mother turned the car onto a dirt road, following the Finches' car. Melodie's mother rolled up the window and adjusted her sunglasses. The Finches' car threw up plumes of dust. They turned off the dirt road and drove down a rutted alley beside the cattail forest. One beat against the side of the car, and the chassis bounced in the ruts that led to the beach. Then the Finches and Melodie's mother stopped their cars. Melodie opened the door and the dog jumped out.

The car trunks were opened, and the apparatus for the beach was hauled down by all of them, even Janine; she swung her pail and shovel as she ran to the pier. Melodie had nothing—she always forgot, she didn't know what to bring to the beach.

From the water, hidden by the seagrass, Melodie saw her mother lift the lid of the cooler, and she heard her call and look up and down the empty beach for her children. The dog bit at a sand flea deep within its fur. Janine lifted the horseshoe crab by its prehistoric tail. Janine was singing; Melodie heard the strands of music across the full tide. Melodie swam

After the Hunger

toward her sister, stroking parallel to the beach, as her mother called again, impatiently.

Melodie paddled her legs slowly; she didn't want to come out of the water, into the element of sand. Janine dragged the creature behind her, its body wending a trail in the sand. A knot of seaweed, coming in with the tide, revolved against Melodie's legs. She jerked her legs away as it pulsed around her, a brownish-yellow mass, flat and thick, serrated at the edges. She kicked at it furiously. She yelled, "Ma, Ma." Her mother looked up, interested for a moment only. She took off her sunglasses and met the eyes of her daughter while Mr. Finch's cold hands wound around Melodie's legs. She kicked, she went under, the seaweed encircled her legs. Melodie tore at it, came up, took the air, the element of air, into her lungs, went down. Mrs. Finch was standing now, looking across the water, as Melodie ripped at the seaweed. She came up, gasping. The seaweed came up next to her. She fled from it, her legs kicking, her lungs spent.

Melodie's knees scraped the shore. Janine dallied on the beach. Her mother took a plate from the cooler. Melodie hauled herself out of the water, gasping for breath. Her bones hurt. She wanted to tell her mother how much her bones hurt and when would they stop hurting, would they ever? Did they hurt her too, when she was growing? Melodie ran up the beach to the blanket. She could hardly see; her hair was slicked across her forehead, and the salt bothered her eyes. It was nighttime. She was afraid of the dark. She gasped for breath. Someone sat on her bed. Her mother said, "Melodie, stop dripping on the blanket. Be a good girl. Can't you see I'm talking to Mrs. Finch?"

Melodie's fingertips were wrinkled and blue. Her eyes stung. It was only the salt water, but they stung as if she had been slapped. She backed away from her mother's blanket.

Janine called, "Mellony," and dropped the tail of the horseshoe crab and its dead body sank into the sand. "Where are you going, Mellony?" Janine asked.

Melodie ran up the stairs. She waited for Janine, trying to take the sting out of her eyes.

"Wet," Janine said.

Melody rubbed her forearm across her face.

Mr. Finch sat in his car, idling the motor. He looked at Melodie, her aching bones, the tracks of her fingernails, her wet bathing suit and hair. Melodie took her sister's hand and stared at him. He pushed the gear shift forward and drove off, leaving a spray of dust behind.

Melodie and Janine stood on the fringe of the cattail forest. The furred spikes were high above their heads. Melodie heard their mother's voice, calling to them across the beach, the embankment, the lot where the car baked in the sun. Janine knelt in front of the cattail forest, and Melodie knelt with her. Janine crawled between the stalks, gaining access to the forest, and running within it, her body a flash of dark skin, pink bathing suit, her jet hair red in the sunlight that filtered down the stalks. The ground was hard. Nothing moved within the forest. The cattails were brittle, ancient— from before roads and houses, much older than Melodie and

After the Hunger

Janine, the girls who lived in the big houses, their mother and father, and their grandmother who cared for them.

Melodie wound her hand around a stalk at the edge of the forest. Janine was singing. Melodie saw her hair's red corona through the stalks. She entered the forest. The cattails parted on a path, an animal path, just wide enough for Melodie and Janine to walk one at a time. Janine waited for her sister. Three pebbles marked the ground where she sat. The pink bathing suit lay at her feet. Her fawn body was the color of the stalks, and her arms and legs were the dark places between them. Janine laughed her high, shrill, beautiful laugh, from before she could speak the language of her god. Melodie released the turquoise straps from her shoulders and pulled the bathing suit from her hips. It fell among the cattails. Janine started on the path through the forest, and Melodie followed her.

Four Evenings

Dinner at Home

The kitchen faced the back of the house. The entire far wall and part of the adjoining wall were framed with windows. The view was of the back yard and of a patio with a metal table and chair for reading or drinking an iced tea. The windows made the light in the room bright and clear, so Francoise worked during the day in a flat, neutral light. Later, when she began taking down pots and baking pans and plates for dinner, the light seemed to withdraw in phases from the room, until she had to turn on the overhead light.

Harold's class schedule at the university made his presence at dinner often irregular, but he would be home this evening as his last class ended at four. Francoise had bought a rib roast and potatoes to crisp around the juices of the roast and Brussels sprouts which Harold loved but which she found had an aftertaste of something unpleasant, of something like dirt and darkness. That morning he left for his first class, walking down the front steps with his car keys jingling in his hand. She leaned out the upstairs window and called to him, "Harold, will you bring some coffee home? We're running low." She closed the window and Harold was at the bedroom door, saying to her in a barely controlled voice, "Don't you ever shout out the window at me, like a fishwife." Then he was gone. She heard his steps on the stairs and the front door being pulled roughly shut and she sat on the freshly made bed as if she had been struck. The children were in the other room, playing together. She had had to arrange her face like an actress before she could go to them. She straightened the hem on a curtain, then pulled the curtain shut and closed the door behind her.

She had bathed the children after their dinner. They ate together in the kitchen. She had made Ronnie a fried patty of ground beef, and sliced tomatoes and carrots from the garden she had planted under the kitchen windows. There was only Harold's G.I. Bill and her work at the department store on Thursdays and Saturdays. So she had planted a kitchen garden. Bella ate mashed food. Anything seemed to do. She loved bananas mashed in milk and sprinkled with cinnamon. Francoise should be giving her more to eat. She should read a book or call her mother or her sister Grace. They would tell her what she should be feeding her children. Bella waved her spoon around; food entertained her. Ronnie ate quietly, steadily. She was a stealthy eater. She ate like a refugee.

When they were first married, Francoise asked Harold what he had eaten at home and he told her he didn't like his mother's cooking and so Francoise cooked the recipes she had been raised on. Harold ate indifferently. Often he came home and claimed he had eaten something on campus. He was thin like all the men were thin who had come back from the war. But his appetite never really seemed to have returned. He smoked and drank coffee and she heard the keys strike the sheet of paper rolled into his typewriter on the dining room table and she waited for him over a magazine on the living room couch and then she stopped waiting for him and went to bed.

Francoise opened the oven door and checked the roast and the potatoes. She drained some of the juice; it would make a good gravy. Her mother used to boil all their vegetables; Francoise used to try to laugh with Harold about it. Her mother made beautiful turnips, thinly sliced, still steaming hot and tossed in black pepper and melted butter. A turnip could use a good boil. But string beans, cauliflower, spinach, sitting in pools of water on her dinner plate in her parents' house, seem to have been taken out of the realm of food and into the realm of the drowned.

She cut the stems from the Brussels sprouts and sliced them lengthwise. She would steam them when Harold came home. The grocery stores were full of canned foods. There were canned fruits and canned vegetables. In the magazines women in beautiful dresses wearing a string of pearls posed over a can opener that practically turned itself. The kitchens in the magazines were modern and efficient-looking. One hardly had to put effort into anything. *Had we put so much effort into the war,* Francoise wondered, *that our lives now were to be effortless?* There was Kraft Macaroni & Cheese and Campbell's Cream of Mushroom Soup and Libby's Fruit Cocktail and Stouffer's frozen dinners and Minute Tapioca and Green Giant Canned

Whole Golden Corn Niblets and Birds Eye Frozen Spinach. Everything was supposed to save time. One could vacuum in one's high heels. Harold was away. He had turned his course load into days and evenings away from her. Francoise spent her leisure time in a state of anxiety.

Ronnie crept into the kitchen. Francoise looked at her with veiled annoyance. She had been thinking of something far away, long before she married or gave birth. She was in a bathing suit on a beach. Someone had taken her picture. She was sitting on the sand. Her knees were bent and her head thrown back and she looked like Betty Grable. She was on a beach with her friends the summer after they had graduated from high school and someone had taken her picture.

There was something stuck to Ronnie's hands. "What is it?" Francoise said. "You're supposed to be upstairs playing with your sister."

"Bella was coughing," Ronnie said. "I patted her on the back."

"Stay here," Francoise said. "Don't touch anything."

Bella was on the floor, saying, "Aug, aug, aug," to the pool of vomit on the rug. Francoise looked at it with disgust. She picked Bella up and brought her to the bathroom, removed her pajamas and wiped her face and hands with a wet washcloth. She dressed her in clean pajamas. All the while Bella was saying, "Ooo, ooo, ooo," and waving her hands and laughing, or clearing her throat, which sounded like a strange kind of laughter, which she did by wrinkling her nose and snorting so that she sounded like a very old man. Francoise laid her on

Ronnie's cot and got a rag from under the bathroom sink and soaped it and tried to wipe the vomit from the rug. The milk and bananas smelled sour and Francoise gagged. She rinsed the rag and sprinkled baking soda over the stain. Her daughter was watching her with curiosity. Francoise looked up at her and said, "Don't move," although what was that to say to a child, and she lifted her into her crib and went downstairs.

Ronnie turned in the kitchen like a ballerina. A ballerina would turn and then perhaps she would bow. She would turn and leap and spread her arms and bow. Ronnie had seen a picture of a ballerina in a book at Lou's house and Lou had explained to her what a ballerina was and showed her a costume her parents had bought her for a school play. The bodice was shiny and pretty and the skirt was made of layers of weightless material with hundreds of tiny holes in it. Lou had let her try on the costume although it was too big for her and Lou had shown her how she had leapt across the stage in the school auditorium with the other girls who were also ballerinas. Ronnie liked the way the cloth felt; she leapt across Lou's bedroom and stopped suddenly and hugged herself.

The windows reeled around. First the windows, then the walls, then the windows. It was getting dark. Ronnie could hear the roast spitting in the oven. She didn't dare open the oven door and anyway she was barely tall enough to reach the handle. Her mother had placed an angel food cake on the counter to cool. Ronnie didn't dare touch it. There were knives on the counter, and the peelings of potatoes. She stood stock still and listened to the house, to the vibration of the air in the rooms. Then she stood on her tiptoes and ate. The peelings were wet from washing and they tasted heavy and damp. She went to the counter next to the refrigerator and turned the catch on the breadbox. She had learned to do it slowly and quietly. She put her open hand under the door and held it as it opened. Inside was a loaf of Wonder Bread. She opened the colored wrapper carefully and slipped a slice of bread out. She ripped the bread in half and stuffed it into her mouth and it seemed to melt there, and then she swallowed and it was gone. She closed the wrapper and then the breadbox and looked around the kitchen. She did another pirouette. Then she sat at the kitchen table and waited for her mother.

Francoise was in the kitchen. She said to Ronnie, "Go back upstairs and look after your sister." She took Ronnie's hands in hers. "What did you do?" she said. Ronnie had wiped her hands on her pajamas. There was no evidence from her hands of her path through the kitchen. "Go upstairs and change into a clean pair of pajamas," Francoise told her. "Clothes don't grow on trees. You have to learn to take better care of them."

"Is Bella sick?" Ronnie asked. Ronnie's voice sounded strangely accusatory.

"Go upstairs now," Francoise told her. "I've put Bella to bed. I'll come up in a while and check on you."

The roast was done. Harold was late. Bella was sighing in her sleep. Ronnie slept at an odd angle, her back hunched up, as if she had been struck. Francoise stood in the doorway of their bedroom for a moment, then returned to the kitchen.

It was fully dark. Francoise had changed into a skirt and blouse. She wore a white organdy hostess apron with a ruffle at the hem and tied in a big bow. Her fingers slipped along it when she went to wipe her hands. She heard the deep purr of the motor of the car and then Harold shut the motor and she heard the jingle of his keys. He carried an armful of books up the front stairs and he looked away from her as he came into the house.

"Hi, Honey," she said from the archway of the kitchen. Harold put his books on top of the book case. "I'll have dinner in a minute." Her husband was home. She lived in the interstices of waiting. All around her there was loneliness. There were floors and rooms and furniture, mops and sponges and brushes, cloths to take the dust away. Her children made her aware of the extremes of her patience. In the rooms the light changed and then it was dark and then the light came and changed again.

Harold took his seat at the dining room table. He had sat through three classes and had spent a number of hours in the library. He was reading the critics now, Trilling and Fiedler and Howe, and the Beats, Ginsberg and Kerouac and Corso and Snyder, and the playwrights, Williams and Hellman. He should have gone to New York. There would be time for the theater somehow, he would take the train and catch a matinee. He lit a cigarette. He remembered the poem, the Corso poem, about kindness. Kindness as a sort of conjuring. A poem about kindness as a lament. He drummed his fingertips on the air. There were nurses and priests in the poem. A knife. People were hurt. There was no mention of kindness after that. He beat out a rhythm with his fingertips on the wood of the table.

Harold looked up as Francoise arrived in the dining room, her hands laden with dishes, looking like someone's imagining of domesticity. A frilly white apron and above it the tired eyes. She had put a bracelet on; it glittered under the overhead light.

Then she brought in candles and lit them and somehow it seemed like the end of a play. Someone should blow the candles out, accede to the darkness.

Harold put his napkin in his lap, an automatic gesture. He took a sip of iced water.

"How was your day?" she was saying to him.

"Good, good," he said. He looked at the table. The food in the serving dishes looked strange to him. He had forgotten to bring the coffee. He hoped she wouldn't mention it. He didn't want to see the look of emptiness on her face that his failures evoked in her.

Then he said, remembering, "How are the children?" She had served him a slice of the roast. The meat was browned and pink inside. He closed his eyes. Then she was spooning gravy on the crisped potatoes.

"I made Brussels sprouts," she said. "They'll be ready in a minute. I thought you might like them with seasoning. I found it in the store the other day—"

"What did Ronnie do today?" Harold asked. "Was she a good girl?"

"She came downstairs with her hands full of vomit, that's what she did," Francoise said. She had turned away. She tried to laugh.

Harold pushed his plate away. He put his napkin carefully next to his plate. Then he got up from the table and walked out the door.

Francoise ate her dinner. She would have to tell her mother or her sister, if anyone would listen to her, how well it had turned out. That Brussels sprouts can be steamed, not boiled, and it gives them a more lively flavor. That the meat had cooked well. She took the plates to the kitchen and wrapped the leftovers in aluminum foil and placed them on shelves in the refrigerator. In the morning the kitchen would be filled with light, seeming without source, and then as the afternoon passed the light would withdraw and she would be standing again in the darkness.

At Bedtime

Her daughter, crying, was a shadowed form in the cot in the shadowed room. Francoise sat on the little trunk at the end of the cot, listening to Ronnie's grief. Her daughter seemed unaware of her. The light was poor. Something—a streetlight, a streak of moon, the light of the stars—lit the stillness of the room. There was just the grief, a clotted breathing, something old already within her young daughter. Francoise got up, reluctantly, and went to her. She was turned on her side under the covers. Francoise put her palm on the warm forehead, damp as if her daughter was in the throes of fever. In the evenings, at bedtime, Ronnie was full of fear. Francoise endured the ritual of opening the closet door and checking under the bed, then firmly closing the closet door and arranging the bedclothes again just so. See, she would say. Nothing there.

Ronnie believed in witches. She believed in the witch who inhabited the closet and the space under her bed. What do you know about witches? Francoise had said, when it all began some months ago. Ronnie was silent, as if the word itself held a malign potency. It must have been from the TV, Francoise realized, from *The Wizard of Oz*, which they had all watched together on the living room couch one Sunday night, before Harold went away. It was supposed to be a happy film, finally, of courage and endurance, of reunion and familial love.

The witch is only an embodiment of our own fears, she wanted to tell her too-young daughter, which we are then able after many trials to overcome. If only in a most haphazard, capricious way. But how does one explain, even to oneself, that the woman with the wart and the crooked nose and the terrible voice, talking, talking at you, threatening to destroy you, is an image in your own mind?

Her daughter's face was wet. Francoise went to the bathroom and returned with a streamer of toilet paper. "Here," she said. "Blow." Ronnie blew weakly into the thin paper. Francoise threw it away and washed her hands in the bathroom sink. She returned with a damp washcloth and wiped her daughter's face. The rough movement of the washcloth caused Ronnie to stop crying; she tilted her face upward, toward her mother's rote attentions. The house was quiet. Bella was sleeping across the hall, in their parents' bedroom. Her father was gone. The house was full of absences. Ronnie looked into the shadows that were her mother's eyes, but Francoise was already done. She returned the washcloth to the bathroom and rinsed it and folded it over the towel rack. She pulled the edges of the cloth so they hung straight and true.

Francoise washed her hands again, in the near darkness. There was the witch, and then the crying. She could hear Ronnie again in her room, crying, trying not to cry, sniffling and then weeping. She wept as if she had lost her own soul. She wept too disconsolately for a child. She wept for her father. Her father who drove away. Her father who drove away in his car. How far away. Then he returned. He returned and sat at the kitchen table. He lit a cigarette. He sat at the kitchen table in the noon light.

Francoise stood over Ronnie's cot. She was so tiny. Four years old. She wore a pajama set that Francoise's parents had given her. Pink and white with little ribbons at the collar and sleeves. It was wrinkled and damp now; Francoise thought she could smell a sour smell coming from her daughter's skin, of sweat and dampness from her tears. She knew she should pick her up and comfort her. But she couldn't. She did not want the child's body against hers, damp and needy, struggling to put her arms around her, to cry onto her shoulder, and then perhaps, exhausted, to fall asleep.

There was too much of the animal in children. They wet themselves, they needed changing, they pooped into diapers, on the changing table, in the soapy water of the bathtub. They spit up their food, they got sick with errant viruses and threw up violently on a rug, they laughed manically over nothing, they threw toys like missiles and kicked their legs, they cried if you caught a fingernail on their skin while dressing them. They insisted on all of your attention. They had no idea how to control their emotions. Everything was new. Pain and happiness and sorrow. They cried and did not know the end to it.

"Mommy?" Ronnie said.

Ronnie's damp hair was plastered to her cheek. Francoise took a step back. Something had come loose in her. She felt unanchored, without solace. "Go to sleep," she said.

"Mommy," her daughter said.

"I can't stay with you, Ronnie. I did that last night and the night before. But you just keep crying. Now what am I to do? You'll wake your sister soon."

Ronnie wept. Francoise realized that she barely existed in that moment for her daughter. She could try to comfort her, but she was not what her daughter wanted. Further, she could not give herself to her daughter in that way. Francoise looked down at the tiny shadow that was her daughter and knew as if a door had opened that she felt a bitter resentment toward her children, for their neediness and obliviousness. What was she to do? Perhaps Ronnie realized too, in her father's absence, that the house was truly empty, that there was no one there for her.

"I'm going to take a walk," Francoise said. "I'm going to

take a walk every night until you learn to stop crying. You can cry and cry and there won't be anyone to hear you."

Francoise walked down the stairs and draped a sweater over her shoulders. There was no sound from the room upstairs. She closed the front door quietly behind her.

The evening was mild. Across the road, a dog barked once in a tentative way. The stars splashed across the sky. Francoise walked all the way down the road and back. On the sidewalk in front of her house she listened for her children, but there was no sign. There were no lights in any of the houses. She walked down the road again. The trees and underbrush were dense and close. The road was a narrow ribbon she found herself walking on. The trees would crowd and suffocate her. She heard her feet on the road, the sound of the soles of her shoes. She was flung into the world again, walking a narrow ribbon, by herself. There were monsters in the woods, of course. She could not convince herself, as she tried to convince her daughter, that they were only an image in her own mind.

She opened the front door softly, took off her sweater, and stood at the foot of the stairs. From the children's bedroom there was only a wet, exhausted breathing. In Francoise's bedroom, Bella turned in her crib and opened her eyes. She looked steadily at her mother. Francoise was suddenly frightened. She sat on the bed. Bella turned away. She had been sleeping all the while; she had not been mutely watching Francoise. Francoise put on her nightgown and got into bed. She slept on the other side of the bed, away from the crib.

She closed her eyes. The house was quiet. Outside she heard the leaves rustle, as if a breath had awakened them.

The Study Evening

The car stopped in front of the house and the men got out. They were laughing and serious at once. They carried books and notebooks. Two of them carried paper bags containing cans of beer. They wore pens in plastic guards on their breast pockets, as if they were engineers. Harold was at the door, shaking their hands as they came inside. They arrived in the living room as if at the end of a race. There was the sound of breath being caught, the pleasant sound of arrival and expectation.

"Put your things anywhere," Harold said. "And yes, welcome." He was bowing grandly. "Welcome to our home."

Some had sweaters. A few items were put over the chairs, on the coffee table.

"Francie," Harold said. "Where are you, gal?"

Francoise shut the back door carefully. She had been on the patio, out of the range of the kitchen light, smoking a cigarette, saved from a visit to Lou's mother Kitty. Everyone smoked. But she kept it a secret. Harold had his secrets. She had hers too.

"Hello," she said. The men had turned from what they were doing and straightened respectfully as she walked into the living room.

"Francie, these are the boys. "Wiley and Sam and Herb and Pinkie and Robbie and Ez."

"Hello," Francoise said.

The boys all said hello.

"Make yourselves comfortable," Francoise said. "I have some things for you to snack on. I'll put them on the dining room table."

Someone stepped forward, carrying the bags of beer. The cans knocked together in the folds of the bags.

"I'll get some glasses," Francoise said.

"We don't need glasses, do we boys?" Harold said. "Give me those. Francie, will you put some cans out on the table and the rest in the refrigerator to cool."

Francoise wore a hostess outfit. That is, she wore a matching turquoise blouse and pedal pushers, with black spots like leopard spots. The collar of the blouse turned up. She wore a pair of black flats. She had bought them at the department store on credit.

She set out coasters and put the beer cans on the table in front of each chair. She and Harold had to take the chairs from the kitchen table to accommodate everyone. She put the rest of the beer away. She carried in a bowl of Chex mix and a bowl of chips. Then a dip made with sour cream and Lipton's Onion Soup and Dip Mix. She took a stack of paper plates and napkins to the table.

"God," Harold said, "there's so much stuff here, how are we to work?" The men were settling around the table. Francoise went to the kitchen. She fingered the collar of her leopard-spotted blouse.

"So, what does Professor Franz have in store for us tonight," one of the men said. "I still think he's a war criminal, he knows German too well."

"You flew one too many missions over Berlin," someone else said. "You have Germans on the brain."

"I'll tell you what, he didn't learn German at the Defense Language Institute," the other man said.

Francoise heard the popping of beer cans. Harold had taken down an ashtray from the sideboard. She could hear the quick scrape and flash of a match; then there was the smell of tobacco smoke. She listened for her children, upstairs, but there was no sound.

"Mann is a lot more interesting than Eliot," she heard her husband say. "He can write a sentence. He can make you cry."

"Does Mann make you cry," someone said. There was laughter, the sound of Chex mix being scooped from the bowl, the crack of nuts and the rectangles of grain.

"He makes me cry," Harold said. "I'll tell you why. If only I had written 'Disorder and Early Sorrow.'"

"Now Eliot," another man said. "He makes me cry. Is crying manly? He makes me melancholy."

"Eliot is an effete banker," Harold said. "He didn't know how to write a line until Pound showed him how."

"Now that would make you cry," someone else said. "The world's greatest editor in an insane asylum."

"He's a Nazi," someone said. "Wherever he is, they should put Professor Franz there too."

Everyone laughed.

Francoise walked into the dining room. She emptied the ashtray. She looked for wedding bands on the fingers of the men at the table. She counted two, three. She stood smiling at the men. She didn't know what to say, how to enter in. "Are any of you married," she said. The men looked up at her with curiosity. They were all lean like Harold and there was something predatory about them. *Maybe they had returned that way from the war.* She thought too, *They were glad to be in the company of men again, out of the war, smoking around a dinner table. Had the war made them this way, men seeking the company of men for the experiences they shared and would never be able to put completely away.* Now they were predatory for the future. It lay in thought, in university and the G.I. Bill.

They were still looking at Francoise. Then someone said, "I married my sweetheart after the war."

"Do you have children?" Francoise asked.

"Pinkie," the man said to her, reintroducing himself, separating himself from the other pairs of eyes that looked at her. "Two boys, twins," he said. "Little hellions," and he laughed, embarrassed that he had been taken so gently and persistently from the world of men.

All the men laughed, and they turned their eyes away from her, and Harold said something, and they laughed again, and someone lit a cigarette, and the smoke floated upward above the men's heads and hovered in layers under the ceiling light.

Francoise went outside and sat in the chair on the patio. The night was mild. She had put the coffee pot out; later she was going to make coffee for Harold's friends from the university and cut into little squares a tray of brownies she had made from a mix. She tried to understand the depth of the men's involvement in their books. The war was over; they would live another year now and a year after that. They were newly born again; they were immortal for a little while, they had hungers and reading perhaps helped still the fear of death that had consumed them.

She had been in school during the early years of the war. She had been a lot younger than these men were when they entered the university, she had begun her studies right out of high school. She went away from home, carrying a satchel for her books and wearing her scarf and mittens. The men smoking at the dining room table had spent the years growing into manhood on battleships and in bombers and crawling across open fields.

She had been in love. That's what she remembered about school, being in love and the news on the radio, the names of countries and battles that were far away and unreal. She was in love and their winter boots made deep impression in the snow. The girls had an eleven o'clock curfew on Saturday nights and a nine o'clock curfew during the week. There was a soda shop in town where the students went. She had learned to smoke there, with her friends and the man who spoke to her and walked with her on the paths on the campus, who took her to a dance and kissed her under the dim lamplight on the path next to the library. He was studying to be a doctor. She loved him and the next fall returning to school from her parents' house, returning to him, he told her something had happened, something had changed, and she spent the year in mourning. Then she went back to her parents'

Four Evenings

house and waited out the war there, the windows covered with black cloth so the German U-boats wouldn't be able to get their bearings along the coast. Her sister Grace married a man who had proposed to her before the war and Francoise was a bridesmaid and she was lonely. Then she went with her racket to play tennis one Saturday afternoon; it was fall, the leaves were turning, and Harold and two other people played doubles with her, and afterward he spoke to her and later, on another Saturday, he took her driving in his car.

The men had stopped talking. *Were they studying or just being together, war veterans on the G.I. Bill?* She couldn't return to the house, she stayed in the chair on the patio, in the atmosphere of the night. Now Harold was speaking about Mann and he was reading from the story he had mentioned, the story about everything out of order, and someone was still complaining about Professor Franz, though Francoise could hear under it a deep respect. The house would be full of smoke and the men would talk about their exams and Harold would tell them about the paper he was writing and someone would get another beer and no one would notice that she was gone.

She would read Thomas Mann. She would read Eliot and Pound, all of the books on her husband's shelves. She thought about the man she had loved and the imprints their bodies made in the snow. He had taken her hand and led her away and abandoned her there. Now she wore her leopard-spotted hostess clothes and made Chex mix and bathed her children and put the coffee on and her hands always felt empty, her hands were wrapped around an emptiness. The man she loved had led her into love and left her there. She looked up into the still, mild night and didn't know where she was supposed to go.

The Car Ride

The acceleration of the car was like a dream. Like the Wicked Witch sailing upward on her broom. How the children had screamed. How Ronnie had screamed. There was a gun now in the drawer by the bed. Harold had bought a gun. There are things out there, he said, we must protect ourselves from. What, where, Francoise had said, looking at the barrel, looking for relief out the window into the quiet, leafy night. Her parents didn't like him. He took her for walks under the lights of the sidewalks, to dinner at a restaurant on the shore. Afterwards they walked along the beach and in the distance was the roll of the surf; low tide, the surf like something that had been finally calmed. She had knitted him a pair of argyle socks; she had a photograph of them together, on the grass, he smiling at her, holding up his trouser leg for the world to see. Who had taken the picture? She couldn't remember.

At the wedding her parents had always seemed to stand apart. It was after the war and her sister Grace was married and who, who would marry her. Boys had been killed and Mrs. Beauford's son had been killed, the letter had come and she left the door unlocked every night for him, and his things all ready in his room. Boys were dead and the nights were so quiet and Francoise could hear the clock on her parents' fireplace mantle ticking ticking ticking.

In the movie theater in the center of town she saw *Mr. Blandings Builds His Dream House*, *Philadelphia Story*, and *The Best Years of Our Lives* and her sister was going to have her first child. Harold bought her flowers and he brought a puppy, a cocker spaniel to her parents' house and her parents refused to let it stay. He brought a blue parrot in a cage and her parents turned it away. That year she went to two weddings of high school friends at the Methodist church on the town Green and she didn't dare invite Harold it would seem so obvious. There were birth announcements in the newspapers and sometimes her parents seemed withdrawn from her as if they were waiting for her to stop living out her life in their house. Harold kissed her by the wall along the beach and she saw the lighthouse light blinking dark, light, dark, light.

In her lap she held a Tupperware container filled with chocolate chip cookies she had baked that afternoon. She wore white wrist-length gloves. Harold's hand was draped casually over the steering wheel, as if he were driving a familiar route. Driving to school. He kissed her on the beach at night and the surf whispered behind them. At their wedding he wore a dark blue suit. In the photographs her parents stood away from him. They had built a home together and they lived in it in peace. Harold's parents stood on the other side, his father so dignified, his mother in a dress with a corsage at the shoulder. Her sister Grace and her new husband

Wes were in the photos too. Francoise was married now, she had a place. She understood the place she inhabited as the wife of a war veteran, starting anew together.

The trees were going by faster and the road was dark. They were lost—probably somewhere in her sister's town; Francoise didn't recognize any of the houses as Harold sped through the stop signs.

"Harold, slow down," Francoise said.

Harold watched the needle inch higher.

"You're going to kill us," Francoise said. Her voice was steady and even. She gripped the container of chocolate chip cookies in her hands.

You would hear the planes as if from somewhere else, a steady whine in the night sky. Then the bombs would drop and there was light all around and whatever they had hit burned and burned. The land was lit as if by phosphorescence and he thought he could see the red sun on the tails of the planes but he knew he was imagining it. In the daytime the world was austere and colorless. His job was to study the sky and dispatch reports of weather conditions for the Allied pilots bringing the straining military transport planes over the Hump into China. He began to think he saw things in it, the faces of dead men in the clouds, and to hear the awful sounds the voices of the Japanese made as he listened to them over the radio.

They had followed him home. The Japs and the dead and broken airmen and the voices that were like some obscene command. And so he had bought a gun. Sometimes he thought Francoise was in league with them but he was never sure. When she tried to put her hands up under his shirt in the candlelight he knew she was in league with them.

The roads were smooth and narrow, the footpaths of the Himalaya and the sky and the animals the yak and the prayer flags and the terraced earth. The roads here were black unlike the roads and footpaths of the Himilaya, the headlights swerved as the car swerved, and up ahead were glimpses of dignified houses in the night. Francoise was his enemy, he had known from the time he played with her on the tennis court and he had wanted to put his racket down and walk away. She was the enemy and you hold your friends close and your enemy closer and Francoise was his enemy. He locked his hands on the steering wheel and glanced at her and she held the grip above the passenger window. He pressed a button on the driver's door and all the windows opened and the night air blew in like the wind after the bombs had dropped.

Francoise was crying. She said, "You'll kill us all."

Then she said, "Harold, Harold, what have I done?" But she knew she hadn't done anything or she had sat in the car in the wrong way or spent too long dropping the children off at Kitty's or she had said something wrong while they were dressing for dinner at her sister's. She had worn the wrong perfume or the wrong lipstick. His mother had said, before they married, "He was not adjusting in school when he was a boy." At school, now, they said, he was a man with a future. A man with a future but beginning to be of concern.

After the Hunger

Francoise said, "Harold, we have two children. Who will care for them?" The wind blew her hair. She felt herself disappearing into the night. When they found the car she would not be there, she would no longer exist.

"Oh that's right, you're a mother aren't you?" he said. His voice was filled with derision.

He had kissed her under the sea wall. The surf moved in and out. Her parents stood to the side in the wedding photos.

His face was lit by the dials on the car. The headlights slashed though the greenery, the trees and gardens and the ivy growing along the stone walls at side of the road. She almost let go of any desire to live. *Why not just lift upward into the night, like a being not of this earth?*

He looked like a normal man. He was driving to the house of his sister-in-law. His wife held a container of cookies in her lap. The wind blew through the windows. They would have a laugh when the car came to a stop in the driveway, because they would look as if they had been in a hurricane.

She recognized the house on the corner and Harold swerved the car onto the street where her sister lived. He turned the car into the driveway and slammed on the brakes. The container of cookies fell to the floor. There were crumbs on her shoes, she could feel them. The container of cookies spoiled. He opened the driver's door and walked around the car and opened the passenger door for her. She was afraid when he took her elbow. He led her up the stairs to the front door. Her sister Grace and brother-in-law Wes answered the door together as if they had been waiting for them to arrive. "Come in," they said, and then her sister said to her, "Francoise, you look like you've seen a ghost. Your face is completely white."

"Oh," Francoise said, "we drove with the windows open. It is such a beautiful night. I was so thrilled I must have bitten my lipstick off."

Wes was already fixing drinks. The women drank highballs. The men drank gin and tonics. Wes was slapping Harold on the back. They had both fought in the war. Francoise didn't know how either had survived. Harold was speaking warmly to Wes. *He looked like a young man out for an evening, taking his wife to dinner at his in-laws'. He looked like any veteran, didn't he.*

Grace was speaking to her. She spoke quietly, in a quiet voice, because her daughter was asleep upstairs. She was telling Francoise about the screened-in porch she and Wes were going to build, off the kitchen. They'd be able to have cookouts in the back yard and eat on the porch. She and Harold would have to come. Grace was leading her into the kitchen to show her the photo from a magazine of the vines she was going to plant to shade the porch. They would grow right up the screens.

"Yes," Francoise said. She looked back at her husband. He had said something amusing to Wes. Wes was laughing. Harold had bought a gun. He looked so well, standing with his drink, talking to Wes.

Grace opened the magazine and showed her the photograph.

After the Hunger

"Oh, how pretty," Francois said. She imagined the vines growing up the screens. A green world. Not crowding and suffocating but calm, the heart-shaped leaves cooling one in the shade of the porch. A cooling drink in one's hand. The light striking the heart-shaped leaves, like light on water, as the sun made its transit across the sky.

The Halloween Witch

It was already full dark outside. Mags and her grandmother Esther stood at the double sink in the kitchen under the globe light, the knotted pull cord hanging like a plumb line above their heads. Esther worked a cloth under the crescent of foam that floated on top of the dishpan. She brought a dinner dish from the steaming water, rinsed it under the hot-water faucet and set it in the dishrack, making little exhalations of exertion. Mags folded a linen towel over the dish and patted it dry. The dishrack rested on a ribbed drain board, the enamel pocked with age, that was fitted over the second sink. Each time Esther placed a dish in the rack the drain board put forth a rush of water that fell over its lip into the sink where she worked. She stirred a long-handled metal basket that held slivers of Ivory soap to reinvigorate the suds. Her hands moved again in the water. Mags dried another dish, the porcelain slippery and warm. There was the silverware too, and the serving dishes (tonight having offered carrot and celery sticks, baked potatoes, sautéed yellow squash and baked flounder), pots and pans, dessert dishes (butterscotch pudding), water glasses and Mags's milk glass, and Esther's coffee cup and saucer and creamer. They still ate in the dining room, dinner for two now, Mags's mother Gail and her sister Suzette having moved away, having been asked by Esther to do so early the previous summer.

Mags returned the silverware to the drawer in the sideboard in the dining room, the serving dishes to the china cabinet, the pots and pans to the shelves under the counter next to the refrigerator, and the dishes and drinking cups and creamer to the cabinet above it. With a fresh linen towel Mags wiped dry the coffee percolator and all its parts and placed it, reassembled, on a small table adjacent to the stove. She blew her bangs from her forehead; she felt flushed and warm from working near the vaporous dishwater. She still wore her school clothes, a white cotton blouse under a cardigan sweater and a pleated skirt, because her grandmother's dinners required a certain formality. She was aware of the darkness outside the kitchen windows and of the contained white light from the globe under which they worked and of her grandmother, standing at the sink, folding the cloth over the faucet, and rinsing the dishpan and turning it on its side, her breathing quiet now, her exertion done. She wiped her hands on her apron.

"Well," her grandmother said. She sat down heavily at the kitchen table, set between windows hung with gauze curtains, the shades pulled just below the sash. Her house sweater hung over the back of her chair. She held it in her lap for a moment, then fitted it around her shoulders and buttoned the top button.

The Halloween Witch

"That was a good dinner," Mags said. Mags entered expectantly each evening into her grandmother's dinners. They were full of ritual, a succession of serving dishes, serving spoons; the glint of cutlery. Then everything cleared away and the dessert dishes at Mag's place at the table, at her grandmother's place, a spoon next to each. Mags felt the presence of her grandmother's ancestors, her parents and siblings, sitting on wide, finely grained chairs at a round table, very similar to her grandmother's, and her parents' parents and their families, into the reaches of time. Her grandmother had objects that had belonged to her mother, very old, placed in the china cabinet many years ago, and never used, never moved. Fluted fruit dishes, a drinking cup with her mother's name and the year of her birth etched into it, china salt servers, and faceted glass rests for one's dinner knife.

"Oh?" her grandmother said. She looked across the kitchen at her granddaughter. Esther's hands rested on the table. Her hands, even in her old age, were beautifully shaped, the flesh under the tapered nails a light pink, the skin like old silk.

"I do enjoy those beets," Mags said. Her grandmother cut them to paper thinness with an old knife, sharpened almost as fine, then drowned them in melted butter. Mags loved her grandmother fiercely, though it felt to her like something calm, large and calm, and her grandmother in the center. Mags used to ask her grandmother what she was making for dinner, and her grandmother would reply that such a question was not polite, and turn to her singular labors in the kitchen. Mags would hear her grandmother opening the oven, and taking a lid off a pot and stirring something on the stove, and the odors would follow her upstairs where she sat at the desk in her bedroom reading *Ethan Frome* until her grandmother called her downstairs. Then Mags put her book away and returned to her grandmother and took the dinner dishes down and set the table and brought the serving dishes from her grandmother's hands to the table, each a surprise, a gift.

"My mother taught me how to prepare beets," Esther said.

"Oh?" it was now Mags's turn to say. Her grandmother didn't often talk about herself. She had lived in another time entirely and Mags, from her grandmother's telling, knew only small parts of it, like a fast-moving image across a great distance: the weekly bath in the tin tub brought to the kitchen and filled with scalding water heated on the wood stove; her brother Charles jumping out from the bushes as she made her way in the early evening dark to the outhouse; her family, led by her father, walking to church on newly installed sidewalks.

"My mother showed me how to peel and slice them, very quickly, fresh from the pot," Esther said, "so they keep their heat. That way the butter melts evenly, though I do leave it out to soften first."

Mags wondered if her grandmother had shown her own daughter how to prepare beets and if her mother would then teach her. But something didn't follow. When her mother and sister lived there, her grandmother had allowed her mother to whip the potatoes or salt and pepper the broccoli but she herself prepared the food. When they spoke at all over their work they spoke in low voices that Mags couldn't decipher. Her sister Suzette came to the dinner table reluctantly and wouldn't eat. She was told by their mother that she couldn't leave the table until her meal was done. It sat in hardening butter and fat and the evening seemed arrested in some vast, dark place full of agony until her sister was released from the table and the misery of the untouched, clotted food and pounded up the stairs to an early bedtime. Mags didn't understand how her sister wouldn't eat because she was thin like someone starving. Every joint in her body was a bony protrusion. When Mags went to her she would turn her head away and pretend to sleep.

Mags sat across from her grandmother. Esther breathed through her open mouth, the lower lip lax, as if there was a far struggle, very faint, at the bottom of her lungs. She wore a dress always with a cloth belt and sturdy black shoes with lace-up ties and low, stacked heels, and when the evenings became cooler the sweater she kept hung over the back of the kitchen chair. Mags would hear her on the stairs in the night, after Mags had gone to bed, after her grandmother had sat in the living room in the quiet, with only the reading lamp lit. Later she would hear her grandmother, in her blue felt slippers, slowly descend the stairs to warm a glass of milk.

Neither of them slept well, Mags realized. Sometimes Mags woke to discover she had been tracking her grandmother's movements in her dreams. Mags wanted to help her with the cleaning and the heavy work of curtains and bedspreads when the seasons changed, and the ordering and putting away and preparation of food, but her grandmother wanted to work about the house by herself, to cook their dinner and prepare oatmeal for her as she got ready for school and fix her an afternoon snack of cold milk and an apple-butter sandwich on bread denuded of its crust. Sometimes Mags returned from school to find her grandmother running a cloth over the fireplace mantle or sweeping the kitchen floor, and she knew that her grandmother was in a great silent meditation with the house that she had lived in with her husband for almost fifty years.

Now her grandmother was standing up. She braced her open palms on the edge of the table, and Mags saw the effort in it. "Is the porch light on, dear?" her grandmother asked. She had begun to untie her apron.

"I'll get it," Mags said. She placed the damp linen towel with the others over one of the wooden arms of the drying rack above the radiator, and she took her grandmother's apron from her smooth, reddened hands and hung it over another wooden arm. In the front hall she pushed the button on the wall next to the door and the porch light came on. She pulled back the lace curtain that covered the oval glass in the door. She saw then a square of the porch, painted the same medium gray as the house, and the broad steps leading to a brief walkway then the sidewalk. There were three high back rocking chairs on the porch, which ran the width of the house, with caned seats and backs, painted a deep green. Her grandmother owned a black-and-white photograph taken there of her husband, who had been gone now twelve years, having died of a heart attack in the upstairs hallway. Mags was just five then, her sister a little baby of two. In the photograph a squirrel was sitting on her grandfather's knee and he was feeding it a peanut, unaware of the camera. The squirrel stood on its hind legs, and her grandfather held the peanut toward it. It seemed a familiar attitude between them, as in an old acquaintanceship.

Her grandfather had played on the town baseball team, he was a councilman, and a salesman for a food distributor, which her grandmother told her had saved them from the worst deprivations of the Great Depression, because everyone has to eat. There were photos of him in his baseball uniform; leaning against a sea wall with his bachelor friends when he was courting Esther; in his marriage clothes with her; holding his own young children; holding Mags and her tiny sister Suzette; but the photograph she liked best was of the animal about to eat a peanut from her grandfather's hand, and her grandfather's calm repose.

There were little shadows on the street now, little ghostly figures in sheets and tutus and monster masks. Mags could hear their high whispery voices. They walked under the streetlights like stark little dreams. Some carried shopping bags that they tripped over in their homemade costumes, some carried plastic pumpkins that they held carefully in front of themselves by a thin metal loop. Esther had gone to sit in the living room, where a tray of Hershey's Kisses and Tootsie Rolls, stacked in a fat mound, rested on the coffee table. Mags was opening the door now, and getting the tray. Other years her mother did this, and she and Mags's grandmother greeted the children, and before that, Mags and Suzette, dressed in old sheets, wandered unaccompanied through the neighborhood, going farther than they were allowed, their prize a bag filled with sweets. They ate as much of the forbidden candy as they could, standing outside of the porch lights and streetlights, unwrapping Mars Bars, Mr. Goodbars, Turkish taffy and Atomic fireballs, shaking boxes of Jujyfruits into their mouths. They brought home the depleted bag, the empty wrappers pushed into hedges and flower pots, and their mother took it from them and doled out the candy each day after that, bar by bar, piece by piece as they stood before her, their eyes turned downward, empty of all associations but for the small weight and texture in their palms, until the bag was empty.

But now her grandmother had set out the candies not from a lack of charity but of an old necessity learned from her immigrant parents and the Great Depression, from raising children where one counted out potatoes and saved string and wrapping paper and elastic bands. So each child that came to the door had his or her costume admired by Mags, who announced to her grandmother who was at the door—a ghost, a pirate, a princess—and received two Hershey's Kisses and two Tootsie Rolls, and when the candy was done, Mags pushed the button on the wall and the porch light went out and she brought the empty tray to the kitchen.

Her grandmother had turned on the TV at the opposite end of the living room, and she sat in her chair under the reading lamp next to the couch, and she and Mags, arranging her skirt on the couch near her grandmother, watched the opening credits of *The Carol Burnett Show*. The lights were off in the house, except for the reading lamp, part of Esther's efforts against want and need which made Mags feel safe and protected under the circle of light. The sound from the television was low, so that one almost had to strain to hear, and the bass of the music was like a light vibration in Mags's body. They heard no more small voices on the sidewalk outside. Esther breathed with a slight catch on the intake of air, as if the evening and all the voices at the door had fatigued her. Carol Burnett was singing. The doorbell rang.

Mags looked at her grandmother. No one rang the doorbell. Mags's mother visited only briefly when she came to pick up Mags after work on Friday and bring her back in time for dinner on Sunday, as if her mother and grandmother were divorced parents sharing custody of her. Mags had taken the risk of asserting her love for one, which by reasoning seemed to declare a lesser love for the other, in discussing with her grandmother her wish then presenting it to her mother, so when her mother and sister moved to a rented house in the town directly to the north, Mags remained with her grandmother. Now they lived in a kind of flowing isolation and peace. The doorbell rang again and Mags, under her grandmother's nod, though her lips were tightly drawn, turned on the porch light and pulled back the lace curtain and appraised the person standing there.

"It's someone in a mask," Mags reported to her grandmother. "Like a witch's mask. It looks like a grown-up."

"Open the door, I guess, dear," Esther said. "But be careful."

Mags opened the door. "We're out of candy," Mags said. "We had turned off the porch light…" Now she could see the person under the light. *It's a woman*, she thought. *A witch, yes.* The rubber mask, the hooked, exaggerated nose, the wrinkled skin. The heavy brows and the crooked mouth. Eyes, the person's, the woman's real eyes, were recessed behind the mask. Her hair was covered by a scarf with tied ends that rested stiffly one on each shoulder. There was a wart on her rubber nose, another on her forehead.

The witch stepped over the threshold and brushed past Mags. Mags said, "Wait," but the person walked into the living room. She sat on the hassock. There was the couch as well and the chair where Mags's grandfather used to sit but the witch chose the hassock, pushed toward the middle of the living room, where Mags sometimes would sit, her arms held out, pretending to find a precarious balance on it. Esther sat in her chair, contained in her old body, not alarmed, but cautious, as if the incomprehensible dramas of history could threaten to overcome her, but nothing could again, not after her husband's passing, not after that. Mags stood protectively next to her grandmother. She said, "Can we help you," but the witch just sat on the hassock, facing them, her arms hanging at her sides.

Esther looked at her, because this is what the witch wanted her to do, with some concern. In addition to her mask and scarf she wore a man's light jacket zipped half-way, and under it a shabby blouse, and loose cotton gloves, and khaki trousers with rolled cuffs and a pair of man's shoes that seemed in their excess to curl up over her toes, like those worn by an ancient woman from another realm. With the tray of candies Mags had imitated the harvest feast of All Hallow's Eve, a time of remembrance of the dead—the saints and martyrs, the faithful departed believers—by giving the treats to children wobbling under voluminous sheets and carrying wands brushed with glitter and fabulous skirts of tulle and little cardboard daggers and wearing a patch over an eye, who seemed like imagined figures of spirits and faeries from an enchanted land. But the person before them who would not speak seemed to have come from another place, from the land of the departed, those who were lonely and frightened in their dispossession. Her witch's face was exaggerated and immobile. Mags couldn't see the eyes, whether they looked at her and her grandmother. The person still didn't move or speak. Mags put her hand on her grandmother's shoulder.

"I think you should go now," Esther finally said. "It's quite late." On the television, the sound so low as to be almost inaudible, Carol Burnett and Harvey Korman were frozen in awkward postures, afraid, it seemed, to move, and Mags knew they had said something, Harvey had said something to Carol, not Harvey's character having said something to Carol's character, and each was afraid to burst out laughing as Harvey and Carol and ruin the sketch. Though Mags knew this often happened and it never ruined the sketch.

Mags took her hand from her grandmother's shoulder and started toward the door. It had been left ajar, and as she moved toward the hall she could feel the chill autumn air on her face and hands. She kept her eyes on the witch; she was afraid of her. She would have something terrible in her pockets or in her shoe; she would speak and the sound would be horrible.

The witch stood. Then she said to Esther, "Don't you recognize me?" and she took off the mask and untied the scarf and shook out her hair. She walked toward Esther in her oversized shoes, like one of the departed seeking solace in the world of the living.

Esther said, "Oh, Gail. You gave us a fright," and looked sharply at her when her daughter went to kiss her. Gail stepped back, her hand awkward for a moment on the arm of Esther's chair.

"I just wanted to say hello," Gail said. "And what better way?"

"You should call," Esther said. "You should remember the niceties."

Mags wondered who had really been sent away. *Do the departed leave or are they banished.* It was Suzette who had started storming up and down the stairs and slamming the door to their bedroom and the paned-glass door leading to the hallway upstairs and the front door and the back door. They had lived in her grandmother's house for five years and Suzette had grown more and more into a violent adolescence, and Esther was by then very old and she told Gail she would have to take Suzette and live somewhere else. Esther, after the sum of all her years, most of which she hoarded quietly and dreamed on in the midst of her daily chores and in her efforts at sleep, seemed to want only peace.

"It was just a whim, Mother," Gail said. She was trying to be cheerful, Mags knew. "I wanted to see you. I thought you'd think it fun."

Mags was standing behind her mother, by the archway to the living room. "Where is Suzette?" she asked.

"Where did you get those dirty clothes," Esther said.

"It was a joke," Gail said. "And they're clean clothes. Old, but freshly laundered. Someone at work was collecting clothes for the Salvation Army. I thought you'd find it amusing. Though I could barely drive in these shoes." She looked at the shoes, which seemed to have immobilized her.

"Is Suzette at home," Mags asked, "or is she out for Halloween?"

"Why don't you go upstairs?" Gail said.

Mags sat on the couch. Her mother's face was familiar. She didn't know if it was pretty. It always looked strained, as if she was under great pressures that couldn't be relieved. Mags was glad for her grandmother, to share the house with her in its peacefulness and quiet. When she stayed with her mother on weekends Suzette was often gone. She ate with them rarely. Her life contained secrets, not old ones, to be meditated on, like her grandmother's, but new, dangerous ones. She came to bed late, after being fruitlessly reprimanded by their mother, and wouldn't speak to Mags.

"Dear, will you turn off the porch light?" Esther said to Mags. "It's getting late."

Mags started for the hall.

Gail stood before her mother, like a figure of the departed who didn't know it had no place there. She said nothing. Then she turned and left the house.

Mags turned off the light. She stood in the doorway and looked into the empty street. Her mother had vanished, leaving a faint stir in the air as she returned to the other world. Mags wanted to call after her in the darkness. She wanted to say, "What will happen to me?"

She shut and locked the door and went to her grandmother. Her grandmother was walking painfully across the living room to turn off the television. They had missed Carol Burnett's closing song. Esther led her granddaughter into the kitchen and pulled the cord on the light. She was saying something. It sounded to Mags like, "I don't know. I don't know." Her breathing was labored. Mags followed closely behind her. Esther sat at the kitchen table, and Mags sat across from her. Esther composed her hands on the table and looked at her granddaughter. All was familiar now. All was well. Esther said, "Dear, will you get down some cups and a pot and the cocoa there in the cabinet and heat some milk."

Mags did all this for her grandmother. She stood over the stove as she had dreamed her grandmother doing and tested the temperature of the milk with her fingertip. Her grandmother was sighing but her breathing was quieter now and the catch in her throat was gone. Mags looked across the room at her. The light from the globe in the ceiling lit the side of her face. Mags thought about her sister, out somewhere in the night, running ahead of the hunter's moon; her mother like an unrestful spirit trying to find her way home. Mags poured the heated milk into the cups and stirred in the cocoa. She brought a cup to her grandmother and watched her lift it to her lips and blow on the cocoa and take a sip of it. She set the cup down. Mags, cold suddenly, wrapped her hands around her cup and let it try to warm her.

Opening Day

They pulled into the driveway, fitting the car along the narrow thread of tar. Ro got out, bringing the lunch things, then Claire, carrying a bag of books. The door to the house was shut, which mildly shocked Claire; always her mother, Ella, hearing the roll of the car tires and the tick of the dying engine, opened the front door and greeted them. Now Claire, balancing the bag against her hip, lifted the knocker and heard her mother, her voice rising briefly like a note in a song, say, "It's open." She and Ro entered the small foyer and stepped into the living room, where her mother sat, as she had every day for almost a year, at the near end of the couch, a blue plaid throw folded over its back. The old TV table, with its design of worn fleurs-de-lis, was positioned in front of her. An aluminum walker rested on the carpet nearby.

Ella extended her arm toward her daughter. "Hello, dear," she said. She wore sneakers and white socks, powder-blue slacks, and a white blouse and white cardigan sweater. Claire could see the marks on her outstretched wrist and on her shins above her socks where the medicine made her skin bruise, spotting it a deep purplish-red. Her eyes looked washed of color, an indeterminate shade of gray-brown. Her hair was white now, no longer rinsed the distant shade of her youth. The layers fell stiffly onto each other, as if her hairbrush had touched only the outer strands. *Is this the first sign*, Claire wondered, *a certain blurriness of form, a certain neglect?* But Ella had let everything go, the details of the household, and the grass and hedges, disinterested even in calling the lawn service, until her other son-in-law, Hugh, forced into utility by Ella's omissions, arrived with mower and clippers.

Claire went to her mother and kissed her upturned cheek. Ro bent over her in his courteous way and her mother said, "Hello Roland." Ro wore an oxford-cloth shirt and a pair of khaki trousers. Sometimes he wore a tie. He always asked Claire if he should wear a tie. He was careful about how he should appear in the company of her family, which for the most part involved visits to her mother, who sat even now with her spine erect, her bearing a reminder of the old manners, the old ways. When Ro stepped back from his mother-in-law's brief embrace, Claire saw that her eyes were fixed in an expression of perplexity, as if she were trying to draw her elder daughter and her daughter's husband from a place in memory. In the rehab facility she had been frightened and in need of the attentions of her daughters, and impatient and suffering under the nurses' care. Now she looked out at the world from the cushions of her couch as if a visitor in it. Her body had become lighter; it was the same body Claire had always known, but as if with less density, less connection to the earth, and it was more angular, and her face was thin, and her brittle-looking hair framed her temples.

Ro hung their coats in the closet by the front door. It was the end of March but they wore winter parkas. They had driven to visit Ella in weather of fog and light rain.

"How are you, Mother," Claire said. She sat on the couch, her calves tucked at an angle to it. Her mother still held her hand.

Ella regarded her daughter with some of the old familiarity. But then there seemed to be a message in it, in the set of her mouth, in the slight turn of her body away from Claire, as if Claire, having been perceived, had been found to be without substance, like an idea her mother had once been attached to and had since set aside. Her mother removed her hand from Claire's and rested it in her lap. Claire laced her fingers together and realized that she was holding her own hands. She was suddenly and deeply sad, as if her mother had shown herself again, in the moment that had passed briefly between them, the mother Claire used to know, who had gone away.

"Daiva has left," her mother said. "Just this morning. It was quite sudden." Her eyes became wide, as if she were reliving the shock of Daiva's departure.

"Annie told me over the phone," Claire said. "Something about her stepmother taking ill."

"I was used to her so."

"She was very good to you," Claire said. Her mother holding up the water glass from the TV table and Daiva refilling it. Her mother calling Daiva downstairs to assist her to the bathroom three and four times in the night. Sending her on errands on foot, a mile up the main street, to purchase a box of crackers at the Stop & Shop.

"I don't know why she would leave so suddenly," Ella said.

"It's a mystery," Claire said. She looked briefly at Ro, who sat across from them in the upholstered chair by the window.

"Her stepmother took a fall," Ella said, "though I don't know the circumstances. But she's probably your age or thereabouts, and making, I would assume, a quicker recovery. Well all that aside. What I mean to say is that it can't explain Daiva's by-your-leave, because her stepmother is still in the hospital, and what could there possibly be for Daiva to do?"

"I don't know," Claire said. They would never know. A second language spoken with pauses and pursed lips helps in safekeeping one's own motives, one's own secrets. Maybe, she and Annie had speculated, Daiva wanted a life of her own again, a young vital woman doing something other than tending to the needs of their mother.

"Where is her replacement?" Claire asked. "Annie told me the agency was sending someone."

"She won't be here till later this afternoon."

"You were here by yourself?"

Ella waved the question away. She spread her fingers on her knees and pressed her lips together. She studied her nails. Claire thought that if she shouted at her, "Mother, Mother," she would not respond. Her mother's hands contained bruises, veins, the smooth polish of skin, the rounded nails. They were like an artifact, a language of symbols. There was a word, some word that would unlock everything. But Claire was never permitted to know what it was, or if it existed.

Ro had been watching her. He got up brought the bag of books to her. She put the books on the couch between herself and her mother.

"Mother," Claire said. "Mother." Ella, startled out of her reverie, looked at her daughter. "We've brought you some books," Claire said. Ella examined the books one by one, turning them in her hands. The books were mostly biographies. Ella liked to read about history that way. She was entranced by the diaries and letters of Anne Morrow Lindbergh. She read the accounts of the Great Depression—the oral histories and the breakdown of the land. The great early aviatrixes taking to the air across Africa, across the Pacific. Adventurers traveling on foot, by camel and elephant across landscapes of dust and sand. Citizens of the occupied countries of Europe emerging from war, having survived on boiled dandelion leaves, having somehow prevailed. Ella put the last book down and nodded her approval. Claire placed them on the coffee table next to the others she had brought on an earlier visit.

"You can take those with you," Ella said. She used to have Daiva stuff each book in the garbage container when she was done, until Claire, on learning their fate, intervened in a kind of horror. Claire refilled the bag with the books Ella had finished and left it by the front door, to take to the Goodwill.

Ella said, "It must be time for lunch. Wouldn't you say so, Roland?"

Ro looked up politely from his phone, where he had been checking his messages. He taught in an advanced mathematics program at a technical college, and his students often sent him e-mails about the progress of their work. Mathematics, he liked to tell Claire, was the language of the universe. Imagine, he would say to her, Einstein ran a nub of chalk across an old slate board, envisioning the structure of the universe. He predicted everything we know about it, Ro further told her, and, in doing so, he dared to refute all the old maxims. Motion, energy, magnetism. This made Ro happy, the idea of a dynamic universe, its profound equations.

Claire wished to remain a few more minutes on the couch. She and Ro had traveled two hours on the throughway; they had spent a good deal of the morning preparing the ingredients for lunch. "We only have to heat the soup and make the salad," Claire said. "It's barely noon. Do you have lunch at this hour?"

Ella frowned at the mantle clock, as if it could answer Claire's question.

Claire stood up. She knew she must go to her mother's kitchen, because her mother wanted her to. She would put the lunch things out and lean her hip against the counter, a paring knife in her hand. Daiva used to help her, cutting the stems from the spinach leaves, getting the plates down. Claire reached for her mother's TV table to give her passage to the kitchen.

After the Hunger

"I'll rest here till you're ready," Ella said.

"Do you want the TV or a magazine or one of the books?"

Ella handed her daughter her water glass to fill.

Ro had made a butternut squash soup that morning, spinning the ingredients in the Cuisinart. Ro took the container from the bag of lunch things, and Claire spooned the soup into a saucepan and set it on a burner. Ro sliced and buttered rolls for the toaster oven. Claire cut the stems from the spinach and with the dull edge of the knife scraped the leaves into a bowl. She sliced strawberries and added feta cheese and chopped walnuts, then tossed them together in a vinaigrette dressing.

She stopped once and returned to the living room to check on her mother. Ella was poised at the edge of the couch, waiting to be called to lunch. Her hands gripped the cushion on either side of her thighs. She seemed to be waiting and listening, her eyes focused on the carpet next to the TV table. She turned her head briefly when she heard Claire approach, then returned to her posture of waiting.

Claire picked up the knife from the cutting board, then put it down again.

Ro tested the soup with his index finger. He was practically a chef; he was a chef. He made beautiful meals for Claire. She stood with him in their kitchen, talking to him, following his movements from refrigerator to counter to oven, getting him a spatula or a jar of paprika, a measure of olive oil, and she turned to take down the dishes and the serving plates, and the whole meal was done, Ro already with oven mitts lifting the baking pan out. He located recipes on the Internet and she wrote up a list and they brought the bags of groceries in and later, the kitchen an aftermath of onion skins and vegetable shavings and opened spice jars and crumpled kitchen towels, they ate together in the dining room, the light softly illuminated above the table.

When Claire used to visit her mother, before she knew Ro, her mother prepared food for her with her body turned to the counter and stove, as if she were guarding a secret. She worked over the sizzle of butter in the frying pan and the intermittent, low conversation between them that Ella discouraged in her need for an ordered assembly of their meal. It seemed to Claire that this could only be achieved in rigid silence, different only in kind from the silence in which she imagined her mother prepared her meals after she and her sister, one by one, left her household. To the press of buttons on the old electric stove and the putting down of cooking utensils on its enameled body, she would call Claire from the kitchen table to take a dinner plate, warmed on a burner, from her, their hands touching briefly, the steam of vegetable and potato and baked fish rising and mingling for a moment with the breath of mother and daughter.

Claire set the dining room table and went to her mother. Ella got up from the couch, her open palms pressing the fabric, as the physical therapist had taught her to do. She ignored Claire's proffered hand. She centered her walker in front of her, then had it lead her down the hall.

After the Hunger

Claire had bundles of letters her mother had sent to her over the years, a fraction of her true correspondence when Claire, on some mission of erasure, would tear them in two and throw them away. Her mother had corresponded nonetheless. There were always telephone calls, too many telephone calls. She learned about e-mail and began forwarding Claire images, having been forwarded to her, of birds with magnificent plumage and beautiful muscular animals and the pastel raiment of suns setting and rising, as if to share the splendors of the world with her. She sent her a clip of the rescue missions by boat on 9/11 which made Claire want to weep because those acts of mercy could break one, after all the hardness and terror. A cascade of e-mails with accompaniments. Now, after her mother's return from the rehabilitation facility, Claire dutifully phoned her, and her mother soon ended the call. Claire began to mentally watch a clock, finding herself stumbling through a conversation that she knew would be done, not from its natural course but rather her mother's indifference to the rituals of salutation. Her mother seemed tired of her, bored with her. She had lost the capacity for conversation, for the mutual gift of companionship.

Ella no longer made phone calls, to Claire, to anyone. She didn't sit at her computer. She didn't address cards at Christmastime. The season had marked almost a year since her fall in the kitchen, in her sleeplessness opening the refrigerator to make a snack, the door not giving then giving suddenly and throwing her onto the linoleum floor. In the months since, her pelvic bone, having suffered three fractures, was healed. She clung to her walker. She had news of no one. Claire would note that there were no signs of visits or habitation aside from herself and Ro, and Daiva's impeccable housekeeping. She and Annie began to understand that no one called or visited anymore, after their mother's first few months out of rehab when friends brought food and books and called her on the phone, having been discouraged by her inattention, her preference for solitude. Ella used to play pinochle and cribbage with Claire, and she played almost professional-level bridge, first, years ago, in people's homes, then at the Senior Center, but all of that was gone.

Claire followed behind her mother's walker to the dining room. Ella put the walker aside and sat down. She began to eat, not waiting as she would have done, as she had taught her daughters to do. She ate hungrily. At the rehab facility she turned away from the institutional food and when she returned home three months later she seemed fragile, unsteady, as if from the shock of her own mortality. She had been put by her doctor on a low-dosage anti-depressant to improve her appetite. She had gained back her original weight. She looked healthier now; her color was good. But she had removed herself from her previous life and lived in inaccessible places, away from everyone.

Ro put his napkin in his lap. "I see you have some bulbs coming up," he said. Claire could tell he was searching for a way to begin a conversation with Ella.

"Oh," her mother said.

"They look like daffodils," Ro said.

"Possibly," Ella said.

"Is Dee helping with the heavy cleaning, with the yard?" Claire asked. "Annie told me Hugh comes over with the mower."

"She hurt her back. I haven't seen her in quite some time. I don't know what this new woman will do."

"Do you want us to stay until she arrives?"

"No, no. I'll be fine. I told the agency so."

"Would you like more salad, soup?"

Ella looked up, her faded eyes fixed on something other than Claire. She folded her hands on the tablecloth.

Claire cleared the table and brought out a bowl of fruit salad and a plate of cookies. She poured a glass of milk for her mother. Coffee was for mornings, for breakfast; Ella didn't offer any to Ro and Claire. They drank iced water. Claire served the fruit salad. She passed the plate of cookies to her mother. Her mother shook her head. Then she got up and gathered herself behind her walker.

Claire heard Ro in the living room showing Ella photographs on his phone. Claire's hands were under the tap. She had turned the hot water up; it felt strangely powerful, annihilating. She ran the sponge over a dish and placed it in the drainer. She let the water scorch her hands.

She stood in the doorway to the living room, holding a dishtowel. Ro was still showing Ella photographs. Claire thought he had shown them to her before. Her mother squinted at them. They were probably Ro's documentary photos of their yard. That winter, from their dining room windows, he had photographed four deer, their fur gray and soft-looking, that had come into the yard at midday and eaten from the shrubs. Ro had gone outside with a pot and lid and banged them at the deer. They moved away slowly, because of the cold, perhaps, or the snows that had deprived them of food. Ro had taken photos at a block party that summer on their street. He told Ella who was in each frame with Claire. Ella listened to the names, her eyes narrowed at the small screen. Ro had a photo of their dining room table, set for dinner, the planes of the water glasses and silverware caught in the slanting movement of the setting sun. Ella's attention began to drift. She sat back on the couch and looked at Ro with a plea in her eyes, as if she had been called upon to do more than she was able. He put his phone away.

Claire sat next to her. "I put the leftovers in the refrigerator," she said. "You should have enough for another lunch or two. There are some fresh ingredients in the hydrator for a salad."

"All right, dear," her mother said.

"Can I get you anything?"

"I can't think of anything." Her mother's voice was low and formal, as if she were speaking to someone else, someone not her daughter.

Claire, turning away, straightened the pile of books on the coffee table.

Ro got her coat and helped her into it. Ella mechanically followed the movement of Claire's arms into the sleeves, the shrug of her shoulders under the cloth, her fingers buttoning her coat. Her eyes had lost their fire, their complications and contradictions. Now she seemed merely withdrawn. Claire didn't know which she was more hurt by.

"When is the new woman coming?"

"At five or so. Maybe later."

"You'll be all right till then?" *We could stay*, Claire wanted to say. *We could watch a movie on the VCR.*

"Oh yes," her mother said.

Ella leaned forward so Claire could kiss her goodbye. Ro, done with that, said, "It was good to see you, Mom."

Claire said, "I'll call you tomorrow."

"Don't lock the door," Ella said. "For when the new woman comes."

Claire held the doorknob and pulled the front door closed. Her mother sat on the couch, not looking at Claire, not waving to her from the door, as she used to, as she got into the car with Ro.

They drove up the main street, then on lesser roads, to a park that Claire had visited with her mother and Annie in her childhood. She remembered the wide expanse of lawn, the ribbed trunks of the trees. Ro had to type in the address on the GPS. They were in a quiet neighborhood, the houses unassuming but surrounded by pine and oak trees and fields bordered by stone walls covered with the skeletons of vines. The parkland had been owned by one of the old families before they donated it to the town. Beyond each of the two entrances from the road was a house, one erected for the patriarch, the other for the patriarch's son. The houses were large, rising three stories, with gables and patterned wood shingles and deep porches. They were protected from the wind by hemlock trees that rose high above their rooflines.

Ro drove onto the property and stopped the car in the driveway of the patriarch's house. The house had fine bones, a fine lineage, but observed closely it looked neglected, having been moved from the purview of the family to the impersonal care of the town. Ro and Claire could see its failures, the cracks in the elaborate trim work, the latticework under the great formal frame of the house broken away. The windows were empty of curtains. The glass deflected the light, the glare as if a small flame guarding the uninhabited interior.

Ro put the car in reverse and they entered the park by the second entrance. The son's house, equally formal, equally insulted by the accrued neglects, had a guest house in the back, the shingling and windows and porch a miniature of the larger house. The light rain had turned to drizzle. Ro turned the windshield wipers briefly on then off. The houses, as if seen through a distorting lens, were still, waiting, drawn into themselves. Ro turned the steering wheel and the car moved slowly down a winding asphalt path, away from the house.

There were odd clusters of buildings beyond the family homes, where the land began to slope away from them: a clock tower museum, a toll booth (Claire reading from the plaques on the buildings), a building made of California redwood, a lighthouse, a windmill. They drove past a coliseum (Claire continuing to read the plaques), a basilica. The grandeur of the family homes seemed changed, reduced by the eccentric placement of the buildings, their inexplicable rendering on the landscape.

Ro drove on, looking for a place to park.

Claire didn't remember the buildings but she remembered the grass, the trees, a group of excited children, herself among them. There had been a man on a tractor. He had taken her for a ride, sitting her next to him on the wide seat, the deeply grooved tires making ruts in the grass as they passed over the open land. It was summer; there was the buzz of insects. He had given her a ring. The man wore a tan shirt and trousers of heavy cloth—work clothes—and she wondered even then how the ring had come into his possession. She was always standing by herself then, as if having been revealed by a blinding light. He had taken her up, sheltering her momentarily, and given her the ring. She thought—looking at it years later, trying it on again after so much time, where it still hung loosely on her finger, made of a thin metal band and fitted with an oblong turquoise stone—*where had the ring come from, and where had it gone.* It had slipped somehow out of her possession. To revisit the old places, its half-told stories that ended with drawn lips, an intake of breath, a brace of knuckles lifted softly against the mouth. She twisted the skin on her naked finger.

Ro shut the engine and they stepped out into the diminishing afternoon. The wind was against their faces. Claire put on her gloves and watch cap and Ro fitted the hood of his parka over his head. They walked away from the curious buildings, down the sloping land. Ro said, "Are you all right?" Claire said,

"Yes, yes," to the cold, the visit to her mother's house, whatever his question was, grateful for him, the man who walked with her into the past, who escorted her there, safely, and safely away, whom she could turn to and say, Yes, yes, and mean it for once. "Yes, yes," she said again, and he took her gloved hand.

They followed a path toward the river. They could see it, one of the great rivers, its course there, almost at its mouth, determined by the tides.

"See that sandbar there," Claire said. "How the water is running past it toward the Sound. It must be low tide."

There was a drop in the land, and below it a narrow dirt road, and the river, close now, through the leafless trees. This is what she remembered. The sound of the wind, the distant rushing of the river. But the wind was cold now, cutting, and they blinked their eyes against it. Across the park, where the land curved toward the horizon line, tendrils of fog enveloped a stand of trees. There were picnic tables nearby, and pits that held the ashes of old fires. They sat at one of the scarred wooden tables, holding themselves against the wind. Ro helped her up and they walked along the perimeter of the park, their heads down, their eyes tearing. Claire leaned against Ro's side. They walked into the wind and around it and through it. Over the sound of the wind was the steady movement of the river. Ro blew into his hands. They turned back, toward the car, moving up the slope of land, the wind urging them like the pressure of a hand against the back.

Ro turned on the heat and their bodies accepted the blasts of warm air. They had to use the GPS again; the roads were familiar and not familiar to Claire. She had come back with Ro and she was a poor guide, finding herself in these places of memory, these imagined places, with no sense of how to enter them, to be within them, and then to leave. There was the park and herself, the girl on the tractor, the girl under the trees. It was a place of flickering light. Ro was driving, watching the GPS, the streets on the monitor shifting and elongating with the turn of the steering wheel. He took her to the shacks once inhabited by fishermen to see middens of clam shells left by Indians on the riverbanks, the battlegrounds of the Revolutionary War, the ruined houses of the Federal Period, the Great Meadows where wildflowers grew thickly along the path and a redwinged blackbird, swaying on a high stalk, called its song. It seemed to her that he was always walking with her, taking her hand. He liked geological time, historic time, the turning of the seasons. She took him to the past, her past, and he watched her enter and emerge, enter and emerge, as if attempting to find it and then return, something finally clarified by her efforts.

Ro turned the car down the road. The clocks had changed two weeks earlier but he had switched on the headlights in the drizzling rain.

The GPS brought them to the restaurant. It was part of a cluster of stores and restaurants a few miles from Annie's house. It served a buffet from stations containing trays of steaming food. Claire and Annie both loved buffets in that they made material the idea that one could eat until one couldn't anymore, that food was in constant abundance, was constantly being replenished. That one could be hungry and hungry again and the hunger could be placated. The restaurant was big enough to support the notion that one could sit in it all evening and eat and eat some more and no one would take much notice. Claire and Ro waited at a table near the front of the restaurant. Annie arrived first and sat across from them. She smiled at them, the delicate skin around her eyes crinkling, even as it did as a child. She took off her big coat with the fake fur collar, put her big pocketbook next to her. She was taller than Claire by a few inches; she had lovely hands.

"Oh, Claire! Ro!" Annie said, and Claire was glad for her, her beautiful crinkling eyes and the way she leaned slightly toward them, anticipating the evening. Hugh arrived with their younger daughter Frankie. Frankie wore the same shapeless wool sweater she had worn each time Claire and Ro had seen her since her return to the East Coast the previous fall. She had been christened Frances Lillian but she went by the name that suited her. She had gone to Hollywood to work in an administrative office at one of the big studios, and she left it with an obsession for money: other people's money, how to get money, what people did with their money. It irritated her that she didn't have enough money to live even remotely among these people. She left her job abruptly and fitted her car with her suitcases, a clothing bag, and a shoebox of CDs.

The family recounting of her return was vague. Claire thought she had got into some kind of trouble at her job and been fired. Whatever it was, Frankie seemed to feel she had to put a whole continent between herself and her life there. She had not made other plans. She was living as the guest of her parents. She had told her older sister, Oma, that she intended to stay "until our parents kick me out," and so for Claire every event with her sister and Hugh was now also attended by her niece.

The waitress took their drink orders.

"How did you make out this winter?" Hugh asked Ro. Hugh sat between his wife and daughter. He had taken off his glasses to pinch the bridge of his nose. He managed a number of family properties. He took care of Ella's bills. She called him frequently about unfamiliar noises in the house and once about a squirrel caught behind the fireplace screen that had mysteriously vanished when Hugh arrived to confront it. It was very old school, Ella's dependence on a man. Hugh looked chronically tired.

"After the last snow we had a leak under the dormer window," Ro said. "Now we have a stain on the living room ceiling. I'm waiting for the weather to turn to get to the bottom of it."

"I kept hearing about those roof collapses farther north," Hugh said. "People taking brooms out their bedroom windows. Lucky for us we made it through."

"The winter broke a lot of records," Ro said.

"How much will a repair like that cost you?" Frankie said to Ro.

Claire looked at Frankie in surprise. An image of Frankie came to her, as a nine-year-old child, rocking her body in a fury because she was losing at a game of Monopoly. She said to Frankie, "This weather must be a shock again, after California."

"Yeah, but I'm used to it," she said.

"She won't take off that sweater though," Annie said.

"Do you remember that park, that big park?" Claire said to Annie. "We saw it again today. You and I went there as children. There are those big houses, those odd buildings."

"That park," Annie said. "At the top of a hill. We ate hot dogs there, at a big outdoor fireplace. We were there with those people, those friends of Mom's. Do you remember that dog, that stray dog. He took off with the hamburger meat, all tied up in white paper, and the father, what was his name, chased him to the ends of the park."

Claire couldn't remember. She wondered if Annie had made it up. But Annie remembered people, conversations. Claire remembered trees, wind, the sound of insects in the high grass. She wanted to tell Annie about the man with the tractor, lifting her up, but she was unsure of her memory.

Frankie was at the far end of the table, one leg under her, her body positioned above theirs, watching them as they conversed.

She said to Claire, "What's the biggest regret you ever had?"

Ro's arm brushed hers. His leg was a wall, a sturdy wall, against her own. "I don't have any regrets," she said to Frankie. "How about you?"

Frankie spat the top of her straw wrapper onto the table and stuck the straw into her iced tea. She adjusted her weight on her folded leg and suctioned the drink up the straw.

They took turns at the buffet so someone would be at the table with their coats. Everyone's plate was stacked with food. Claire and Ro were eating sushi.

"How was your visit with Mom," Annie said.

"Okay. A little distant. As usual."

"Did the new person show up?"

"Later today. Mom said she'll be all right till then. After lunch she seemed tired, so we left. She misses Daiva."

"That has to be the most difficult job in the world."

"Hand and foot. I would imagine."

Frankie cut a stuffed mushroom in half. She said, "Grammie should be converting her stocks to mutual funds. If the market tanks again she'll be in real trouble."

"What do you know about her stocks?" Claire asked.

"She has all stocks. No one her age should have all stocks."

"Frankie wants Mom to put our names on her account so we can have access to her funds," Annie said, "so we can help her make decisions about selling her stocks. Her regular account is drawn way down, paying the agency every month."

"I wouldn't know how to make a decision about selling her stocks," Claire said.

"I could help her with that," Frankie said.

Ro got up from the table.

"I think her broker should help her with that," Claire said to Annie.

"Frankie thinks she could do a better job because she wouldn't have a vested interest," Annie said. "And Mom's broker isn't having any conversations with her at all."

"If I were Mom, or anyone, really, I don't know if I'd want another person, even my children, to have access to my funds," Claire said. "That's most of her money. She could do that transfer thing instead, for, you know, later on." Claire saw her mother again, in her house, among her lamps and her furniture. She wondered what she was doing while they talked about her. Was she preparing dinner? Did she stop at her work over the stove, listening for the new woman, listening for her daughter's voice?

"Her broker said she did that but I don't see any evidence of it on her statements," Hugh said.

Claire raised an eyebrow at Hugh.

"We took in her mail while she was in rehab," Hugh said.

Claire had stabbed her palm with her chopsticks. She had meant to place them next to her plate. She closed her hand and laid it in her lap. Then she said, "She's not going to do anything at this point, anyway. She likes having those stocks. It's like the old days when you bought a stock in a good company and watched it grow. Very optimistic. Very American."

"It's more complicated now," Frankie said. "Someone in the Federal Reserve says something and the market falls. Someone in Europe does something and the market falls."

Frankie was eating a plate of General Tso's chicken now, picking up each nugget by her fingertips and biting it in half.

"She should have her house in a trust, too," Frankie said. "So it goes to you and Mom free and clear. Otherwise it'll get held up in court. You'll have to do an inventory of every little thing."

Ro returned to the table from the carving station.

"I wouldn't worry about our mother," Claire said. She didn't want to be having this conversation with Frankie. "She's not going to do anything different. No matter what you say to her."

Claire had stopped eating. There was something at the bottom of her lungs. Her breath moved around it. She had read in the history books about the Mongol warriors. They rode their compact, short-limbed horses across the steppes to conquer the great cities of the East. The warriors' saddles were made of carved wood and hung with brightly colored cloth. They wore a length of gold-colored silk wrapped tightly below the waist to keep their internal organs in place.

"I'm not worried," Frankie said. She was looking at her aunt in a covertly offended way.

Ro cut into his baked ham. He had finished the grilled pineapple slice on top of it.

Claire thought about the houses of the patriarch and the patriarch's son at the head of the park, built on the rise of land, their windows in the rain empty and reflecting a shimmering glare of light. Frankie would be there, in her mother's house, overseeing the appraisal and removal of objects, overseeing Claire's grief. She would want to know her mother's liquid assets. She would have suggestions for Claire and Annie on how to invest them. Claire would look up, trying to find her mother in the house, and see Frankie holding up a dish, weighing it, having reduced her mother to a blanket, a pot holder, a bowl, a sheet of paper with an accounting of her worth.

Opening Day

Her mother had gone away. Perhaps that was her response to her encounter with mortality. Perhaps she was trying in her way to be honest with Claire about being old and often sleepless and hearing sounds in the night.

Einstein asked the profound questions of the physical world and it returned to him the shape and substance of the universe. The Mongols created a calendar for their vast empire in order to manage the movement of armies and trade goods. Her mother found order in silence that she leaned into as a refuge, a place of grassland and solar wind, the old abandoned patrimony vivid and halted in time, where she cooked hot dogs over an open fire in a park for her children, the curl of her young daughter's hair in her cupped hand.

Frankie had returned to the buffet. She stood at a station, a plate balanced on her open hand. It was completely dark outside. The front window was streaked with drizzle. When Frankie was a child, she had seemed to be Claire's adversary. She cheated at Monopoly. Claire pointed out that her roll of the dice did not lead to Boardwalk but one space after it. She cheated at tennis. She walked off the court, leaving Claire gaping after her, rather than play fair. Claire's mother had been her familiar, at least in terms of the old ways, the old manners. It was the only way Claire would understand her, finally, that this is what she had loved, the correct performance of a life. Her mother would turn to her sometimes, while Claire waited for her, and stroke her hair. But Frankie would be there, speaking not to her but about her mother's things, her mother's money, as she tried to locate her mother among her forsaken objects, so carefully put away.

She said to Annie, "There was a man there, on a tractor. That day in the park."

Annie shook her head. She was eating an oyster.

"I saw it," Claire said, "from that seat high up. The fire pit, the hot dogs. There were balloons, all those other children, some sort of celebration."

"It was opening day, probably," Annie said.

"Opening day," Claire said. The dog, a short-haired mixed breed, drawing its paws to the picnic table and closing its teeth around the string that held the butcher's paper, then turning its gaunt flanks and loping across the great lawn. Everything so small, high up, so far away. The dog dropping to its haunches and wriggling under the brambles with its quarry. The man's broad hands, lifting her up, up, and she small beside him, leaning into the metal seat, up, above the tumult of opening day, the smell of the cooking fires and the river, as the heavy tires tracked across the grass.

.

The Ruins

Lise and her husband Dom traveled in the open jeep west through town on Highway 89A. The wind blew their hair but at the traffic lights there was no wind and Lise waited for the light to change, for the wind created by the speed of the jeep to pick up again. Lise and Dom and the other four passengers clung to the bars bolted to the interior of the jeep or pressed their hands against its side. Their guide drove with a certain recklessness. He was athletically built and his skin was a dark golden color from the sun. He looked to Lise to be in his early thirties. Lise wondered how he felt about driving a jeep full of tourists for a living. Not while speeding through traffic, on the way into the desert, but later, when the day was done and he was unfolding the bills he had earned in tips and placing them one on top of the other. If he looked to himself and saw only this. But this was a way of thinking Lise had brought from the East, she reminded herself, and it did not belong in this landscape of red sandstone rock, the horizon ringed by buttes and mesas and formations of fantastic geologic invention, and so she tried to stop thinking. She lifted her face to the wind.

Their guide downshifted and took the jeep off the highway and onto a gravel road. The jeep lurched and settled again, and the passengers, tossed like so many pebbles, found themselves sitting in slightly different places than a moment ago. Everyone carried a pack. The driver, before boarding the jeep, had stashed his backpack under the empty passenger seat. Lise held a backpack on her lap by its straps. In it was a bottle of water, a tube of sunscreen in case she and Dom needed an extra application, a pair of binoculars, a camera, a guidebook, and a King James Bible with a worn leather cover. She and Dom each wore, slung around their necks, a canvas sun hat that Lise had purchased back home for their trip. They put on their hats when the jeep turned off the highway, into the desert. A man sat behind the driver's seat, against the side of the jeep, carrying a backpack strapped over his shoulders. Across from Lise and Dom were a man and two women, each with a small pack clipped around their waists. The jeep bounced again and the slumbering pain in Lise's left leg turned like a gyre. She took Dom's arm.

In a parking lot behind a bank and a real estate office, before the tour was to begin, the driver jovially asked for introductions, and everyone obliged, but Lise's intelligence about the others nevertheless was slim. The driver's name was Josh, and she felt that it was an alias, though if asked she wouldn't be able to explain why. The lone man's name was Steve. Steve said nothing when asked where he was from

The Ruins

but instead ran his hand moodily down the stubble on his cheek. Dom introduced himself and Lise in the even, formal voice she had heard him use over the course of their long marriage with strangers and with subordinates at his work. He gave their home as Warwick, Rhode Island, but she supposed that was like saying New Haven, Connecticut, or Bath, Maine—someplace on the known map. The three passengers who sat together in the jeep each had said their names clearly but shyly, as if having been called upon for a recitation. They spoke in flat voices that rose at the end of each name, as if making a wonderful pronouncement.

Lise was so busy listening to their voices that she didn't catch their names. The man in the group told the others that they were from San Antonio, Texas. They had creamy brown skin and wore aviator sunglasses. The women's black hair fell straight down their backs. The man's hair was pulled back in a ragged ponytail. They wore scuffed sneakers and faded T-shirts that bunched over the waistbands of their jeans. They were overweight, the man more so than the women, as if deliberately so, as if from an old rebuke of hardship. *Brother, sister, sister-in-law?* Lise wondered. Their body language gave no hint of a familial connection. Josh ushered the group into the jeep and started the engine. The three from San Antonio sat formally across from Lise and Dom and the jeep sped out of the parking lot.

They were traveling now on a one-lane forest road with old tire marks in the dust. Josh braked the jeep marginally as it crossed a cattle guard. Lise looked across the landscape and saw no animals, only the red rocks against the sky and a foreground of rough gravel and stunted-looking shrubs. Josh slowed the jeep and turned halfway in his seat, as if having remembered his charges. The stirred dust settled behind the wheels. The landscape seemed to settle with it, into view: the flat land held by a buttress of rock that was striped with orange and red, the great striations like wounds, like markers of the slow workings of time. In profile, mouthing words, Josh looked as if his voice had been captured by mischievous spirits, unawares. Lise looked to where Josh was pointing and saw in the distance the imposing red rocks of a canyon wall, and slabs of rock lying below, disordered and broken as if dropped from the sky; and nearer, a desert floor she recognized from her guidebook of manzanita shrubs and yucca plants, the pale yellow flowers hanging like bells. Along the dirt road and in the near distance were green-gray clusters of prickly pear cactus, a large yellow flower that had come with the advent of spring blooming at the top of each pad. The pads were pierced with spines that looked like small lances protecting the flowers.

Dom took the straps of the backpack from under Lise's hands. He unzipped a compartment and took the camera from it and placed the viewfinder to his eye. He suddenly looked as strange to Lise as the landscape, something that hadn't before been imagined. She heard the shutter click and wondered if, later, on seeing the photograph, she would find the landscape apprehended, because she did not yet have eyes to see it. It was a mystery and a terror and a thing of beauty, like birth, like God, the experience of it on the rough dirt road unexpected and disturbing.

The jeep came to the end of the forest road. Josh braked briefly and turned the steering wheel smoothly to the right. They had been traveling west, and now they traveled north on another dirt road. "Agave," Josh shouted as the jeep sped by a plant with spikes of dusty yellow, saucer-like flowers rising from a cluster of green-blue leaves. Lise leaned forward, into his voice. "It blooms once, at the end of its life cycle," he said, "and there it is." It was the only one on the landscape, a weedy-looking, tenacious thing, reaching for the sun. Dom held the camera up and clicked the shutter.

The man with the beard stubble leaned into the flow of air coming over the windshield. The three passengers across from Lise and Dom sat tranquilly, as if used to certain discomforts, as the wheels rolled over small rocks in the road. Lise shifted in her seat and the pain in her leg reached forward with a tentative claw. Dom took her hand. He began to take it to his lips, as he often did, driving with her in his car or sitting with her over dinner, and she felt the familiar rotation of her arm as he moved it first toward him, then up, and brought her fingers to his mouth. But he stopped and returned her hand to her lap, as if having remembered that they were traveling in a jeep across a desert with strangers.

Lise looked up at the rocks. The striations of color, now white and yellow, orange and red, had a startling majesty. There seemed to be no water on the landscape, no wildlife, only a few cactus plants, and stalks bearing flowers that come forth once in a lifetime. But to be among the rocks, if one dared, that were red like Mars, like a vision across an unbridgeable space. Not like the East where there is color in grass and tree and flower, and in winter only the gray of boulder and tree trunk, but a place that glowed red and orange like fire in the procession of the equinoxes. Lise looked into the distance, into crevices and overhangs, as if looking for Mithras, born from a rock, whose followers practiced forgotten rites in underground temples. But there was nothing, just the startling blue sky, the eternal rocks, and the desiccated ground, as they traveled farther north on another forest road. The pain in Lise's leg was now finding shape and dimension. She felt a quick stab like the stab of a pick in the muscle of her thigh.

The evening before, Lise and Dom sat at an outdoor table in an Italian restaurant situated among a group of stores selling carpet remnants and lawn ornaments, having arrived at the restaurant by climbing a set of wooden stairs. Lise tried to sit in the chair that Dom pulled out for her, but the muscles in her leg had locked and she looked at Dom imploringly and he knew then to leave her alone. She put her palms flat on the table and sat sideways in her chair, waiting for the muscles to relax.

Earlier in the day she and Dom had reached their hotel by rented car after a visit to the Salt River, from where, by letter, Dom's Aunt Sarah had summoned them to her house, roofed in Spanish tile and surrounded by gardens grown from seeds she had brought forty years before from the East. Aunt Sarah sat on her sofa and ran her blue-veined hand over and over the photo Lise had brought of their son Julian, taken at seventeen, the year before he became ill. Aunt Sarah rose and withdrew from a drawer in a side table a Bible that had belonged to her late husband, Herbert, given to him by the members of his church in Dalkeith to carry with him on the ocean crossing to the United States. Inside its front cover she had placed a sealed envelope addressed to Julian. She sat next to Lise again and delivered the Bible into Lise's hands and touched her damp eyelids with trembling fingers.

Dom was speaking to Lise of their trip as they waited for their dinner at the table on the patio. "It will do us a world," he said. They had ordered beers. Dom clicked his glass against hers. "When else would we have had the chance to be here if it hadn't been for old Aunt Sarah demanding an audience," Dom said rhetorically again, as he had said while looking up airline schedules and taking their suitcases down from the attic. But to Lise the landscape seemed treacherous—rock and gravel, desert and a hard, cloudless sky—a world unforgiving of error. She did not know if it was a place that could provide whatever Dom had hoped for her.

At home she listened to her son Julian's breathing as he lay on the couch tucked under an afghan, so he wouldn't be far away from her during the day, so his bedroom wouldn't seem a sick room, a place he had been banished to. His breath was quick and shallow, like a sleeping kitten's, spent from the top of his lungs. Or she couldn't hear it at all as he slept, hours of heavy sleep where he didn't move after she had brought him home again from the hospital, but then suddenly his eyes were open and looking at her calmly as if he had been awake all along under the closed lids, as she worriedly knelt next to him, ready to place her hand searchingly over his heart. The chemo exhausted him and made him ill; he retched behind the bathroom door while Lise, as if struck, sobbed silently into her hands in the hall. When he slept again she went to brush his hair from his forehead, out of habit, as she used to, but his hair had fallen out, and his eyebrows and eyelashes were gone.

He was the youngest and most beautiful of their five children, a boy of eighteen, tall and broad-shouldered, with hair like flax. In high school he was a lacrosse player, netting the ball with his stick and rising into the air like a young god, then hurling the ball like a discus toward the goal. The diagnosis of a malignant tumor had come after she had, on a hunch like a terrible knowledge, taken him to see a bone man after his complaint of a dull pain in the knee was diagnosed by the family doctor as a sports injury and the prescribed therapy had failed. That was nine months ago. He had lost thirty-five pounds. On the couch, sleeping under the afghan, he looked like an old man, his skin wrinkled and yellow, his body a shade of itself.

"Do you know," Dom said, lifting his glass of beer, "that some people believe there are energy sources among the rocks here. People apparently come from all over the world to experience them." Lise looked up at him, pulled away from her thoughts, as she knew he had hoped. "There's supposed to be some connection, some exchange, you see"—he held his hands up demonstrably, or helplessly—"between a person and the place where this energy originates." He looked at her, amused by his own credulity. But he went on, "I suppose the tour tomorrow won't take us to one of those places exactly, but we should see what the day brings us. A change of scenery if nothing else."

Lise put her hand over Dom's and wrapped her fingers into his palm.

The scar on her son's leg was raw-looking, red, slow to heal, like an injury to the beauty of his youth that continued to declare itself, where the surgeon had opened his knee and, working upward to the femur, removed tissue and bone. The surgeon had come to the waiting room, his mask hanging from his neck by the cotton straps, his surgeon's scrubs disconcertingly immaculate, to tell Lise and Dom that the leg had been saved, the knee rebuilt, and the shortened femur bone attached by screws to a titanium rod. Lise had to help her son now to the bathroom, and she cut his food and watched over him as he ate. She helped him into the car for the drive to the hospital for a cycle of therapy in, it seemed, an eternity of cycles where a needle was inserted into his arm and a bag hung from an IV stand slowly dripped poison into his body. A cell could be anywhere, the doctor had told them, a rogue cell, which had to be found and destroyed.

Most mornings Dom went to work to try to earn a living so they could all go on. He knotted a tie under the collar of a freshly laundered dress shirt and went quietly into his son's bedroom, as if into a kind of darkness, before making the commute on the throughway. She helped Julian out of the car and braced her arm across his chest and helped him into the house and onto the couch. He curled his body up the way he used to when he was a child and she held him in her arms and sang "Little Boy Blue." She checked his forehead for fever. There was always the fear of infection. A slight cold could be his undoing. She kept teammates and classmates away, extended family away, his brothers and sisters away. Even Dom kept a certain distance, more, Lise knew, from hurt, as if his heart had been flayed at seeing what had been done to his boy. Then, when Julian slept, exhausted, or didn't sleep at all under his closed lids, she would, on the pretense of shifting his weight, of adjusting a pillow, take him into her arms and hold him, and hear his breath pull quickly in and out, like an injured animal.

The pain in her leg had come on with Julian's diagnosis. It seemed natural to her, a sympathetic condition, but once when the pain held her like a pair of jaws she fell hard on the driveway and felt the shock of the fall with her whole body. Dom took her to the same hospital where Julian was being treated and the doctor told her that her bones were bruised, quite badly, quite beyond the expected outcome of such a fall. He called the pain in her leg and the corresponding muscle weakness a nervous response to a traumatic event. An injury of the nerves.

Lise and Dom had finished their beers. The service in the restaurant was slow. The patio overlooked a ravine, and beyond it were the red rocks, caught in the light of the setting sun. Dom was holding her hand and looking into her eyes. He was telling her what else they could do on their imposed holiday: they had the rented car, they could drive anywhere. Up into the San Francisco Peaks. Or to the Canyon de Chelly. They could buy a heap of turquoise. He would buy her a necklace. He would buy Julian a carving, a charm to wear from his dad, on a silver chain, why not, of some old deity to protect him. A New World rebuttal to Uncle Herbert's notions of God. Lise absently turned the wedding band on Dom's finger, a flicker of a smile on her face. A hawk flew on the air currents above the ravine. Lise watched it climb in front of the rocks. The sun moved over the rocks in a band of light, leaving some of the formation in shadow, some lit, as if a living force had crossed it. A rainbow, borne of light, arced over the ravine. Dinner came, and the sun set, and the rocks retreated into darkness. Lise looked toward the veiled rocks that she could no longer imagine.

Dom was watching her. She was a casualty of Julian's illness, she knew. It was as if she held him with all her might and in doing so had taken some part of his illness upon herself. The months had gone on like the slow circuit of a mill stone. The infusions had worked; her care had worked. Julian had been off chemo for a month. There had been only one scare, a fever; Lise took him to the hospital and after two days it was brought under control. His suffering had had some meaning, at least in the most basic medical terms. He would survive, practically intact. She thought of the turquoise stone mined from the earth that Dom wanted to give her, a keepsake from a trip to a land of stone. She knew he was telling her that she would have to decide what to bring back with her, impoverishment or strength, fear or courage, not the courage to survive catastrophe, but to live beyond it. Hadn't she by the force of her will, or so Dom had told her, helped make their son well again? He was free from the knife, off the IV, he would go to college in the fall, having spent what should have been his first year there wrestling with the devil instead. He just had to accept his fortune, fatten up, grow back his hair, and toss a football again in the back yard with his dad. There would be regular visits to the doctors, of course. He would be followed. He would live his life aware of the miraculous, of chance and fear.

Lise sat back in her chair. The pain in her leg throbbed once or twice. Small white lights strung from the patio roof had come on with the fall of darkness. Dom looked so handsome in the light. He was leaning toward her. He wanted something back again. An ordinary day, a hawk flying, a rainbow formed from particles of light. She looked into his eyes. She said to him, "Take me back to the hotel and hold me." He stood up and held her chair out and she placed her hand around his arm and he led her down the stairs to their rented car.

Driving north, Josh brought the jeep to an abrupt stop in a gravel lot. The passengers climbed out. Dom took Lise's hand and helped her step from the running board to the ground. Lise felt something in her leg, sharp like a sharp object. She encountered the pain as she went up and down stairs and into rooms on unfamiliar errands and into the violently busy hospital lobby and its corridors and across waiting rooms and now on the hard ground among the red rocks. The man with the stubble bent over a match flame and lit a cigarette. Josh said genially, "Hey, no smoking here." The man crushed out the cigarette with his boot tip, and Josh picked up the flayed butt and put it in a plastic bag, which he then zipped into his backpack. The three from San Antonio looked in embarrassment at the ground.

Josh walked out of the lot, and the others followed. Lise pulled her arms through the straps of the backpack. Dom took her hand again. They climbed a path along the rock. Josh stopped and waited for the small group to collect. They looked at him expectantly, but he only turned and led them upward.

Juniper and pinyon pine grew among the rocks, the branches stunted above the ancient trunks. Lise could hear the people from San Antonio breathing regularly, huff, huff, huff, behind her. They spoke to each other in low voices. It was not Spanish or English. *Who are you*, she wondered. They had faces like Indian faces, broad and calm. Their voices were like music. The group traveled on. Lise held onto branches and the bark of tree trunks on the mild ascent. The trail dissolved into stepping stones and she braced her hiking boots along them and pressed her palm against a vertical rock. *Good to touch something*, she thought, *to know something this way*. The presence in her leg was quiet now. It did not announce itself with any predictability. At home, someone in a room in a house across the street played "You Are My Sunshine" endlessly on the piano. There was a black scrape on her car bumper, found after returning to the parking lot from buying groceries. She walked every morning, before Dom woke, before she went to Julian's room, when the streets were empty of traffic and she could hear in the trees the song of the cardinals and the screeching jays and the chuckling call of squirrels, and the pain slept within her. But then she would lie down, tired and falling, falling into dreams, at the end of the day, waiting for Dom to return to her, or opening the day's mail, and the pain would bore into her like something endlessly turning. She stopped on the trail to catch her breath. Dom took the bottle of water from their backpack and offered it to her.

Josh led them upward, off the trail, to a series of stone steps carved into the rock, where they had a harder ascent. The pain slumbered in Lise's body but its presence within her made the muscles in her leg begin to lock. She leaned into Dom's arm. The man with the stubble spit into the trees. Dom waved the others around them, and one of the women, removing her sunglasses, looked with concern at Lise, making small noises of sympathy with her tongue. Lise looked into her dark brown eyes and smiled at her. The woman had deep lines at the corners of her eyes and between her eyebrows that seemed to flatten and return her face to an earlier beauty when she shyly returned Lise's smile. Lise regarded the stone steps under her feet, measured their distance, and began to climb again.

The ruins were straight ahead, built along a cliff. Broken columns of sand-colored bricks looked as if they had been toppled or smashed. There was the outline of a doorway in the brick, the outline of a window. Josh stood at a place with a clear view of the ruins and the group collected around him. "We don't know much about the people who built these dwellings," he said. "They're called the Sinagua, but that's a Spanish name, it means 'without water,' and it was given to them by an American archaeologist. So you see how far away we are from history. The Sinagua lived here for about two hundred years, and then they vanished. The dwellings had been abandoned. Some stresses—internal or external, we can only guess—must have overwhelmed them." Josh looked down, as if he had been required to tell this story too many times and he was trying to locate again the meaning within it. "They disappeared a hundred years before the arrival of the Spanish," he continued. "They may have been eliminated by enemy tribes. They may have moved on because of drought. No one can really know."

The group looked toward the fallen brick. Dom took the binoculars from the backpack and handed them to Lise. She pushed her canvas hat from her head and held the binoculars to her eyes. The ruins came into sharp focus; they were too near, like a catastrophe. She was met with disordered bars of brick and dust and silence in the mild heat of the day. One of the women stood close to her, shading her eyes with her hand, straining to see the ruins. It was the woman who had looked with concern at Lise as she leaned against Dom on the stone steps, parrying the pain in her leg. Her son had survived. He would be well again. She was on vacation with her husband. They would see a different landscape, he had said. A different point of view. They had left Julian in the charge of his two elder sisters, a physical therapist, and a Visiting Nurse. Lise held out the binoculars to the woman and said, "Would you like to use these?" The woman smiled at her and made a brief gesture of acquiescence. She politely took the binoculars from Lise's outstretched hand and held them to the bridge of her nose. She scanned the fallen brick, the outlines of abandoned rooms. She took the binoculars from her eyes and looked up at the cliff, then returned the binoculars to Lise, nodding formally to her. Lise held out the binoculars to the other woman and the man but they shook their heads and took a half-step backward, as if in doing so they were attempting to right the transgression of their companion.

Josh brought them across a face of rock and they climbed upward, above a grouping of pinyon pine, and they were suddenly looking up into a curved wall that seemed blank at first, a mute formation of rock. Dom followed the line of the wall with the binoculars. He handed them to Lise. Carved forms came into view, figures; slowly, as if emerging from under water. There were tightly formed spirals, and circles like moons or suns, and zig-zags like lightening bolts; stick figures of men with their upper arms held out and their forearms drawn up; the outlines of hands. There were pictures of animals, turtles and lizards and deer. Lise saw an elementary face, a circle and within it three small circles and a curved line for the lips; more figures of men with their upper arms held out and their forearms hung downward. The pictures seemed random, telling a story, if there was one, that couldn't be read. Lise gave the binoculars to the woman who stood now like a familiar next to her. She took them again politely. She held the binoculars tightly against her eyes and scanned the rock. She looked at the roof of the formation, and across it, and down the cliff wall. The others shaded their eyes with their hands and squinted upward. The woman brought the binoculars down and abruptly turned away, toward the fringe of pine.

"The two sites," Josh said, adjusting his backpack on his shoulders, "rather surprisingly, aren't related. The rock drawings date back about six thousand years, long before the Sinagua. It is thought that the pictures were made by a number of different prehistoric peoples, as if they all used the same canvas, as it were." He looked up at the rock face that did not speak to him.

The woman returned the binoculars to Lise. She looked at Lise's leg. She regarded Lise questioningly. Lise touched her thigh, as if demonstrating to the woman where the pain lived, and said, "My leg bothers me quite often. Sometimes I think I don't know quite what I will do." The woman pushed her lips together and frowned. Lise did not think she spoke English very well. But she understood that Lise was in pain; she seemed to want Lise to understand that. Lise looked upward and tried to see the drawings in the rock with her naked eyes. She wondered who had made the drawings, priest or supplicant, poet or hunter; if a woman had made any of them. *Was there a picture of a woman giving birth to a beautiful child and what is the image for sorrow.*

She looked at the sky, beyond the mute rock, and even its color seemed dense, impenetrable. They were leaving now. Josh was leading them away, down a series of stones like stairs, and then to a descent over rock and sand and the roots of trees, back to the waiting jeep. Lise took Dom's hand and they stepped slowly over the uneven ground. The others in the group had hiked downward and out of view on a path around a juniper tree. Lise and Dom were alone on the path with the woman. She had stayed with them, solicitous of Lise, of the pain she carried. Now she walked before them, bending over the path, lifting small rocks and pieces of branch from it into the underbrush. Her black hair shone in the afternoon light. She was thanking them, Lise knew, for the use of the binoculars. Lise wondered what the woman had searched for, with her naked eyes, among the drawings on the rocks. She stopped and looked back, toward the rocks, which were shielded now by the branches of the pines, removed again into the silence of time. Then Lise turned and rejoined the procession downward, Dom now behind, having relinquished his place to the woman who led them.

Lise stepped carefully over the roots of a tree. The pain in her leg was like the stab of a knife, like a wound. But her son would be well again; her son had survived. Lise followed the woman who led them down from the ruins, as if there could be no other way to return. The sky was indigo. A juniper tree held green clusters of needles above a dust-brown trunk twisted as if by the force of the desert, as if by a stinging wind. The woman walked before them, her faded T-shirt falling outward like a robe, her black hair streaming along the curve of her back, as she cleared the path for Lise among the rocks.

The Sisters

The kitchens of the well-to-do are elaborately appointed—stainless steel pots and frying pans, serving bowls with designs of flowers in bloom and of fish floating against a wash of cerulean blue, trays of painted wood. Crystal water goblets, pressed glass dessert dishes, and soup ladles with designs raised against a background of silver. There are cookbooks by famous chefs, cookbooks about famous restaurants. Otherwise the reading material of the well-to-do is mostly a discouragement. Thrillers, mysteries, romance, every sort of modern-day pulp fiction. All in hardback in floor-to-ceiling bookcases in living rooms overlooking the Sound. The best collection Mac and I found was in the home of a doctor, an endocrinologist—we could tell by his medical books—he read widely from the canon. We bought quite a few of his books: a set of Faulkner's novels in an embossed case, *Works of Herman Melville*, Cooper's *The Last of the Mohicans*, Flaubert's *A Sentimental Education*. We do not often find fiction in these homes. We are starting to see a concern at work here, hidden or no, about the heart laid bare. Who can abide the fate of literature's great figures? It is the essence and burden of our humanity, and who can truly endure it? In another house I find a book on natural remedies. Then I remember that I already have purchased a number of books on home remedies, natural medicine, holistic medicine, healing that is spontaneous, healing that is remarkable, healing that is extraordinary. A preoccupation I am surprised to find I share with the well-off, the comfortable, and the insulated.

Clothing hanging in the spacious closets of foyers and master bedrooms is another disappointment—bulky cotton jackets, unwieldy neckties, dresses of polyester and rayon. The houses are magnificent, but the minds of their owners, at least as evidenced from what remains on bookshelves and in closets, seem narrow and weedy, suffering from a lack of vision. But then of course the best surely has been put away or taken away long before the doors of these homes are opened to strangers. Mac and I pass the artwork on the walls—blurry dabs of paint that we don't want to take the time to comprehend; paintings of seascapes; a lithograph. We like the walls of our own house—situated not that far in the measurement of geography from the homes we walk into, invited by a posting on the Internet or signs along a road—interrupted occasionally by an etching of a heron, its shoulders hunched existentially, standing on one foot in a marsh; a Chinese paper cutting of butterflies and dragonflies hovering over a waterscape of lilies and lily pads; a line drawing of a herd of horses that seem to be running downward from the sky.

It is as if, walking through the rooms of the houses along the shore, or hidden among the meadows and rolling hillsides of the shoreline towns, so well proportioned, so exactingly constructed, one understands immediately that the expenditure of the imagination was on walls and floors and on chairs fitted with damask, and having been spent before it could ever be urged forth again. But here perhaps the uninteresting, the overlooked, is too a design, like the arrangement of furniture in a room: the predictable books and second-drawer clothing a protection against a betrayal of one's true monetary value; one's true life. Then who are we, who are we to judge the dead, the newly divorced, the unaccounted for?

Mac took me driving on a Saturday morning. He took me, he likes to say, for a drive. Most roads we didn't know, we still don't know. Woods, the rush of trees, stone walls that run perpendicular to the road, all out of the usual order. To the north there's a route that transverses the entire state. We entered it at a round-about, drove on. We noticed a sign affixed to the trunk of a tree. Fifteen-by-eighteen-inch cardboard, electric pink, directions written in lime green. We followed the sign. Then another. We arrived at a house, very old, built on a foundation of fieldstone, with stone steps leading to the front door, itself massive and heavy, held by hammered iron hinges. Wide pitch-pine floors. A number of people were walking in and out of the rooms, sitting in a chair, testing it, standing back from a painting or a table, taking its measure.

The back room, the largest room, overlooked a salt marsh, an endless perspective of seagrass. I sat in one of the chairs and watched the wind disturb the grasses. In the kitchen, among its anomalous granite countertops and recessed lighting, Mac spotted a plate, almost entirely hidden under another plate. He pulled it carefully away, held it at arm's length, turned it over, read the lettering below the mark. He called to me across the threshold, a low note, just above a whisper: "Jet." I turned reluctantly from the seagrass. Mac held up the plate. It was the color of cream. A marriage plate, a Lenox plate, large and having its own particular weight in the hand, decorated with ribbons and chiming bells in high relief. We bought it for $12 from a pleasant woman who sat in the front room behind a folding table, a metal cashbox at her elbow. She wrapped it for us in newspaper and slipped it into a plastic bag. I wrote our e-mail address on the legal pad on the table. We drove home with the plate on the floor of the car behind the passenger seat, aware of its beauty. We baked an Italian pear cake that evening and placed it in the precise center of the plate. We ate it with a good dessert wine. So we began.

There are lesser sales closer to home. Tag sales, yard sales, moving sales. Mac and I always look for books. The better books come from these lesser events, these lesser homes. This we cannot explain. The books at every sale go for the same price: $2 for a hardback and $1 for a paperback. This also we cannot explain. From a book I found at one of these sales I learned of the New England states' involvement in the slave trade and the ivory trade. And in others Michael Pollan's many declarations about food—people read all of his books. I found a book of stories and journals by M.F.K. Fisher, with a black-and-white cover photograph of a flower in a vase and its elongated shadow, about the deprivations of the Great Depression and the early years of the war, and running beneath them, alongside and around them were the other, deeper hungers, so much more difficult to describe.

Some books were just beautiful, and so we bought them: books on quilts and rivers and feng shui and the ruined plantations of the South, the great sailing voyages of the 19th century, the art in the Hermitage before the Nazis looted it, Audubon's watercolors, photographs of America—of people, trains, cars, fields—or what the photographers think America is. We buy every picture book we come across. The books are stacked on the coffee table in our living room. We carry objects out of these houses in plastic bags, in paper bags, under our arms, in a backpack, in a canvas carry-all, and our bookcases and tabletops and cabinets slowly begin to fill. But of course what we are really a part of is a dismantlement, a disruption. Someone is being taken away or someone is moving away or someone has passed away.

In an old basket under a side table in a house in the interior I found two paperback tour books on Connecticut. As we were new when we first started inexplicably but it seems now inevitably spending our Saturday mornings walking around in other people's yards, garages, and houses, I purchased the tour books so I would know something else about the state, what it was like now that I had returned. At least the more apparent facts than I used to know. Mac has brought me back here, he says, to help in meeting the approach of the inevitable. I suppose I think the search for beauty will somehow forestall it. Mac looked through the house for CDs. He considers a Saturday morning a success if he finds CDs. They sell for $1 or $2. He has five shelves of CDs now, above the shelf that holds the CD player, and more in his basement work room (with its tag sale CD player), and most of them have come from our Saturday mornings. When he finds CDs we play a few on our way home. We listen to Bruce Springsteen, Norah Jones, the Grateful Dead, the songs of George and Ira Gershwin. At home we play "Don't Know Why" and dance together on the stone floor.

On Saturday we drive to visit my mother. We drive on the throughway. The exits flow by. There is nothing to distract me. We knock on her front door, turn the doorknob. My mother does not come toward me to greet me. She has begun to turn away from me. We have brought for lunch a large pepperoni pizza from Captain's Pizza. She eats hungrily then seems to fall away—from us, from her attending to the world. She has let her hair grow out, it is starkly white now. I no longer recognize her hands.

We went again on the roads of the interior, driving along dense borders of trees. We started looking for more Lenox. It has a glow, like the glow of flesh. One can identify it by the thin band of gold along its rim. Food looks inviting on it. I am able to eat from it without sadness. We are careful with our knives and forks.

After the Hunger

We never know where we will find it, or even if we are in fact at that moment looking for it. It just appears on a countertop or a shelf. In a house having belonged to a professor of Judaic studies at the university (there were professional journals, a rocking chair with the university seal, the old books of Jewish literature and history), we found a Lenox vase and bowl among the disorder of the rooms he once inhabited. Everything seemed to have been taken down from walls and out of cabinets and placed on old sofas and patio furniture and utility tables. Someone was running the sale, a professional and her assistants who tallied prices and wrapped purchases, but the house, with concrete steps poured so imperfectly that the railing was hung in warning with yellow police tape, had been thrown open, as it were, as if while in the midst of some internal upheaval.

A man was seated on the floor near a sofa, going through a box of papers. He spoke to us in an affronted tone. "These papers should be in the university library, not here," he said. We murmured our agreement. Something had occurred too suddenly for the papers to have been taken to the university. Or perhaps nothing had occurred for some time. We picked our way through the house. I found the vase on a table among tired kitchen items, and the bowl in a cabinet stacked with plastic dinner plates. We paid $25 for them. We took them home. I put the vase on the sideboard. Mac placed sweetbriar cut from the roadside and a gold-colored Christmas ornament in the bowl. He set it on a table in the living room.

We had begun to leave our e-mail address with the people who run the estate sales. Now we get one or two notices each week. I type the words in Google that will lead us to the other sales. "There are so many," I say to Mac. I have begun to be alarmed.

This work, this inquiry, whatever it is, is an efficient business. You go in, look around, pick up something, purchase it, the people running the estate sale or the tag sale or whatever sale it is help you wrap it, and you leave. It is a fast-moving underground capitalist enterprise. The houses, the great houses, now empty of any memory, any connection, have no smell, as if no one had lived there, sweated, smoked, had a drink, spilled something, made a roast, burned a piece of toast. What has taken place in these homes that the professionals now come to in order to manage the dispersal of their possessions? Sometimes one knows what has happened, from small clues left behind. But you never know the real story. It is not meant for you.

Everyone is polite, everyone speaks softly. But maybe it is because Mac and I are always late, as if the enterprise requires some internal preparation, or as if a certain reluctance accompanies us, that we miss the first waves. A few times, having arrived early or having arrived at the wrong moment, we witnessed the proprietary surveying of a table of knickknacks, the refusal to let someone by in a narrow hallway, the way some people are able to own all of the space around them so that you are in effect told to look elsewhere, in the search for something that is impossible to find.

After the Hunger

My mother likes sugar-free vanilla wafers and chocolate-covered cookies that come in pleated cups in a large colorful box. She is mildly diabetic but eats them anyway. Sometimes I forget and bring her a jar of marmalade or raspberry preserves. I place two chilled mangoes on her kitchen table and take from my pocketbook a plastic bag containing cardamom seed powder, purchased at the health food store, and tell her it is delicious sprinkled on the fruit of the mango. She looks at me with disbelieving eyes.

Whatever it is we have come to, it is a place of cleavage, of finalities. In the great houses, lamps, pieces of furniture are arranged not for living but for sale; whole areas of rooms are a blank space. There are closed doors, sometimes with tape in the shape of an X over them or a handwritten sign reading Do Not Enter. There are of course no letters folded into envelopes addressed in script, no post cards, no framed photographs, no scrapbooks or awards or diplomas or family albums. All of this has been put away or taken away. The real lives, the true possessions are hidden or gone. But you can see what people liked to look at in glass cabinets and the type of furniture they favored and what was important—a large efficient and beautiful kitchen or a view of the Sound or heavy drapes falling to the floor in folds. One feels a brief sense of safety, of predictability, standing in the large rooms with their carved moldings and deep sills. But once in a home on the shore, we saw in one of the upstairs rooms the accessories of misfortune—a wheelchair, a pair of metal forearm crutches. No one is exempt.

I try to interest my mother in conversation. I realize I have lost the art. I fumble through a recounting of my week or try to tell her about a book I'm reading. My mother is silent. She sits on the couch as if waiting for something to occur, something that doesn't involve me. She has no news. Mac stays away, even while in the same room. I am angry at him, I want him to help me, but he seems to understand that my mother has other preoccupations, that it is death that interests her now.

The objects we bring home have no provenance—were they a wedding gift, a birthday gift, a purchase from a department store? I give them all a provenance, all except the CDs and the books—the objects we find and take away have one now, abbreviated as it is. In a spiral-bound notebook I write the address of the sale, the name of the object, the date of the purchase, and what we paid for it. Did the porcelain bowl painted with wisps of green and orange, the suggestion of flowers, belong to someone's grandmother? We don't know. But I have something, anyway, something written down of its history.

I sit in an overstuffed chair in a house at the end of a cul-de-sac while Mac goes upstairs. He climbs narrow stairways, steep stairs with no backs, stairways with railings that don't go all the way to the top. He wants to see a house, how it was built, where a hallway ends and what a window overlooks. I wait for him; I am suddenly tired. Tired of objects, homes, strangers' lives. But we are new, our house is new, there are so many beautiful things to bring to our cabinets and tabletops.

In this house where I sit in the overstuffed chair, display tables are arranged along the walls. I spot a Lenox dish and a bowl painted with a basil plant, the delicate roots fixed against the ribbed white porcelain. We look for these too, the bowls from Italy, England, Bavaria, Austria. Mac comes downstairs, shrugs his shoulders. I nod at the display tables. We buy the dish and the bowl for $8. We put the dish on an end table. We make a mushroom and spinach risotto for dinner and serve it in the bowl.

We decide to put out bird-feeders in the back yard. This seemed to be the logical thing to do. In each of them, separately, we put three kinds of feed: mixed seed, suet, and thistle. The woodpeckers come to the suet and feed all day. They are little bullets, holding themselves against the wire mesh of the feeder with their feet. The cardinal pair performs its mating ritual on the ground under the bird-feeder, the male feeding his mate seed by seed. The mourning doves, too heavy to land on the feeder, bob on the ground and eat the seeds dropped by the other birds. The blue jays, when they can't get a purchase on the feeder, flee to the trees and scream and complain. The chickadees come to the thistle, and walk boldly up to us as we sit very still on the deck.

Some Saturday mornings we drive to an address and there are no cars parked along the road in front of the house, no cars in the driveway. The front door is shut. No one is in the garage. We check the address again on the piece of note paper I hold in my hand, and then on Mac's phone, and check again the street number on the mailbox. Mac puts the car in gear and pulls away from the curb.

I leaf through a Zen cookbook, Mac files a few CDs on a shelf. We bought them that morning from what was advertised as an estate sale, but it was immediately obvious that the woman holding it was merely cleaning house. This idea, this event: we question its definition. Or are we too rigid? Can't one have, as it were, a living estate? Or, can't a person who hardly owned a thing who has passed on have an estate? Can't his relatives sell his mismatched china and broken lamps and call it an estate sale?

We went to a house in a modest neighborhood a few exits to the south on the throughway. In the garage I bought two tea cups and saucers, hand painted in England, from an elderly man, and in the kitchen a lead glass vase for my sister Angela, from a middle-aged woman, and each took my ones and fives and wrapped the objects in newspaper and plastic bags. An elderly woman was sitting in a chair in the living room, and it was her house, and her husband and daughter were selling her things. I said to her, standing in the room with her now bereft of almost everything, "You have a lovely home," and she turned to me with the face of a woman who used to know her own home, her own place in it, but didn't anymore, and I left and got into the car with Mac and was quiet a long time afterward.

The moon arcs across the sky; it rises over the woods to the east and sets in the woods to the west. But many nights there is just darkness. The neighbors' houses retreat into the dark. I am awake, still; I lie awake and hear a hoot owl, searching for prey.

Mac uses the GPS on his phone to get us around, but sometimes he just likes to drive. I take one of the tour books with me but he follows a tree line or a stone wall running for once parallel to the road. We enter a park. Woods, stone walls, great granite outcroppings, picnic tables in a clearing. The state is full of parks. We follow a trail, its edges a riot of Queen Anne's lace. A black squirrel scolds us from a rock ledge. I look up, up, beyond the reach of the trees, into the electric blue sky. We drive again, to the north, over bridges that span the great rivers that flow into the Sound. "Some day," Mac says, "we'll drive to Canada, where these rivers begin, and follow them home." We see a gas station. Mac fills up. There are dirt roads leading off the secondary roads. Something about them admonishes us, No Trespassing. The woods are endless. The trees stir.

I dream I am wearing a black bathing suit, my arms are at my sides, one leg is bent, the other extended. My chin is up, I am floating in the ether toward what I don't know. A man's hand reaches toward me. His hand runs over the fabric of my bathing suit, over my stomach, around my waist. He presses his hand across my chest. He is trying to find the exact place on my body that will be most comforted, and at the same time he is trying to keep me from floating away.

Sometimes I wonder why Mac drives us on these roads. What is the point? I am crying sometimes, weeping, away from Mac, in another part of the house, so he won't see me, so he won't ask me anything.

We drove to a house in disrepair and difficult to walk through, the floors on a slant. The rugs were thin and frayed. The house was so old and no one had taken care of it and now someone was selling all the old tired things. Mac found a copy of *A Child's Garden of Verses* in a cabinet in an upstairs room. The book was illustrated with line drawings in the style of the 1920s. The pages smelled of mildew. Mac paid 50 cents for it. I held it on my lap on the way home.

Sometimes we find things in books. A pair of airline tickets to Chicago. A Mass card for the man who used to live in the house; his wife's business card. There is no one to return these things to, so I keep them in a drawer. I don't know how we are supposed to throw them away.

The grackles have come again. They land in a great beating of wings on our back lawn. It is covered in black birds. More web the sky. The birds' bills dip into the grass, looking for insects. Their heads are iridescent, like dark jewels. They rise together and fly above the house and land on our front lawn. They move over it like pieces of a puzzle. They fly to the lawn next door, their wings stirring the air. They land on all the lawns in the neighborhood. Then they fly upwards and away. The sky is blue again, and empty.

We walk into a den with built-in cabinets on three walls and a sliding glass door leading to a patio with a view of the Sound. The cabinets are marked with a water stain, three feet high. "Hurricane Sandy," we say to each other, these years later.

We have come upon sales—yard sales, tag sales, moving sales—run by the homeowners, the affluent but not spectacularly rich, and the women especially seem somehow insulted by the idea of people coming to their yards and garages (never into their homes) and looking through their things. We bought a wool needlepoint runner for the upstairs hall at one of these sales, for $5, and at another a L.L. Bean canvas briefcase for Mac, for $1. The husband was friendly and voluble, but the wife was withdrawn. She sat at a table in the garage piled with folded linens and blankets, looking at no one. She did not like it that people were touching her things.

We have brought lunch again. I look across the dining room table at my mother. Behind her the window is hung with silvery blue drapes that are almost as old as I am. I wish to take my mother's hand, to try to know her again. I would like to open an old photo album and place it across our laps, sitting on her familiar couch, and turn the pages together and remember what is there. The parents and aunts and cousins, her two daughters, we sisters, growing up. The three of us sitting on a dock on a lake somewhere in upstate New York, Angela in her early teens, I a few years older, her knees, my knees, bent toward our mother, framing her.

I would like to give a name to everything again, an embroidered handkerchief I brought her from a trip, the turquoise dress I wore to a high school dance, the Rocks glasses I gave her many years ago from which we used to sip whiskey sours and play games of Scrabble at her kitchen table. I want to bring myself to her and tell her that before I belonged to anyone else or anything else I belonged to her, that this is where I began. For a few moments I would like to return to her, to be held and comforted. But there is nothing left of her desire for us, for the world. I wonder how she can turn away from her daughters, from Angela and me, from our husbands Mac and Ed, from everyone. I look at her and want to ask her would she please be with us just once again. But lunch is over and she looks at me not as a familiar and I think then she has always looked at me this way. She stands, goes into the living room. Mac has put way the lunch things. He gets my jacket, helps me into it. There is nothing left to do.

We are inland, at a sale being held in a garage, up a long drive. I feel my lungs working as we climb the driveway. We buy a vegetable steamer, a roasting pan, and an asparagus steamer for $10 from a woman with long gray unkempt hair. She tells us that she and her husband are retiring to South Carolina, where property taxes are $400. She is selling her mother's china. At home we steam garden peas and toss them in butter and pepper and serve them in the bowl painted with the basil plant, the roots trailing among its ribbed spaces.

The woodpeckers, not satisfied with the suet we feed them day and night, have begun to attack our house. They drill the wood, stop, drill the wood. Mac thinks it may be some kind of mating ritual. They attack the wood along the upper floor—at each end of the house, in the back at our bedroom window, and in the front at another bedroom window. I open a window and clap my hands. The woodpecker pauses, puts its beak to the wood. We have actual holes in the wood now, and great scars pit it.

These sales aren't difficult to find, we have our GPS, there are directions in the e-mails and on the Internet. But they are often difficult to get to: large areas of exposed rock one has to negotiate in crossing a lawn; steep brick stairs leading to a front door; failing concrete steps at a side door; a railing coming away from its moorings; rotting floorboards in a screened-in porch; a long passage by foot up a road, to the house, because there are so many cars, so many people ahead of one; living rooms, once one has achieved them, with the curtains drawn or on the north side of the house in a shadowy darkness so that the objects one seeks seem hidden and inaccessible. At a tag sale the owners sit in a room off the kitchen drinking coffee. The stairs to the upper floor are narrow and steep. Mac goes ahead, and after a few minutes returns, opening his empty hands. We buy a book on minerals that Mac found in a bookcase in the living room.

Objects shift ownership, place, and all that we have assembled will be disassembled someday as well. I say to Mac, holding a plate upside down, "Remember the woman in that house who said that someday it would be her things being picked up, examined, all that she had collected from sales just like this?" Perhaps that is the true provenance, the continual assembling and reassembling of objects from places lost or unknown. The need for beauty, continuity, even if brought together by utter chance by one's own hand, from one's own yearning, and with it the peace one hopes it can bring. But

Mac is looking for CDs. He does not need these objects as I do. How does one make a home from a conflux of abandoned objects? How does one consecrate a room, a bookcase, the table at which one eats? But then they too, all of them, are like the predictable books and the clothing that feels wrong in the hand, the edifice that bars inquiry into the real story, the real life. Only I know it of course, I am beginning to learn it, though I don't want to.

We bought four realistic-looking plastic owls and placed them strategically around the outside of the house. For a while there was no sound of beaks drilling wood. Then the woodpeckers returned. We bought holographic tape and Mac cut it into ten-foot strips and hung it out the windows, except for the front, because he worried about our neighbors' estimation of us. The tape furls and snaps in the wind. The woodpeckers stay away. From the couch in our living room I see a tape unfurl in front of a window. It is like a mother's arm, reaching for her child, then gathering her up, and the gesture is repeated, reaching and gathering, reaching and gathering, until all is well.

We move on to larger objects, an upholstered chair and ottoman for our bedroom, a country kitchen table that we put in the bedroom with the front-facing window, so I can attempt something on it—writing a letter, reading the first pages of a book. I look instead out the window. Mac now has an easy chair for his basement work room. The people who run the estate sales have pick-up trucks, drivers; they have thought of everything.

After the Hunger

Other times the tape unfurling in the wind sounds like the rustle of clothes, the rustle of a skirt against a nylon slip, the slip moving over a stockinged leg.

Sometimes Mac and I don't go anywhere. We just drive. We open the car windows. We drive away from everything I used to know.

It is early evening when my sister Angela calls. She says, "Juliet." I can tell by her voice that it is over. I begin to sigh, I begin to breathe through my mouth. Then I am crying. She says, "I'll call you later tonight. We'll see each other tomorrow." I forgot to ask where our mother is. I seem to have lost her in this world a long time ago. I try to understand what I will mourn so I can prepare for it.

Mac drives and drives. We are somewhere along the coast. He turns onto a dirt road. We are driving into a wildlife refuge. It is full of marshland, the sound of frogs. Mac and I get out, walk along a border of reeds. Our shoes make imprints on the damp ground.

The homes of the well-to-do seem removed and inaccessible in their own way, built on a rock outcropping or reached at the end of a winding gravel driveway. The rooms are large and calm, painted pale green or pale taupe, or with white wainscoting, the upper part of the wall painted the color of the sky in summer. One room has white valences and white drapes cascading to the floor. A precisely cut depression along a walkway is filled with tumbled gray stones. Of course nothing is familiar here. This is not my house or the house of anyone I know. I lift a bouquet of porcelain blush-red roses from a mantle, purchase it for $9. Mac unwraps it, places it on our mantle. The backdrop of brick is of course all wrong.

We purchase an olivewood spatula at a house that at mid-afternoon is nothing but detritus, the objects in the rooms impossible to match to their purpose. But there is the spatula, shining and new, arranged in an old vase like a flower. Mac turns the onions and garlic with it. I take a sip of wine, cut the ends of the green beans. I have promised myself not to drink wine while I work, there are lit burners, sharp knives, spices to measure, a kind of forgetfulness that can descend upon me. Mac is an efficient cook. I try to keep up.

We are at a professionally run estate sale in a modern-design house. There are older houses on this street too, the bloom of forsythia. Furniture has been sold or moved around, I don't know what room I'm in. I leave Mac to his hunt for CDs and follow some people to the basement. In a plastic box on a shelf I find an improbably beautiful chiffon scarf in a design of blue and yellow flowers. A girl of about twelve has been running through the rooms of the house. She excitedly picked up a clarinet from a bookshelf upstairs and turned it around and around, as if it were a baton, then she rocked back and forth on a hassock as if to show off its functionality. Mac and I were unable to connect her to any of the adults in the house. In the basement, where I stand holding the chiffon scarf, the girl climbs onto an exercise bicycle, and pedals and pedals, and the wheels turn maniacally, and the room fills with the sound of the turning wheels. I want to find Mac. I want to tell him that a chiffon scarf that one could trail deliciously around one's throat any number of times does not belong in a plastic box in a basement.

Angela and I sit on an old couch in our mother's attic surveying the room. The men, Mac and Ed, are downstairs, in the living room, and we hear their low voices going back and forth. They are waiting for us to ask them to do something, to take something down or take something away. There are a few cloth suitcases at our feet, an old fan, a box of Christmas ornaments, some stacked shoeboxes, a shelf containing photo albums with dusty leather covers, a large cardboard box filled with gift boxes from all the old department stores. In addition to the couch on which we sit there is a metal wardrobe, an old blond wood chest of drawers, and a large mirror propped against a sloping wall. The household is compact, functional, without the excesses of crystal water goblets or bowls from Italy or Bavaria. Angela and I each seem to recognize that there won't be any kind of sale of objects from our mother's house, though I don't tell Angela that we have seen sales of the most meager household items put on display in the hope of some reasonable sum at the end of the day, or that one won't have to keep handling an object again and again and feeling its awful weight.

Mac and I took a drive farther inland to a house that was so large it seemed like an error, an embarrassment, in a neighborhood of similar houses. We parked in the driveway. It was raining lightly, and the day was progressing, and we were the only shoppers. There were objects arranged on a table in the driveway, and in the garage three women sat in from the rain, drinking coffee and leaning toward each other behind an empty display table. All of the objects on the table outside were getting wet. There was jewelry and household items and some books spine-up in a cardboard box. Mac said, "They'll get ruined in this rain." The women leaned toward each other; one of them laughed. I wiped the spine of a book of recipes and bought it because the cover was beautiful and it was written by a woman who had collected the recipes her mother had brought to the U.S. with her from Cuba at the time of the revolution. I opened the book on our dining room table and saw all the old family photographs the mother had brought with her from Cuba and the daughter had saved and arranged each by each next to her mother's recipes.

On one of our drives, which Mac takes me on for the sake of driving, for the sake of something else, we see birch trees growing on a granite cliff. Mac pulls over, stops the car. The wind in the leaves is like the rustle of clothing, like the movement of clothing when a woman walks into a room and sits in a chair. Her daughters follow her, called to her by her perfume, and her outturned arm languidly reaches for them.

Mac makes breakfast. He makes *revoltillo de acelgas con jamón* from the recipes rescued from Cuba. We have black coffee and toast spread with marmalade from the unopened jar I took from my mother's house. The plates from which we eat are of glass, and their color is red.

It is hot in the attic, though only May, but the room is so close, the one window, which Angela has opened, so narrow and small. We cannot seem to leave this room. It seems like the hidden heart of the house, in all its disorder. We do not know how to begin to try to discover it, not in one object but an accumulation of them from which we will try to understand something, something we hope to be able to name. The men wait downstairs for us, they are waiting for us to move.

The Rock Gardens

Along the Post Road, on a grassy tract of land behind a barricade of wooden guardrails, a half-acre of closely packed shrubs and flowering plants stood in green plastic containers. The prices were listed on a hand-painted board. The plant sale took place from mid-May to early June and benefitted the state park that lay adjacent to the town's borders, a coastal area of meandering trails, dunes spiked with sea oats and bear grass, great ribbons of kelp discharged onto the shore, a nature center, and the Sound lying bluely beyond. Lucia and Douglas walked across the gravel parking lot toward a guardrail that marked the straggling edges of the half-acre. They had heard about the sale the previous spring, their first year in town, from a neighbor's mother strolling her baby granddaughter along their street, who told them to look heading east on the Post Road for a white tent on a meadow of grass.

 The tent was like the tent of a traveling show favored by bountiful weather and fortune, its twined ropes staked to the ground. Already in mid-morning, the hour the plant sale began, the parking lot was filling, and Lucia and Douglas could see a number of would-be buyers, some under the open scalloping of the tent, and some examining the plants laid out on large metal flats on the grass. In the distance, at the head of a paved walking trail, were the moving silhouettes of bicyclist and bicycle, the heads of the bicyclists otherworldly in their padded helmets. The sign before the turn-off from the Post Road read PLANTS BELOW WHOLESALE, and Lucia and Douglas had come with a list of the plants they hoped to find.

They had been away three weeks, called away by the obligations that had made possible the purchase of their house, so that they could see an end to them some day, here, in this new place. Before their departure they had volunteered for a three-hour stint on the half-acre, taking short-bladed scissors and cutting away the dead growth from the flats of arborvitae then bringing each plant to be put out for sale. The others, the more damaged plants, they separated to be sold at a discount or discarded. It had been a hard winter; people were still talking about it this late into the spring. Lucia and Douglas could see, driving the country roads, that the shrubs especially and the fir trees had suffered severe damage from the unremitting cold and the weight of the snow, the needles brown or fallen away from gray stricken branches.

In their own yard the plants they had set in the ground the previous spring and summer and watered and fertilized with such profound care had come up this year irregularly or not at all. Douglas tried to tell her that it was a foreseeable consequence of making a garden; some survived, some did not. It could be a failed connection of root to soil, he told her, a bad winter, the quality of sunlight, something unknown. Now there was one bleeding heart where they had planted two, three weak-looking peonies and two strong where they had planted six, tangles of blackened branches where there had been a rose bush. Starting in the fall the deer had bitten into the newly planted Rose of Sharon and eaten from the old established hydrangeas.

Douglas was telling her now, as they walked between the flats of the remaining arborvitae, that deer, eating plants they usually had no interest in, had probably been a sign that the winter would be hard. Lucia had planted crocus bulbs in a clay pot on the patio, but something had unearthed and consumed them. The squirrels destroyed a painted bird-feeder Lucia bought Douglas for his birthday. They returned to the house to find the feeder ripped off its pole and lying in the grass. Lucia tried to make peace with these encounters. She had come to their small rectangle of land so hopefully and earnestly, and she often experienced the frustration of her ambitions, some betrayal of her desires for it.

They made a quick pass inside the tent, where the annuals were displayed in bright hanging baskets and on long side tables. They admired the flowers, the begonias and petunias and fuchsias, but Lucia could not see the point in purchasing the radiantly colored plants that would die and never return. The act of permanent death offended for her every notion of life and its predictable cycles. Outside, the plants on the flats seemed to change each time she and Douglas came there and Lucia thought of them as if on a revolving platform, these plants this week, these plants the next. They were donated by a local nursery, depending on its overstock, though Lucia could not imagine hundreds of arborvitae as being a mere miscalculation. The morning they volunteered to trim the arborvitae they bought three witches' broom bushes, and Douglas planted them by the fence in their back yard. They looked again now for bleeding hearts and peonies, so plentiful last year, but instead they found rhododendron, mountain laurel and Scotch broom. They loaded four mountain laurel onto a rusting red wagon set among a nest of wagons outside the tent. Lucia carried the containers of Scotch broom to the table where a man and a woman, sitting in the shade of a small open tent, oversaw the sale of the plants. Among the flats Douglas had found a boxwood to help repair the one that had been partially destroyed by the plow that winter.

The man stepped around the table and helped Lucia. She said, "Hello, Gerald," and the man, dressed in a gray T-shirt and worn khaki pants and wearing a sun visor, said, "Hello," in a barker's voice and she realized he didn't recognize her from the morning he showed her and Douglas how to cut the dead, scale-like leaves from the arborvitae. Standing somewhat painfully to his full height from the tedious chore, Douglas had said to him, "We bought a house here about a year ago. We plan to retire there eventually. But then, how does one do that exactly?" He was trying to make a joke of it but it had occupied him ever since they had bought the house. Now they had a place, a definite place. But no plan. Many plans. What does one do? Douglas may as well have been talking to Lucia, or himself.

Gerald swept the visor from his forehead and put it back again. Pointing up the Post Road, he said, "There's an archaeological dig just beyond those trees. I sit in every once in a while. They've begun to unearth Paleolithic artifacts made from flaked chert and quartzite." Douglas took a step toward him and said, "Arrowheads, I imagine. Stone tools." Gerald arranged his visor on his forehead and said, "It should take a good while. They're always in need of volunteers." Douglas said, "Well, well," in an interested but noncommittal way.

Later, after they were done with the arborvitae, Douglas told her that he would volunteer for the dig when he was done with his work; it was one of his many other ambitions, an interest he had never been able to follow, because how many can a man have at one time? Lucia foresaw nothing but rest and peace and she thought here she would have the clarity to account for herself in this lifetime in ways she was just beginning to understand.

Gerald had continued to converse with them over the damaged arborvitae and had led them to a better understanding of the mind of the town, which Douglas later pronounced to Lucia to be good. Gerald was speaking to Douglas now about the wisdom of their purchases in the same impersonal voice. Douglas, taking out their checkbook, said, "I take shovel to dirt and immediately the blade hits, as if by divination, a monster rock." He held his arms out to show Gerald what he meant. "New England," Gerald said, as if announcing it to a crowd. Douglas wrote out the check. The woman behind the table, who had been smiling pleasantly at the scene of selection and purchase, took Douglas's check and placed it in a metal cash box. "This will go to the nature center," she told them. "We have plans drawn up for a new one, a green one, with more space. We've been holding the plant sale for fifteen years. Now we can go ahead."

Lucia imagined the woman there, every day for six weeks of every year for fifteen years, under the spring sky. She had short graying hair, deep wrinkles in a handsome face, and a strong body. She was dressed much like Gerald. "We were looking for bleeding hearts and peonies," Lucia said to her. "We wondered if we missed them."

"There haven't been any this year," the woman said. "We never know what we're going to get." Lucia knew then that there wouldn't be any bleeding hearts or peonies this year, that there wouldn't be any plants to fill the barren spaces the hard winter had left.

They said goodbye and Lucia said good-bye to Gerald and he said good-bye to her in his barker's voice. Lucia returned the rusted red wagon from their car and the woman helped her with it. Gerald was asking her if she would like him to get her a sandwich for lunch in a voice he used for people he knew.

The Rock Gardens

They drove back along the Post Road, the plants secured in the back seat on a cushion of old towels, past glimpses of marshland and farther, past the low trees that bordered the marsh, brief sightings of the Sound. In the center of town they drove under a banner strung across the road that changed with regularity, announcing an event sponsored by the Lions Club or the Exchange Club or the Historical Society. Lucia read the banner and said, "Look. Lunch on the Green." Douglas slowed the car and turned it onto a narrow road. He parked in the shade of a tree, checked the plants, and left a window cracked in the locked car.

The centerpiece of the Green was the Congregational church, set back on a sloping lawn, with tall white columns and the steeple rising above it. The parsonage, beyond a stretch of lawn, was almost completely hidden by thickly leafed trees. Across a narrow side road and sidewalk was a wooden one-room schoolhouse, a relic of history, and the Memorial Hall. Lucia and Douglas knew by now that if no other event was taking place on the Green there were always the food trucks with their menus hand-painted on the side panels featuring lobster rolls and tacos and elaborately frosted pastries. But often there were fairs and festivals, people sitting under small open tents selling jewelry and soaps and hand-made bird-houses, or farmers' markets with freshly baked breads and cheeses resting on beds of crushed ice and bunches of spring onions and leeks heavy and long as rope.

Douglas took her hand. They walked past a table laid with beaded necklaces. He said, "Do you want anything?" He bought her things. He bought her a necklace of seed pearls at Christmas; a radio. He bought her books and CDs of the old songs she used to sing. He bought a Laura Nyro CD for her and she sang "Stony End." In their yard he could use his phone to play music and she knew where he was by the songs she heard. She would go to him and they would sit together on some impossible rock uncovered of leaves by Lucia or unearthed by Douglas's shovel and he would sing "Wooden Ships" to her or "Tuesday Afternoon." He would say, "Does anyone sing like this anymore? Does anyone write a song like this anymore?" He had his arm around her. They listened to "Hello Cowgirl in the Sand," the high tenor voice emerging from the phone in Douglas's pocket that seemed to have no source, that seemed to exist in their minds.

Lucia glanced at the table of jewelry, all handcrafted but all the same at every fair, and she squeezed Douglas's hand. People were stopping at booths and Lucia and Douglas moved around them and then at the end of the tables were open spaces. Lucia could feel the grass on her ankles. There were generations of people, children and young parents and people their age and elderly people, and it seemed to her as if the Green had gone still and there was only the slow movement of their forms on the grass. She became aware of a band playing, a jazz band, and Douglas said to her, "Hear that, that beat right there? It's a drumstick beating against the rim of the drum."

Lucia listened to the beat of the drum as if from far away. She watched a young father walk quickly behind his small daughter toward some destination only the child seemed to know. She looked up at the sky, a high, thin blue, and behind it, a darker blue, dense and turbulent, as if containing something yet to be revealed. A few plump white clouds seemed not to move in the windless sky.

"Look at them," Lucia said. "Even the young parents. They're all moving about as if in a dream."

"No one's in a dream with young children, not in that way," Douglas said.

The young father now had his daughter's hand. They walked together on the grass. "Jeff and Debra look to be that way," Lucia asserted about their new neighbors across the street. She wanted to be part of a place that made one feel like that, walking on the Green on a spring day, after such hardship.

"They can't be, not with two kids," he said.

"Jeff takes his son for a ride on his bike with the training wheels. Debra's mother walks the little girl in her stroller."

Douglas was quiet. She knew he didn't want to talk about children. If they talked about children perhaps next it would be other children and he didn't want to talk about other children. But often he looked at children, sitting with her in a restaurant or waiting in line at the grocery store. He would say, "Look at that beautiful child," and Lucia would hesitate to look. How would they seem to others? A couple longing for a small child. It was a dream, another dream. At the line in the grocery store he flirted with the little girls in their mothers' arms, playing peek-a-boo. He wanted a little girl. He wanted to go back in time with her and have a daughter. He would spoil her, he said. He would carry her in his arms. Lucia thought he was telling her he would love this child in a different way that didn't involve any of the bitterness of the past.

To perhaps divert her, Douglas pointed to the branch of a tree. Lucia looked upward. She could see nothing. Douglas was always pointing out the miraculous that Lucia could not see. She thought there must be something deeply wrong in this. He would say, "See, by the garage," and she would look by the garage when he meant twenty feet in front it, a rabbit appearing now against the gravel like a figure in a puzzle. Or driving he would point to something out the window that his head and shoulders and the slope of the car roof hid from her. He wanted to show her things and she often failed at seeing them. But sometimes together they saw a chipmunk sprinting in kinetic bursts across their lawn, its tail rigid, or a mourning dove calling as it flew upward and landed on the branch of a tree.

Once, standing in their front yard, they had seen a pileated woodpecker, though they didn't know its name at the time, its long, prehistoric body held straight against the trunk of a tree, then watched it fly across their neighbors' yards into the woods. They saw it again in the back yard, a severe, angulated profile in a far tree, and heard its terrible call. In the evenings sometimes they heard the call again, and Douglas was certain he heard a return call. He liked the world in pairs or small families. He planted shrubs and flowering plants that way, arranged in orderly lines or in groupings facing each other.

Working in the yard, they saw two red-tailed hawks gliding above the trees. Lucia brought Douglas to the yard at dusk to see the risen moon, a white irregular shape pale and almost translucent, while the dying sun lighted the tops of the trees with a radiant yellow light. Once she showed him an indigo bunting. So she had things for him as well, to bring to him, as he did out of some continuous wish to witness the miraculous that often, here, seemed to hover before them.

Douglas pointed again so Lucia could see. She took her cupped hand from her brow and stopped squinting into the tree. She had finally seen the hummingbird, a dark outline against the sky. It didn't move. Then it was gone. Douglas took her hand.

At a booth, Lucia bought their tickets: eight tickets at a dollar apiece bought two strawberry shortcakes, the purchase of which was to support the Congregational church. They moved up the line to a table overseen by three women, one slicing biscuits and placing them open-faced in a cardboard container, one scooping cut strawberries over each biscuit with a large metal spoon, the third taking a large dollop of whipped cream from a ceramic bowl with a serving spoon and snapping her wrist over the berries. Lucia placed their tickets in a glass jar with the others and they said "Thank you" to the women and carried the shortcakes across the grass to a table under an open tent. They sat in recently vacated chairs. Lucia waited until the strawberry juice had soaked the biscuit before she began to eat.

Douglas was watching the dogs on the grass in front of the tent. The dogs were on leashes. There was a standard poodle, its fur black, its bearing noble and contained, and a white, its fur bobbed and reminding Lucia of a plant whose branches have been forced to twine or bend, and three or four golden retrievers, one a pup with ash-blond fur being sniffed by an Airedale, its tail tucked and quivering.

An Aussie, its fur freckled and in patchworks of color, crossed near the table. Lucia thought it a strange breed, the coat oddly patterned, the tail usually clipped, the shape of the body to her eye slightly distorted in the neck and in the slope of the hindquarters.

"That one's about the size of Bonnie," Douglas said. "The color's right too."

"You should get a dog," Lucia said. Douglas's dogs seemed to haunt him, ghost dogs that appeared in the bodies of dogs they saw in a park, or from the car window.

"They die," Douglas said. "You outlive your dog by any number of dog lives. It's too sad."

"It is," Lucia said.

"We travel too much, back and forth. And what if we wanted to get away?"

Lucia let the argument go. He was, she knew, convincing himself more than her. But she was the one who always brought it up. She didn't know what else to say to him.

The Rock Gardens

"See how that Aussie keeps turning to look at its owner," Douglas said, "even on its leash. Bonnie would sit at the threshold of the living room and follow anybody who dared leave and then attempt to herd them back." Douglas had told her how the family he was part of then was in such disunity, but the dog didn't seem to realize this. She had wanted them together. She herded them back. At night she slept at the head of the stairs, listening for any movement. Then she followed the transgressor to the kitchen or to the closed door of the bathroom and waited until she could herd him back. Their other Aussie, Otto, Douglas described to Lucia as "twice Bonnie's size and stupid as a stone." He told her how Bonnie would drop a tennis ball before Otto then pick it up swiftly with her laughing mouth and dance away when the bigger dog turned his great head to investigate it. Douglas imitated his bark, a low, bass assertion of protest.

An earlier dog, Lucky—which Douglas described to her elaborately but Lucia imagined otherwise as a terrier with dirty white fur and alert ears—one day, left momentarily alone in the kitchen, chewed through the flimsy wooden gate and upended the potted plants, shaking their roots as she ran through the house. When Douglas drove the car on an errand the dog sat up from her place in the back seat and rested her chin on Douglas's shoulder. He had a Tuxedo cat named Little Bit who brought gifts of squeaking mice and writhing garden snakes to the back steps. The cat liked to be carried around in Douglas's arms, belly up, like a dog or a baby. Douglas often reverted to these stories and Lucia wondered what was really on his mind. The cat died one day of no apparent cause, a handsome, still-young creature. Lucia didn't know what had happened to the other animals, where they went or how they died, for they must be dead by now; that wasn't part of Douglas's need to tell her these stories. But she suspected they were sent away by Douglas, adopted out, in brief moments of clarity while enduring the unexpected redirections of his life.

They had seated themselves a number of empty chairs from two elderly women who sat in repose at the head of the table. Whatever they had eaten was gone; or perhaps they had just come to sit for a while. They held themselves as old people do, beautifully erect and motionless, as if to hide the slow betrayals of the body. Only their heads moved, dipping slightly one toward the other. They spoke to each other confidingly in their old voices. "You will have to see my garden," one of them said. "Are the roses out?" the other asked.

Lucia pressed her fingers against the tines of her plastic fork. They had finished their shortcakes. She wanted another, she wanted five others, she wanted the sun to remain fixed in the sky. Douglas was turned away from her, looking toward something she couldn't see. The women held their arms in their laps. Their skin was pale, thin it seemed, not aged by the sun but as if having been cared for, protected, all their lives. Lucia leaned toward them. She thought she should acknowledge them. She did not yet know the protocols of the town. "It's a fine day," she said. "It's a beautiful day," the woman nearer to her said. The day was green, and blue, the clouds suspended in the sky like an intake of breath. The woman held Lucia's eyes as if to say, *This is all, this is all. This is what I know from all these years, and all I need of today and the next day and the next, after the hardships of the past.* Lucia and Douglas pushed their chairs back. Douglas had collected their containers to bring to a trash barrel. He nodded to the women and they regarded him politely with their old eyes. They sat under the tent still as idols, turning their heads to each other and speaking in murmurs.

They drove north on roads that angled sharply then led straight through woodland. Douglas turned the car into their driveway. He set the Scotch broom by the fence and the mountain laurel in the front yard, triangulated with an oak tree. "As the laurels grow they'll form and interest point in the yard," Douglas said. Lucia did not know this phrase, perhaps it was a homeowner's phrase, but she thought the laurels as they grew would form a place of shelter. Douglas set the boxwood next to the larger, plow-damaged shrub by the driveway.

They changed into their work clothes and Lucia spread sunscreen on Douglas's arms and face. They tucked their pant legs into their socks and Douglas sprayed himself and Lucia with Cutter's along their socks and shoes and on their clothes and arms. He sprayed Lucia's palms so she could protect her face and neck. The deer carried almost microscopic ticks and they dressed themselves as if for battle and immediately afterward, when they were done in the yard for the day, they unpeeled their sweat-stained clothes and put them in the washing machine then took hot showers and scraped their skin with loofas lest one had found them.

From hooks on the garage wall Lucia took down a trowel and a small rake and a larger one and Douglas brought down his shovel. They wore thick gardening gloves. He was going to plant the Scotch broom first. At the fence line Douglas put the blade of the shovel to the ground and stepped on it to make the first cut. He would dig and invariably find a rock and if it was a big one he would call Lucia from her work and show it to her, large and damp with soil and lying on the grass. Sometimes he used a rail from an old bed frame, left behind by the former owner, as a lever, lifting the rock and pushing dirt under the rail then working the rock; sometimes he used a crowbar and brought up the rock in sudden propulsion like a strongman performing a feat of strength.

There were thick stone walls in the woods behind the house, demarcating a long-abandoned field or pasture. Farmers once pulled the rocks from the earth with chains and oxen but still the land defeated them, the topsoil a poor mixture of clay and broken rock, the rocks revealed by the plow again each spring. On their rectangle of land, removed from the elementary concerns of survival, Lucia could admire a rock that Douglas had harvested practically with his bare hands. He would perhaps still be panting a little from his victory over it, and then wonder what they were to do with it.

It was hard work, not just planting but keeping the lawn, keeping their rectangle of land. The woman they had purchased the house from had relinquished it after a long struggle. She had left much of her life there behind. They arranged to buy her furniture, living, as they were, somewhere else with nothing of their own to bring with them. She left a kitchen full of utensils, a chest full of summer blankets. Lucia found a photograph of her in her wedding dress, a woman younger then by twenty years, smiling at her new husband. There had been a divorce. The house, her own house that she had purchased and moved into, was beautifully appointed. But Lucia found that the furniture they had bought from her held scrapes and cracks as if from carelessness or some larger failure. The yard was overrun with dandelions. The bushes grew to untoward heights, straggling toward the sky.

The former owner left them a congratulatory card. They heard from her once, from where she had gone to undertake the task of recreating herself, when she sent her new address, should, she wrote, any mail slip through. Lucia wondered if she wrote to hear about her house that she had appointed so beautifully and then had to abandon. Lucia wrote to her with a brief paragraph of news, careful not to intimate that the house she had left behind had become a place of refuge. That would seem unfair. Further, Lucia believed that that sort of thinking could harm this newborn truth.

There were small rocks embedded in the lawn and Lucia gave herself the job of dislodging them with the trowel and bringing them to the woods so the mower would go more easily for Douglas. She picked up sticks and branches that had fallen in their absence and raked the debris into piles. She listened for the muffled, chopping sound of Douglas's shovel. If she didn't hear him she went in search of him. If the lawnmower stopped she went to find him, to see her husband standing over it or having decided to break up the slow shearing of the lawn to bring a trash barrel full of the sticks she had collected to the woods. She feared sometimes he would disappear, not of his own will but out of a cruelty that could take everything important away. The world used to feel sharply that way. Of course now, too, everything could be taken away, her husband and all that they had made together of their lives. In the night she held him in her arms, and he was still and aware of her as if conscious of this moment of need and rest that was felt by him being held and her holding him. She held him in piques of love when he sat back in his chair after dinner or when they lay together in their bed listening to the tree frogs and the howl of the neighborhood dogs over some perceived disturbance or some reality they could not imagine.

    Lucia brought the rakes and trowel to the strip of yard by the driveway and propped them against a tree. The yard was ringed by years of leaves, fallen or swept by winds to its edges, and caught in the brambles and the rocks and the elaborate roots of the trees. She had raked the leaves for three seasons now and part of this, their second, spring. The yard itself had been neglected in another way; the soil was thin and depleted. Douglas told her it was impossible for the soil to hold, patched as it was with sparsely growing tufts of grass, and the top layers washed away under the rains and melting snow. The yard, especially the front yard, which sloped toward the road, was full of rocks and exposed tree roots. Douglas wanted to order a truckload of loam and bury it all but Lucia liked the rocks, they were so severe and somber. They seemed to be a part of the land—of granite cliffs blasted through to make the throughway they traveled to get there, of ancient ledges and of spruce and white pine and some austere way of thinking brought from across the sea that the landscape seemed to have already articulated.

She went to Douglas, who was leaning on the shovel near another hole he had dug for the Scotch broom, and put her gloved hands around him and kissed him with her mouth tasting of Cutter's and told him where she would work. The soil under the rocks was rich with a compost of decayed leaves. The previous year she had raked a line of demarcation in the back yard. Now she could look out the window or go with Douglas and see the rocks, heavy and immovable, against the deep-brown soil and the background of woods. At the border of the woods was a formation of two rocks Lucia had uncovered, set one on top of another, exhibiting glacial scratches made by the drag of the retreating ice sheet. Douglas proposed edging the dirt where the rocks lay to make a more defined space, to incorporate them into the design of the yard. They would plant ferns and lily of the valley there. Lucia didn't have these words—defined, space, design—as he did. But she could see in her mind's eye what he meant.

Lucia took the small rake to the leaves by the driveway. The rake allowed her a finer precision, to bring the leaves from the spaces between the rocks whose tips and edges she could just only see, to reveal them completely. Douglas worked within her sight so she could look up and see not the absence she feared but he himself pushing dirt around the newly planted Scotch broom and emptying a watering can over them.

She put her rake up and turned her forearm and looked at her scar. She had tried to show it to Douglas but he couldn't see it. She had held her forearm this way and that. It was another evidence of the miraculous, she wanted to tell him, like a red-tailed hawk or a sharp sliver of moon in a lavender sky. When she was two she lived with her parents in a rented house in Montreal, and her mother, in a gesture of friendliness, went to visit her next-door neighbor and left Lucia in the back yard with the boy, the son. The boy was four. She remembered now nothing of this except that the boy suddenly bit her arm. Was it a sunny day? Was she wearing a summer dress? Were they playing with blocks or following the trail of an ant? Had she held a dandelion to him? Did he lift her arm, or stand over it?

She remembered the shock of his teeth, the terrible pain. It was her first experience of pain. It seemed to her she had known that moment her entire life. She screamed in shock and pain. Her mother ran out the back door. There was a wound, a red welt; then a crescent of white, serrated skin; then a fading line of silver. They never visited the neighbor again and she moved back to the States with her parents and every once in a while her mother would say, Do you remember that boy who bit your arm? and she would

The Rock Gardens

turn her arm and run her fingertips over the silver crescent that no one could see.

Lucia raked the leaves away from the rocks. The scar rose above the movement of muscle in her forearm. It was clear to her that the rocks had deliberately been moved to form a natural boundary. They were too large to be used for a stone wall. *Had the plow turned up more rocks in the endless task of clearing the land? Or had they been uncovered in excavating the foundation for the house, or, littering the yard, deemed unsightly there?* They were surely glacial boulders, broken and carried from granite ledges and the bedrock itself with the retreat of the continental ice shelves. So they too were a product of violence—a larger violence of more duration, but nevertheless—of the glacial invasions and in their slow retreat the northward dragging of rock and soil.

When she was done with her rake Douglas gathered the leaves into the trash barrel and carried it to the woods. Douglas admired the rocks, their irregular shapes beginning to be revealed by Lucia in their severe beauty, the product of unimagined forces come to rest in their yard. They seemed half formed, their bases covered yet with wet under layers of leaves. Lucia and Douglas sat together on one of them. Lucia embraced Douglas with the spent muscles of her arms. Every once in a while she was angry at the woman who had sold them the house she had so carelessly looked after. The rectangle of land was too much. They raked and mowed and planted and watered. And did so again. But something would come of it, some design.

Douglas went back to work. He brought the watering can and the shovel to the containers of mountain laurel under the oak tree. She could see him from where she worked. She was pulling the leaves away again, making a long line of them at the edge of the driveway. She stopped and flexed her fingers in the heavy gloves. To uncover a rock took many steps. First one raked; then one raked the farther leaves, making a path; then one raked again. She wondered what she would be here and what she would do here when the yard was done and all around it the woods breathed. Putting her rake down, she went to the back of the yard, to the rocks she had already uncovered, scarred by the glacial invasions and neglected under the leaves, now somber and eternal in the shade of the woods, the deep striations visible under her eye. Douglas's phone was playing a song, and as she got nearer she heard the words, and she followed them to find him.

Fomite

About Fomite

A fomite is a medium capable of transmitting infectious organisms from one individual to another.

"The activity of art is based on the capacity of people to be infected by the feelings of others." Tolstoy, *What Is Art?*

Writing a review on Amazon, Good Reads, Shelfari, Library Thing or other social media sites for readers will help the progress of independent publishing. To submit a review, go to the book page on any of the sites and follow the links for reviews. Books from independent presses rely on reader to reader communications.

For more information or to order any of our books, visit
https://www.fomitepress.com/our-books.html

More Titles from Fomite...

Novels
Joshua Amses — *During This, Our Nadir*
Joshua Amses — *Ghatsr*
Joshua Amses — *Raven or Crow*
Joshua Amses — *The Moment Before an Injury*
Jaysinh Birjepatel — *Nothing Beside Remains*
Jaysinh Birjepatel — *The Good Muslim of Jackson Heights*
David Brizer — *Victor Rand*
Paula Closson Buck — *Summer on the Cold War Planet*
Dan Chodorkoff — *Loisaida*
David Adams Cleveland — *Time's Betrayal*
Jaimee Wriston Colbert — *Vanishing Acts*
Roger Coleman — *Skywreck Afternoons*
Marc Estrin — *Hyde*
Marc Estrin — *Kafka's Roach*
Marc Estrin — *Speckled Vanities*
Zdravka Evtimova — *In the Town of Joy and Peace*
Zdravka Evtimova — *Sinfonia Bulgarica*

Fomite

Daniel Forbes — *Derail This Train Wreck*
Greg Guma — *Dons of Time*
Richard Hawley — *The Three Lives of Jonathan Force*
Lamar Herrin — *Father Figure*
Michael Horner — *Damage Control*
Ron Jacobs — *All the Sinners Saints*
Ron Jacobs — *Short Order Frame Up*
Ron Jacobs — *The Co-conspirator's Tale*
Scott Archer Jones — *And Throw Away the Skins*
Scott Archer Jones — *A Rising Tide of People Swept Away*
Julie E. Justicz — *Degrees of Difficulty*
Maggie Kast — *A Free Unsullied Land*
Darrell Kastin — *Shadowboxing with Bukowski*
Coleen Kearon — *#triggerwarning*
Coleen Kearon — *Feminist on Fire*
Jan English Leary — *Thicker Than Blood*
Diane Lefer — *Confessions of a Carnivore*
Rob Lenihan — *Born Speaking Lies*
Douglas Milliken — *Our Shadow's Voice*
Colin Mitchell — *Roadman*
Ilan Mochari — *Zinsky the Obscure*
Peter Nash — *Parsimony*
Peter Nash — *The Perfection of Things*
George Ovitt — *Stillpoint*
George Ovitt — *Tribunal*
Gregory Papadoyiannis — *The Baby Jazz*
Pelham — *The Walking Poor*
Andy Potok — *My Father's Keeper*
Frederick Ramey — *Comes a Time*
Joseph Rathgeber — *Mixedbloods*
Kathryn Roberts — *Companion Plants*
Robert Rosenberg — *Isles of the Blind*
Fred Russell — *Rafi's World*
Ron Savage — *Voyeur in Tangier*
David Schein — *The Adoption*
Lynn Sloan — *Principles of Navigation*

Fomite

L.E. Smith — *The Consequence of Gesture*
L.E. Smith — *Travers' Inferno*
L.E. Smith — *Untimely RIPped*
Bob Sommer — *A Great Fullness*
Tom Walker — *A Day in the Life*
Susan V. Weiss — *My God, What Have We Done?*
Peter M. Wheelwright — *As It Is On Earth*
Suzie Wizowaty — *The Return of Jason Green*

Poetry
Anna Blackmer — *Hexagrams*
Antonello Borra — *Alfabestiario*
Antonello Borra — *AlphaBetaBestiaro*
Antonello Borra — *The Factory of Ideas*
L. Brown — *Loopholes*
Sue D. Burton — *Little Steel*
David Cavanagh — *Cycling in Plato's Cave*
James Connolly — *Picking Up the Bodies*
Greg Delanty — *Loosestrife*
Mason Drukman — *Drawing on Life*
J. C. Ellefson — *Foreign Tales of Exemplum and Woe*
Tina Escaja/Mark Eisner — *Caida Libre/Free Fall*
Anna Faktorovich — *Improvisational Arguments*
Barry Goldensohn — *Snake in the Spine, Wolf in the Heart*
Barry Goldensohn — *The Hundred Yard Dash Man*
Barry Goldensohn — *The Listener Aspires to the Condition of Music*
R. L. Green — *When You Remember Deir Yassin*
Gail Holst-Warhaft — *Lucky Country*
Raymond Luczak — *A Babble of Objects*
Kate Magill — *Roadworthy Creature, Roadworthy Craft*
Tony Magistrale — *Entanglements*
Gary Mesick — *General Discharge*
Andreas Nolte — *Mascha: The Poems of Mascha Kaléko*
Sherry Olson — *Four-Way Stop*
Brett Ortler — *Lessons of the Dead*

Fomite

Aristea Papalexandrou/Philip Ramp — Μας προσπερνά/It's Overtaking Us
Janice Miller Potter — Meanwell
Janice Miller Potter — Thoreau's Umbrella
Philip Ramp — The Melancholy of a Life as the Joy of Living It Slowly Chills
Joseph D. Reich — A Case Study of Werewolves
Joseph D. Reich — Connecting the Dots to Shangrila
Joseph D. Reich — The Derivation of Cowboys and Indians
Joseph D. Reich — The Hole That Runs Through Utopia
Joseph D. Reich — The Housing Market
Kenneth Rosen and Richard Wilson — Gomorrah
Fred Rosenblum — Vietnumb
David Schein — My Murder and Other Local News
Harold Schweizer — Miriam's Book
Scott T. Starbuck — Carbonfish Blues
Scott T. Starbuck — Hawk on Wire
Scott T. Starbuck — Industrial Oz
Seth Steinzor — Among the Lost
Seth Steinzor — To Join the Lost
Susan Thomas — In the Sadness Museum
Susan Thomas — The Empty Notebook Interrogates Itself
Paolo Valesio/Todd Portnowitz — La Mezzanotte di Spoleto/Midnight in Spoleto
Sharon Webster — Everyone Lives Here
Tony Whedon — The Tres Riches Heures
Tony Whedon — The Falkland Quartet
Claire Zoghb — Dispatches from Everest

Stories

Jay Boyer — Flight
MaryEllen Beveridge — After the Hunger
L. M Brown — Treading the Uneven Road
Michael Cocchiarale — Here Is Ware
Michael Cocchiarale — Still Time
Neil Connelly — In the Wake of Our Vows
Catherine Zobal Dent — Unfinished Stories of Girls
Zdravka Evtimova — Carts and Other Stories
John Michael Flynn — Off to the Next Wherever

Fomite

Derek Furr — *Semitones*
Derek Furr — *Suite for Three Voices*
Elizabeth Genovise — *Where There Are Two or More*
Andrei Guriuanu — *Body of Work*
Zeke Jarvis — *In A Family Way*
Arya Jenkins — *Blue Songs in an Open Key*
Jan English Leary — *Skating on the Vertical*
Marjorie Maddox — *What She Was Saying*
William Marquess — *Boom-shacka-lacka*
Gary Miller — *Museum of the Americas*
Jennifer Anne Moses — *Visiting Hours*
Martin Ott — *Interrogations*
Christopher S. Peterson — *Amoebic Simulacra*
Jack Pulaski — *Love's Labours*
Charles Rafferty — *Saturday Night at Magellan's*
Ron Savage — *What We Do For Love*
Fred Skolnik — *Americans and Other Stories*
Lynn Sloan — *This Far Is Not Far Enough*
L.E. Smith — *Views Cost Extra*
Caitlin Hamilton Summie — *To Lay To Rest Our Ghosts*
Susan Thomas — *Among Angelic Orders*
Tom Walker — *Signed Confessions*
Silas Dent Zobal — *The Inconvenience of the Wings*

Odd Birds
William Benton — *Eye Contact: Writing on Art*
Micheal Breiner — *the way none of this happened*
J. C. Ellefson — *Under the Influence: Shouting Out to Walt*
David Ross Gunn — *Cautionary Chronicles*
Andrei Guriuanu and Teknari — *The Darkest City*
Gail Holst-Warhaft — *The Fall of Athens*
Roger Lebovitz — *A Guide to the Western Slopes and the Outlying Area*
Roger Lebovitz — *Twenty-two Instructions for Near Survival*
dug Nap — *Artsy Fartsy*
Delia Bell Robinson — *A Shirtwaist Story*
Peter Schumann — *Bread & Sentences*

Fomite

Peter Schumann — *Belligerent & Not So Belligerent Slogans from the Possibilitarian Arsenal*
Peter Schumann — *Charlotte Salomon*
Peter Schumann — *A Child's Deprimer*
Peter Schumann — *Faust 3*
Peter Schumann — *Planet Kasper, Volumes One and Two*
Peter Schumann — *We*

Plays
Stephen Goldberg — *Screwed and Other Plays*
Michele Markarian — *Unborn Children of America*

Essays
Robert Sommer — *Losing Francis: Essays on the Wars at Home*

Made in the USA
Middletown, DE
21 June 2020